"Bentley," she whispered. "Do you really think I'm beautiful? Desirable? Do you desire me . . . ?"

She was doing this, he tried to remind himself, because she'd been hurt. Young women were like that. He'd seen it—and steered clear of it—often enough. Older women, the kind he always sought out, were wise enough to know that there was always another lover just around the corner who would soothe the sting of their wounded pride.

She pressed her body against his again.

"Sweetheart, don't," he warned. "Don't do this. Don't ever slip off into the dark with a man like me."

She looked at him, half innocent, half seductress. "Don't you want me?"

"Desperately." Somehow he managed to give her a brotherly peck on the tip of her nose. "Madly. In the worst possible way. Now disappoint me, Freddie. Go up to bed. Alone."

Praise for Liz Carlyle
No True Gentleman

"One of the year's best historical romances."

—Publishers Weekly (starred review)

"Carlyle neatly balances passion and danger in this sizzling, sensual historical that should tempt fans of Amanda Quick and Mary Balogh."

—Booklist

A Woman of Virtue

"Sensual and spellbinding. . . . Liz Carlyle weaves passion and intrigue with a master's touch."

—New York Times bestselling author Karen Robards

"With *A Woman of Virtue,* Liz Carlyle shows she deserves fan support from mystery aficionados as well as romance lovers."

—Affaire de Coeur

"*A Woman of Virtue* is a beautifully written book. . . . I was mesmerized from the first page to the last."

—The Old Book Barn Gazette

"I can't recommend this author's books highly enough; they are among my all-time favorites."

—Romance Reviews Today

The Devil You Know

Liz Carlyle

POCKET STAR BOOKS

NEW YORK   LONDON   TORONTO   SYDNEY   SINGAPORE

An *Original* Publication of POCKET BOOKS

 A Pocket Star Book published by
POCKET BOOKS, a division of Simon & Schuster, Inc.
1230 Avenue of the Americas, New York, NY 10020

ISBN: 0-7434-3787-X

First Pocket Books printing April 2003

10 9 8 7 6 5 4 3 2 1

POCKET STAR BOOKS and colophon are registered trademarks
of Simon & Schuster, Inc.

Front cover illustration by Alan Ayers

For information regarding special discounts for bulk purchases,
please contact Simon & Schuster Special Sales at 1-800-456-6798
or business@simonandschuster.com

Printed in the U.S.A.

To my friend and editor,
Lauren McKenna

⚵

Thank you for your undying support and
boundless enthusiasm.

Prologue

In which we Commence our Tale of Woe.

Do you believe in universal truths? Admonitions, beliefs, or even morality tales passed down through families like so much well-worn linen? The Bard once said that all the world's a stage and we mortals merely players. If you subscribe to that, as many amongst us do, then the misbegotten life of Randolph Bentham Rutledge could have been termed a comedy to some and a tragedy to others, depending upon one's point of view.

To his partners in debauchery, it was a comedy, so long as the money held out. To his wife, his children, and his debtors, it was a tragedy, and one with far too many curtain calls. But the gentleman himself (and one must use this term loosely) once laughingly declared that his life was really just one great farce, and it was appropriately titled *The Rake's Progress*—or would have been, had the title not been snatched up by some proselytizing cartoonist who was most likely fated to sink into the swamp of literary obscurity.

The family saga really began long ago, some eighty years prior to the arrival of William the Conqueror, when an ambitious peasant from the market town of Chipping Campden heaped his worldly goods onto a creaky old ox-cart and set out on a journey deep into the countryside. Posterity knows not the reason for this adventure, taken as it was during a time when most Saxon peasants would live cradle to coffin in one place. But we know he did not go far—just twenty miles south as the crow flies—and yet the distance was to alter his family's fortunes forever.

The traveler was called John of Campden. And legend says that when he reached the verdant valley of the River Coln, he paused on a swath of bottomland which rolled out to meet the wolds like a lush green carpet. There he unharnessed his ox, unloaded his cart, and sank the first of many spades deep into the fertile earth. And thus began his family's climb toward that lofty stratum of blue-blooded rural gentry.

How a simple Saxon came by such a fine property, whether by honest labor, clever deceit, or perhaps even a shrewd marriage, we know not. But throughout the many centuries which followed, his descendants labored hard and long to build sturdy cottages, tidy villages, and powerful wool churches, so called because their every keystone and candlestick had been paid for by that common currency of the Cotswolds. Sheep.

Six centuries later—long after the Campdens had somehow lost a *p* and become the Camdens—yet another John came along with yet another grand plan. He used his wool money to build a fine manor house on the very site where legend held that his ancestor had stuck his first fateful spade into the earth. This house was built, as were all such houses of its time and place, of butter-brown stone, and it was so symmetrical, so exquisite, and so grandly and perfectly proportioned that the villagers stood in awe, as well they should have done. With its crenellated bays and steep, soaring roofs, and the parish church of St. Michael the Archangel standing quite literally in its shadow, Chalcote Court evoked the wealth, power, and influence which this ambitious family had so assiduously acquired.

But the tides of fortune and the wheels of history were destined to turn against the Camden family. When, almost two centuries later, another John Camden was born at Chalcote, he unwittingly brought with him a time of great uncertainty. Though there was no want of money, years of pox, plague, and civil unrest had somehow ripped entire branches from the family tree. And this last John Camden was an ill-fated fellow who had spent four decades, and almost as many wives, striving to beget an heir for a dying dynasty, until at last he gave himself a heart seizure in the midst of one last thrust of the family sword.

He awoke some two days later in his vast, barrel-ceilinged bedchamber to see his twin daughters, Alice on the right and Agnes on the left, bent like sorrowful angels over what John Camden knew was to be his deathbed. The mattress was so narrow, and his daughters' hair so soft and fluffy, that their heads quite literally brushed one another. Weak and disoriented, the old man fancied they were smothering him and waved them away. Being biddable girls, they leapt back at once. But, as luck would have it, Alice's comb caught in Agnes's hair, and they had a devil of a time getting themselves disentangled.

Watching the tussle in mute amazement, the old man suddenly decided it was a sign from God. With what strength his maker had left him, John Camden sent to Oxford for his solicitor. He drew a complicated will, one which tore a gaping wound down the middle of his heritage. The property which his family had held so proudly and so wholly for eight centuries was to be slashed in two. Alice, the elder by a quarter-hour, was to have the piece on which Chalcote stood. The more distant portion was to go to Agnes, a young woman more prudent than pleasant.

John Camden expressed but one dying wish: that his daughters' progeny intermarry and thus reunite—or reentangle, if you will—the family estate. But, more importantly, none of the land was ever to leave the family's possession. For if it did, he vowed his soul would never rest.

Alice moved quickly. During the very first week of her very first season, she caught the eye of a fellow who was thought by all who knew him to be the most attractive, and the most profligate, gentleman in all of England. Alice was rich, silly, and madly in love, and her wedding bells had scarce stopped ringing before Randolph Rutledge began laying waste to eight hundred years' hard work.

By the time this miserable mistake of a marriage had produced three children, there was very little estate left to reunite, and John Camden's ghost was nowhere to be seen. As for Agnes, she had moved on with her life, marrying well and building what amounted to a fully fortified castle on her half of the land. But, still vexed over Alice's having got the famous family seat, Agnes barely acknowledged her disreputable brother-in-law's existence—or her sister's suffering.

"Well, we cannot very well sell the blasted thing," said Randolph to his wife one rainy afternoon as he squinted through the parlor window into Chalcote's forecourt. "No one with the sense God gave a goose would wish to live in this wet and dreary place."

Alice let her head fall weakly against the back of her brocade divan. "But it is spring, Randolph," she replied as she modestly shifted her nursing infant beneath his blanket. "Cam says one must be grateful for spring rain. Moreover, we cannot sell Chalcote, or even mortgage it, for Papa tied it all up. You knew when we married that all would go to Cam someday."

"Oh, stop sniveling about someday, Alice," said Randolph bitterly, flinging himself into a leather armchair. "Your perfect little prince shall have it all soon enough, I'll wager, for if I cannot lay hands on some blunt soon, I'm apt to expire of boredom."

Alice looked at him through weary eyes. "You might spend some time with Cam or Catherine," she suggested, her gaze going to their children who were bent over a backgammon table in a distant corner. The young man sat with his long, booted legs stretched out beneath the table, while the girl dangled her feet above them. On the floor beside them sat one of a dozen copper pots. Caught up in the game, the children seemed oblivious to the annoying *plop! plop! plop!* of the leaky roof above their heads.

Randolph snorted, then turned on his wife. "M'dear, I would not think of interfering," he snarled. "That dull yeoman farmer over there is all your doing. And I pray to God he's the savior you think him, for this miserable excuse of an estate direly needs salvation. As to the chit, I reckon she's a taking little thing, but . . ."

But she is just a girl.

This last disparagement hung unspoken. Alice Rutledge sighed again and, unable to resist the overwhelming fatigue which had plagued her since the birth, let her eyes drop shut. She must have dozed for a time—she often did so—and awakened to the sound of the babe's flailing and squalling. Her breasts, it seemed, were always too soon emptied, and the child was forever wailing his frustration.

"Greedy little devil," she heard Randolph say with a chortle. "Never enough, eh, my boy? Women are ever like that."

Alice forced open her eyes. Her husband was bent low over her divan, his hands reaching out for the child. She had not the strength to refuse him, and so, as she often did, Alice simply let the babe be pulled from her grasp. Arms waving eagerly, the child went to his father with a happy gurgle.

In short order, Randolph had soothed the babe by bouncing him enthusiastically on one knee whilst singing a coarse tavern ditty. Alice forced her eyes open and thrust out her hands to snatch back the child. "Stop it, Randolph!" she demanded. "That is excessively vulgar. I shan't have him exposed to your disgusting habits."

Still bouncing the happy child on his knee, Randolph shot her a sour, quelling look. "Oh, shut up, Alice," he said. "This one is mine, do you hear? The choirboy and the chit you've already ruined, but this one—ha! Just look at his eyes! Look at that grin! By God, this one has my spirit and my appetites."

"I pray not," snapped Alice.

Randolph threw back his head and laughed. "Oh,

Alice, you may as well surrender him gracefully. You've had your way with the other two, but this chubby little devil has my name and my nature, and I shall do with him just as I please." And then, quite deliberately, he let his eyes run over her. "Besides, m'dear," he added, a little too cheerfully, "I don't think you've the strength to stop me."

Alice let her hands drop away empty. Empty like the whole of her life. The only good which had come of it was her children, Camden, Catherine, and the baby. And Randolph was right. Damn him to hell, but he was right. Her days on this earth were numbered, and she knew it with a fearful certainty. And then what? Dear God, then what?

In Cam she had instilled a rigid self-discipline which would ensure that he would always do the right thing. And Catherine's sweet nature and simple beauty would eventually win her a good husband, one who would take her away from all this. But the baby, her sweet little Bentley, what would become of him when she was gone? The grief and fear swallowed her up again, and Alice's eternal wellspring of tears burst forth.

Chapter One

꙳

In which Mrs. Weyden's warnings go Unheeded.

"Tout vient à celui qui sait attendre," muttered Frederica d'Avillez. Her tone made it sound more like a curse than a proverb. It was, she supposed, just a remnant of some long-ago French lesson which now kept repeating itself over and over in her head until it became maddening, rather like that big green and yellow bird she'd once seen swinging on a wire in a Piccadilly shop window. *All comes to him who knows how to wait.* What a bloody stupid saying. And an egregious lie, too.

At the stable door, she stared grimly into the night for a long, uncertain moment, then forced back her shoulders and marched off in the direction of the terraced gardens. As she paced, Frederica tapped her crop impatiently against her thigh, the muted sting somehow keeping her tears at bay, much as her silly proverb had done for the last several months. The words had given her hope during a miserable come-out season in London. And they had sustained her at home here in Essex while she anxiously awaited Johnny's return from his grand tour.

Well, much good her patience had done her! She should have gone to Scotland with Zoë and the little ones. Instead, she was stuck here with Aunt Winnie and the menfolk, and she and Johnny were done for.

Ruthlessly, Frederica shoved a bough of hemlock from her face and pushed on through the shimmering moonlight, her riding boots digging hard into the gravel as she hit the garden path. Here, at the bottom terrace, the gardens were allowed to grow thick and natural. High above in the distance, someone had left a lantern burning by the back door. Frederica should have found it welcoming, but she didn't.

The night was cool but not damp, the air thick with the scent of freshly turned earth. She drew in another steadying breath, and a sudden sense of despair almost overwhelmed her. It drew at her lungs and wracked her shoulders, but she fought it down and picked up her stride. Anger was a better emotion. And she was angry. Spitefully so. The fierce desire to hurt someone was almost frightening. She had come home from London for no good reason. She had been mistaken. Despite all his whispered pleas and smoldering glances, Johnny Ellows, it seemed, had not meant to marry her at all.

Abruptly, she jerked to a halt, scarcely seeing the next flight of steps which loomed up in the moonlight ahead. How could she have been so mistaken? How could she have been so stupid?

Because she was a silly little girl.

Well, the truth hurt, did it not? Things were no different here at home than they had been in London. The surroundings were just more familiar. Society, and apparently even the rural gentry, could always find cause to look down on her. Suddenly, Frederica felt as inadequate in Essex as she had in town. At that thought, something inside her snapped. As if it possessed a will of its own, Frederica's riding crop struck a whacking good blow at the next swag of evergreen, sending snippets of foliage spinning into the night. Unleashing her rage felt oddly satisfying. She was tired of being so perfect, so placid, so bloody damned . . . *restrained.* So, again and again, she thrashed at the greenery which verged on the paths and steps, all the while making her way briskly up the terraces.

"He loves me not!" she hissed, striking a blow at the juniper on her left. "Not! And not! And not!" A row of bare-branched forsythia fell victim, dry twigs splintering hither and yon. Stems of yew twirled wildly off into the darkness. The sharp tang of evergreen surrounded her, and still she pushed on, venting her wrath on whatever shrub the moonlight spilt over. The hot press of tears threatened. *Oh, Johnny!* She had thought . . . he had said . . .

But apparently not.

He was to wed his cousin in May. On his father's orders, he had said. He loved Frederica madly, had always loved her, but he could not risk being cut off. There would be no estate, no lovely manor house.

Frederica had reminded him of her generous dowry, but it had done no good. Perhaps his cousin had one larger? The lump in her throat had kept her from asking. So, with a sad smile, Johnny had lifted her hand to his lips and had taken his leave of her forever.

And yet Frederica had heard too well what had gone unsaid. Her blood was not blue enough—or English enough—for the virtuous Squire Ellows. And her cousins' titles, money, and influence notwithstanding, Frederica had been born on the wrong side of the blanket, and so she was a bastard—an *orphaned foreign bas-*

tard—the worst thing you could be in England, or so it seemed tonight.

She had almost reached the upper terrace which was rimmed with a low stone wall and flanked with a row of boxwoods. The lantern still swung from its hook by the back door, the pale yellow light spilling across the flagstones. Drawing back her whip, she gave the nearest boxwood one last thrashing.

"Jesus Christ Almighty!" exclaimed a raspy masculine voice.

Frederica leapt back, her hand flying to her mouth.

A broad, dark shape emerged from behind the boxwood, his hands working furiously at the close of his trousers. "Bloody hell, Freddie!" barked the man around the stub of a glowing cheroot. "Give a chap an apoplexy, why don't you?"

Heart in her throat, Frederica leaned forward to peer into the shadows. And then, as he buttoned his trousers, she saw a familiar gold signet ring winking at her in the moonlight. "Oh, good Lord!" she groaned. "Bentley Rutledge, is that you? What, pray, are you about?"

Rutledge gave a bark of laughter and hitched up his last trouser button. "What's it look like, Freddie love?" He unclamped the cheroot between his teeth and cocked one hip against the stone wall. "Try to give a little warning next time."

"For pity's sake, Rutledge! Didn't Tess put a slop pot under your bed?"

But her initial shock having faded, Frederica was not especially embarrassed. She had known Rutledge forever, it seemed. He was her cousin Gus's best friend and a favorite at Chatham Lodge, a house which was usually filled cheek-by-jowl with visitors. And although Aunt Winnie could often be overheard exclaiming that Rutledge was an unconscionable rake, her eyes were always twinkling when she said it. Frederica looked Rutledge up and down. Winnie had said some other things, too. Things unmarried young ladies probably weren't supposed to overhear.

But Frederica had overheard them, and she did not doubt for one moment that they were true. Rutledge was a tall, handsome devil with melting brown eyes, a wicked grin, and thick, dark hair which was always too long. In fact, now that she thought on it, he seemed to get handsomer with every passing year. And bigger. And broader. He was strong, too. On Boxing Day, he had caught her beneath the mistletoe. She remembered how he had set his big hands about her waist so that his thumbs almost touched. And then he had lifted her effortlessly into the air, twirling her round as he kissed her—full on the mouth, too.

But it meant absolutely nothing. Every year around Christmastime, Rutledge would catch and kiss all the ladies—Aunt Winnie, Cousin Evie, and even Zoë, whom no one else dared to kiss, because even though she was illegitimate, her father was the great Lord Rannoch. But this year, Rutledge had snatched Frederica up when no one else was about. He had given her the usual swift, smacking kiss. And then, strangely, he had seemed to falter. He almost forgot the twirling part, then the kiss softened somehow, as if their mouths had parted slightly. Then he had lowered her very slowly, their bodies brushing, his eyes never leaving hers. When her toes again touched the floor, Frederica had felt all hot and strange. But Rutledge had turned away at once. And that had been the last time he'd kissed her—or anyone—beneath the mistletoe.

How strange that she should remember that tonight. Good Lord, she had a tragedy on her hands. Her grief over Johnny flooded back. "I'm sorry to have startled you, Rutledge," she said, fumbling awkwardly with her riding crop. "But it is a bit past midnight. Shouldn't you be in bed?"

"Oh, *I* should?" In the moonlight, she could see his very large, very white teeth as he grinned. Rutledge was always grinning at her. "And what of yourself, sweet? Slipping back from the stables so late? Who's the lucky fellow?"

For a moment, she couldn't breathe. "None of your business," she finally snapped.

At that, Rutledge slid away from the stone wall and stood a bit unsteadily. "Why, Freddie!" he whispered, grinding his cheroot beneath his boot heel. "It's young Ellows, isn't it? Ah, those Cambridge men have all the luck!"

The jest was like a knife in her heart, stabbing swift and deep. Frederica placed a steadying hand on the stone newel post. "Why must you always tease me, Rutledge?" she demanded, fighting her tears with scorn. "And why is it that you never turn up here unless you're avoiding some scandal? Or her husband? And speaking of scandal, why are you wandering the gardens alone? Can you find no better company than me?"

In the lamplight, Rutledge crooked one eyebrow and moved toward her with his easy, loose-limbed grace. "I was just finishing a smoke, Freddie," he said more gently. "Your cousins and I got back late from the Wrotham Arms, that's all. Gus thought we'd best walk Trent up and down the terrace for a bit. He and Theo just hauled him up to bed. The poor lad will pay for his sins on the morrow, I'll wager."

Frederica swished her skirts past Rutledge and started up the last three steps. "His sins?" she echoed, her back already turned to him. "And the rest of you are pure as the driven snow, I'm sure."

"Pax, Freddie!" Rutledge laughed, seizing her lightly by the shoulder and turning her face back toward his. "What the devil's got into you?"

And then he saw. Frederica realized it when the sparkle slowly melted from his eyes. "Aw, Freddie, what's all this?" he murmured, his hand heavy through the wool of her habit. He lifted the other hand to cup her jaw and slid the ball of his thumb beneath her eye. "Crying? Why? Who? Give me a name, love. I swear to God, he'll be dead by dawn."

At that, Frederica erupted into something which was not quite a laugh and not quite a sob. Killing Johnny— or at least maiming him—was just the sort of thing Rutledge might do, too, if she asked. But her tears were flooding forth now.

On a sharp sigh, Rutledge caught her hand and hauled her hard against him, sending her hat tumbling into the grass. "Oh, shush, Freddie, shush," he crooned, wrapping a strong arm about her waist. "Don't cry, love. Oh, don't cry. I'm sorry I teased you. I oughtn't have. Just don't cry."

His sympathy made it worse. Or better. She wasn't sure. But on the next awful sob, she threw her arms around his neck. Rutledge settled one big hand on her spine and began to ease it up and down. It was a strong, heavy hand, and Frederica needed someone's touch. It didn't much matter that it was Bentley Rutledge, the worst rogue in all of Christendom. One couldn't help but like him, and, for all his wicked ways, he always made her feel comfortable. He was never arrogant or formal or cold. He was just . . . Bentley.

He was patting her back now. "Shush, shush," he crooned.

"Oh, Bentley, I'm just so miserable!" she whimpered. And then Frederica allowed herself the rare luxury of burying her face against his lapel and sniveling pathetically. He smelled of horse, tobacco, and far too much brandy, yet his strength and his touch were inescapably masculine.

But she should be hugging Johnny.

The notion came out of nowhere, blindsiding her. Frederica drew breath again, and another sob shuddered through her. In response, Rutledge tucked her head firmly beneath his chin and drew her tight against his length. "What happened, Freddie?" he whispered, brushing his lips against her hair. "Did someone hurt you? Who? You can always tell old Bentley."

And in that instant, she knew that he was right. Bentley Rutledge was just the sort of gentleman one could confide in, because he'd doubtless seen every sort of wickedness life could offer up—and he knew how to keep his mouth shut, too. "It-it-it's Johnny Ellows," she sobbed. "He doesn't want to m-marry me after all."

She felt his hand stop, felt his fingers dig into her spine. "The deuce!" he softly cursed. "That two-faced dog! He's been hanging out after you since you put your braids up."

"I know!" wailed Frederica into Rutledge's coat. "But now his father says he has to m-m-marry his cousin!"

"Oh, *his father says!*" The derision rumbled in Rutledge's broad chest. "Well, his father is a pompous prig! Ellows doesn't deserve you. Not by half. Gus and I have always said so. And now we know he's gutless in the bargain."

Frederica sniffed again. "What do you mean?"

Rutledge tucked her a little closer. "Ah, Freddie, a man would be a fool not to put up a fight for you," he murmured, patting her lightly on the head now. "I would, were I in his shoes. But—well, I'm not. Wouldn't do at all, of course! All I'm trying to say is that if Johnny Ellows doesn't have the ballocks to—damn! Your pardon, Freddie, but if he doesn't have 'em, then you can do better. Much better."

But Frederica could only shake her head against the rough wool of Rutledge's coat. "But no one else has ever wanted me," she managed to whisper. "And no one ever will. I know! I spent a whole season in London, and not one gentleman proposed. It's because they think I'm not good enough. Not legitimate enough. So it just seemed easier to come home and m-marry Johnny after all. But even Johnny doesn't want me! And now I'm destined to just shrivel up and die an old maid."

She felt Rutledge's body go rigid. "Hush, Freddie." It was an unmistakable reprimand. "Your cousin Gus said you were the prettiest girl in London last season. Those town fops just heard you were already spoken for. Or maybe they were intimidated by your guardian, Lord Rannoch."

"Oh, it's not Elliot!" Frederica sobbed. "It's because of m-my mother. And—and, well, no one can be pretty enough to overcome that."

"Balderdash!" His voice was oddly choked. "You're beautiful enough to overcome any obstacle. Trust me on this, love, because I'm about as jaded as a man can get."

At that, Frederica lifted her face to his, and almost wished she hadn't. Rutledge was staring at her with a gaze that made her breath catch. His mouth was no longer smiling, and his deep brown eyes had gone curiously soft, just as they'd done on Boxing Day.

A long, strange moment held sway. Later, Frederica wasn't perfectly sure why she did it, but she lifted herself onto her tiptoes, pushing her breasts flat against Rutledge's chest. And, oddly, while she was doing it, Frederica was thinking of Johnny—or, rather, thinking of how she had wasted herself on him. She was almost nineteen years old, and she was ready to experience life—real life. Perhaps Rutledge was right. Perhaps Johnny did not deserve her. A mean-spirited little part of her wanted to make him sorry for what he had done and was wondering if she should just ask Bentley to break his legs after all. But most of her brain had already forgotten about Johnny and was thinking only of how Bentley's hands and mouth had felt on hers all those weeks ago.

"Bentley?" Her voice had gone all croaky somehow. "Do you remember last Christmas?"

He was very quiet for a moment. "Might do, Freddie. Why?"

"I mean, when you . . . you kissed me? On Boxing Day?"

He drew in a slow, deep breath. "Er, vaguely."

"Well, it felt nice," she confessed. "And I was wondering if you—if you might do it like that again?"

There was a long, heavy silence. "Not a good idea, Freddie," he finally answered.

His resistance was intriguing. "Why not? I thought . . . well, I thought you liked it just a little."

"Oh, I did."

"Then do it again. Please, Bentley?"

His resistance was short-lived. "Oh, hell, Freddie!" he choked. And then, with a soft sound deep in his throat, he bent his head and lowered his mouth to hers.

In the future, Bentley noted, *be very, very careful where you take a piss.*

It must have been his last clear thought before his lips brushed Freddie's. And somehow, despite a brain slightly clouded by brandy, he had the presence of mind to kiss her tenderly. Sensing her hurt and confusion, he settled his mouth over hers, spread his palm wide against the back of her head, and slid his lips gently over hers until they parted on a breathless gasp. Freddie kissed like an eager virgin, uncertain at every motion, but sweet. So sweet. And all he had to do, or so he told himself, was to make her feel desirable.

Which was precisely the bloody trouble. She *was* desirable. And wildly beautiful with her honey-warm skin and heavy black hair. He'd first noticed three or four years ago, and the thoughts which had begun to run wild through his head had made him feel like a lecherous dog. Which was why he'd found it prudent to treat her—and tease her—like a sister. Well, he bloody well wasn't kissing his sister now, was he?

Bentley knew he should stop, but, as with most of his sins, he simply didn't. Once begun, it just felt too good to quit. So he settled his other hand low against her back and urged her gently against him as he eased his tongue into her mouth. Freddie gasped, drawing cool air into his mouth and bringing home the reality that all of this really was new to her. But she was twining her arms about his neck now and pushing herself against him with an unmistakable feminine hunger—an invitation he had never in his life refused.

Then, to make matters worse, she began to return his strokes, slowly and sinuously sliding her tongue along his, pushing it into his mouth, and making incredibly seductive sounds in the back of her throat. He really wished she hadn't. He might have had a prayer, might by some miracle have dredged up the fortitude to tear his mouth from hers and go the hell upstairs. To his bed. Alone.

But self-discipline had never been Bentley's strong suit, and when she deepened the kiss, he tightened his grip in her hair and savagely tilted her face fully into his, exposing the curve of her throat. He kissed her there and across her high, beautiful brows, then down her cheek. Frederica gasped again, and, in return, Bentley explored her body with his hands, plundering her innocence with his mouth while stroking her waist, the length of her spine, and the generous swell of her bottom.

He kissed her and kissed her until his head swam with some sort of dark, seductive haze. Somehow,

Freddie always had a way of making him ache for something. She made him crave—an emotion he'd damn near deadened with life's excesses. It had to be her innocence. The wanting of a woman whom no man had yet touched. But when he slid one hand beneath her perfect derrière and pressed her more fully against him, Frederica's breath ratcheted instantly upward, her delicate nostrils flared, and he realized, ever so fleetingly, that it just might be something worse. It had been a long time since he'd been able to keep his eyes off the chit.

God. Oh, God. *He could not do this.* Not to her. And not to Gus. Whatever Bentley's sins, he was a good and faithful friend.

Suddenly, to his great surprise, Frederica tore her mouth from his. "Bentley," she whispered. "Do you really think I'm beautiful? Desirable? Do you desire me?"

In the darkness, Bentley stared down at her. "Ah, Jesus, Freddie! If you were any more desirable, Rannoch might be meeting me at dawn."

Frederica licked her lips uncertainly. "Come with me," she whispered, the words tumbling out in a rush. "We cannot linger here. Someone might see."

Like a lamb to the slaughter—a bizarre simile if ever there was one—Bentley caught her hand and allowed himself to be dragged back down the steps and into the shadows of the next terrace. He was already hating himself when Freddie turned to face him, allowing a shaft of moonlight to slant across her perfect, slightly exotic features. It was her eyebrows, he suddenly decided. God, he'd always loved her eyebrows. Bentley felt his control slip another notch.

She was doing this, he tried to remind himself, because she'd been hurt. Young women were like that. He'd seen it—and steered clear of it—often enough. Older women, the kind he always sought out, were wise enough to know that there was always another lover just around the corner who could soothe the sting of wounded pride. Freddie, heaven help her, did not know that. And it was up to him to explain it.

She pressed her body against his again. Though his hands were trembling, he set them firmly on her shoulders and gave her a good, hard shake. "Sweetheart, don't," he warned. "Don't do this. Don't ever slip off into the dark with a man like me."

She looked at him, half innocent, half seductress. "Don't you want me?"

"Desperately." Somehow he managed to give her a brotherly peck on the tip of her nose. "Madly. In the worst possible way. Now disappoint me, Freddie. Leave. Go up to bed. *Alone.*"

Wordlessly, she reached up and curled her fingers about his. With an impish smile, she tugged him down onto a wrought-iron bench, then turned her face to his for a kiss. Bloody hell, the chit was a beauty. When he had been away from Chatham for a while, he could make himself forget how beautiful she was. And now she wanted him to kiss her.

"No," he whispered.

"Yes," she answered. "Now. Please."

So he obliged her. Damn him for a rogue and a scoundrel, but he did, crushing her mouth hard beneath his, as if the harshness of it might shock some sense into her. He did it roughly, crudely, forcing her head back even as he dragged her body against his. He shifted his weight, trapping her between the bench and his body, so there was no way she could miss the jutting weight of his cock. He kissed her and kissed her until the tenderness left, and only the visceral need remained. It ceased to be a game. The breath sawed in and out of his chest. He drove his tongue inside her mouth in what should have been an alarming parody. A clear sign of what he really wanted. What he ached for. And still, she did not falter.

Somehow he found the strength to rip his mouth from hers. "Freddie, stop!" His voice was deep, slightly strangled. "This is not a Christmas kiss. No more. We have to stop. Now."

She looked at him through heavy eyes. Eyes which looked suddenly sure, suddenly knowing. The little girl was gone. And with a slight choking sound, Bentley opened his mouth against the delicate flesh of her throat and let his lips slide down and down.

"Freddie." The name was torn from his chest. "Love, if you touch me again—if you so much as brush your lips over my face—I swear to you, I won't be able to stop myself from pushing you down into that patch of grass and f—" He squeezed his eyes shut and shook his head. "And . . . and doing something to your body that is really, really wrong."

She put her lips against his ear. "Bentley, I'm tired of being really, really good," she whispered. "Do you want me to die a dried-up old virgin?"

"Oh, dear God," he whispered. And for the first time in his life, the phrase was not a blasphemy.

It was Freddie who slid out of her coat first. His own

soon followed and, with it, the last of his restraint. His desire for her was like a living, breathing thing, a thing he could not contain. Swiftly, before he could rethink it, Bentley coaxed her mouth open again and began to slip loose the buttons of her shirt. It was a task he'd done a thousand times, often in the dark, often drunk— drunker, that is, than he was now. And yet his hand shook, and it took longer than it should have done.

Freddie knew what Bentley was about the instant his fingers began to toy with the buttons of her shirt. *I can't pretend,* she told herself. *I can't pretend I don't know. Or that this is somehow his fault.*

She did know. And she did not care. She even had some vague notion of just what she was giving up. But Johnny had never kissed her the way Bentley Rutledge did. She doubted—oh, yes, she deeply doubted—that he even knew how. She doubted most men knew how.

Bentley was and always would be a rake. But he clearly wanted her, and Frederica was tired of saving herself for a marriage that would never be. She had desires, a feeling sometimes like white-hot fire in her blood, which she neither knew nor understood. It was a fire that Bentley, she somehow sensed, would understand.

"Freddie." Bentley choked out the word just as cool air breezed across her breasts. "Freddie, for God's sake, say something. Sweetie, I'm no good. Say *no.* Stop me."

But Frederica just bent her head and rubbed her cheek over the bristles of his day-old beard. It felt so rough and so good. And Bentley smelled the way a man was supposed to smell. Like smoke and soap and sweat all caught up together.

"Oh, bloody hell," he whispered. And then, with hands that shook, he shoved the cambric shirt off her shoulders and into the grass.

She could feel the heat of his breath on her breast. Then he opened his mouth over it and began to kiss it—suck it—through the thin lawn of her shift. Over and over, he drew the tip against his teeth, sending something slow and sweet spiraling through her body. And when Frederica thought she could bear the torment no longer, she arched and gave a soft, strained whimper. But Bentley made a low sound in his throat and turned his attention to the other breast, sucking until the fabric clung obscenely to her hardening nipples.

It was hot, and heady, and frightening. His hands were splayed firmly over her back, pressing her to him. She could smell his hair, the essence of him in the heat which escaped his clothing. It made her ache to touch him back and left her ashamed that she didn't know how. But she trembled when his hands skimmed down her waist to fist in the heavy wool of her skirt. Effortlessly, he dragged it halfway up her thighs and then, on a groan, all the way up. His mouth still on her breast, he eased one hand between her legs.

"Freddie." The word was a desperate plea. "Is this a yes? Sweetie, do you know what I'm asking? If you do, then say *yes*. Or *no*. Please."

Freddie slid her hands up his broad expanse of chest and lifted her eyes to his. His powerful muscles shuddered beneath her touch, a testament to his desire. "Yes," she said. The syllable was soft but certain.

"Good Lord, Freddie, this is suicide," he said, then

tumbled with her into the stiff winter grass, taking the force of her weight on his chest. She sprawled over him, her thigh pressed against the hard, throbbing ridge which she'd noticed beneath the close of his trousers. She knew what *that* was. She'd been raised in the country. With three very male cousins. She splayed her hands across his chest and looked down at him through a wild tangle of hair.

With a touch that was gentle, he threaded his fingers through it and pushed it from her face. And then, after a moment's hesitation, he pulled her full against him and kissed her long and deep.

When he broke the kiss, Frederica found herself panting wildly. Gracefully, he rolled to one side and shifted his weight over her. In the heat of passion, boots, stockings, and drawers were stripped away. The chill night air breezed over much of her body. With his weight braced on powerful forearms, Bentley hung over her, his face cast in shadows.

His eyes. Oh, how she wished she could see his eyes again. Funny that she'd never noticed how warm they were. "Yes," she said again, and Bentley's hand went to his trouser buttons, swiftly jerking them free. In the darkness, she could see little and thought it might be for the best. She felt his hand slide between her thighs to touch her intimately. He gave a little groan of satisfaction and, with his knee, gently pushed her legs wide. "Ah, God, Freddie." The words were an anguished whisper. "I hope I can do this right."

And then, without another word, she felt the hard, hot weight of his erect shaft pressing against her body. It was then that she felt a moment of panic. As if he sensed it, Bentley dipped his head and brushed his lips across her ear. "If you say stop, love, I will. I can."

He sounded as if he were trying to convince himself. She shook her head and felt her hair scrub against the grass. "No, no," she said on a gasp, her hands clawing blindly out for him. "Take me. Give to me. Oh, Bentley, I don't care. I don't care what happens." And in that moment, she spoke the truth. She wanted the pleasure his body promised. Wanted it, and feared it, too. But she was so tired of waiting. The heat in her blood was throbbing through her now. The weight of him pinned her, forced her down against the unyielding earth as his legs pushed hers wider still.

He was going too fast. Bentley knew it when he heard another sharp intake of breath. Ruthlessly, he checked himself and shifted his weight to slide first one finger, then two, back and forth through her soft, curling hair. He ached with lust for her, this girl he knew better than to want. But he did want her. And now he was lost—almost lost—in her sweet virgin's body. With each stroke, he slid deeper into the hot, inviting heat until one fingertip was grazing her clitoris with every motion. Freddie began to pant, then to whimper, and the sound of it brought back the full import of what he was about to do.

This is it, old boy, he warned himself. *Do it, and you are as good as married. Caught by your codlings. Snapped up tight in the parson's mousetrap.*

Or maybe not.

Freddie's family was—well, just a little unconventional. And Freddie might not be fool enough to have him. Her cousins might prefer to simply kill him. Gus would surely try. Rannoch would likely succeed. But he had the most terrifying notion that just once with Freddie might be worth it. The sounds of night and the scent of fallen leaves washed over them, making him somehow more aware of the woman beneath him.

God, she was wet with desire, audibly so, and the thought gave him an incredible sense of power. He wanted her writhing beneath him, wanted to hear her soft, breathless voice against his ear. It would be different, he knew. Sweeter, somehow. And yet he was more than a little scared. Would it hurt? Would she cry? God, that he could not bear.

On the next stroke, he slid two fingers fully inside her, and Freddie gasped. With delicate precision, he drew out and slid in, deeper with every stroke, until he could touch the thin wall of flesh which nature had drawn taut inside her. And suddenly he wanted to rip through it with a ferocity he'd never known before. *She was going to be his.* The insane thought slammed into him like a brick wall. *His.* She had been touched by no man save himself, and the need to lay claim to her, to ram his body past that delicate barrier and take her for himself, raced through him like a lightning strike.

And he could wait no longer. Bracing himself above her shoulder with his hand, he took the weight of his cock in the other and gently probed her silken folds of flesh. To his shock, she rose to meet him, and she was so slick and wet he almost lost control.

"Easy, sweeting, go easy," he whispered. "Oooh, no, no, Freddie. Let me, love. Let me do it."

But there was, he knew, no avoiding the next step. Still, he resisted, trying almost unconsciously to draw back. With eager, innocent motions, her body kept rising with his, following him, her nails digging deep into the flesh of his shoulders. He pushed her hips hard against the grass, but when she arched again on a strangled moan, he slid half inside.

Her head thrashed, and she whispered something. Pleading? Begging? Oh, sweet heaven, she was so beautiful he thought he might die. And then, on a soft, jubilant cry, he thrust himself inside. He remembered little after that, which was devilish odd. He usually just watched himself have sex, distantly and dispassionately, not that that made any sense.

But this time, it was as if heat and light rushed through him, driving him into her. He tried, oh God, how he tried to hold back. He squeezed his eyes shut and dug his fingers into the grass, and then into the very earth itself. But he could not hold back the fierce desire which seemed to possess him.

He was drowning. Drowning in her perfect, virginal softness. Her tender flesh drew at him, sucking the very essence of life from his body. Over and over, he pushed and explored. He wanted—no, needed—to make it good for her. She possessed him, was him, and yet he was afraid he could not take her with him. It might have been seconds, or it might have been hours. And then, dimly, he heard Freddie's sweet cry of urgency. Felt her leg hook round his waist to drag her body against him. Her motions were awkward, artless, and beautiful. Oh, so beautiful. His arms—his entire body—shook now.

Freddie arched again with a choking whimper, then her mouth opened on a silent cry, the sound of perfect ecstasy. *La petite mort.* The little death. And then all hell broke loose inside his head. Never once did he think to slow down, to pull out. Instead, shudder after shudder wracked his body as he drove and pumped his hips into her, until at last, that exquisite light exploded in his brain, and his seed spurted forth, hot and ravenous, marking her as his.

Chapter Two

The mysterious Affair of the Vanishing houseguest.

There was dirt under his fingernails.

Bentley shifted his head on the pillow, but even in the feeble dawn, he could see it. Lord, that was a tad uncouth, even for him. Shaking himself fully awake, he stretched out his hand, and it was then that he noticed the grass stains on his knuckles. His heart lurched, his stomach knotted, and on a groan of despair, he rolled over to see Freddie curled about her pillow like a sleepy kitten.

Her pillow. Her room.

Despair became alarm. Bentley leapt from the bed, and bare-arsed naked he was, too. But one ankle caught in something. Blister it, his drawers. Shaking himself free, Bentley stared down at the telltale heap of clothing which lay strewn on his side of the bed. As if he were a man facing death, his life—or at least the last six hours of it—flashed before his eyes. And then every detail settled over him like a lead weight. After lighting a candle, he sat down in a chair, his head falling forward into his hands.

Dear God. He remembered swaggering off to the Wrotham Arms with the Weyden brothers and letting young Lord Trent come along. He remembered drinking too much and letting Trent play too deep. And then hiring a buxom, flame-haired tavern wench to distract the lad. But Trent wouldn't have her. "Old enough to be my mother," he'd grumbled, red-faced.

So to salvage her pride, Bentley had taken her upstairs, paid her again, and started to have her himself. And he was well on the way to doing a bloody good job of it, too, given how much he'd had to drink. Then Trent had disgraced himself by retching all over the taproom, and the racket had drawn Bentley back down again. Thank God he'd still had his trousers on. But given that the wench was just the type he usually consorted with, he'd be dashed lucky if he hadn't given Freddie the French pox.

Freddie. Oh, Freddie.

That, too, he remembered with painful clarity. Last night, after what he'd done to her in the garden, Bentley had found himself unwilling—no, unable—to leave her. It had seemed ungentlemanly. Or so he had told himself. As if it were considered perfectly good *ton* to tear asunder a young girl's virginity without the benefit of clergy. And so he had brought her here, to the privacy of her bedchamber, knowing that she would wish to bathe away all evidence of what they had done. Then, when he should have taken himself off to toss and turn with guilt in his own bed, he had surrendered to temptation again.

It was odd, but something deep inside him had yearned to undress her. To do it properly, to admire her, this bold, beautiful prize he had claimed. But Freddie's bravado had fled. She had been suddenly shy, and to soothe her, he had kissed her again, slow and long. In response, Freddie had melted. And that had been that, so far as their self-control went.

He had loved her again, but gently, with his hands and his mouth, until her soft gasps of pleasure settled into the night and she had settled into his arms. And again, he'd been unable to tear himself away. But this was the morning after. Something had to be done. But what? Or, rather, how? Scrubbing his hands down his face, he turned a complete circle of the room. Freddie had one of the coveted tower rooms in the oldest part of the house. The ceiling was braced with massive beams, black with age and barely visible in the faint dawn. An old casement window overlooked the side garden, its wavy diamond-shaped panes awaiting daylight. Otherwise, Bentley was trapped in a circle of stone—and in more ways than one.

And yet nothing but honor was stopping him from walking out. In fact, now that he thought on it, leaving—at least until tempers cooled—might just be for the best. But first, he had to talk to Freddie. He drew near the bed again and settled his hand over her bare shoulder. But Freddie did not stir, and he could not bring himself to wake her. Part of it, admittedly, was guilt. But part of it was the peaceful beauty which she radiated in sleep.

How strange it all was. For a long time, Freddie had been the merest slip of a girl, not at all the sort to turn his head. He'd never had a virgin. Never had a woman who hadn't been had a hundred times before. He liked them older. Wiser. And he wanted a clean getaway when he was done. He rarely bedded the same woman two days running, and he rarely went two days without bedding someone. He was—or so his brother often sneered—unrepentantly promiscuous.

Only once had he been foolish enough to take a lover whom he could not leave. The memory of that still turned his stomach. And only once had he taken a mistress. Not because he'd really wanted one, but because he'd liked her, and because the life he could so easily offer Mary had seemed so much better than what she had. But in the end, he'd left Mary, too, with disastrous results.

So why Freddie? She had caught his notice more than once these last few years. So often it had begun to alarm him. Now he could see the gentle curve of her hip beneath the counterpane, could hear the slow, steady rhythm of sleep in her breathing, and he found it all strangely soothing. Her long, heavy hair was down—he vaguely recalled pulling the pins and ribbons from it— and spread across her pillow like an inky waterfall. Soft, sooty lashes fanned over olive skin which always glowed with warmth. Strangely, there was nothing of her fair, blue-eyed cousins in her, though he knew her father had been Trent's uncle Frederick, an army officer who'd died a hero's death in Portugal, leaving his fiancée to bear their child alone.

In her sleep, Freddie smiled and wriggled a little deeper into her pillow. On another strange stab of longing, Bentley turned away from the bed and went to the hearth. Naked, he knelt and stirred up the fire which had been banked for the night. An armoire the size of a dray horse stood opposite, and beside it a giltwood escritoire which looked absurdly dainty. He glanced about the room again and, not knowing what else to do, pulled on his drawers, then lit the branch of candles atop the escritoire.

Ink and a fresh sheaf of paper were already laid out, and Bentley tossed what seemed like a score of pages into the fire before he'd written anything which suited him. It had to suit; he was out of paper. So he sat back in his chair and turned it to the candlelight. He was shocked to see the page tremble in his grasp.

Bloody hell, he thought, his eyes skimming over it. These were words which ought well make a man's hands shake. In truth, Bentley felt just a little ill. But there was nothing else to be done. He had Freddie's reputation to think of. And then there was his obligation to her family. What would they decide? And what did he want?

He leaned back in the tiny chair and considered it. What did he want? To waltz through life unencumbered and unfettered, of course. To be thoroughly irresponsible. It was all he knew, all he'd ever wanted or expected. Besides, he tried to reassure himself, Freddie wasn't apt to want him. Not for anything save a moment's pleasure, right? If she thought otherwise—if her heart somehow formed a girlish attachment to him—Rannoch could always surgically remove it with his dirk. And then turn his knife on Bentley.

Yes, he was most likely a dead man—or would be, once the ink was dry in the parish marriage register. Ah, well. They didn't call him Hell-Bent Rutledge for nothing. It had been bound to come to something like this in the end. So, with a shrug, Bentley folded the note, gave it an impulsive kiss, and propped it up on the windowsill. He meant to tiptoe back to his room, bathe, dress, and await the inevitable. He even went so far as to place one hand on the doorknob. But he still could not quite tear himself away.

On a sigh, he returned to the bed and lifted one hand to touch her hair. But in that instant, an awful clatter arose from deep in the stairwell beyond the door. *Oh, Lord.* His hand froze, and his mind raced. A servant? Yes. With a mop bucket? No. No, a coal scuttle, more likely. His eyes shot to the window. Daylight was almost upon them. He had no way out. A servant would shortly pop in to build up the fire, and Freddie would be irrevocably, hopelessly ruined.

The scuttle clattered again, closer. A little desperately, he strode to the casement window, popped the latch, and swung it wide. Two stories up. Rhododendron and holly beneath. Well, he'd had it worse. At least this time there wasn't an irate husband with a pistol to his back. Snatching up an armful of boots and clothing, Bentley hurled it into the breaking dawn, then hitched himself onto the windowsill. Afterward, he never could remember having actually jumped, yet he must have done, for he landed with a crash and a thud, twigs and shrubbery splintering all about him.

But no one seemed to hear, which was a bloody good thing, for it took him all of two minutes to suck the wind back into his lungs. His right leg was bent awkwardly but not broken. His face was bleeding; an unmistakable warmth was trickling down his temple. Gingerly, he elbowed himself up, the Essex scenery whirling about his head as if he were a top spinning slowly off balance.

Somehow, he staggered to his feet and fished his boots and coat out of a patch of ivy. One stocking was caught on a sprig of holly, and his trousers had sailed over the garden path to land on the lawn beyond. With rough, impatient movements, Bentley gathered them up and jerked them on. He glanced back up at the window just as a draft caught the white underdrapes, billowing them outward. Good Lord, someone really had opened the door! The close call almost buckled his knees.

Unfortunately, it now occurred to Bentley that having escaped the house, he had no way to get back in. Had he been in his right mind, he would have simply crawled under the boxwoods out back and claimed to have passed out drunk, which, given his proclivities, would have been perfectly plausible. But he was not in his right mind. And so he did something unutterably stupid.

It might have been his hangover. Or his guilt. Or a mild concussion. Or—and he hated to admit this—it might have been just a plain old fear of the inevitable. But whatever it was that drove him, in that moment, it somehow seemed as if his best alternative was to start walking, or limping as it were, in the direction of the stables. And to keep on going until he'd hitched up his horse and got the hell out of Essex.

In all likelihood, no one at Chatham Lodge would notice or care. He often came and went without invitation or announcement. And he'd already told Gus that he had to take his leave directly after breakfast, for in less than three days he was due at Chalcote Court for the christening of his newest niece, a child whom he had inexplicably been asked to godparent. Besides, his note told Freddie very plainly where to find him.

Yes, it explained everything, and sweetly, too. The

words had been charming, confident, and laced with just enough honesty to make his offer sound sincere. Not one word of trepidation or doubt could be elicited from his carefully crafted lines. He would await her response, he had said. And he hoped, or so he had claimed, that Freddie would soon make him the happiest man on earth.

And so the soon-to-be happiest man on earth slung his cravat round his neck and hobbled off in search of his horse. But just as he turned the corner, the wind kicked up again, riffling through his hair and flapping at his coattails. Too obsessed with thoughts of marriage, lust, and fear, Bentley just bowed his head and pushed on toward the stables without ever noticing that the breeze had caught something else, something far more important than his coattails. A folded slip of paper came sailing through Freddie's curtains. Away it drifted, like a butterfly just set free, spinning and fluttering as it made its way high above the gardens, over the lawn, and off into the woodland beyond.

The scene at Chatham's breakfast table was usually one of mildly subdued mayhem, for the household was generally large, busy, and informal. Each morning from eight until half-past, teetering trays laden with steaming bowls were toted up and down the kitchen stairs and plopped directly onto the table, rather than the sideboard. It was safer that way, claimed the ever-practical housekeeper Mrs. Penworthy, what with so many hungry young men rushing haphazardly about.

On this particular day, however, only a half-dozen places had been laid round the big table. Mrs. Winifred

Weyden, the household's doyen, had not yet taken her seat. Instead, she was pacing back and forth along the windows and talking to herself, her head bowed over a letter. "Oh, my!" she said on a spurt of laughter. "How shocking!"

"Chafing dish!" sang Mrs. Penworthy, hurling a covered platter onto the table. "Hot kidneys!"

Winnie was undeterred. "Listen to this!" she said to the three young men gathered round the table. "Lady Bland writes that last week the King's hounds chased a stag through the middle of Paddington, and then through the canal, and right into the church!"

"Catching up on all the gossip, Mama?" murmured Gus Weyden, watching his cousin, the Earl of Trent, and praying to God the lad did not disgrace himself over the steaming pile of kidneys which Theo had just uncovered.

"And then there's this!" said their mother, turning Lady Bland's missive a little toward the light. "This coachbuilder—oh, Theodore, what *is* that name?" She thrust the letter at her son Theo.

Theo glanced at it. "Shillibeer," he supplied, forking up kidneys and plopping them onto his plate. "George Shillibeer. Keeps a good livery in Bury Street."

Winnie smiled dotingly. "Yes, Shillibeer. Anyway, it is all very queer, for Lady Bland says he has inventing this thing . . ."

Already chewing, Theo thrust out his fingers and snapped them.

Winnie surrendered the letter.

"An omnibus, Mama," said Theo, glancing at the page as he swallowed. "Got 'em all over Paris. Gus and I rode one once."

"Did you indeed, my dear?" marveled Winnie. "Well, this one is meant to haul passengers up and down the New Road, twenty at a time for one shilling six!"

"Just a bob if you ride up top," corrected Theo, tossing a glance at Lord Trent. "I daresay that's where the bolder fellows ride, eh, Michael? Of course, they jostle and sway like a ship at sea, but you—oh, what?" He had forked up the last kipper as he spoke, and now thrust it, still dripping, at Lord Trent. "Sorry, Michael, did you want this?"

With a faint gagging sound, Lord Trent shut his eyes. At once, Winnie tossed down her letter and rushed to him, barely missing Mrs. Penworthy and a bowl of boiled eggs. "Michael!" She bent over the young man in a crush of pink silk, pressing her hand dramatically to his forehead. "Oh, my dear child, you look dreadful! Have you a fever? Is it your throat? Your lungs? Oh, pray do not take ill just now! You don't even have an heir!"

"An heir?" choked Michael.

"He's sick, Mama, not dying," scoffed Theo.

"Still, Rannoch will think me at fault!" complained Winnie. "He'll scowl and say that perhaps I've not watched all of you properly, but really, I'm quite sure that I have *tried* to do so."

It was clear that Winnie's guilt was speaking, for she was a notoriously lax chaperone and easily distracted from her duty. "Michael is almost of age now, Mama," Gus reminded her. "And I am sure neither Evie nor Elliot expects you to *watch* anyone."

At Winnie's elbow, Michael drew a ragged breath. "Don't fuss, Win," he managed, easing back his chair. "I'm just a tad dyspeptic."

Theo jabbed a fork in his cousin's direction. "Best go back up to bed, old chap."

Michael rose unsteadily, and Winnie sank into her chair. A knowing look passed over her face as her gaze shifted back and forth between her sons. "I see the way of this," she said crossly, once Michael was out of earshot. "No, no! Do not dare play the innocents with me! Michael is still too young to fall in with your riffraff crowd. And Bentley Rutledge! I shall strangle him, too! Where is that rascal?"

Gus and Theo shrugged just as Frederica's shadow fell across the table. "Good morning," she said. The gentlemen stood at once, and Theo pulled out her chair. "If you're looking for Michael," she continued, "he just passed me on the stairs."

"Not Michael," said Theo dramatically. "Rutledge. Mama has sworn to kill him."

Frederica gasped. "Oh, no!" she said, half rising from her chair again. "Indeed, Winnie, he did not—I mean, it was all my—"

Winnie cut her off. "My dear, you are very kind to take up for these scamps, but Rutledge is a bad, wicked man. And I know perfectly well that they were all four in their cups last night."

"Oh." Frederica fell back into her chair and hid her trembling hands.

Just then, Mrs. Penworthy bustled back up the steps with a coffeepot and tipped it adroitly over Frederica's shoulder. "Is it Mr. Rutledge you're wanting, Mrs. Weyden?" she inquired, pouring a steady brown stream. "For 'tis a very queer thing, but Tess says he's gone off without his valise, and nary a sign his bed's been slept in!"

Suddenly, Frederica seemed to choke. Amiably, Theo reached out to pound her across the back, making her gasp. "All right there, Freddie?" he asked.

Eyes watering, Frederica pressed the back of her hand to her mouth and lowered her gaze. "Wh-what do you all imagine has become of Mr. Rutledge?"

"It's a bit of a poser," mused Gus.

Theo swallowed again. "Well, he certainly came back from the Arms last night. We left him on the terrace when we—"

"The *Wrotham* Arms?" interjected Winnie shrilly. "That ramshackle roadhouse?"

Gus smiled tightly. "Yes, Mama," he said. "Anyway, we did go upstairs before him." He turned to his brother. "Theo, you did not, I hope, lock the door behind you?"

"Someone did!" sang Mrs. Penworthy from the stair-well. " 'Twas locked this morning."

"Freddie!" Alarmed, Gus's gaze went to her. "Freddie, you were not, by some chance, out late last night?"

Frederica's bottom lip began to tremble. "Wh-what on earth do you mean to suggest?"

Gus looked at her strangely. "Nothing, Freddie. Nothing at all. It is just that I know how you some-times like to—to *walk* of an evening." From across the table, he tried to wink at her without his mother's noticing it. "And I thought, or rather hoped, that per-haps you'd left the tower door unlatched. As, er, you sometimes do?"

Winnie waved her hand dismissively. "Oh, Gus, the child went to bed with the headache," she reminded him. "Right after supper. Do you not remember?"

"Quite so," said Gus swiftly. "And I hope, Freddie, that you are fully recovered?"

But Theo was not concerned with Frederica's feigned headache. "So we left a guest locked out last night?" he interjected. "Is that what it comes to?"

"Do not be ridiculous," said his mother, motioning impatiently for the toast rack. "Bentley Rutledge is not a guest."

Gus laughed. "But does it not horrify you, Mama, to consider that we may have left him to sleep in the stables?"

It was Theo's turn to laugh. "Oh, ho! That one never slept in the stables, depend upon it! More likely, he returned to the Wrotham Arms and bedded down with that red-haired wench he'd already paid."

"Really, Theo!" Now Winnie was horrified. "Recollect, if you will, that there is an innocent at this table!"

Ingenuously, Theo looked about. "Who? Oh. Freddie."

But Freddie did not look insulted, or even especially innocent. Instead, she looked quite ill. Awkwardly, she jerked from the table. "Your p-pardon," she said weakly. "I am afraid my headache has returned." And on those words, she bolted from the room.

Winnie's face softened with worry, and she began to make maternal clucking sounds. "Oh, dear me, first Michael and now Frederica? Perhaps there really is something going round!"

Chapter Three

In which the Prodigal Son limps home.

"Dearly beloved, ye have brought this child here to be baptized, and ye have prayed that our Lord Jesus Christ would vouchsafe to receive her, to release her from sin." Caught in a shaft of jewel-colored light, the Reverend Mr. Basil Rhoades droned on, his gaze flicking periodically to his prayer book.

Bentley Rutledge stood opposite the rector, with every intention of listening. But as with so many of his good intentions, this one slipped from his grasp. Somehow, he lost his place in the liturgy—another metaphor, no doubt—as his gaze drifted away from the squat Norman font in which countless generations of his mother's people had been baptized. He found himself staring along the length of the nave and through the arch, until his eyes were focused somewhere in the murky depths of the chancel, and his thoughts were drifting deep into the shadows.

He had few memories of this place, the church of St. Michael the Archangel. There had been the occasional christening or wedding, yes. And in the Rutledge family, funerals aplenty, for they were prone to live hard and die young. But the very essence of this place, the smell of musty hymnals and cold, damp stone, felt unfamiliar, despite the fact that for most of his twenty-six years, he had lived in its shadow. The quiet cadence of the prayer book was like a foreign tongue. The refracted splinters of light which stabbed through the stained glass and spilt across the flagstones were almost otherworldly. His father hadn't been much of a churchgoer, and Bentley had followed suit.

Basil cleared his throat sharply. "Dost thou believe all the articles of the Christian faith as contained in the Apostles' Creed?" intoned the rector. "And wilt thou endeavor to have this child instructed accordingly?"

Beside him, Bentley's sister, Catherine, gave him a subtle nudge. His eyes caught hers in alarm. "I—er, I do believe them," he said awkwardly. "And by God's help I will . . . I will endeavor so to do."

Basil's lips thinned in mild irritation. "And wilt thou endeavor to have her brought up in the fear of God?" he asked, glancing at the prayer book. "And to obey his holy Will and Commandments?"

"I—I will," Bentley managed. "By—ah, by God's assistance." Then he squeezed his eyes shut and waited for lightning to strike him dead.

But no lightning struck. It ought to have done, given such a dubious promise from such an unlikely instrument of the Lord. Basil seemed to have expected it, too, for he'd also lost his place. But somehow, the rector jerked back into motion and continued, eventually reaching out to take the babe from Bentley's sister-in-law, Helene.

After settling the infant in his arms and draping the lace christening gown carefully over his elbow, Basil looked again at Bentley. "Name this child."

Bentley felt a moment of panic. "Er—Alice," he

answered. That much he knew, for it had been his mother's name. In desperation, he looked down at the words he'd scribbled in the margin of his prayer book, but his perspiring fingers had blurred them. "Alice Marie Emelyn Rutledge," he read, rushing through the words and praying he'd got it right. He must have done, for Helene was smiling at him proudly.

"Alice Marie Emelyn Rutledge," echoed Basil, dipping his fingers into the font, and crossing the child's forehead. "I baptize thee in the name of the Father, and of the Son, and of the Holy Ghost. Amen."

But little Emmie took exception to the cold water. She went rigid on a loud squall, one fist swiping Basil across the nose, knocking his spectacles askew. Disconcerted, the rector moved as if to thrust the child out at arm's length, but Emmie snatched hold of his surplice, requiring Basil to disentangle himself. Helene stepped forward to pry the fistful of white linen from Emmie's hand with an apologetic look.

God help us all, thought Bentley. *That one's a Rutledge for sure.*

Soon it was over, and they were flooding from the church and into the wintry sunlight. His elder brother, Cam, Lord Treyhern, led the way, carrying Emmie, who was marginally calmer now. Bentley's sister, Catherine, and his cousin Joan herded the children out. They darted off into the sun like brightly colored fish in a pond. With a shy smile, Joan turned back and slipped her arm companionably through Bentley's. They chatted quietly for a moment while Helene and Cam accepted congratulations all around.

It was good to see his pretty cousin. It was especially

good to see her looking well, happy, and, if he was not mistaken, expecting again. Before his run-in with Freddie, Joan had been the only woman he'd ever considered marrying. Thank God she'd eloped with Basil and saved them both from his stupidity.

"You must call at Bellevue soon," Joan said softly. "We will have a long walk, Bentley, and a long talk, too. I have a secret to tell you. It will be like old times."

"Yes," he said quietly. "Like old times, Joan."

Only two months apart in age, he and Joan had once confided everything in one another. But they had been children then, and he was not at all sure he could endure those old times again. Drawing her arm from his, Joan slipped away to chase after one of her many children. Her husband, Basil, was still smiling benevolently at the small crowd which had finished filing from his church door.

Of course, all the village tabbies were there to scowl disapprovingly at Bentley. And then in turn—when each thought the others weren't looking—the old girls would cluck, straighten his cravat, and then kiss him on the cheek as if magnanimously forgiving him for some mortal sin.

If they only knew.

Yes, he now carried one which was weighing a tad heavier than all the rest. Well, perhaps save one. Of course, what he'd done with Freddie wasn't, strictly speaking, a mortal sin, but it bloody well felt like it. And after three days, he was tired of waiting for the ax to fall. He wondered just how hard on his heels the bad news was.

He could almost see poor Freddie now, tearfully confessing all to Winnie Weyden. He could see Winnie screeching, wailing, then penning a hysterical note to Lord Rannoch. He could see that black-hearted devil's carriage careening back from Scotland, Rannoch polishing up his claymore as he came. Could see himself being marched down the nave with one of those nasty little Scottish daggers at his back and a rope drawn tight around his ballocks, choking off his life's blood.

Marriage. A wife. A life of bondage.

God help him.

Suddenly, cool fingers touched him lightly on the cheek. Bentley blinked and looked down at his sister-in-law, Helene, whose eyes were melting with warmth. "Ah, you did not fail me, my dear," she said in her faint French accent. "I knew you would not."

Sometimes, he thought, *I get a little tired of her faith in me.* But Bentley did not say that aloud. Instead, he just snorted. "You were bloody lucky, Helene." Suddenly, a chill wind chased over him, and Bentley looked up to see that they stood in the shadow of the bell tower. The others were leaving, filing off toward the village gate or onto the path which circled through the churchyard and back up to Chalcote. Dutifully, he returned his gaze to his brother's wife and offered her his arm.

With another smile, she took it, and they followed the others at a distance, making their way between the gravestones in silence. The churchyard was separated from Chalcote's orchard by a stone wall, set with a thick wooden door. Bentley helped her through, then turned to push it shut.

"Bentley, I fancy you are limping," Helene remarked as he dropped the latch.

"Wrenched my knee," he admitted.

"Oh, dear." She stared at his leg. "How?"

He tried to glower at her. "None of your business."

Amiably, Helene shrugged, took his arm again, and changed the subject. "You have changed, Bentley, since we saw you at New Year's," she mused. "You are quieter than usual. A little grim, I think. It is not like you, my dear. I hope nothing is wrong?"

Bentley felt his fists clench. "Did my brother put you up to this, Helene?" His words were low and hard. "Is it to be an inquisition?"

His sister-in-law jerked back as if he'd struck her. *"Nom de Dieu!"* said Helene quietly. "How can you ask this? And do you imagine Cam would notice anything amiss in someone's manner? Like most men, he sees only deeds."

Yes, and maybe that is what troubles me.

The thought came out of nowhere, and at the last instant, he bit back the words. Instead, Bentley slowed to a halt and covered Helene's hand where it lay upon his coat sleeve.

"Forgive me, Helene," he said quietly. "I spoke wrongly."

They strolled through the orchard in silence, the grass brittle beneath their feet, the bare branches clattering above their heads. Catherine, Cam, and the others were well up the hill now, and Helene seemed disinclined to hasten after them. And so Bentley slowed, matching his pace to hers and allowing a measure of peace to settle over him.

As if to stir him from his reverie, Helene gave a little squeeze on his arm. "Pray do not be so quiet," she said.

"You worry me. Tell me instead of your adventures—at least those fit for a lady's ears. Did you come straight here from London?"

"More or less," Bentley replied, bending down to pluck a twig from Helene's cloak hem. "I'd been in Essex for a few days. Went by Hampstead just long enough to put up my kit and turn round again."

Helene smiled. "And you've dressed for the occasion, I see. Most impressive."

"Almost respectable, do you mean?" He looked up, squinting into the sun. "I daresay my brother finds that most gratifying."

She did not answer but continued on in her musing tone. "The season is almost upon us, Bentley. Will you spend it in town?"

"What, doing the pretty with all the debs?" He laughed and began to snap the twig into pieces, tossing them over his shoulder as they strolled. "No, I fancy not."

"But you might enjoy it, Bentley. Don't your friends go? Wouldn't you like to meet—well—new people?"

Bentley tossed her a dark look. "Good Lord, Helene, do you think to marry me off?"

At that, she laughed. "Heavens, no! You are not the marrying kind, Bentley. Still, you might consider cultivating a better class of friends, you know."

Bentley stopped abruptly on the path. "I cannot believe I am hearing this from you, Helene, of all people! What happened to your fine notions of egalitarianism? Besides, not all my friends are as ramshackle as Cam makes them out to be. Augustus Weyden, for example. He is quite well bred."

"Precisely my point," Helene gently insisted. "He and his brother Theodore seem quite nice gentlemen. You should spend more time with them. And of course they will be in town for the season."

"Will they?" Bentley shot her an odd look. "I thought they went only under duress."

Daintily, Helene skirted a patch of mud. "Lord Rannoch's eldest daughter is to make her come-out this year."

Bentley was taken aback. "Do you mean little Zoë Armstrong? Helene, she is but a child!"

"Ah, but all of seventeen, at least," murmured Helene.

With a stab of guilt, Bentley remembered that Zoë was but a year or two younger than Freddie. And Zoë seemed a child to him. He vaguely recalled the invitations which had landed on his desk last spring when Freddie debuted. He had been surprised by them, even as he had declined them. He had been quite sure that Freddie was too young for such a thing.

But she had not been too young to lust over, had she? He had been a little ashamed of his feelings then. Now he was mortified. And suddenly, he felt very, very old.

"And so you will do it?" interjected Helene brightly. "You will stay in town for the season and accept at least a few of the invitations which come your way?"

"Absolutely not, Helene." Bentley quickened his pace, tugging gently on her arm.

But suddenly, an appalling chill settled over him. The truth was, he might have no choice about attending the season's events. By the time invitations went out, he might well be married. Once wed, a man belonged as much to society as he did to himself. Appearances would matter. A fellow wouldn't dare get himself carried out boots first from any sordid pubs or rowdy whorehouses. A man's public conduct reflected on his wife. And a gentleman never, ever embarrassed his wife.

Nor would he, Bentley sadly realized. Instead, he would have to learn to be tactful, to partake of his indulgences with a newfound respect for discretion. That much, at the very least, he would owe to Freddie. And so Bentley strode up the rest of the hill, imagining himself to be a very magnanimous and put-upon fellow.

Winnie Weyden folded her newest letter neatly and laid it in the center of the drawing-room tea table. "Five weeks!" she exclaimed, gazing absently at the crackling hearth. "Oh, dear! So much to be done! I think we must take on another laundry maid. And notify the dress-maker, too. We'll want a bolt of ice-blue silk put back for Zoë. And the hats and gloves . . ."

At the pianoforte, Theo stared across the room at his brother and rolled his eyes without missing a note. Gus lifted his gaze from the chessboard which he and Frederica shared. "Five weeks until what?" he asked lightly. "Really, Mama, you are beginning to have entire conversations with yourself."

Already hopelessly beaten, Frederica fell back into her chair. "She's reading a letter from Cousin Evie," she said in a low tone. "Evie and Elliot are coming home from Scotland."

"And then we're to go straight to town," added Winnie in a suffering tone. "There is Zoë to be got ready for the season, and in so little time! And you, Freddie! Last year's ball gowns simply will not do."

Freddie turned from the chess table in horror. "My gowns?"

But Winnie was already calculating. "At least six new ones," she murmured, ticking them off on her fingers. "Unless we can take the ruching off the neckline of your ivory silk. You are not, after all, a debutante now."

Gus slid his knight dangerously close to her queen, but Freddie paid it no heed. "Winnie, surely I need not attend another season?"

Winnie lifted her brows. "You are out now, my love," she responded tartly. "Surely you wouldn't see poor Zoë launched without your support? Besides, Squire Ellows and his family are going this year." This last was said suggestively.

Dramatically, Theo banged out the last three notes of his sonata. "We! Are! Doomed!" his beautiful baritone voice proclaimed.

"Aye, Freddie, we are," agreed Michael, stirring from his position by the hearth. The young Earl of Trent let his foot slide from the brass fender and drained the last of his sherry. "We'll all go, or my sister Evie'll know the reason why. At least you ain't cursed with a standing order to dance with all the wallflowers."

"No, because I'm one of them!" Freddie jerked from her chair, almost upsetting the board. "And I can't go, do you hear? I just can't!" And with that, she hastened from the room.

"Dash it, there she goes again!" she heard Theo mutter. "What's got into old Freddie?"

A cavernous silence settled over the drawing room,

but Frederica did not stop. Instead, she rushed up the main staircase and down the passageway until she reached the stone steps which led to the old tower. Around and around she went until at last she reached her door, pushed it open, and flung herself across her bed.

She hated this. Hated to behave so appallingly. So childishly. She certainly wasn't a child any longer, if ever she had been. But lately, she seemed unable to get a grip on her emotions. A bad hangnail could make her cry. What on earth was wrong? Since the night Johnny had broken off with her, life had seemed as if it would never be normal again. On a sob, Frederica buried her face in a bed pillow.

She wished she had someone to talk to. She missed Zoë. They had been best friends for almost ten years. When Cousin Evie had married Zoë's father, Lord Rannoch, Frederica had been thrilled. Her older cousins—Evie, Nicolette, Gus, and even Theo—had always seemed so grown up. But when Zoë had come into their lives, for the first time Frederica had had another girl to share her secrets with. Yet she now had a secret she was not comfortable in sharing with anyone, certainly not with Zoë.

Bentley Rutledge.

He was her secret. Her sin. Her shame. What she had done with him in the dark that night had been wrong. And dangerous. She was appalled by what she had done. By what she had *asked* for. And yet, given the opportunity—and this was the most appalling part— Frederica was not at all sure she wouldn't do it again. And this time, it wouldn't be for spite.

Frederica did not understand how she could think of Bentley Rutledge and still feel that incredible yearning deep in her belly, when he had treated her so shabbily. But what had she expected? That she would awaken in his arms to hear his vow of undying love? Ha! She knew him better than that. Thank God she'd never been fool enough to fancy herself in love with him.

Still, there was no doubt that he could light up a room with his warmth. And it was hard not to notice the way he could throw back his head and laugh—really laugh—and often at himself. He was sweet to everyone, especially women. And especially when he wanted something. Once she'd caught him in the kitchen trying to kiss Mrs. Penworthy, who was sixty if she was a day, and all of it over a raspberry tart he'd wanted made for supper. Mrs. Penworthy had taken a wooden spoon to his skull. But they'd had raspberry tart—enough to last a week.

Lord, what a scoundrel, thought Frederica, dashing her hand beneath her damp eyes. And now, she was stuck with the memory of how comforting it had been to drift off to sleep in his arms. Even worse, Evie and her husband, Elliot, Lord Rannoch, had commanded that the family return to London soon. It would look to all the world as if Frederica were back for a second go at the marriage mart.

Suddenly, her heart dropped from her chest into her stomach. Good Lord, what if someone actually did offer for her? She had always dreamed of having a home and a family of her own. It was the hope, no doubt, of most orphans. But she could not in good faith wed a man without telling him the truth. And she had not the courage to do that. And how would she explain such a refusal to her cousin Evie? Or to her guardian, Lord Rannoch? But there was one thing worse, even, than that. What if she went to London and came face to face with Bentley Rutledge? Oh, God! How humiliating. She would never be able to face him again.

It was only later—days later—that Frederica realized how odd it was that the prospect of running into Johnny did not distress her half so much as the thought of seeing Bentley again.

Chapter Four

In which Miss Armstrong is sworn to Secrecy.

Three days passed at Chalcote. Three days of utter silence. The first—the day of Emmie's christening—Bentley occupied himself by ambling aimlessly through the house and garnering the strange stares of the servants in return. He could not blame them, he supposed. He had never been much of an indoors sort of fellow.

On the second day, he packed his niece, Lady Ariane, into his curricle and set off for Aldhampton Manor, where they spent the afternoon with his sister, Catherine, and romping with Anaïs and Armand, her twin toddlers. But Unka Benky could play horsey for only so long before his twisted knee would seize up, leaving him feeling not just old but decrepit, too. Matters did not improve when, over afternoon tea, those black, all-seeing eyes of Catherine's husband began to send shivers down Bentley's spine.

Max de Rohan, Lord de Vendenheim, was a former police inspector, but, his odd background notwithstanding, there was something unnatural in the blood of his family. Not just in Max but in his spooky grandmother, too. Old Signora Castelli was someone a fellow definitely wanted to avoid. She was a crapehanger from hell who could make a man feel as if his soul were being turned inside out and examined for stains, like yesterday's laundry.

By the third day, Bentley felt like a caged animal going slowly insane, and so he shrugged on his drab duster, grabbed his gun, and headed toward the stables to set loose his pack of setters. Halfway along the path, however, he met one of the housemaids, fetching up a jar of beeswax from the gardener's cottage. Queenie paused on the path, set the jar on her hip, and gave him a saucy wink. "And top o' the morning to you, Mr. B.," she said, letting her eyes run over him. "Don't the sight o' you fair warm a game gal's heart!"

And then, because the old girl expected it, Bentley drew up alongside her and gave her a good, solid grope on the arse. "Ah, Queenie," he answered wistfully. "There's not a backside so fine in all of London, I'd wager. I wonder I can stay away from Chalcote at all."

At that, she actually batted her lashes and blushed. "Oh, go on w'you," she answered. "You ain't got the time o' day for the likes of me."

Bentley tossed his gun over one shoulder and smiled. "Now, Queenie love, you know that's not so," he said, sauntering backward down the path while holding open his other hand plaintively. "But old Saint Cam would string me up by my clock weights if he caught me trifling with his staff, wouldn't he? Perhaps, though, it might be worth it, eh? Would you make sure it was, Queenie?"

He was several feet away by then and secretly praying she didn't take him up on it. Queenie just laughed, tossed her hand dismissively, and turned toward the house. But suddenly, Bentley was struck with a notion.

"Queenie, wait!" he called, hobbling back up the foot-path. "Look here—d'you still bring in the morning post?"

Mystified, she nodded. "Aye, me or one o' the footmen."

Bentley considered his next words. Queenie might be a little too experienced even for his tastes, but he was genuinely fond of her. She was a former prostitute who had once done the family a great service by rescuing Ariane from a terrible danger. They had all been deeply grateful, and afterward, Bentley had persuaded Cam to give her a position, for he had known too well the look of a worn-out trull on the long downhill slide.

Queenie was still looking at him, her round, plump face almost maternal. "Wot is it, now, Mr. B.?" she urged. "Come on, it's awright to ask Queenie."

Bentley felt suddenly embarrassed. "Well, it's just the post," he began awkwardly. "If anything comes for me, pull it out, will you? Tell Milford not to leave it on the hall table but to give it to me personally, all right?"

At that, Queenie's expression softened. "Aw, poor lovey," she murmured, patting him on the shoulder. "In a spot o' trouble again?"

Somehow, he managed to laugh. "Queenie," he said, dipping his head to give her a swift, smacking kiss. "You don't know the half." And with that, he hobbled on off to the stables.

The dogs began leaping and wagging before he'd shot back the bolt on the kennel. Suddenly, they were surging around his knees, and as he knelt in the stable yard to ruffle their ears and accept their breathy canine homage, Bentley found himself both surprised and relieved that his dogs had not forgotten him. It was a secret fear of his. A fear of being shut out, cast off from this place he both loved and loathed.

The setters milled about, yapping and prancing, so he made his way down the hill, over the river, then onto the high wold beyond. Here and there, lazy sheep dotted the fields, tugging resolutely at the drab, wintry grass. The dogs snuffled their way through every little spinney and copse they passed, their white-fringed tails fanning eagerly until the occasional bird burst forth, when they would freeze stock-still to await the shot that never came.

Instead of shouldering his gun, he praised the dogs quite shamelessly and kept walking. He had not come to shoot, he realized. It was not even the best time of year for it. No, he had come to think. And to consider how they all lived now—Helene and Cam at Chalcote with all the children, Catherine and her brood at Aldhampton Manor. Even his cousin Joan and her rector had settled into a life of blissful domesticity. But Bentley was still just drifting. Though he supposed he was somewhat fixed, at least so far as the Royal Mail was concerned, at Roselands Cottage, Helene's former home in Hampstead.

When he'd moved in, the place had been empty, save for Helene's old nanny, who occasionally clucked at him but mostly just let him come and go as he pleased. And the place had an utterly fabulous rose garden, though he really did not talk about that a vast deal—after all, a man had an image to maintain. But most importantly, Hampstead was next to London and far from Chalcote, a fact which suited him well. He and Cam often needed a little distance.

When he had been young and foolish, he'd told himself that Cam was just jealous because Bentley was their father's favorite. Randolph Rutledge had seemed to despair of his eldest son, seizing upon every opportunity to mock him. In hindsight, his father's behavior seemed appallingly cruel, and Bentley was sorry for having fallen in with it. And he was sorry for some other, far uglier things, too. Cam had always been a bit of a nose-to-the-grindstone sort of fellow, yes. But thank God for it, else they'd all have drowned in the River Tick. Bentley was old enough now to see that someone had had to do the miserable job of dragging them out.

And yet Bentley had never been able to bring himself to thank Cam for the unutterable sacrifices he had made, the worst of which had been his first marriage, a disastrous union which had saved them all financially, even as it damned each of them emotionally. Cam had been forced to live with a vindictive, amoral bitch who despised him, Catherine had been impelled to marry too young merely to escape, and Bentley . . . well, no point plowing well-furrowed ground. Still, seeing the past so clearly now only made what had happened next seem more unspeakable. He would be bloody lucky now if he did not reap just what he'd sown.

Bentley tried to put it from his mind as he hobbled up the next hill, his favorite place. And when he topped it—the highest for miles around—Bentley could see his cousin Joan's house, Bellevue, gleaming grandly in the distance. The place looked as foreign as a chunk of chalk in the midst of the Cotswolds, for his Aunt Belmont had had white Portland stone hauled halfway across hell just to build something grander and more unique than Chalcote.

Joan wanted to see him, she had said. And he wanted to see her, too. They were to have a long walk, and a long talk, and then Joan had something to tell him. But Bentley was not in the mood to share any more confidences, not even with Joan.

Suddenly, the dogs burst from beneath a raspberry thicket, their pink tongues lolling out as they raced up the hill, darting around the placid sheep. Planting his feet firmly on the ridge top, Bentley turned away from Bellevue to see Chalcote, now equidistant away. The manor house was like a little topaz gem nestled in a sea of olive velvet. Below it, he could see St. Michael's and the churchyard, its gravestones so small and white against the grass they seemed as insignificant as flakes of snow. But they were not insignificant. No, not in the Rutledge family plot.

About a sen'night after her run-in with Bentley Rutledge, Frederica found herself persuaded to a game of bagatelle in the parlor with Michael one blustery afternoon. Winnie had dragged Gus and Theo to the vicarage for tea, but Michael had begged off, and Frederica had pled another headache. Thus far, the excuse had served her well, for she'd not stirred from home in days.

"Poor child!" Winnie had exclaimed as Gus stood in the hall, helping his mother with her cloak. "I do hope it won't come to spectacles, but I daresay no one can suffer the headache as often as you and not be quite near-sighted."

Theo had thundered down the stairs, pulling on his

coat as he came. "My head aches, too," he sullenly remarked. "Perhaps I oughtn't go."

Still holding her kid gloves, Winnie smacked him a cracking blow across the arm with one of them. "Do not be ridiculous, Theodore!" Her guinea-gold curls trembled with indignation. "Get yourself into that barouche this instant! You shan't put off your duty another moment."

Looking more like chastened boys than grown men, Gus and Theo helped their mother down the short flight of steps, casting a mournful look back at Michael and Frederica as they went. They set up the game table, and Michael offered her the choice of cues. Miraculously, Frederica potted the first six shots she called, and a quarter-hour later, she had the upper hand on Michael.

Suddenly, a shadow appeared at the door. "My lord," said the butler. "Mr. Ellows has called. Shall I put him in the parlor?"

Frederica suppressed a gasp. Michael rested his cue on the toe of his boot. "Old Johnny, eh?" he said, shooting her a crooked grin. "What d'you reckon he wants? Send him in here, Bolton. Maybe Freddie can whip us both."

Bolton bowed and left. At once, Frederica laid her cue across the table. "I shall let Johnny finish this match with you," she said quietly. "I must see Cook about dinner."

She had already turned toward the door when Michael caught her by the shoulder. "What's this, Freddie?" His clear blue eyes searched her face. "No time for Johnny?"

"No."

"Surely you don't mean to cut him?"

For a moment, she held his gaze warily. "I just need to speak with Cook."

But it was too late. Johnny stood just outside the door, sliding out of his elegant greatcoat and handing it to Bolton. "Good afternoon, Frederica," he said, making a perfunctory bow. "And Trent, I trust I find you well?"

Michael merely laughed and tossed his cue down next to Freddie's. "Well enough, considering I've just been thrashed," he answered, turning to face her. "Freddie, I'll see to some tea, if you and Ellows will excuse me. May I give Cook your message?"

Frederica eyed him darkly. But in truth, it was hard to blame Michael. He knew nothing of Johnny's perfidy. "I am sure," she said stiffly, "that Mr. Ellows has come to see you—"

"Actually, I haven't," Johnny interjected. And for the first time, Frederica realized how acutely uncomfortable he looked. "A word with you, Frederica, if I may?"

What sort of trickery was this? Freddie looked back and forth between Michael and Johnny. Left with little choice, she acquiesced.

Michael departed, leaving the doors flung wide for the sake of propriety. Frederica motioned toward a chair near the fire. "Will you sit, Mr. Ellows?"

But Johnny dipped his head and stared at her almost shyly. "Ah, you are still angry with me," he said quietly. "Well, I cannot blame you. But I had to call, Freddie. I had to."

"Why?" The word was sharp.

Johnny's face colored. "We leave for London in the

morning," he muttered. "Papa has leased a house, you know. And I wanted to ask . . . well, if I would see you there."

Frederica placed her hand on the back of the chair Johnny had refused and hoped he could not see her fingers digging desperately into the upholstery. "Why, I daresay you might," she answered, her voice surprisingly calm. "It is not, after all, such a very large place."

Johnny came deeper into the room. He stopped but a few feet from her and dragged one hand through his well-coifed hair. "Now, see here, Freddie, that is not what I meant."

Very deliberately, Frederica lifted her brows. "Then what did you mean, pray?"

Johnny made a hissing sound between his teeth. "What I mean is, if I call for you at Strath House, will Lord Rannoch receive me? Will *you* receive me?"

A wave of confusion washed over Frederica, and she felt her knees almost buckle. Surely he did not mean . . . no, he couldn't possibly. Out of stubborn pride, she regained herself. "I cannot think why it would matter to you, Mr. Ellows, but by all means—"

His hand came up, one finger touching her lightly on the lips. "Johnny," he corrected, his eyes suddenly melting. "I am still Johnny to you, am I not, Freddie? Please say that I am."

Slowly, she shook her head. "No, you cannot be," she whispered. "Surely you see that? We cannot go on as if—as if we are still playmates. Or—or something else. Your affianced bride will frown upon it, as well she should."

Johnny mumbled something under his breath.

Frederica did not dare believe what she thought she'd just heard. "I am sorry," she said, her heart suddenly pounding. "Wh-what did you say?"

At last, Johnny sat down, his posture rigid. "I am not betrothed." She heard him plainly that time. "My marriage to Hannah has been—well, it shan't take place after all. There was, it seems, a difference of opinion."

Frederica felt a cold horror steal over her. "What?"

Johnny lifted his eyes to hers, his mouth twisted with a wry smile. "Hannah has bolted to Scotland with her father's steward," he admitted.

But Frederica was slowly shaking her head. "Johnny, no." Her voice was a horrified whisper. "No. This cannot be. You were to marry her. You said . . . why, you said you had no choice."

Johnny shrugged. "Hannah, it seems, made herself a choice," he admitted. "And a bloody bad one, too. Now she is to be cut off without a shilling, and I am to inherit Uncle's property anyway."

"Dear God, I cannot believe this!" Frederica felt suddenly ill. "Your cousin has given up everything to marry for love? And now her father will disinherit her? She has been brave."

"Why, I daresay she has." But Johnny had a satisfied look in his eyes, and Frederica wondered that she'd never noticed it before. "But she's been rather foolish, too. Still, I am off the hook. I am free, it seems, to do as I please."

"As you please?"

"We'll take up, Frederica, where we left off." He smiled and held out his hand.

But, still shaking her head, Frederica took one step backward. "No."

The smile melted from Johnny's face. "What do you mean, no?" he asked. "Freddie, don't be stubborn. I did what I had to do. You cannot punish me for it now."

Frederica sank slowly into the opposite chair. "I think you should leave," she said hollowly. "I think it best you go this minute. And later, if—if you should care to leave your card at Strath House whilst in town, I am sure my cousins will receive you with pleasure."

"And you?" Johnny challenged.

"I am sorry," she answered. "But I shan't."

Johnny jerked to his feet. "My God, I cannot comprehend this!"

"I believe, Mr. Ellows, that you'd best try to come to grips with it." Somehow, Frederica found the strength to stand, throw back her shoulders, and walk gracefully into the corridor and up the steps.

"But Freddie!" His voice echoed up the stairs. "Why are you doing this? Nothing has really changed."

Oh, Johnny, she wanted to cry. *Everything has changed.* She had changed.

Her mind still reeled from shock. Should she laugh? Or cry? Johnny Ellows was hers for the asking now. And yet she could not have him. Because in a fit of anger and confusion, she had done something far more foolish than his cousin Hannah, and she had done it for spite, not for love.

She slowed on the next landing, her hand grabbing hard at the stair rail. A part of her was tempted to marry him anyway. He deserved no better. And a part of her was appalled she could even contemplate such a thing. Then, hard on the heels of that came the knowledge, from somewhere deep in her heart, that it wasn't Johnny she wanted. No, not anymore. It was a frightening realization.

It was a full fortnight after his arrival in Gloucestershire that Bentley spent a late and somewhat intemperate evening at the local public house. Memories and shadows had begun to torment him, and the urge to escape Chalcote had become almost tangible. Moreover, the Rose and Crown did a lovely rack of lamb, and the barmaid, Janie, had a bountiful rack of tits.

Janie had always been dear to his heart—and some of his other organs, too. But on this night, nothing—not even the lamb—had been to his taste. And so he'd merely propped himself up on his elbows near the tapster and bent the poor chap's ear as Janie swished from table to table, looking daggers at his back. Bentley had stumbled back up the hill to Chalcote sometime past two.

Milford came at once to take his coat, then gave a little cough. "You had asked, Mr. Rutledge, that we give you your mail personally?" he said, draping Bentley's coat over one arm.

Bentley was instantly on guard. "What has come?"

"Just this," he said, withdrawing a letter from his pocket. "Her ladyship received it this morning. I apologize for the delay."

"You gave *my* mail to Helene?"

"It was addressed to her," he explained. "But when she opened it, she found a letter enclosed for you, forwarded from Roselands."

Bentley snatched the letter, his stomach bottoming out.

Oh, God. There it was. Gus's handwriting scrawled across the velum. Fleetingly, he wondered why Gus had sent it to the Hampstead cottage when he'd plainly told Freddie he'd wait here in Gloucestershire. He thundered up the three flights of stairs to his bedchamber, but once there, he couldn't dredge up the nerve to open it. Instead, he tossed the letter onto his dressing table, then went to the bureau to pour himself a drink. He oughtn't have needed another, but he did. With a shaky hand, he pulled the stopper from the decanter and sloshed out two fingers of Cam's finest cognac. Then, with a carelessness which would have made a Frenchman faint, he tossed it back in one swallow and waited for the burn.

And still, he couldn't do it. For the next quarter-hour, he paced the floor of his room, considering what the letter might say. Well, not what it might say—that much he knew—but how it might be worded. Would Gus be after his blood? Or would he, perhaps, be glad that they were to be cousins? He tossed the letter another look where it lay, pristine and white upon his dressing table, and gave a bitter laugh. No, it most assuredly did not say that. It was one thing to be friends with a scoundrel, and quite another to have him marry into one's family.

Perhaps it was a challenge? Not likely; Bentley had never been bested with pistols, rarely with swords. No, this was probably just a demand that he present himself at once at Chatham Lodge, fully sobered up and appropriately attired, with a special license in his pocket. His bachelorhood was ending, and a life of responsibility was beginning. At that thought, nausea roiled in his stomach, sending Bentley diving for the slop pot, something he'd not done in an age.

But as it happened, he couldn't do that right, either. He found himself simply staring at a crack in the porcelain bottom. Good Lord. This would not do. He set the pot down and somehow got hold of himself. He was suddenly ashamed. He had to do right by Freddie. She was a sweet and tender thing. Better than he deserved. And now she was to be stuck with him, poor child. Finally, he sat down and slit Gus's black wax seal. With an ice-cold calm, his eyes skimmed the words. And then skimmed them again.

What the devil?

The letter was little more than an apology! Gus had somehow got it into his head that Theo had locked Bentley out of the house. The entire family, or so the letter purported, was mortified. His valise, Gus wrote, had been carefully packed and sent on to Hampstead. They hoped he would favor them with another visit soon. Gus closed the missive with a slightly off-color remark about the redhead left pining for his attentions down at the Wrotham Arms.

Damn.

Damn and blast and bloody hell! That deceitful little witch! She had not told them! Not one word. It was obvious. Good God, how could she do this? How could she do this to her family? To herself? To him? What did she think? Did she think that he would not care? Did she somehow imagine that she could simply offer up her virginity to a fellow and then expect him to slink off quietly into the night? Suddenly, his hands were shaking again, but not with dread. It was with anger and with indignation.

By God, that girl was *his*. Surely she had better sense

than to try to pass herself off as anything else? Surely marriage to him could not be the worst of her options? Could it? Well, good God! He did not know. He really did not know. Had he not proposed very prettily? Utterly begged her to marry him?

Well, those had been his words, anyway. And he had never once let himself believe that they would not be wed. He had not wanted it, of course. This was a lucky escape. He should account himself most fortunate. So why did he feel such a black, boiling rage? Why did he suddenly yearn to get his hands around Freddie's lovely throat? And why had he suddenly thrown open his wardrobe, yanked out his portmanteau, and begun to stuff his clothes into it?

Because there was no point in cooling his heels here. No point in waiting on a letter which was never going to come. By God, he would just forget about Freddie. When next he went to Chatham Lodge, he would pretend that . . . well, he just wouldn't go. He would never go there again. Gus and Theo—even that pup Trent, if he wished—would just have to come down to London, where they could have some proper debauchery.

On that thought, Bentley stalked back to his dressing table, snatched up Gus's note, and tossed it onto the coals which were now dying in his hearth. Then, flinging himself into his favorite armchair, he propped his elbows on his knees and watched the edges glitter hotly with yellow, then with red. And suddenly, the letter burst into flame and was gone.

For Frederica, the days dragged on, one into another, with a disheartening sameness. Johnny left for London, and she could not get Bentley Rutledge out of her mind. And when at long last Zoë came home, bursting with her usual exuberance and filled with tales about the cold, barren beauty of her father's seat, Frederica could only listen with half-hearted attention. Nor could she bring herself to confide the depth of her folly to Zoë. And so, early one morning when she longed for a friendly face, she slipped into Zoë's room and, in bitter, hushed tones, told her only of what Johnny had done.

Zoë, a dark little sprite of a thing, simply laughed her tinkling laugh and shrugged. "Good!" she said, padding across the room in her dressing slippers. "He does not deserve you, Freddie. You have crushed his heart with your boot heel, and I am glad. Now we will go to town, you and I, and take London by storm!"

"Take London by storm?" Frederica echoed dryly. She lay stretched across Zoë's bed, flipping through a fashion periodical which Winnie had forced upon her. She rose onto her elbows and eyed her friend narrowly. "We're more apt to set London on its ear, Zoë. The bastard debutantes! I can hear it now."

Zoë lifted her head from the trunk which she had already begun to pack. "Me, I do not care what they say," she insisted, her brown eyes glittering. "And gossip is not always a bad thing, Freddie. It will make us all the rage, you'll see."

"I was not any sort of rage at all last year," Freddie retorted, thumbing impatiently through her pages.

Zoë just laughed again and forced a fistful of stockings into one corner of her trunk. "Ah, but this year, your necklines will be lower," she said. "And this year, you go with me. Before, you were so beautiful and proper. So unattainable. Besides, your parents were quite respectable. A brave officer. A beautiful widow. Such a sad story of true love." Zoë lifted her chin and batted her eyes dramatically.

"Your point, Zoë?"

"My parents were not respectable." She giggled. "A wicked French dancer for a mother! A disreputable rake as a father! Society craves even the scent of scandal, and oh, I will seem very, very accessible. And in my company, you will seem so as well. I will make sure of it. We will turn heads, break hearts, and find our true loves!"

In response, Frederica hurled her *Ladies' Quarterly* at Zoë's head. "Hush up, Zoë."

But the younger girl caught it and began to dance it merrily round the bed. "April and May! April and May!" she sang. "You'll be wed before All Hallows Day!"

Frederica pressed her hands to her ears, shutting out the sound. She wouldn't be married in this lifetime, she now realized. Nor would she turn heads or break hearts. And she prayed she did not find her true love, for the pain would be too bittersweet. Tired of Zoë's song and dance, Frederica sat up and clambered off the bed. But when her feet hit the floor, the room dipped and spun wildly, then something sucked her down into a big, black roar.

Next she knew, Frederica was staring at the ceiling, and Zoë was on her knees beside her. "Freddie!" she cried, pressing a cold hand to Frederica's forehead. "Oh, my! Are you all right?"

Frederica felt her face bead with perspiration. But

the awful roar slowly receded, and she was able to lever herself gingerly onto one elbow. It was then that the nausea gripped her. Eyes flying wide, she clamped one hand to her mouth, and the sensation relented.

Perhaps it was good old feminine instinct. Or maybe just Zoë's innate French insight. But whatever it was, suddenly, Zoë knew, for a sorrowful suspicion passed over her face. "Oh, Freddie!" she said very softly. "Surely not . . . ?"

Frederica hesitated. "Oh, Zoë, I'm so afraid."

"Dear God!" whispered Zoë. "Papa will strangle Johnny. And he'll lock you up for the rest of your life."

Frederica let her head fall back onto the floor. "Oh, Zoë!" she cried, one hot, stinging tear slipping from her eye. "Don't tell! Oh, please don't!"

Zoë blanched and sat weakly back on her heels. "Freddie, oh, my dear, is that wise?"

Frederica shook her head, her hair scrubbing over Zoë's carpet. It was not the first time such a wave of sickness had hit her, and she, too, knew the signs. "Just a few more days," she whispered. "Oh, Zoë, I have to be absolutely sure! And then, I will tell Cousin Evie. I swear it."

"Yes, all right," Zoë reluctantly agreed. "But you'd best write to Johnny at once."

"Oh, Zoë," whispered Frederica sorrowfully. "There is something—someone—I'd better tell you about right now."

Chapter Five

In which Lady Rannoch concocts a Most devious Plan.

Strath House, the London residence of the Marquis of Rannoch, was not in town at all, but just a merry jaunt away, in the fashionable suburb of Richmond. Rannoch's life was a perfect example of the old adage "Be careful what you wish for," because once upon a time, whilst wallowing in the depths of self-made misery, the marquis had wished for a big, happy family to enliven his days, and a very lovely wife to enliven his nights.

So it was his own fault that beneath the marquis's vast and paternalistic roof lived not just himself but his precious daughter, Zoë, his beloved wife, Evie, their two young children, and—when he fell out of favor with whatever lady's sheets he'd been wrinkling—the Marquis's disreputable uncle, Sir Hugh. And that was just the second floor. Above lived her ladyship's young brother, now the Earl of Trent, her sister Nicolette, who was at present in Italy, and their paternal cousin, Frederica d'Avillez, an orphan of the Napoleonic wars.

Above lived Lady Rannoch's friend and former governess, the merry widow Weyden, and sometimes even her handsome, slightly dissolute sons, Augustus and Theodore, who were called, somewhat incorrectly, cousins. This huge house, stuffed with dear relations, near-relations, and no-relations, was presided over by his lordship's very Scottish butler, MacLeod, whose brows flew haughtily upward at the very mention of the word *pension,* and whose age no one—not even the marquis—dared to ask.

With a few unfortunate souls, however, the marquis's bite still rivaled his bark—and then some. And so, on one lovely day in early April, when no cloud marred the sky, Lady Rannoch entered her husband's private library with every intention of leashing and muzzling him. This was a room she seldom frequented, for, despite her years of happy marriage, it remained every inch a man's room. Heavy velvet draperies still reeking of cigar smoke hung from the windows, and beneath them sat an eight-foot mahogany sideboard, its gleaming surface laid with crystal decanters filled with every sort of single-malt whisky known to man and its little doors stuffed with chamber pots, playing cards, ivory dice, and the like. The marquis, alas, had never been a saint.

As with the rest of the house, here and there sat priceless objets d'art—Grecian sculptures, Capodimonte porcelains, and vases from a half-dozen Chinese dynasties. Rannoch couldn't get his faint brogue round most of the words, and so he simply referred to it as *gimcrackery,* for all of it had been hand-selected by his former valet, a prissy, particular man with the taste of a museum curator, who had thought his master a cultural philistine. Kemble had long since become more of a friend than a servant, but the gimcrackery remained, because Lady Rannoch liked it—and could even pronounce it.

But today, the marchioness saw neither the burgeoning beauty of spring nor the decorating genius of Mr. Kemble. She had come as the harbinger of grim news, and once she'd sucked up her courage, she lobbed it like a hot mortar casing, right into the middle of the room.

Her husband gaped as if she'd just gone stark raving mad.

"Freddie has been what?" Rannoch's powerful voice rattled the windowpanes. "Good God Almighty, Evie! Swear that my ears deceive me!"

But his wife did not need to repeat herself. The word *ruined* still hung in the air, like a red flag waving at a volatile bull. "I'm very sorry," she whispered. "And Frederica is, of course, quite shattered."

Rannoch's tread was heavy as he left the desk and strode to the windows. "By God, I blame myself for this," he said, his fist falling against the window frame. "They should have been made to go with us to Scotland, she and Michael."

Evie saw his jaw was already twitching. She turned back to the window. "No, it's my fault," she answered. "But my brother is an earl now, almost of age. And as for Freddie—" Her voice broke almost wistfully. "Well, she was so eager to see Johnny upon his return. I had not the heart to refuse her."

Her arm snaked around her husband's waist, and, on a sob, she buried her face against his cravat. Rannoch patted her shoulders. "Ah, well," he said, his voice rueful yet gentle. "She saw him right enough, didn't she? And now there's the devil to pay."

"Oh, Elliot," Evie whispered into the silk of his waistcoat. "You don't understand."

"My love, it will all come aright in the end. Ellows is a bit callow and arrogant, but what young man is not?" Rannoch patted her again. "And he'll do his duty by Freddie," he added grimly. "Or I shall know the reason why."

"Oh, I wish it were that simple." Her words were a thready whisper. "But it wasn't Ellows."

Not Ellows? At last, Rannoch caught the dawning horror in his wife's voice. His blood chilled, and his heart nearly stopped. Someone—and not the fellow she'd so clearly hoped to wed—had violated his sweet little Freddie? What man would dare? The quiet, elegant girl, who was in many ways his favorite amongst all the children, had been seduced? *Or worse?*

The first thought left him reeling. The second left him rabid. One hand fisted at his side, and one purpose seized his brain. *The name.* By God, a traitor had been harbored beneath his roof. And that traitor was going to die.

"Who?" he growled. "By God, I'll have his head!"

But Evie was weeping. A fragment of memory—a vision of Frederica as a little girl—began to torment him.

When he'd first fallen in love with Evie and her family, Frederica had been nothing but coltish legs and big, brown eyes. And amazingly gentle and wise. As the runt of the litter, she'd often been teased, and somehow, he had become her champion. Often, she had returned the favor. Yes, in a way which defied explanation, Freddie had been his friend. A friend he had direly needed. Was it any wonder he'd so quickly developed an abiding tenderness for the child who had known neither mother nor father?

And now, someone—someone who held his own life mighty damned cheap—had dared to touch her. He took his wife by the shoulders. "Evie," he said, trying to keep his fingers from digging into her flesh. "Who did this?"

Evie bit her lip, and her eyes pooled with fresh tears. "She says it was Bentley Rutledge," she answered bitterly. "The Honorable Mr. Randolph Bentham Rutledge. So, shall I have the announcements engraved and welcome him to our family?"

"Rutledge!" the marquis roared. "Rutledge? Why, I'd sooner be damned!" Blood was pounding in his head. Driven by it, Rannoch stalked toward the bell pull, very nearly ripping it from the wall. "And I'd sooner welcome him to his own funeral!"

Evie's voice followed him. "I fear it shan't be that simple, Elliot," she said, fingertips pressed to one temple as if her head, too, was pounding.

Rannoch stormed back. "I should like to know who's to stop me."

But his wife just shook her head. "Frederica may," she said softly. "She says that—I mean, I think that—oh, Elliot, it seems almost certain she carries his child."

A deadly silence held sway for three heartbeats.

"God damn him!" And then came a bloodcurdling roar, echoing off the walls and through the house. As if his hand were not his own, Rannoch's fingers encircled the throat of an exquisite Chaffer bust—George II, to be precise—and with no effort at all, he hefted it up and hurled it through the window, a good twenty feet into the gardens beyond. Glass shattered and wood splintered. Shards of precious porcelain rained onto the draperies and bounced off the floor. George's nose, never his best feature, clattered off the windowsill, then tumbled across the parquet floor. Outside, for an instant, even the birds went still.

Evie could only gape at the destruction. And then Rannoch resumed his diatribe. "Damn him!" His fist pounded the sideboard where the bust had sat. "Damn him straight to hell! I'll gut him like a hare! I'll slit his throat an inch at a time!" The decanters of whisky were rattling now. "I'll pike his frigging head over Tower Bridge! I'll—"

At that instant, the door swung open. MacLeod, the butler, stood impassively on the threshold. "You rang, milord?"

Rannoch whipped around. "I want *my horse,*" he snarled. "And I want *my knife.* And I want *my whip.* And I want them *now.*"

MacLeod barely lifted his brows. "Aye, milord. Your whip, and not your crop?"

"My whip, damn you."

Unperturbed, MacLeod bowed and shut the door.

Evie laid one hand on her husband's arm. His head snapped around, his eyes burning through her. "Elliot," she whispered. "You cannot do this. We—why, we don't even know where Rutledge is. And think of Freddie. The gossip. The child."

The child?

The child. With a hand that shook, he touched his fingers to his forehead. Freddie was going to have a child? Dear God in heaven! He couldn't absorb it. Rannoch drew in a deep draught of the cold air now washing over his face and willed his mind clear of the fiery haze. Slowly, the roar receded, and the room came back into focus. He realized that a breeze was playing with his wife's hair, and he looked past her to see that the window was shattered.

He blinked again. "Aye, then," he said quietly. "He'll wed her first. Then I'll kill him."

Evie drew him forcefully toward a chair near the empty hearth. Stiffly, he sat. "Listen to me, my love," she gently insisted. "We cannot jump to conclusions. Freddie says—"

"Says what—?"

Evie pursed her lips. "That it was not his fault."

Rannoch looked at her incredulously. "An innocent girl is raped, and she says it was not his fault?"

Vehemently, Evie shook her head. "What if it wasn't like that, Elliot?" she asked. "What if she . . . well, the fact is, Freddie says—"

"What?" he interjected violently. "That she was willing?"

His wife closed her eyes and spoke very slowly. "Frederica claims that she was as much to blame as Rutledge—more so, in fact. And I cannot but believe her."

"Well, I bloody well do not!" insisted Rannoch. "And I mean to tear that cad limb from limb. I'll pound him into pond scum. I'll poison his wells and burn his village—"

"He lives in Hampstead," Evie dryly interjected.

"Who gives a shite?" snarled Rannoch. "The place is overrated, anyway. I'll make him rue the day he set foot in my house and tainted—"

His wife cut him off by pressing a finger firmly to his

lips. "Watch your language," she cautioned. "And, strictly speaking, Chatham is Michael's house, and Frederica is my cousin."

"Then you tear that scoundrel limb from limb," growled Rannoch, a little embarrassed. "And don't bat those big blue eyes at me and pretend you cannot do it, for I know too well your temper."

"Oh, I could do it," Evie readily agreed. "If I thought him guilty."

"You think she lies? You think the babe is Ellows's?"

"No." As if considering her words, Evie slowly shook her head. "No, Freddie has changed since last year," she answered. "She thinks, I believe, that she did not take during her season. And yes, there may have been some high sticklers. But mostly, everyone was awestruck. Still, behind all that polish there yet hides a child who feels like an orphan. One who is lonely and insecure, but deeply passionate."

Elliot narrowed his gaze. "What are you trying to say, Evie? It sounds like gammon to me."

Faintly, she smiled. "Zoë says there was some sort of trouble over Johnny," she answered. "A rumor that he might wed a cousin. Perhaps it overset Frederica? Made her do something foolish?"

Rannoch laughed harshly. "Oh, let me guess! You think she seduced Rutledge? Is that it?"

Evie shrugged. "I once tried something similar myself," his wife answered softly. "To quite good effect, I might add."

Rannoch tried to glower and failed. "I recall it," he snapped, but there was little bite in his voice now. And then, suddenly weary, he propped his elbows on his knees and let his face fall forward into his hands. *Oh, God!* Rutledge was worthless, the worst kind of rogue. He should never have been invited into a home where innocent young women lived.

"Gus and Theo shoulder much of the blame, Evie," he finally said, addressing the carpet. "They knew what Rutledge was, and they didn't keep an eye on him. And I should have ordered them to keep their dissolute friends from Chatham. We have lived too lax a lifestyle. We have always let the children run wild. Now we will reap what we've sown."

"Change is not the answer, Elliot." His wife's voice was stern. "It is how we have always lived, a choice I made quite willingly. I will not see us shut up in some sort of moral prison made of society's strictures. You, of all people, should know how wrong that is."

Just then, MacLeod returned, bearing a long black horsewhip neatly curled on a silver tray. "Your mount awaits, milord."

Evie placed one hand lightly on her husband's knee, as if to hold him down. "We are so sorry, MacLeod," she said gently. "But his lordship will not be leaving just yet."

From the corner of his eye, Rannoch saw the butler wink at his wife. "Verra gude, milady."

Suddenly, Rannoch sat straight up. "Fetch Miss d'Avillez down, MacLeod," he commanded. "Her cousin and I wish to speak with her."

The door closed without a sound. "Do not be harsh with her," said his wife, in a tone that brooked no opposition. And in a few short moments, the door softly opened again.

Rannoch jerked to his feet and turned toward the

door. Freddie's eyes were swollen from crying, but she was otherwise composed. She crossed the room, her movements graceful and precise, as always. Her heavy black hair was coiled in a simple arrangement at the nape of her neck. Pale blue silk framed her lovely shoulders and set off her honeyed skin. She was beautiful. Elegant. And a grown woman. Dash it, why was it so hard for him to admit that?

He motioned her to join them in the chairs before the hearth. At once, Evie bent near, to brush the back of her hand across Frederica's pale cheek. But Rannoch was a brusque and sometimes bad-tempered Scotsman, and he saw no need to pretty up their task with a long preamble or any polite euphemisms.

"Freddie, I'm told you're breeding," he began rather bluntly. "And that Rutledge is the sire?"

Frederica's lips trembled, but her composure held. "The f-father," she corrected, lifting her chin a notch. "And I'm sorry for it, though I daresay regret does me no good now."

Rannoch nodded. "It does not," he agreed. "Have you told him?"

"Told Rutledge?" Frederica's eyes flared wide. "Lord, no!"

Weighed down by grief and responsibility, Rannoch rubbed one finger up and down the side of his nose. "Aye, well, that's a bit of a problem, is it not?" he finally said. "We'd best fetch him down here. And then, as much as it pains me to say it, I think you know what must happen next."

"No!" Frederica's bottom lip began to quiver. "No! He doesn't want me. He won't marry me."

Rannoch's short tether snapped. "Oh, no?" he snarled. "I'd not be making a great wager on that, lassie."

He almost jerked to his feet, but his wife's hand again stayed him. Frederica blinked back tears. "Wh-at I mean, sir, is that I won't marry him," she snuffled. "I won't do it. I'm s-sorry, sir. But I cannot compound one bad mistake with another."

For a moment, Rannoch sat, quietly seething. *Bad mistake* was a rather apt description of Rutledge's whole existence. But it was Evie who took the lead. "Freddie, we will not let him mistreat you," she said, leaning intently forward. "I swear to you, he won't."

Freddie looked startled. "Why, I never dreamt he would!"

Rannoch snorted. "Then you've more faith in the rascal than I."

Evie's blue eyes turned on him, dark as a stormy sky. "Many young men have black reputations, my love." She fairly bit out the words. "Some of those reputations are deserved, but a vast deal are not."

And once upon a time, Elliot, yours was blacker than any.

Those words he heard without his wife having spoken them. Theirs was a close marriage, and he knew her well. And again, she had him with her damnable logic. He crossed his arms stubbornly and glowered back. But he also shut his mouth.

Evie turned again to her cousin. "Then why will you not marry him, Freddie? Really, I'm not at all sure you have any choice."

Frederica's shoulders sagged. "Well, I do not think he

is deliberately cruel," she answered slowly. "Indeed, I think he can be rather kind. But he is so full of charm, and far too handsome. And I could not bear a husband who flirts, gambles, keeps whores, and runs with low company, no matter how charmingly he did it."

Evie eyed them both quite skeptically. "Very plain speaking, my dear," she said dryly. "Rather too plain."

Rannoch plunged back into the conversation. "Frederica, we would be irresponsible guardians if we did not force this marriage," he said. "Evie tells me you insist upon shouldering half the blame and—"

"Oh, at least half!" Frederica interjected, staring up at the ceiling and sniffing.

Rannoch shook his head. "Well, God knows I'd like to be spared the details. But what's done is done, and now you must pay the piper. You and Winnie will leave for Essex immediately after Zoë's ball. I shall wait upon Mr. Rutledge at his lodgings. A special license will be arranged."

Knowledge dawned on Frederica's face. "No!" she cried, bracing her hands on the chair arms as if she might leap up. "No! He does not want me, Elliot! Why must you make me do this? Indeed, you cannot make me."

"Cannot—?" echoed Rannoch in a lethally soft voice.

Evie's fingers dug at once into his knee. But Freddie would not be still. "You had a child out of wedlock!" she accused him. "You were no saint! So how dare you tell me how to live my life?"

Rannoch felt his face color. "I am a man, dash it," he growled. "Society permits men a measure of latitude. And though I love Zoë with all my heart, I take no pride in the circumstances she suffers for my thoughtlessness.

It is a hard, hard burden my child must bear. And you bear it, too, Frederica."

Evie leaned intently forward. "Would you wish your child to go through what you have gone through, my dear? England is a judgmental place, and you know it as well as I."

One tear slipped from Freddie's eye and rolled down her chin. "Oh, yes, I do know!" she said softly. "So s-send me away! Let me go home. To—to Figueira. It is a far better place than this. Legitimacy does not matter there, for no one gives a jot which side of the blanket you were born on."

Evie jerked back as if she had been slapped. "Oh, Freddie," she whispered. "Do you feel we were wrong to keep you here? We had only your welfare at—"

"Enough!" roared Rannoch. "Freddie is saying things she cannot possibly mean. Portugal is out of the question."

"Why?" Frederica's voice was strident.

Rannoch jerked from his chair. "Your homeland is again at war, in case you'd not heard." His voice was edged with a fury he could not hide. "A bloody civil war, not apt to be soon settled. Just as it was at the time of your birth, Portugal is unstable and unsafe. That is why your father's fellow officers brought you out of the bloody place to begin with. And that is why you will remain under my protection until you are either *wed* or *dead*. Is that clear?"

Just then, the door flew open, and Gus started into the room. "Oh, hello!" he said, jerking to a halt by the windows. "Terribly sorry! I was just coming in to fetch a—good God, what's happened to George?"

"He fell," snapped Elliot.

"What, through the window?" Unwisely, Gus laughed. "That's almost as queer as old MacLeod's doings! Did you see what he was carrying through the house? A horsewhip! Curled up on a salver, neat as the morning post!"

Elliot stood and, with a leisurely grace, turned to face him. "Speaking of that horsewhip," he said grimly, "I wonder if I mightn't have a use for it yet."

Gus blinked. "Beg pardon, sir?"

"Come here!" barked the marquis. "Freddie, out. Gus, sit."

It was not a request. And Frederica looked happy to go. As she rose to leave, Gus stared at her swollen eyes with grave apprehension.

"What the devil's wrong with Freddie?" he asked as soon as the door clicked shut.

His booted feet spread wide, Elliot stood looking down at the young man. "She is with child," he gritted.

"Dear Lord!" Gus blinked uncertainly. "You cannot be serious."

"I am quite serious," Rannoch snapped. "And I hold you responsible."

Uncertainly, Gus half rose from the chair. "Why, good God, sir!" he choked. "I take great umbrage at that! How can you think it? Of either of us? That's—that's appalling."

"Oh, Gus," said Evie witheringly. "That isn't what he means."

Rannoch sat down and stared at Gus. The silence which surrounded them was a heavy one. "I'll tell you what's appalling—that an innocent girl cannot be protected from such wickedness beneath her own roof," said the marquis. "You got us into this, and now I've half a notion to make *you* marry her."

"Sir, that's a bit harsh," Gus sputtered. "I had nothing to do with it, and I should very much like to put a bullet through the scoundrel who did!"

Rannoch's eyes narrowed. "Then go with God when you do it, Augustus," he said grimly. "Because he's got a near-perfect aim, and yours won't be the first grave he's dug."

Evie's hand fluttered to her forehead as if her head pounded. "Gus," she said softly. "The babe belongs to Rutledge."

Gus looked fleetingly mystified. "Rutledge?" he said, as if he'd never heard the name before. "What—old Hell-Bent? And . . . and *Freddie?*"

Rannoch jerked from his chair. "And Freddie," he confirmed, moving restlessly toward the hearth. "And now she says she won't marry him."

"There must be some mistake." Gus's voice was weak. "He would never do such a thing."

Rannoch's face was a mask of anguish. "He did it, and now I bloody well ought to drag him in here with a knife to his throat," he bit out. "I ought to make him do right by that child. But I cannot bear her tears. She says he'll make a bad husband, and I cannot say she's wrong. Oh, God, Gus, have you any idea how badly I want to do murder for this?"

Evie rose to her feet. "Sit down, my dear," she said, urging her husband back into his chair. "We must think only of Freddie, and how to mitigate the damage."

"I would to God I knew how," muttered Rannoch.

Evie began to walk back and forth along the carpet. "Frederica has asked to be sent away," she said quietly. "That isn't the solution I'd choose, but it has much to recommend it. Perhaps we should engage in a little subterfuge."

Gus let his shoulders slump. "Anything!"

Evie smiled weakly. "Perhaps we could send Frederica to Flanders? That, at least, is safe. Uncle Peter will take care of her, and we have many loyal friends. My parents' house is not leased at present."

"And what is the subterfuge in that?" asked Rannoch.

"In London, we will put about the rumor that she is going away to wed someone on the continent."

Rannoch looked doubtful. "Who?"

Evie shrugged. "A distant cousin? An old family friend? We'll be vague, and imply that the connection was formed whilst we were abroad."

Gus relaxed a little. "We might pull it off."

Evie turned and crossed the room again. "Gus, Winnie, and Michael can take Freddie to Bruges in a week or two, ostensibly to finalize the wedding plans," she suggested. "Then, as soon as Zoë's season is over, the rest of us will join them."

Rannoch shook his head. "Evie, love, the rumors will start the moment she returns with a babe and no husband."

A look of grief sketched over Evie's face. "Freddie cannot return, Elliot," she said quietly. "At least, not soon. I shan't leave her, of course, until the child is born. Afterward, I'll visit when possible. And after a year or two, we can kill off her husband in some tragic accident."

Gus was warming to the topic. "Then she can return to her family to be comforted," he said. "It does make sense."

Rannoch gave them both a sour smile. "We can try it," he said. "But this will put an end to any chance she might have had of making a good marriage."

Evie's face fell. "Yes, it's one thing to mislead the gossip mongers, and quite another to deceive a prospective husband. But as for rumors, who is going to ask questions?"

Gus laughed bitterly. "Rutledge won't."

Rannoch gave a disgusted snort. "Not bloody likely," he agreed. "He'll just be so damned grateful we didn't come a-knocking with a tight noose and a special license, he'll be beside himself. And I have no doubt the scoundrel knows better than ever to darken our door again."

Chapter Six

In which Mr. Kemble's expertise is Direly Needed.

For three decades, the brokerage house of Goldstein & Stoddard had been situated within spitting distance of the Royal Exchange and the Bank of England, in the heart of London's financial district, a place as different from Mayfair as chalk from cheese. In the City, streets bore sturdy, hardworking names that hinted at their earliest purpose: Cornhill, Threadneedle, Poultry, and the brokers' haven, Exchange Alley. Stoddard's sat in Lombard Street, so called for its first residents, Lombardian moneylenders who had arrived in the thirteenth century and proceeded to make themselves, and a few fortunate others, wildly rich.

Very little corn or poultry was traded in the City nowadays, but in Lombard Street, not much had changed. Old Goldstein was long dead, but a succession of able Stoddards had trod up the firm's marble steps, the most recent of whom was Ignatious, who had a voice like steel wool and possessed, not the traditional English green thumb, but something better: a forefinger of solid gold. Stoddard was at present using that finger to count out a pile of banknotes.

"Yes, yes, all there," he rasped to the gentleman seated by his desk. "Three thousand exactly." With an expert flick of the wrist, Stoddard whacked the edge of the stack on his desktop and thrust it at a clerk near his elbow. "Take it to the counting-room, and enter it in the cash book."

When the clerk left, Stoddard laid aside his spectacles and scowled at his client. "Really, Mr. Rutledge," he chided. "You court the thieves with all that poking from your pockets."

"Oh, blister it, Stoddard!" Rutledge opened his arms expansively. "Do I really look the sort some craven cut-purse would trifle with?"

Stoddard let his eyes drift over the cynical lines of Rutledge's face, the coat stretched across broad shoulders, and the dust which coated his heavy boots, noticing that the butt of a knife could be seen peeking from one leather turndown. And today, despite his outward indolence, there was a strained, brittle look about his eyes. "No," he finally admitted. "You don't look worth the damage you'd likely do."

His client roared with laugher. "See, that's why I hired you, Stoddard. Your brutal honesty."

With an acerbic smile, Stoddard drew a fat leather ledger from a distant corner of his desk. "Then let's get to it," he said. "We've several matters requiring your immediate and undivided attention."

Rutledge sat up a little straighter. "Well, I'm here, devil take it! In short, Stoddard, am I not your bloody slave?"

The older man flicked a sardonic glance up at Rutledge. "Would that that were so," he murmured, pushing forward a fat document. "Now, here is Lloyd's latest trust deed. The changes are minor, but—"

"Good Lord!" Rutledge scowled at the papers. "Am I to read all that?"

Stoddard, to his credit, did not roll his eyes. "When you've this much money at risk, yes, especially if you mean to continue on as a subscriber at Lloyd's. Let me warn you again that insurance underwriting is a risky investment. I should sooner put you in the funds, or perhaps gold."

Rutledge stretched lazily. "A faint heart never filled a fellow's purse, Stoddard," he remarked. "I mean, we may lose our drawers tomorrow, but we've had a devilish good run so far, wouldn't you say?"

The older man smiled dryly. "Indeed," he said. "So if that's decided, let us move on to other matters. As I'd hoped, Tidwells' has made a quite nice offer for the *Queen of Kashmir*—if, that is, you are still bent on selling her?"

"Lord, yes, shed it," he said, lacing his fingers behind his head. "I won it quite by accident, you know, and whilst it's been vastly diverting to own a boat—"

"A *ship*," corrected Stoddard a little impatiently. "It is a merchant ship, Rutledge, not some leaky sailing skiff."

"Aye, well," answered Rutledge, shrugging. "Anyway, let 'em have her. I don't care to keep up with it any longer, do you?"

"Shipping," harrumphed Stoddard, "is not my field of expertise." And then he shoved a second pile of papers across the desk and handed Rutledge a pen. "Capital allocation, however, is."

Lightly, Rutledge lifted his brows. "What's this?"

"I mean to reinvest your proceeds in American steel," said Stoddard impatiently. "You are carrying too much risk, Mr. Rutledge, as you always insist upon doing. The

Baltimore and Ohio is creating quite a demand for steel. A steady, dependable demand."

"More of those railroads, hmm?" said Rutledge doubtfully. "Reckon they'll ever come to much?"

"You'd best hope so," snapped Stoddard. "Twenty percent of your capital is invested in them. If, however, you wish to piss away your money with better certainty, sell out, and go back to your pernicious gaming hells."

Taking up the pages in his left hand, Rutledge smiled, showing two rows of flawless white teeth. "Never left 'em, Stoddard," he said good-naturedly. "Do you think pixies left that three thousand pounds under my pillow? Besides, if we're honest about it, what is your office here but a large, opulent dice box? And our underwriter friends across the street—" Here, the young man gestured in the direction of Cornhill. "Aren't they just a gang of bookmakers? Well dressed, aye, but Lloyd's is—"

"*Bookmakers—?*" sputtered Stoddard.

Rutledge smiled wider still. "Gambling, Stoddard, is gambling. And it matters very little where a man does it or what he calls it." Then, as if he barely read them, Rutledge's eyes flicked up and down the pages, one after another.

But he was reading them, every bloody word, and Stoddard knew it. And he knew, too, that Rutledge was not half as reckless or blithe as he wished people to think. Though why the man would not keep a decent haircut and a better wardrobe when he could so easily afford it was beyond his broker's understanding.

In the silence of the office, the *skritch-skritch* of

Rutledge's pen continued as, here and there, he paused to sign. When at last he was done, he leaned back and crossed one knee over the other in a gesture which should have seemed effete but instead looked faintly dangerous. "Next chore, Stoddard?"

With an impatient motion, Stoddard punched the bell on his desk. "I work for you, Mr. Rutledge," he said as the clerk snatched up the papers and scurried away again. "Pray do not look at me as if I am your governess."

"Never had a governess, Stoddard," he said on a yawn. "Not yet, anyway. How much d'you reckon an especially fetching one would cost?"

Upon leaving Stoddard to despair of his client's future in private, Bentley headed across town to his club in Pall Mall, where he hoped to find a measure of peace. The Traveler's Club was one of the few upper-class establishments in which a man could actually relax. Bentley liked the eclectic clientele the club drew—and, after all, they had let him in.

On the steps, he surrendered his slipshod ways just long enough to draw out his handkerchief and give his boots a desultory dusting. Once inside, he tossed his topcoat to a waiting porter and headed toward the morning room. It was not crowded. He took a seat at an empty table by the massive bank of windows, resisting the urge to prop his boots up on the polished surface.

At the next table, several fashionably dressed young men were chatting over tea and newspapers. His young friend Lord Robert Rowland was amongst them, along with his elder brother, the Marquis of Mercer. They murmured civil greetings. Mercer even motioned him toward a chair. Feeling decidedly unsociable, Bentley shook his head. They shrugged and returned to their conversation.

Bentley's habits were known to the staff, and a waiter had followed him in with coffee and a freshly ironed copy of the *Times*. He'd skimmed but a half-dozen pages, however, when the younger men rose and began to drift away.

As he passed Bentley's chair, Lord Robert leaned across and gave him a hearty slap on the back. "Bad news, Hell-Bent, about old Weyden, ain't it?" he said cheerfully. "And a dashed dull business, if you ask me. After all, the season's barely begun."

"I beg your pardon?"

"What?" Lord Robert grinned. "Has Weyden not told you?"

"Told me what?"

"Rob and I saw him in Lufton's last night," explained Mercer. "Weyden's piking off. Taking the family back to Bruges. There's to be a wedding, he says."

"Gus getting married?" Bentley snorted. "I doubt that."

Robert shook his head. "Lord no, not Gus!" he answered. "Weyden's cousin, some fellow on the continent."

"A banker," interjected Mercer. "Swiss, I heard the Earl of Trent say."

"No, no, it's some minor Prussian nobleman," asserted another gentleman. "A nephew of Lady Rannoch's mother."

Bentley gave his newspaper an impatient rattle. "Rob, you're standing in my light," he said dismissively. "But if you fellows ever decide who is getting married, let me know, and I'll send the bride a monogrammed soup spoon or some damned thing."

"Oh, no secret there!" said Lord Mercer glumly. "That's the bloody point, Rutledge!"

A strange feeling crept over Bentley. "What?" he asked, tossing down his paper.

Robert looked at him quite seriously. "It's the lovely Miss d'Avillez, Rutledge. Reckon young Trent will be giving away the bride?"

Bentley's heart stopped. "Miss d'Avillez?" he croaked.

Robert nodded. "We'd heard the chit was all but betrothed to some Essex nobody."

Mercer laughed a little bitterly. "I had it from Weyden himself last season," he complained. "A dashed unsporting thing to do, if you ask me—put it about that a lady is engaged if she really isn't."

"Ah, well!" sighed Robert. "No one had the ballocks to court her. No wonder she's leaving town."

The young men moved as if to depart. Bentley pushed his coffee cup away and shoved back his chair. *Good God!* This could not be. It could not. She would not dare.

Mercer shot him a strange look. "Well, it doesn't much matter now, does it?" Bentley heard him say as they left. "They're to leave at the end of the week."

For a long, still moment, Bentley just sat, grappling for self-control. *How could she?* How could Freddie do this? What could she possibly be thinking?

One thing was plain—he had to find her. They had to talk. And quickly, too. In fact, Bentley had left his table and was halfway along the corridor before he realized he was leaving. In the hall, he brushed past Lord Mercer and his stunned companions, then hit the front steps at a run. Behind him, the porter shouted, "Sir, your coat!"

The fellow caught up with him just as he snapped his fingers at a servant who darted off to fetch his horse. Bentley shoved his arms into the coat and began to pace up and down the pavement, the long, heavy hems slapping at his top boots each time he whirled about to retrace his steps. He had to think. Around him, the afternoon traffic clattered up and down Pall Mall, fine carriages and lowly carts equally oblivious to him in his fury. At last, his mount arrived, and Bentley was halfway to Vauxhall before his fury turned to something worse. Panic. And a feeling of having been betrayed.

It made no sense, he told himself. None at all. But why should he care? And yet he did not turn around. Did not once consider the prudence of his actions. And before he had finished thinking things through, he was riding beneath Strath's clock tower and into the cobblestone courtyard. He swiftly dismounted and passed his reins into the hands of a groom attired in Rannoch's livery. Two arching staircases curved about either side of a magnificent fountain, then rose up to the classical paladian entrance. He had been here only once, but the house was unforgettable. Bentley went swiftly up the right staircase and dropped the knocker, still uncertain of what he would say.

"Miss d'Avillez," he blurted to the footman who answered the door.

But Strath was a formal place, in stark contrast to

Chatham Lodge. "Miss is not in, sir," he said with a bow. "Would you care to see Lady Rannoch?"

Bentley felt his anger spike. For an instant, he toyed with the notion. But what would he say to her? *"I took your cousin's virginity, so by rights she's mine"*? No, even in his confused state, Bentley knew better than that. "I'm very sorry, but I must insist. You must tell Miss d'Avillez that I am here."

The footman smiled faintly. "I am sorry, sir. Miss d'Avillez is not at home."

"No." Bentley shook his head. "She has told you to put me off, I am sure. Well, I shan't have it, do you hear? You will go and tell her that I demand to be seen."

The footman exhaled impatiently and turned away. He turned back again with a little silver salver and thrust it at Bentley with a look of someone vastly put upon.

It was only then that Bentley realized the depth of his confusion. He hadn't given the poor devil a card. He hadn't even bothered to introduce himself. The footman did not know him. And here he was, standing on the doorstep in clothes which hadn't looked especially grand when he'd put them on eight hours ago and now looked slightly disreputable. Worse, he was demanding to see an unmarried young lady. Freddie probably was out. And he probably looked like the village idiot—if not something a little less pleasant. Moreover, if he left a card now, it would surely tip his hand . . .

"Sir?" inquired the servant. "Your card?"

Bentley could feel his face flush with heat. "Sorry," he stammered to the footman. "Seem to have forgot the bloody things. I, er, I shall just go home and fetch 'em."

And with that, he turned and went back down the stairs again. Behind him, the door closed with a hearty thump, as if to say *good riddance*. Bentley was humiliated. But, by God, he was not daunted. No, not by any stretch. He got back on his horse and headed toward the river, his mind in a whirl. He had to see Freddie. And he'd little doubt she meant to avoid him. So how? *How?*

Then, as he went tearing back through Richmond, something finally stirred. There was something . . . yes, something just beyond his reach. A fragment of memory. A chore. A task. Something examined, then tossed aside out of habit—and anger.

By God, he had it!

Suddenly, Bentley spurred his horse, and the mighty beast sprang as if he'd just been freshly saddled. This time, he went all the way to Westminster Bridge and turned toward the Strand. Late afternoon was settling over London, the sun sinking behind the westerly rooftops. In its wake, the glow of red which should have been visible was muted to a ruddy haze by London's air. He found the Strand choked, too, and it took him all of ten minutes to go the short distance to his destination. When he reached it, he slapped a bob into the hand of a grubby but cheerful lad who dawdled near an adjacent lamppost.

"I've another just like it," he said, settling a firm hand over the boy's narrow shoulder. "Hold that horse, and do not stir from this spot."

He went along the pavement but a few feet, plowing his way through ink-stained clerks and weary shopgirls who were flooding down to Charing Cross and leaving their workaday world behind. He edged his way between two snugly corseted matrons who were brandishing black umbrellas, and finally, he reached the door. Bentley paused just long enough to read its only marking, a discreet brass plaque which was inscribed: *Mr. George Jacob Kemble, Purveyor of Elegant Oddities and Fine Folderol.*

Good God, he really did not want to do this. But, unable to think of any better idea, he wrenched ruthlessly at the knob and went in with such force that he set a little bell to dancing madly somewhere above his head. A handsome, very elegant young man tripped from behind the corner, his hair beautifully pomaded, his feet almost floating toward the door.

"Bonjour, monsieur," he said, sliding a dubious glance over Bentley's attire. "How may I help? Gems? Silver? Antique porcelain? We have some really lovely Egyptian pottery recently excavated near Cairo."

"No, thanks," Bentley managed.

The clerk lifted his nose another fraction. "Something more traditional, then? We've a collection of sixteenth-century Chinese *fahua* just taken in an estate purchase."

"Thanks, no," said Bentley, his attention distracted by the curious little shop. The place was a bit like St. Michael's, redolent with the mustiness of old things, but here the smell was overlaid with the clean scents of beeswax and vinegar. The floor—at least the parts not covered with Turkish carpets—was polished to a blinding sheen. The glass cases which lined the room glistened. The shop looked, on the whole, like a St. James's jeweler had bought out the British Museum, for the room was stuffed with curiosities of every sort, much of it secured in showcases but some of it displayed on tabletops or even hanging from the walls and ceiling.

The clerk gave him a condescending smile. *"Trés bien!"* he said, steepling his fingers. "A cup of oolong whilst you browse?"

"Thank you, no," said Bentley, returning to the present. "Is Kemble in?"

Suddenly, the velvet curtains behind the counter ripped open. "Just speak of the devil," said a soft, wicked voice, "and up he jumps!"

It was quite an entrance, Bentley would give him that. "Afternoon, Kemble," he said to the veritable fashion plate who stood framed in the bottle-green draperies. "A word in private?"

Kemble arched one brow and tapped one perfect fingertip against his lip. "Now what, one must ask oneself, could the infamous Hell-Bent Rutledge possibly want of a simple shopkeeper such as *moi?*" But, with a strange smile, he relented, pulled the drapery open invitingly, and gestured at the clerk. "Jean-Claude, put the kettle on."

Bentley blurted out his confession as soon as they were seated near Kemble's desk. "I need your help."

"Oh, that I do not doubt," trilled Kemble. "What is it now, Rutledge? Jewel smuggling? Gun running? A dead body in an alley?"

"Nothing like that," muttered Bentley, wishing it were something so simple.

Kemble set his head to one side. "You are't mixed up in that opium business again, are you?" he asked warily.

"Good Lord, Kem! I never knew they'd stashed that opium in my hold and you know it!"

"Then did your brother-in-law send you here?" Kem sniffed. "Really, dear boy, I can't keep getting mixed up in Max's politicking and crime detecting and what-not. The police—not to mention all those Reformists—are making some of my business associates quite nervous, you know."

"Not Max. Not that sort of trouble." Bentley stared at his boots. "It's just that I, well, I need to attend a ball."

With a dramatic flourish, Kemble cupped one hand about his ear. "I do beg your pardon?"

"A ball," said Bentley more certainly. "I have to go to a ball, Kemble. And I don't have a valet. But you—why, you *know* people. So I want you to—to get me rigged out, so to speak. Fixed up. In something, you know, *smart.*"

At that, Kemble tossed back his head and laughed. "Oh, my God, there's a woman in this!" he said, rising, then lifting his hands as if to conduct a choir. "Well, up! Up! I owe old Max a favor, Cinderella. So let's see what we've got to work with. I can have Giroux & Chenault in Savile Row stitch you up in a trice, but we'll want a few measurements."

Feeling like some great, lumbering ox standing next to Kemble's svelte figure, Bentley watched as the man swished back and forth, taking inventory. "My God, you're tall," he muttered. "Really, what do they feed you Gloucestershire boys? And the cut of that coat—what a nightmare! Have it off at once; Jean-Claude can use it to polish the silver. No, don't scowl, and give me the waistcoat, too."

Bentley sighed, and did as instructed because he was desperate.

"While we're at it, I'll have Maurice whip you up something for everyday," muttered Kemble, pawing through his desk drawer and coming up with a box of pins. "You can't get by on your good looks forever, Rutledge. Eventually, everyone must dress."

Or undress, thought Bentley sourly.

By the time the uppity Jean-Claude came through the curtains, Bentley was down to his smallclothes. "Ooh, *à bon derrière!*" murmured the clerk appreciatively as he put down the tea tray.

"Don't even think about it," warned Kemble round a mouthful of pins. "This one will only break your heart."

Bentley narrowed his eyes. "What did he say?"

"He said you'd look good in blue," muttered Kemble, spitting out the last of his pins. Jean-Claude smiled and began to pour. "And you're quite trim, Rutledge, underneath that sagging fabric," continued Kemble, standing back to eye his handiwork—a careful pinning of Bentley's shirt. "Yes, a tuck here, a tuck there, and I think that rag you're wearing will at least serve Maurice as a pattern."

"You mean, he'll cut it up?" It was Bentley's favorite, worn soft with age at the collar and elbows.

"*Mais oui,* into little pieces!" proclaimed Kemble, making a little *snip-snip* gesture with his fingers. "And I think—yes, I do think blue is your color."

Bentley shrugged. "I like blue."

"That is of no consequence." Kemble smiled at him as if he really were the village idiot. "You've put yourself in my hands. So when, pray tell, must my miracle of transformation be ready, Mr. Rutledge?"

"I don't perfectly recall," he confessed. "The invitation came weeks ago, and I tossed it aside. But I think it said this Friday."

"*Friday*—?" interjected Kemble. "I'm a former valet, not God Almighty. It took him six days to create perfection."

"Well, you and Maurice have two," said Bentley. "And I don't have to be perfect, just presentable. It's a come-out ball for Rannoch's chit, Zoë."

"Rannoch's daughter?" Kemble's expression shifted to one of horror. "Oh, my God, are you completely insane?"

Chapter Seven

In which Miss Armstrong speaks her mind—
and Then Some.

On the morning of Zoë's come-out ball, Madame Germaine and her seamstress called at Strath to personally attend the ladies' final fittings. Frederica gathered with the others in Evie's sitting room, ready to be poked and prodded. She had not made it through the first volley of gossip, however, before she succumbed to another nasty bout of morning sickness—the fifth straight in as many days.

She darted behind the dressing screen and heaved up her breakfast, but not before she caught the speculative gleam in Madame's eye. Frederica had been resigned. It was rather obvious whom Madame's next juicy bit of tittle-tattle would concern. But it wouldn't much matter, would it? She was to be exiled to Flanders soon.

Eventually, her queasy stomach settled. The fittings were finished, and the seamstress, the dressmaker, and all their speculations were packed up and sent back to London. Winnie shooed Zoë from the room, the latter still in a snit over her demure white dress.

"I wanted ruby red like Freddie!" she fumed. "I hate this silly white! I hate it! No one will notice me."

"Red is no color for debutantes, Zoë," scolded Winnie as they stepped into the corridor. "The gentlemen will think you fast. Why can you not behave like Freddie? Last year, she wore only pastels and looked so sweetly virginal—"

Zoë cut her off with a snort of laughter. Winnie's face burst into color. On a small squeak, she cast Frederica a horrified look and promptly shut the door. Frederica burst into tears and threw herself onto Evie's brocade sofa.

Evie sat down beside her and brushed the hair back off her forehead. "There, there, Freddie," she murmured. "Winnie meant only to compliment your good sense."

"I can't think why! Especially when I so obviously haven't any!"

With a look of chiding affection, Evie opened her arms. On a loud, damp snuffle, Freddie dived into them. "You are just overwrought, love," Evie murmured into Freddie's hair. "It is just the babe, you know—both the qualmishness and the tears. Trust me, in another month or so, you'll be fine."

But Frederica knew she would never be fine again. Her hand went to her stomach, still as flat as ever. She was glad, deeply glad, for this child. Still, she knew too well that it would be no easy task to raise a child without a father. She had dreamed of something better for her children, something more secure than she had had.

Though her parents had been deeply in love, and Frederica had their letters to prove it, they had died in the midst of war. When at long last it ended, her father's fellow officers snatched her from what was left of her mother's homeland and brought her safely to England, to her grandmother, the powerful Countess of Trent.

But Lady Trent had sneered, called her a little brown by-blow, and sent her away again. They thought she did not remember. But she did.

They had taken her then, her English saviors, to her father's elder brother, only to learn that Maxwell Stone was himself five months dead. But his daughter, Evie, little more than a girl, had opened her home and her heart. It should have been enough. But it wasn't. It never had been, and the knowledge left her feeling guilty and ungracious.

So Frederica had pinned her hopes on romantic love. And her dream lover, she had vowed, would be different. Perfect. Dependable. Secure. And very, very ordinary. She would marry someone who could keep her—and, more importantly, their children—safe. Someone who was wise and well grounded, someone she could love with her whole heart, and who would be worthy of her deepest respect.

She had tried to convince herself that person was Johnny. But nowadays, when she was alone with what was left of her dreams, Frederica could admit that even in Johnny she had been willing to settle. His chief attraction had been his familiarity. He was the boy next door. A simple country squire. And all of those things had seemed safe, secure, and ordinary. It had all been a façade, of course. But only after Bentley Rutledge had blown her grand plans off their hinges had she grasped that fact.

Certainly she could not love such a scoundrel as he! After all, he met none of her criteria. He was not secure. He was not safe. He certainly was not ordinary. And if he had cared for her one whit, he would never have run off

without so much as a fare-thee-well! And on that
thought, for some reason, Frederica burst into tears again.
Good God, ever since that night with him, she'd been a
mindless, spineless watering pot. And she wished—oh,
how she wished—she could strangle him for it.

"There, there, now," murmured Evie, rocking her
gently back and forth, as if she were four years old and
homeless again. "It will all work out, Freddie. It will.
Just trust me, love."

By design, Bentley arrived at Strath House quite late
on Friday evening. Already, a ring of carriages lined the
circular driveway, and a few of the more staid guests
were beginning to trickle down the front stairs. True to
his word, Kemble had rigged Bentley out in a fine style.
Jean-Claude, the haughty salesclerk, had pronounced
him *tres soigné* and tried to pat him on the arse. But
Bentley just smiled, gave him the slip, and dashed off to
Richmond wearing an evening coat and matching
breeches in a color Kem called deep twilight, which
Bentley reckoned was just an overblown word for
bluish-black. The waistcoat was made of pale gold silk,
like the color of good champagne, and on the whole, he
thought he looked quite presentable, though the new
shirt itched a bit, and his stockings left him with no
place to hide a knife. Ah, well. That was a temptation
best left at home, anyway.

At the end of the carriage drive, he tossed his cloak
and top hat into his curricle, and when Rannoch's footman turned his back, Bentley ambled off into the darkness. He'd no wish to be announced. Not until he knew
which way the wind blew. Behind the house near the

river, all lay in darkness, the soft *slosh-slosh* of the Thames barely audible above the laughter and music. As expected, the rear doors of the ballroom had been thrown wide.

Still, the weather was chilly, even for spring, and few guests had ventured from the ballroom onto the veranda. It was a simple matter to vault over the low stone wall and make his way through the gardens. The ballroom was full, but it was not a crush. Through the doors which gave onto the adjoining drawing room, he could see Lady Rannoch standing with her husband as they greeted guests.

Gus and Theo Weyden lingered in one corner. The musicians had struck up a lively country dance, and Theo was leading Zoë Armstrong onto the floor. Gus stood near his mother, who was obviously gossiping with her bosom-beau, Lady Bland, a lush, dark-haired widow whose age was as uncertain as her morals. Normally, she was just Bentley's type, but tonight, she stirred no interest.

Instead, he began to make his way around the fringe of the crowd, his eyes raking the room for any sign of Freddie. This, despite the fact that he did not even know what he meant to say to her if he found her. What he wanted to do was snatch her up by the scruff of the neck, give her a little shake, then kiss her senseless, but he was fairly sure that was not at all the thing.

Indeed, when he let himself think about it, the entire situation bewildered him. The need to talk to Freddie, to touch her again—not in any sexual way but in a way he could not explain—was beginning to disturb his sleep. To counter it, he'd taken to prowling the pubs and hells of London until dawn. Sometimes, he didn't sleep at all. It was not unusual. He'd lived that way for much of his life, carousing for nights on end, then crashing into bed for a two-day recuperation. But this time, it was not the past which drove him.

Once his initial rage at being spurned had died down, he had told himself that he was simply concerned for Frederica. That he had a certain responsibility to her. And that was true. But he had the oddest notion that if he could just stare into her eyes, if he could just feel the warmth of her skin and the throb of her pulse beneath his fingertips, then he would somehow understand why she was doing this.

By the time the last strains of the music died away, he had casually made his way around the whole of the ballroom without sighting his quarry. The dancers were flooding from the floor now, and just a few feet away, Theo was returning with Zoë. Then Gus and Theo left, headed for the card room, no doubt. Throughout the cavernous chamber, the buzz of conversation swelled to fill the void left by the music, but the musicians quickly struck up again. Winnie Weyden returned to her conversation with Lady Bland, leaving Zoë to stand on her tiptoes, casting an expectant gaze about the crowd.

Bentley seized the moment and approached. "Miss Armstrong?"

Zoë whirled about, her eyes flaring wide as saucers.

Bentley offered his arm. "Might I have the honor?"

For a moment, she was speechless, a rare circumstance indeed. "Oh, hullo, Rutledge!" she finally managed. "Frightfully sorry, but this one's promised to—"

Bentley laid a finger to her lips and winked. "Ah, perhaps!" he whispered. "But the poor devil isn't here, is he?"

Zoë seemed to consider his offer, then, like a sudden burst of sun, her mischievous smile returned. "Do you know, Rutledge," she said, "I have always thought you wise beyond your years." And without a word to Mrs. Weyden, who was still chatting, Zoë took his arm.

Then a harrowing thought struck. "You have permission to waltz, I hope?"

Zoë's eyes flashed with laughter. "More or less!"

"Zoë—!" he said warningly.

"Oh, don't worry! Tonight I'm on my best behavior."

Bentley set one hand at her waist, careful to keep a decent distance as he swept her onto the floor. Zoë was a delicate, elfin creature with raven hair and soulful brown eyes. But those eyes were deceptive, for there was nothing soulful about her. Though the chit was adopted, everyone knew she was Rannoch's. It was said her mother had been an expensive French courtesan, and Bentley didn't doubt it. Zoë was a minx in the making—a vixen, a scamp, and pure, unpredictable trouble. He almost felt sorry for Rannoch.

"How beautifully you waltz, Rutledge," said Zoë with a sly grin. "And such elegant attire. Another decade or two, and they might have to let you into the Athenaeum."

He could not miss her good-natured sarcasm. The Athenaeum was a club which admitted only the staid and the scholarly. Bentley frowned down at her. "Dash it, Zoë. I do have a few graces."

As the other couples swirled about them, Zoë tipped

back her head and laughed. "Aunt Winnie says you are a wicked rake with rough edges," she said. "But tonight you look quite civilized, really. Still, I prefer you in your boots and that long duster. They make you look just a little dangerous. And ladies, you know, think dangerous even better than dashing."

Lightly, he lifted one brow. "I was not aware of that, Zoë," he murmured. "Perhaps I ought to invest in an eye patch and a scimitar? I fancy I could even learn to clutch the blade between my teeth. After all, a man has an image to maintain."

Zoë began to giggle in a most unladylike fashion. "You can always make me laugh, Rutledge," she said as he steered her past another couple. "But I'll confess I'm shocked to see you here."

"I'll just bet you are," he said dryly. "I don't ordinarily accept your family's formal invitations. But tonight I couldn't resist."

"Ah!" Zoë drew her brows into a pensive knot. "I daresay those invitations went out some weeks past."

"So they did," he agreed. "Why? Am I suddenly *de trop*?"

Zoë lost a little of her color. "Oh, indeed not!" she murmured. "N-not on my part."

Bentley had not missed her ambiguity. But Zoë was still chattering nervously. "Besides, it is my come-out ball, is it not? And I am glad that you are here. Until now, the evening had been wretchedly ordinary, but I somehow suspect you shall find a way to enliven it."

"Miss Armstrong, your intimation shocks me," he said with mock gravity. "I mean to be the very soul of propriety."

"Do you?" Zoë batted her eyelashes coquettishly. "I wonder why I cannot entirely believe that."

"I have no notion," he said quietly. "Is there some reason I ought not?"

Zoë chewed at her lip, never missing a step. "Propriety," she finally said, "can be a vastly overrated virtue, if you ask me. Sometimes a person must take matters into their own hands and throw society's strictures to the wind."

Bentley swept her gracefully into the next turn. "Why is it, Zoë, that I begin to suspect that you, too, are wise beyond your years?"

The mischievous smile curved her mouth again, and for a moment, they danced in silence. "Have you seen Freddie tonight, Rutledge?" she asked, as if changing the subject.

Bentley felt a bitter smile tug at his mouth. "I have not," he said quietly. "Though I should very much like to."

"Oh, I thought you might," confessed Zoë airily. "But she almost didn't come down. She's been a bit faintish lately, which is very odd, don't you think? Still, she's looking quite splendid in her mama's pearls and her favorite ruby gown. Madame Germaine even had to let the bodice out."

"Really?" Bentley felt his face flush.

But Zoë was still prattling. "Isn't that frightfully unfair when I am thin as a rail and stuck in this dratted white lace, and Freddie is rounding out so nicely? Anyway, she finally went upstairs to hide from that awful Johnny Ellows. He's gone now, but he'd been making a dreadful nuisance of himself."

"Had he indeed?" Bentley managed.

Zoë nodded innocently. "Freddie's bedchamber is on the third floor, but she sneaked up the gallery stairs, so she'll eventually return that way, don't you think?" she remarked, staring up into the vaulted ballroom. "You'll notice the doorway to the stairs set in that stone arch below the minstrel's bay. Every level is interconnected, you see. Isn't classical architecture interesting?"

"Why, I begin to find it perfectly fascinating," murmured Bentley.

Just then, the music ended, and Bentley escorted Zoë back across the ballroom. Lady Bland had melted into the tide of dancers, and Mrs. Weyden's icy gaze had zeroed in on Bentley. Even worse, in the distance, Bentley could see Rannoch pushing his way through the crowd, his rage almost palpable. But why? Because Bentley had danced with his daughter? That made no sense. Had Freddie confessed? No, were that the case, they would have come knocking on his door long before now.

But never one to be intimidated, Bentley bowed and lifted Zoë's hand quite deliberately to his lips. "Miss Armstrong," he murmured, holding her eyes intently. "I shall look greatly forward to seeing you again. Your lecture on classical architecture was nothing short of inspiring."

On his way out, several gentlemen, including Lord Robert Rowland, greeted Bentley convivially. Others stared, no doubt because he was so rarely seen in polite society. And a few had the audacity to whisper behind their hands. But Bentley had never given a tinker's damn for the opinions of others, not even Rannoch's.

Besides, he'd stripped more than a few of those fine fellows of a small fortune and would likely strip the rest of them before all was said and done.

It was a matter of simple subterfuge to leave the house and then reenter the ballroom near the gallery stairs. He slipped unnoticed through the door Zoë had pointed out, bounded up two flights of steps, and came out on the balcony which encircled the dance floor.

Tonight the gallery was unlit, indicating that it was not open to guests. What seemed like a thousand candles burned in the chandeliers which now hung below him, casting eerie, flickering shadows along the balustrade. Leaning over, Bentley looked down into the minstrel's bay and watched the violinists draw their bows in perfect synchronization. In the ballroom below, the dancers swirled in a rainbow of hues, working through the steps of a country dance. Cloaked in the gloom above, Bentley could see and not be seen.

He found that oddly pleasing. Life along the shadowy edges of society had always suited him best. He stepped back from the balustrade and went along the gallery until he found the passageway to the main staircase. Then he paced back a few feet, slid behind a marble column, and began his vigil. He suspected Zoë Armstrong had been sending him some sort of message amidst all her banter. He only hoped he'd understood it.

Apparently, he had. In a matter of minutes, a flash of ruby silk floated across the landing and turned down the darkened corridor. Bentley moved as if to step from behind the column, but at the last instant, he froze. He recognized Frederica's tense whisper and strained to make out the words.

A masculine voice responded. "But how can you do this to me, Freddie?" he complained. "I've arranged everything! Even Papa has come round."

Bentley could hear their soft footfalls coming down the last flight of stairs. "Take your hand off my arm," Frederica hissed. "Life is not so simple, Johnny, as you make it out."

Abruptly, the footsteps stopped, mere inches from Bentley's hiding place. "Oh, you're bitter now, but I swear I'll make you forget that," whispered Johnny hotly. "I swear it. Just let me—"

Bentley heard a soft, strangled gasp. "Why, how dare you!" Frederica cried.

His every muscle suddenly jolting, Bentley lunged. Seizing Johnny Ellows's coat collar in one fist, he jerked the lad off his feet and gave him a shake which rattled his teeth. Slinging his victim aside, Bentley looked at Frederica. Even in the gloom, he could see her eyes flared wide with alarm.

"Hello, Freddie," he said quietly. "Careful in the dark, love. Remember, you never know who you might run into."

But Ellows had staggered to his feet. "See here, Rutledge," he growled, planting one hand on Frederica's shoulder. "This is none of your concern."

Gently, Bentley lifted his hand away. "I'm afraid, Johnny boy, that I've just made it my concern." His voice was lethally soft. "Touch her again without her express request, and the next thing you'll be touching is the trigger on a dueling pistol. And if those clever Cambridge dons of yours gave you any grasp of ballistics, physics, or the laws of probability, then you'll be pissing down your leg and praying to your maker when you do it. Because I *don't* miss. Now, take that bit of wisdom back to Essex, and stuff it up your priggish papa's arse."

Ellows's face had gone white. Anxiously, he looked from Bentley to Frederica and back again. Then, muttering a curse under his breath, the young man scuttled away.

Bentley waited for Frederica's expression of gratitude, but none came. Instead, she tried to slip away. Bentley caught her elbow. "Whoa, Freddie." Their bodies were just inches apart. "Going somewhere?"

Her expression froze. "None of your business, Rutledge," she coolly answered. "And I appreciate your help, but I can manage Johnny."

Her indifference was like a slap in the face. On a stab of anger, Bentley yanked her hard against him. "Can you, now, sweetheart?" he growled into her ear. "I'm awfully glad to hear it."

He felt a moment of panic course through her. She tried to wrench away. Ruthlessly, he tightened his grip. He didn't know what he'd expected, but it wasn't this.

"Let go of my arm!" she snapped. "Why can't people leave me alone? Why are you even here?"

His anger ratcheted sharply upward. "Maybe I've come to kiss the bride, Freddie."

"Are you and Johnny both run mad?" she hissed. "Get out, before you're seen."

"How the warmth of your welcome touches me, Freddie." His voice was a cold whisper. "Are you this hospitable to all your invited guests?"

Frederica tried to look disdainful as her eyes swept

over Bentley Rutledge. But more than six feet of accursedly handsome and thoroughly outraged male glowered back. And this male would not be so easily dispatched as the last. "You w-were invited?" she stammered. "There must be some mistake."

Rutledge cocked one of his arrogant eyebrows. "Now, why is it, Freddie, I begin to wonder if someone forgot to scrape the "rough edges" off Rannoch's guest list?" His hand tightened on her elbow. "What a bloody shame. Does that mean I won't be invited to the wedding?"

Frederica's heart leapt into her throat. "No—I m-mean yes." In the face of his fury, all rational thought was fleeing.

"By the way, Freddie, what was that date?" he gritted. "I'd like to get you penciled into my social calendar—assuming I can wedge the happy nuptials in between my rampant bacchanalia and my debauching of virgins."

"Bentley, please!" Too late, Frederica realized she sounded desperate. "I cannot be seen talking to you. Don't you realize that?"

His hard, sour smile taunted her. "Now, that's a strange one, Freddie. I mean, we're such old friends. And you were more than cordial last time we ran into one another."

"I don't understand," she whispered. "Why are you doing this?"

His eyes glittered maliciously. "Well, now, I'm not perfectly sure, Freddie. Maybe I don't have anything better to do than waste an evening with people who are overdressed, overfed, and overly self-important. Or maybe I'm just trying to understand how a woman can make such passionate love with me one day, then marry someone else the next. Yes, by Jove. I think that was it."

Frederica turned her face from his. "Please just go, Bentley. What we did was a dreadful mistake."

"By God, it was no *mistake!*" he growled. "We did it quite deliberately."

"Please." Her voice trembled. "I'm begging you. Don't make trouble."

"Then answer me, damn it!" He seized her chin and jerked her eyes back to his. "Tell me, how could a woman do that—do it twice, actually—then turn around and announce her betrothal to someone I never heard of? Perhaps you could explain? And if you can, why, I'll leave on your next breath."

She tried to shove him away. "Take your hands off me. I mean *now*. I am free to marry where I please."

"Are you?" He stood over her, lean, tall, and deeply dangerous—not a man to be trifled with. "Tell me, Freddie," he whispered silkily. "Does that old flame realize he's getting damaged goods? And does he know who had you first?"

A spike of rage seized hold of her then. Unthinkingly, Frederica drew back and slapped him hard across the face.

"Why, you vicious little hellcat," he growled, snaring her other hand in his.

"Let go of me, you pig! Next I shall scream."

There was a slight, scornful curl to his mouth. "Go ahead, Freddie love. Scream. Have the whole bloody lot of 'em up here. I've nothing to lose, and I'll give them plenty to gossip about."

She looked at him hard and swallowed. He meant it. Oh, he really did.

He sensed her uncertainty. "Just tell me, Freddie," he growled, pulling her back to him. "Why are you marrying someone else? Tell me why."

This time, she heard the strange little catch in his voice. And that telling phrase—*someone else*. Frederica tried to reason. What was he thinking? What did he want? Did she owe him an explanation? He clearly wasn't leaving without one, and she just wasn't up for a fight. "I must do what my family thinks best," she said vaguely. "That is a woman's lot in life, Rutledge. Others decide what is best for us, and then we do it."

Fleetingly, something which looked like grief twisted his beautiful face. "Oh, Freddie," he said softly. "That does not sound like you. You are far too stubborn for that."

Suddenly, she could bear it no longer. "Yes, and what has my stubbornness gained me?" she exploded, fighting down her tears. "Nothing but trouble, that's what. And do not lie, Bentley, and say that you're jealous, for we both know it isn't so. You didn't really want me all those weeks ago, and you don't want me now. I accept the blame for what happened. I was stupid, and now I am sorry. But I don't know the rules of this game you seem to wish to play. I don't know what I am supposed to do. And I certainly don't know why you would care."

Her tirade ended on a quavering note. In the ballroom below, the music, too, melted into silence, and for a long moment Bentley simply stared down at her, his gaze burning white-hot with an emotion she did not understand. Yet something in it touched her, almost broke her heart. And then, just as a strangled sob escaped her throat, Bentley caught her firmly by both shoulders. For a moment, it was as if he sought to hold something back, some raging emotion, a physical blow, she hardly knew what. And then she felt a tear slither down her cheek, and he snapped, shoving her hard against the marble column and covering her mouth with his.

For a moment, Frederica could not think, could not even breathe. She tried to twist her head. Tried to shove the heels of her hands against his shoulders. But his mouth was unyielding, his touch desperate. His hands slid from her elbows to her shoulders, the broad palms searing the skin laid bare by her evening gown. He forced his tongue into her mouth, and somehow, Frederica came fully against him. Then he was cradling her face in his hands, imprisoning her between his palms, stilling her mouth to his. Tonight there was nothing of the lighthearted rogue in his kiss. Instead, a raw, unfettered emotion seemed to drive him. A gasping hunger. An untamed need.

Fleetingly, he tore his mouth away. "Don't cry, Freddie," he rasped. "Oh, God, please don't."

Then his long, strong fingers slid into her hair, gently restraining her as he thrust deep, plumbing the depths of her mouth and leaving her body trembling. Frederica could smell the starch in his cravat, the spice of his cologne, and his simmering male heat. Again and again, he slanted his mouth over hers, raking her skin with the faint bristle of his beard. Frederica was frightened, more frightened now than when he'd taken her virginity. Then he'd been just devil-may-care Rutledge. But this man was an emotional tempest.

She must have cried out beneath him. Still framing her face in his hands, he lifted his mouth just a fraction, his breath hot and swift on her skin. For an instant, he hovered. And then, as suddenly as it had come, his grip relaxed, and the raging storm died.

Only then did Frederica realize she'd been kissing him back, that her hands had slid down his shirtfront, around his waist, and beneath his coat. Her breath, too, was coming in short, urgent gasps. She had to fight the urge to follow his lips with her own.

"God." His whisper was like a prayer. "Oh, God."

Then he dragged her hard against him, his arms binding them chest to chest. For a moment, she gave in, surrendered to the madness, and let herself go limp in his embrace. She could feel the incredible power in his arms. His body thrummed with vitality and strength. And she felt so weak. So tired and so confused. Beneath the silk of his waistcoat, she could hear his heart pounding.

"Now, tell me, Frederica," he rasped, his voice unsteady. "Is that what you feel when your fiancé kisses you? Does his touch steal your breath? Leave you weak in the knees? Tell me *yes*. Just say it. And I swear to God, I will walk down those stairs and out of your life."

But Frederica made no answer at all. How could she? There was no one else, and there never would be. Worse, she knew, suddenly and instinctively, that no one would ever make her feel the way this man did. That was a part of the danger, wasn't it? Just a few short weeks ago, she had been a foolish girl who had thought she'd understood what passion was. And now, she was a ruined woman who knew too well the power of pure human lust.

She was afraid to speak, afraid to trust her own emotions. She had a child to consider. A child she whose security and well-being she could not jeopardize. No, not even for this—this plunging, dark desire which drew her down into its depths and promised such sweet, perfect pleasure. She did not want to want Bentley Rutledge. She wanted desperately to forget his perfect pleasures. But her body answered his, and she was suddenly afraid. Afraid she did not possess the experience—perhaps not even the will—to fight it.

Her silence seemed to frustrate him. A little roughly, he set her away, and Frederica slid gratefully from his grasp. Bentley did not turn to look at her. Instead, he braced one hand high on the marble column and stared down at the spot where her feet had been. Then he drew a breath which shuddered through him. For a long, expectant moment, the silence was broken by nothing but the laughter and gaiety below.

Finally, he spoke, his head still bowed as if he'd been beaten. "Just say it, then, Frederica," he rasped. "Just tell me what you want, and have done with me, damn you."

Frederica felt her heart stop. "Have done—?"

Without lifting his hand from the marble, Bentley slowly swiveled his head until his gaze caught hers. It was a look of torment and of despair. "I have been trapped in a damned perdition these many weeks, Frederica," he managed. "If you don't want me—if you absolve me—by God, say so. Set me free of this hellish guilt I've been wallowing in."

Hellish guilt.

The phrase rolled off the tongue, awful, ugly words. Was that what he felt? And what was he offering? She had never dreamed he could look so enraged and distraught. It seemed so totally out of character.

Later, Frederica was not sure where she found the courage, if one could call it courage to tell a lie. But somehow, she steeled herself. "I am leaving England, Bentley," she whispered. "I cannot take risks. I need a life that is safe, dull, and ordinary. And that is what I think best for the . . . for all concerned. You have no cause to feel guilty." Her hand reached out, almost of its own volition, and came to rest lightly on his shoulder.

His entire body went rigid at her touch. He looked away and made a harsh, guttural sound.

"Do not feel guilty, Bentley," she repeated. "You are right in one thing. What I did with you I did willingly. And what I do next I do willingly, too. Is that what you needed to hear?"

Bentley straightened his spine and stared into the murky gloom. Frederica held her breath, and she wasn't sure why. "Aye, that was it, I guess," he said softly. Then, without so much as a backward glance, he walked rigidly toward the gallery, turned the corner, and disappeared.

For what felt like an eternity, Frederica stood, simply listening to the fall of his footsteps as he moved through the gloom toward the gallery. Suddenly, an awful sense of regret seized hold of her. Her stomach went weak, as if with dread. As if she'd just made the worst mistake of her life. *Had she?* Good God, surely not? He'd offered her nothing; she'd asked for nothing. That was how it had to be. Even if he wished to try, Bentley Rutledge was not the sort of man who could be a good father. Nor would he ever be a dependable, faithful husband.

But the truth, it seemed, did not stop her. Frederica found herself catching her skirts in one fist and flying round the corner toward the balustrade. She threw herself against it, caught it hard in her hands, and leaned over so fast her head swam. Desperately, her eyes searched the crowd below. But the supper dance had ended. The ballroom was swiftly emptying. And Bentley was nowhere to be seen.

Do not stop. Do not look up.

Bentley moved down the steps and into the ballroom with those two thoughts in his mind. *You are well out of this one, old boy,* he told himself. *Now, just keep moving.*

As though it were a sluggish tide, Bentley forced his way through the crowd flooding from the ballroom. Color and sound blurred. The laughter about him rang with an artificial shrillness. One greeting, and then a second, went unheeded. His elbow caught someone's arm. Glass tinkled. A champagne flute? He did not stop. Instead, he pushed from the ballroom into the corridor beyond, swiftly making his way toward the front door.

In the entrance hall, a footman stepped forward, murmuring something about his coat. Bentley did not answer. Another servant held open the door for a gentleman who was departing. Without a word, Bentley pushed blindly past them, bursting out into the chill spring air. A light fog had scuttled up from the Thames to float surreally about the forecourt and the fountain, which still spouted twenty feet into the air. In the murk made yellow by the lamplight, he hastened down the wrong flight of steps, and a cold, cascading mist settled over him.

At the bottom, Bentley pushed his way through the clamor of servants, horses, and vehicles in the carriage drive. Opposite the house, all was cloaked in shadow. Bentley plunged into the gloom until his fingertips touched the moldering stone of the distant courtyard wall. He turned then and fell against it, staring back up at the steps. He should have been thanking God. Or at least heading gratefully homeward. But instead, he wanted simply to stand in the dark and hate Frederica d'Avillez with his every fiber. Why? *Why?*

What did it matter? He could not do it. He'd not been able to kindle up pure, unmitigated hatred since he was a boy. Instead, there was just an old, familiar emptiness where that cathartic emotion should have burned.

He did not know how long he stood there, hatless, coatless, his clothing damp from the fog and the fountain. From time to time, his ears caught the rumble of conversation or the wafting strain of a violin as it carried through the night. Strath's every front window, better than a score of them, blazed with a glow that looked warm and inviting. Yet he wasn't wanted there. Not any longer. And that was his fault. He knew he should leave. But instead, he simply stared through the cold fog and listened as the gaiety continued.

After a time, the anger began to recede. He began to wonder what she was doing and with whom. He even let himself imagine her face, let himself hear again her coldly dismissive words, until it began to feel as though he were pricking at his own flesh with a keen blade. He must have stood in the shadows for some hours, but time held no meaning.

Eventually, however, the trickle of departing guests became a surge. Carriages circled through, horse hooves clattering smartly off the cobblestones as they spun under the clock tower and into the night. And then, ever so slowly, the lights of Strath began to go out. First the main floor, and then those above, until, at last, only the lower service rooms were lit. Except for one feeble flame far, far to the left. On the third floor.

Frederica slept on the third floor. Was that her room? He shut his eyes and imagined that it was. Her maid would be undressing her, preparing her for bed. He imagined that he could see the ruby silk sliding off her honey-colored shoulders. The frothy, feminine under-things sliding down her body and into a pool of white about her feet. He could almost see her small, high breasts, their nipples so dusky and perfect. Tonight, they had all but burst from her ruby ball gown, and when he thought of it, he could remember how they had tasted in his mouth—a trace of rose water, a hint of salt, and the warm essence of woman.

Suddenly, and very strangely, something struck him. Zoë's deceptively light banter began to return to him in strange bits and pieces.

Madame Germaine had to let the bodice out.
She's been a bit faintish lately, which is odd.

It had all sounded so meaningless. But perhaps Zoë's words hadn't been banter at all? He couldn't forget how Freddie had leapt into flame at his touch and yet had refused to answer his questions. Questions which were really quite simple. Or were they? An appalling certainty began to settle over him. My God, how could he have been so blind? He jerked away from the wall, indignation coursing through his veins. This was not about what Freddie wanted, was it? It wasn't even about what he wanted—not that he knew what that was. By God, this travesty was all Rannoch's doing! He felt it in his bones.

With motions which were resolute and angry, Bentley strode toward the lone servant who yet lingered in the courtyard. At last, it was time to leave. But he would be back. And then Rannoch—or someone inside that house—would have hell to pay.

Chapter Eight

In which Mr. Amherst does the Lord's Work.

The Marquis of Rannoch was an early riser, a habit hard built by years of dissipation, when, as a matter of sheer survival, he'd learnt how to stay up most of the night and still draw a steady bead come dawn. Though most of his less obliging tendencies had been long since conquered, he still struggled with a few, chief amongst them his vile temper and the occasional bout of insomnia. Of late, both had worsened, because—though no one save his wife would have guessed it—the marquis was a man riddled by doubt.

This morning, Rannoch stood before the newly glazed library window, staring pensively across his coffee cup and into the gardens, which he could not really see. Last night's haze had become an impenetrable pea soup which had swathed Strath House in cotton wool, leaving it still and silent, like some spun-glass ornament packed away after Christmas. Much of the family yet lay abed; only his wife Evie and his ward, Frederica, had risen. He feared they had slept no better than he, and for much the same reason.

The marquis was jerked from his reverie when, behind him, the library door swung open. He turned from the window and was surprised to see MacLeod. The butler carried a small silver tray with a calling card laid square in the middle of it. Rannoch made a sound of disgust in the back of his throat, one which only a fellow Scot could interpret.

"Aye, milord," answered MacLeod, his expression quite put-upon. "Verra early, it is."

"A damned fool, then." Rannoch grunted. "Well, go on. Who the devil dares plague me at such an hour?"

MacLeod smiled sourly. " 'Tis the de'il himself, if his black look can be believed."

Rannoch picked up the card and flicked it a glance. "My God!"

"Oh, I doot that." MacLeod bowed. "Shall I fetch him?"

By the time Bentley Rutledge appeared, Rannoch had fortified himself with another cup of coffee. Fleetingly, he had considered something stronger and discarded the notion. God only knew what this meeting might come to. The doubt which had driven him from his bed at dawn returned twofold.

Rannoch rose stiffly when Rutledge entered. With a purposeful stride, the younger man crossed the room. Then he flicked his wrist disdainfully, sending a sealed sheet of foolscap sailing into the middle of Rannoch's desk.

The marquis was not a man given to niceties. "It is but half past nine in the morning, Rutledge," he growled. "What the hell do you want?"

The young man glowered across the desk at him. "Only that which is mine," he said, stabbing one finger at the paper he'd hurled onto the desk. "And I have come to take it."

Rannoch let his eyes drift over Rutledge. He recognized too well the glittering eyes and rigid posture of a man's barely contained fury. And he did not for one moment underestimate his adversary. Rutledge was decidedly dangerous, as he'd proven time and again. At seventeen, he'd blown his first man to kingdom come, and that hadn't been the last. He was a seasoned gamester who ran with low company, and he'd been implicated in smuggling, drug running, blackmail, and worse. One mistress, a docklands whore, had got her throat slit in an opium deal turned nasty. Another lover—a very wealthy, much-married countess—had been throttled in her own bed. But Rutledge had a way of always ending up on the fringe of scandal, never quite in the middle—in part because, like a lion lazing in the sun, he gave the impression of being too handsome and too indolent to be dangerous. But believing that was a grievous error.

Without another word, he picked up Rutledge's paper and slit the seal. His eyes flicked over it once. Then again. Good God Almighty. This did not bode well. "You must be quite insane," he snapped, tossing the paper onto his desk. "Certainly you are mistaken. There is nothing here which belongs to you. Frederica d'Avillez is my ward, and apt to remain so as long as I wish it."

He scarcely saw the hand slash out and snatch him by the coat collar. "Your ward is to be my *wife*," Rutledge snarled, dragging the Marquis halfway across his desktop. "And before this day is done, you *will* wish it. In fact, I may have you on your knees begging for it."

Rannoch seized Rutledge's wrist and tore it from his coat. "Bold words, you fool," he retorted, shoving the younger man back. "And bolder moves, I see. You must have wanted that special license rather badly to rouse a bishop from his bed at such an hour."

Rutledge planted both palms firmly on the desk and leaned into him. "We've no more time to waste, Rannoch," he snapped. "You and that idiot Weyden have botched this so thoroughly there's no saving her from embarrassment now. We'll get on with it. And we'll get on with it today."

He was, Rannoch saw, entirely serious. And in part, he was right—a fact which served only to enrage the marquis. "Oughtn't you to have considered the potential for embarrassment before you seduced her, Mr. Rutledge?" he sneered. "Perhaps, before you lured her into your bed and stripped her of her maidenhood, you might have considered that she is little more than a child? A gently bred child, who is no match for a man the likes of you?"

For the first time since entering the room, Rutledge dropped his gaze and backed off. "I'll not deny you're right."

Rannoch had half expected Rutledge to slough off the blame, and when he did not, the marquis inexplicably exploded. "But you didn't, damn you!" he roared, pounding one fist on his desk. "Instead, you— a guest in our home!—took the most indecent liberties imaginable and violated our trust in a way which ought to get you shot at dawn. No, do not look to me to sanction your sudden self-righteousness. Do not expect me to offer up an innocent girl on the altar of matrimony to some worthless scoundrel, merely to appease his newfound notions of propriety. By God, I ought to put a bullet through you purely on princi—"

Rutledge cut him off. "You may find that harder than you hope," he snarled back. "But once the vows are spoken, and Miss d'Avillez has the protection of my name and my family, then, by all means, send your second to wait upon me."

"Hell, no," said the marquis. "I'd rather watch you suffer. And suffer you surely will, for I mean to see to it."

Scorn curled Rutledge's lip. "And you'll rue the day you set eyes on me, Rannoch."

"Many men have, I'm told," he agreed. "But you've made an ill choice in your victim today, Rutledge. Now, get out of my house, and account yourself fortunate I've not splintered both your kneecaps."

But to his shock, Rutledge set both hands flat on the desktop again and leaned forward with an ugly snarl. "No, you will fetch that girl down here, Rannoch," he demanded. "And you will tell her what her duty is. I've sent for the parson, and I want this deed done, do you hear me? I'll own my sins, yes. But I know the law of this land, and I know she carries my child. I'll drag this through the courts until hell freezes over. And by the way, this is England, Rannoch, not your godforsaken Caledonian wilderness. We have laws here."

"Oh, bravo!" Someone near the door began to applaud slowly. "Spoken like a man who has acquired a passing familiarity with the judiciary."

Rannoch looked past Rutledge's broad shoulder. Gus Weyden stood in the doorway, one elbow propped casually against it. "By the way, Elliot," added Gus dryly, "your cousin-in-law is coming up the stairs and looking very much as if he's on a mission from God." Then he turned his attention to Rutledge. "As for you, old friend, I look greatly forward to rearranging that beautiful face of yours in a more private moment."

Before Rutledge could reply, a golden-haired man in clerical black appeared behind Gus. With a tight smile, Gus stepped fully into the room, and the Reverend Mr. Cole Amherst followed him in, still attired in a sweeping merino cape and carrying his elegant beaver hat in his hands. It was hard to believe that this tall, serene gentleman was stepfather to such a young hellion as Lord Robert Rowland. Even more outrageous was the fact that he was Rannoch's kin by marriage. But the vicar had what some might call the misfortune to be both those things.

Rannoch stepped from behind his desk. "Damn you, Cole, must my very family turn on me?" the marquis snapped. "Haven't I enough crosses to bear?"

The vicar smiled faintly. "God never gives us more than we can bear, Elliot," he said quietly. "Just pray for a little patience, and all your burdens will seem lighter."

"Patience?" Rannoch felt as if the blood vessels in his temples were about to explode.

The vicar's eyes lit with humor. He looked at Rutledge and spoke. "I have done you the favor of interceding with the bishop, Bentley, and at a most unreasonable hour. Now, return it by permitting me to speak with his lordship in private."

When the younger men were gone, Amherst set his hat on one corner of Rannoch's desk. "Is it true what Bentley claims?" he asked, stripping off his driving gloves and tossing them down with his hat.

"True enough, damn him." Rannoch fell into his chair and waved vaguely at the coffee service. "Help yourself."

The vicar did not move. "She carries his child?"

Tightly, Rannoch nodded. "Though I cannot believe she was fool enough to tell him."

"And yet you meant to marry the girl off to someone else?" asked Amherst gravely. "Really, Elliot, was that wise?"

Rannoch shoved a hand through his hair. "It was just a ruse," he admitted. "Freddie got her back up and said she wouldn't have Rutledge. Nor did I wish to see her bound for life to such a one. What was I to do but take her away under some pretense? She has always been a good girl, and I love her like a daughter."

Amherst moved to the tea table and poured himself a cup of coffee. "But I fear Rutledge has a point, Elliot," he said, returning to his chair. "In the eyes of the church, they should marry. He might carry through with his threat and drag this into the ecclesiastical courts. It will be futile, of course. But nasty. However, if you wish to charge Rutledge with something very unpleasant—I think you know what I'm getting at here—and hold this matter up to the bright light of the law, you might best him quite thoroughly. But you will need Frederica's cooperation. You will need her to accuse him of something which I fear is simply not so."

Rannoch stared into his empty cup for a long moment. Frederica had never denied her complicity in this appalling affair. And Rannoch had somewhat exaggerated her naïveté. He wanted Rutledge to be wholly at fault, but damn it, it simply was not so. "I take your point," he grumbled. "But Rutledge is a rake and a scoundrel."

"Elliot, Elliot!" murmured the vicar, slowly stirring his coffee. "When we are young, we are none of us much better than the world expects us to be. You know that. Besides, he is no longer young. And I have found I quite like him."

Rannoch grunted. "Do you indeed?"

Amherst grinned weakly. "Yes, and on some level, Frederica is fond of him, too, Elliot. Else she'd never have done such a thing. Surely you know that much of human nature?"

"I suppose so," muttered Rannoch. "Tell me, just what do you know of him?"

The vicar fell silent for a moment. "In the past," he finally said, "I have had occasion to be greatly in his debt. If you require the tawdry details, you'll have to get them from my wife."

Rannoch caught the faint stench of an averted scandal. "Young Robert, eh?"

Amherst nodded. "And Rutledge, despite everyone's expectation, proved himself over and over to be a loyal friend, even when Robert scarce deserved it. And that, Elliot, is in part the measure of a man's maturity."

Rannoch took up one of his quills and began to draw it back and forth between his fingers. "You think he will make Freddie a good husband?"

The vicar smiled again. "Only God knows that," he answered. "But remember what Erasmus said. Better the devil you know, Elliot, than the one you don't. What will her future hold if she does not marry him?"

Rannoch shoved away his empty cup. "I don't know."

"Ah, and there's our quandary!" said Amherst, setting his cup aside, too. "It is a hard world, Elliot, and we
cannot always protect our children from it. At least
Rutledge is from an excellent family. I account his
brother Lord Treyhern a good friend. If—and I do say
if—he does not properly care for Frederica, you may be
sure the family will. So I have put my prayer book in my
pocket and my faith in Bentley Rutledge. What do you
say, Elliot?"

For a long moment, Rannoch sat perfectly still. Then,
with the swift decisiveness of a self-confident, slightly
arrogant nobleman, the marquis jerked from his chair.
"Wait here," he said over one shoulder. "I'll have to go
and ask my wife."

In the end, Amherst prevailed over Lord Rannoch,
and Lord Rannoch's wife acceded to Amherst's wisdom.
However, Lady Rannoch emphasized—and it was a big
however—the marriage would have to be Frederica's
decision. They had already promised her one thing and
could not now fairly go back on it.

And so the marquis met again with the devil he
knew, banked his temper, and explained to Rutledge—
as best any man could—Frederica's feelings. Then
Rannoch and his wife found Freddie in the music room
and told her of their change of heart. The young lady
was not pleased. Nonetheless, half an hour later, Bentley
found himself being pointed in the direction of the
music room and given an encouraging thump on the
back by the vicar.

When he entered the room, Freddie was seated at the
pianoforte, plinking out some gloomy tune with one fin-

ger. She did not look like a woman who was with child. She just looked like—well, like Freddie, with her inky black hair swept up in an elegant twist. And her eyebrows. Those beautiful, bewitching eyebrows. She lifted them now as she rose, a vision of graceful, exotic beauty.

"Good morning, Frederica." The words were spoken calmly and firmly. *So far so good.*

Freddie showed her nervousness with a stiff half-curtsey. "Thank you for coming today, Rutledge," she coolly began. "I'm sorry Elliot could not make plain my position."

So she meant to brazen it out, then. "Your position?" he inquired, cocking his head to one side.

She swept across the room toward him. "It's kind of you to offer for me, but I do assure you it is not necessary."

"And I do assure you that it is," he challenged. "Freddie, you are carrying my child."

She gave a faint smile. "As I'm well aware, having spent the better part of the morning vom—ah, but never mind that."

Bentley felt a moment of alarm. "Freddie, are you unwell?" he asked, sliding a hand beneath her elbow. "Shall I send for a doctor?"

She smiled again, that curving, bitter smile he feared he might grow to dread. "Thank you, but it is not necessary," she said, stepping away again. "No more necessary than my marrying. Perhaps you do not understand, but in my country, illegitimacy is no great stain, and once this dratted civil war is finished—"

Something in her tone made him snap. "Oh, no, Freddie," he interjected, holding his palm up. "I've already heard this from Rannoch, so don't even start. You aren't running off to Flanders, and you aren't going home to Portugal. And you aren't marrying some imaginary fiancé, which is just what I suspect you were up to."

Her eyes flared with anger. "You are not yet my master, Mr. Rutledge."

Bentley felt his blood begin to boil. So much for persuasion. "Perhaps Rannoch did not make plain my position, Freddie," he said, biting back his anger. "But by God, *this* is your country. And that is my child. And if you think for one moment that you are going to poke so much as a toe off English soil with my babe in your belly, then you are about to get one hell of a rude awakening."

Her entire body went rigid. "Why, I daresay I just have!" she said softly. "Is that a threat?" Beneath the blue silk of her morning dress, he could see her shoulders begin to tremble with rage.

"That child is mine, Frederica," he said tightly. "And I mean to take care of it. Do not even think of getting in my way."

Her black eyes mocked him. *"Your* child! *Your* way!" she spat. "How dare you suggest I do not care for the welfare of this babe? Trust me, Rutledge, I know too well the importance of having a parent. Of having safety and security. Consider being a child with none of that, as I once was, then give me your high-handed attitude."

Bentley tore his gaze from hers and stared blindly into the depths of the music room. Oh, yes, she did know. Perhaps she knew far better than he. She was also young, and emotionally wrung out. But she was no one's fool. Frederica had been left an orphan. And in his own heedless way, Bentley had left his first child—his and Mary's daughter—an orphan. Because of his thoughtlessness, Bridget was dead. But this child was different. He *knew* about this child. He would not commit the same sin twice. Nonetheless, as husband material went, Frederica obviously believed him worse than nothing. And he couldn't say she was wrong.

He walked to the windows and stared out into the colorless fog, his hands clasped tightly behind him. In a way, Frederica's words had cast just such a pall over the room. Over his hopes and his dreams. Even his dread and his fear. Because, again, it all came down to this. The child. And a marriage that must be made the most of.

He left the window and returned to her. Frederica had sat back down on the piano bench, her shoulders slumped. Bentley knelt at her feet and took both her hands in his. "Oh, Freddie," he said, squeezing them tight. "We must make this work. There is a great passion between us. Surely we can build something more. Aren't you even willing to try? Do you think this is easy for me?"

"No," she said sorrowfully. "I am sure that being saddled with a wife is not at all your idea of pleasure. Men like you do not want wives. I cannot think you want a child, either."

He leaned into her then and lightly kissed her cheek. "And girls like you do not want husbands like me, Freddie," he whispered. "Do you think I don't know that? But we'll survive. And as for pleasure, I daresay that whether or not we find that in our marriage will be up to us."

Her eyes had widened at the unexpected kiss. "You must think that I have trapped you." She sounded perfectly wretched. "Oh, Bentley, I just—I just didn't consider the consequences. I did not think about having a child!"

Bentley rose to his feet and set his hand on her narrow shoulder. "It's my fault, Freddie," he said. "We shouldn't—I mean, I wasn't . . . prepared."

Freddie's face twisted with confusion. "Oh? And you think I am?"

Bentley lost her for a moment. "Am what?"

"Prepared."

Bentley smiled and shook his head. They had best get this one straight here and now. "Freddie, sweet, not that kind of prepared. Don't you understand, every time one does, er, it—"

"It—?" she interjected.

"Sex." He strangled out the word. "Every time you engage in—er, that, you run the risk of having a child."

She looked at him blankly, and then a spurt of sardonic laughter bubbled up. "Good Lord, Rutledge! Probability being what it is, you must have sired a veritable cricket team."

Bentley felt his jaw begin to twitch. "Freddie, that is none of your damn—" He checked himself at once. He'd been about to tell a lie. And curse. His business was, for the most part, her business. Or would be in a matter of hours. "Just one," he finally bit out, stabbing a finger at her perfectly flat belly. "And that makes two. And even if this hadn't happened, I would still be honor bound to marry you."

She lifted her delicate chin and stood. "A matter of gentlemanly honor, now, is it?"

He tried to smile. "Absolutely."

She arched her exotic brows, shot him a strange look, and then began to pace the room. Bentley was enough of a gamester to know when a person held a worthless hand and was desperately looking for a way out. But why was he not doing the same? Why was he going so easily up the steps to that guillotine of domesticity? He told himself it was because of Mary and what he'd done to her. Because he had failed their child, and the result had been horrific. He would not willingly do so a second time.

But what if he couldn't do it? What if he failed anyway? He would be trapped. Again. And this time, he'd have trapped someone else with him. His chest began to tighten with that old, familiar panic. His hands began to sweat. Then shake. *Good God, not here. Not now.* But all the air seemed to have been sucked from the room.

Questions tormented him. Could he be a steadfast husband? A reliable father? Could he promise never to leave her? He braced one hand on the piano and forced his breathing to calm.

When he'd first assumed they would marry, he had told himself it was a mere inconvenience. That nothing would really change. But everything was going to change. Freddie wouldn't accept anything less. They found one another physically desirable, yes. Even looking at her now, he could feel something deep and profound stirring inside him. But Bentley feared that mightn't last. And Frederica, at least, deserved something better.

He studied the lovely angles of her face as she turned and paced again toward the windows. And suddenly, he was struck by the unnerving realization that in wedding her, he would be giving up the one thing which had always sustained him through every personal relationship in his life. The freedom to simply storm out—out of the room, out of the country, even out of someone's life, if they got too close, too demanding, too . . . anything which he found uncomfortable. No one, not even his sister, Catherine, held him in thrall. No one could force him to do their bidding. No one could bully or blackmail or shame him into love, obedience, or any other emotion. Never, ever again, he'd sworn, would he live like that. And if the price he'd paid for his freedom had been a life lived in a measure of isolation, he could not say as how he'd overly suffered from it.

But was it fair to let Frederica suffer from it?

At last, she stopped pacing and turned to look at him, her narrow shoulders set stubbornly back. "We'll just end up hating one another," she said.

But *"I'll end up hating you"* is what she really means, thought Bentley. "No, we won't," he said firmly. "We can't. We have a responsibility to the child."

It was as if she could read his thoughts. "Oh, Bentley," she said in a quiet, sorrowful voice. "Can I count on you? *Really* count on you?"

The question was asked so sincerely that Bentley's inner doubts seized a chokehold on him again. And he let that uncertainty drive him toward her, let it compel him to take her hand in his. "Just a year, then," he said swiftly. "We'll marry and give ourselves a year. To see how we go on."

"A year?" She sounded horrified.

Bentley drew a deep breath. "All right, six months," he managed. "We'll try it for six months. In the end, if it does not work—if we are making one another miserable—then we will live apart. But I must be able to see the child. I have to know, Freddie, that all is well. You must promise that you will never go far away. I will provide you with a house and servants and whatever the child needs by way of education or dowry."

"Bentley, it takes more than those kinds of things to raise a child!"

Bentley misunderstood. "Very well. Five thousand a year for your expenses."

"Five thousand pounds?" She looked at him as if he'd just sprouted horns.

Christ Almighty! Bentley had never believed Freddie mercenary. But then, he did not know the terror of finding oneself unwed and with child, either, did he?

"Ten thousand, then," he said gently.

"Fine," she snapped. "If that's how you want it."

"Or fifteen?" he hastily added. "Whatever it takes. Oh, hell, if I marry you, my worldly goods are yours. But you must promise to try, Freddie. And I will do my damnedest—I mean, my very best—to be a good husband."

Freddie's face crumpled. "Oh, Bentley!" She was staring at him, her eyes wide, her expression incredulous. "This all sounds so . . . so appalling. You are speaking of money and of separation and—oh, my God, how on earth could we have let this happen?"

He shrugged, opening his hands wide. Good Lord, someone needed to lighten the moment. "Well,

Freddie," he quipped, propping one hip casually against the pianoforte. "For my part, I was half sprung. And as for you——" Here, he somehow managed to shoot her his cockiest grin. "Well, I'd like to think I was just flat-out irresistible. But you tell me, Freddie. What was it?"

Later, Bentley couldn't understand why he'd teased her with such a foolish question. Had he hoped she might confess to having harbored some sort of unrequited passion for him the whole of her life? Or for worthless rogues in general, perhaps?

Freddie drew a deep breath, clasped her hands before her like a schoolgirl, and leveled him. "Oh, I don't know! I was just so—so hurt. So mad. And I think——" She stopped and shook her head as if trying to clear her thoughts. "Yes, I think I just wanted to get back at Johnny. I wanted to punish him."

Bentley stared at her, incredulous. "To get back at Johnny?"

Her lips trembled. "Well, you know, to m-make him sorry he threw me over?"

Anger and hurt welled up in him anew. "You just wanted to bed me out of *spite*?"

Frederica had the good grace to stare at the floor. "In part," she whispered. "And I w-wanted to know what it was like to, well, to *do* it. And I heard Winnie say that you were something of an expert."

"Well, damn me for a fool!" he swore, pushing himself away from the pianoforte with a violence. Freddie hadn't even found him irresistible! She'd just wanted to spite another man! It stung far more than it should have done and conjured up too many bitter memories. Bentley lost his temper again.

"Let me tell you something, Frederica," he growled, wheeling on her. "I've been used, abused, and blamed for a lot of wickedness in my day. But, by God, I don't like being used as somebody's vengeance fuck, and I bloody well won't be dropping by old Johnny's house to tell him about it over tea. And I swear to you, Freddie, if you ever pull another trick like that, I'll blister your arse with the back of my hand."

Freddie drew herself up an inch, lifted her stunning eyebrows, and stared down her pert little nose at him. "I'd just like to see you try," she hissed. "Rannoch will have your head on a platter—if there was anything left when I got done with you. And just so you know, I find your language deeply offensive."

Bentley caught her by the shoulder and dragged her pert little nose right into his face. "Darling," he snarled. "I hate to be the bastard who bursts your romantic bubble, but most everything about me is deeply offensive. And you can just get used to it."

She lifted her brows another notch, opened her mouth, then crumpled at once into tears.

Bentley just looked at her in gape-mouthed astonishment. *Oh, bugger all!* he thought. *Now I've really done it.* He let go of her shoulder and shoved both his hands into his hair. "Aw, Jesus, Freddie, don't cry!" he begged. "Oh, please, oh, please, don't. Anything but that. You know I can't bear it."

Then somehow, and very suddenly, Freddie was in his arms, snuffling against his lapel again. Which was just what had got him into this mess to begin with. He was afraid—really quite terrified—of crying women. And when it happened, his solution was to either bolt, buy them jewelry, or tumble them senseless. No wonder Freddie was pregnant. They really would have a bloody cricket team before this was done. If she stayed with him.

"Oh, I can't help it!" she sobbed, her fingers digging desperately into the fabric of his coat. "I just can't. I feel so queer all the time! Laughing and crying. Hungry and queasy. It's as if—oh, as if I'm not myself. Evie says I'll be right again when the baby comes, but I just d-don't believe her."

Bentley made himself another mental note. *Figure out what makes her cry. And then never, ever do it again.* Then he kissed her atop the head and curled one arm around her still-slender waist. "Well, I'm sorry, Freddie. I swear I am. I guess it doesn't much matter why we did it."

"Well, you j-just make it sound so appalling," she wailed. The words were muffled in his cravat now. "I d-didn't mean it the way you m-made it sound, Bentley. I didn't. I just thought—oh, I just thought—oh, I don't know . . . I felt so awful and so angry. And you smelled so good, and you're always so sweet."

Sweet—?

Christ Almighty. She thought he was sweet? He kept forgetting how young she was. He did not want anyone looking up to him. He damned sure didn't want to be anyone's hero. And suddenly, it dawned on Bentley precisely why that might be.

The proverbial shoe was slowly easing onto the other foot, wasn't it? And a tight, miserable fit it was, too. He had always had the luxury of being the reckless one. The person who could always be depended upon to do the worst thing instead of the right thing, and get away with it by virtue of a hangdog look and a dose of damn near infallible charm. The person who was always pretending everything was fine, even when it obviously wasn't. He was not so wholly lacking in self-insight that he did not understand the mechanics of the thing.

But what he did not perfectly understand was how to be something else. Like the man of the family. Before, Cam had always seemed willing—annoyingly willing—to do that. And now . . . well, this wouldn't be Cam's family, would it? Suddenly, he set aside his wounded pride, his crazy, conflicted feelings for Freddie, the ugliness of his past, and thought only of his future. He was to be a married man. The reality of it left him shaking. It was here. It was happening. He was to have a wife, and then a child, and he would be responsible for their care and their happiness, until they hefted his coffin into a hole in back of St. Michael's. If she stayed with him.

There it was again, that awful, niggling thought.

"Bentley?" Freddie's voice came at him as if from a distance. "Bentley, are you all right?"

He looked at her and blinked. Freddie looked wan and tired. And so very, very young. Somehow, he managed a smile, and then, to soothe himself as much as Freddie, he pulled her snug against him and buried his face against her neck. And, to his shock, she felt . . . well, she felt as if she just might be worth all the fear and sacrifice. "Ah, just hold on tight, Freddie," he whispered. "We'll get through this."

"All right," said Frederica into his cravat. "I'll try."

Bentley kissed the top of her head again. "Good girl," he said. "Now, come on, let's go downstairs and get the deed done. The Reverend Mr. Amherst is waiting."

Her head jerked up at once. "Now—?" she screeched, her eyes horrified. "Bentley, are you quite mad? We cannot do it now! You aren't dressed! And look at me! My eyes are red, and my nose is pink, and—why, I don't even have a bride cake or a ring or any of the other trappings!"

Bentley felt a stab of irritation. "Freddie, love, you're pregnant! How much more trapped can you get?"

Frederica's face screwed up like little Armand being put down for a nap.

Oh, Lord! thought Bentley. What a damned coil this marriage business was! "God, I'm sorry, Freddie," he somehow managed. "Please don't cry. I'll come back tomorrow."

"Tomorrow?" she sniffed, sounding a little grateful.

"Tomorrow," he said wearily. "But darling, that's it. If you aren't ready by then, I'm throwing a sack over your head and carting you off to Gretna Green."

At Bentley's insistence, he spent another hour at Strath sequestered in the library with Rannoch hammering out a draft of the marriage settlements. As distasteful as he found it, Bentley meant to honor the six-month promise he'd made to Freddie. And he needed to put it in writing, to make to her some small gesture of good faith. But what he did not need was Rannoch's money.

The marquis's brows had lightly lifted when Bentley mentioned that he and Frederica had already agreed upon the conditions of any separation. Then Rannoch made a little strangling sound in the back of his throat when Bentley explained the financial terms he'd offered. But when Bentley insisted they apportion

Frederica's rather significant dowry to any children born to the union, the old boy quite literally choked on his coffee.

It was, Bentley suddenly realized, a most gratifying sight. He was one of those brash gamesters who had often known both penury and prosperity in the same month, and was never much troubled by either condition. Now, for the first time in memory, Bentley actually took great pride in the fact that his present situation was extremely flush. And on his next breath, he was struck with the realization that he was now obliged to keep it that way.

His heart in this throat, Bentley left Strath almost as quickly as he'd come and went straight to Lombard Street. He was, quite literally, but a shipwreck away from abject poverty. His remark to Stoddard had been but half in jest; if a fellow had a bad day in the insurance business, the underwriters really could take his drawers, and probably grind out his bone marrow, too. The profits one made were obscenely high, yes, but the downside was total ruination. And as thrilling as that risk might be, it was one he could no longer afford.

Stoddard, thank God Almighty, had not yet delivered his latest agreements. He was quite pleased to toss them into the grate and almost deliriously happy when told to deposit every sou of unallocated capital into the safe and sound five percents. And so it was that Bentley's three-year love affair with that most faithless of mistresses, Lloyd's of London, ended in a puff of coal smoke.

Stoddard fairly beamed as he showed Bentley to the door. "I collect you've seen the error of your investment habits, Mr. Rutledge!" he chortled, brushing a little soot from his coat sleeve.

"You collect right," agreed Bentley a little morosely. "I daresay hazard will be the next thrill to go. Soon I'll be suffering the gout and wrapping warm flannel about my throat."

It was a shame, but there you had it. Life as he'd known it was about to change. And so Bentley ambled down to Hanging Sword Alley—a bit subdued by the symbolism of the name, given the day he'd had—and wolfed down an eel pie and a tankard of ale at a grimy little pub whose ambiance he especially liked. Somewhat cheered, he sauntered on into the Strand.

Kemble was stuck halfway inside his bow window, arranging an assortment of enameled snuffboxes, when Bentley ambled past. The jangling bell caught his attention, and he looked up, his eyes instantly mistrustful.

"You again!" he said when Bentley wandered inside. "And don't give me that pathetic puppy look, as if you just pissed on the carpet."

"Arf!" said Bentley with a shameless grin. "But it's something rather more serious than carpet, I fear."

Kem's eyes rolled. "What now?"

"A wedding."

"Good Lord!" said Kemble, backing his haunches out of the window. "When?"

"Tomorrow." Bentley just leaned against the door and feigned a pitiful expression.

On a sigh, Kemble shut the window and snapped its little lock shut. "Have you a proper morning coat?" he challenged, swishing around a table piled with an arrangement of old mantel clocks. "No, I thought not.

Where is it to be? And for God's sake, don't say St. George's. I can't possibly manage that."

A church? Bentley had never considered that. If Frederica wanted a bride cake and a ring, she probably wanted a church, too. Bloody hell. This was more work in one day than he did in a week. Then he remembered Freddie's soft, trembling lips, and all the inconvenience slipped from his mind.

"Where?" Kemble demanded again, throwing open the green draperies which led to the back rooms. "Remember, Rutledge, one must dress for location! Not just occasion!"

Bentley jerked into step behind him, giving the delicate-looking clocks a wide berth. "I did not think to get a church," he said honestly. "Do you reckon I ought?"

Kemble whirled about, horrified. "My God, not your wedding?"

Bentley tried to smile. "Wish me happy, Kem."

But Kemble just pressed his hand to his forehead. "Good God!" he muttered. "I've been saddled with Bentley Rutledge, Man of Action! I thought you were supposed to be indolent, charming, and dissolute."

"Well," said Bentley a little wistfully. "Things change."

Kemble plunged through the draperies. Bentley followed him to his desk. Kemble snatched a pen from its stand and began to scratch out a note. "I pray that Maurice still has your measurements," he snipped as he scribbled. "And the choirmaster at St. Martin-in-the-Fields owes me a favor. We'll walk round there in a moment. And flowers! We'll need flowers—lilies if we can get them. Good Lord, Rutledge! You're going to make me a candidate for sartorial sainthood! How do you expect me to get all this done today?"

"Well," said Bentley very quietly. "You're going on quite splendidly, Kem. But I only came in to buy a ring."

Chapter Nine

In which Lord Treyhern suspects The Worst.

On the morning of her wedding, Frederica shook out her favorite blue dress and gave it to Jennie, the maid she and Zoë shared. It was to be her last clear thought. The rest of the day flew by in a flurry of packing, hugging, crying, and chaos. It was just as well. She was afraid to slow down, afraid that her fears might catch up with her brain before the deed got done. And yet the morning was not without hope; a tiny little flame of it burned now in her heart.

Frederica had passed a sleepless night. But to her surprise, few doubts had assailed her. The sleeplessness was due, in part, to hope. And to the thoughts of what came after marriage. No, he was not her dream husband. But he certainly was her dream lover.

"Better the devil you know, I daresay," Elliot had sighed, kissing her gently on the nose.

At least her child would have what Frederica had always longed for, a good old English surname and a legitimate lineage which went back a dozen generations. Moreover, though she would never have confessed it, Frederica was also just a little bit afraid that a piece of her heart had begun to hold out yet another hope, and one which was surely wasted. Nonetheless, the Bentley Rutledge she'd thought she knew had not been precisely the same man who had proposed marriage to her yesterday.

Zoë spent the early hours of the morning lazing about Frederica's bedchamber, making a general nuisance of herself. Apparently, Frederica's soon-to-be husband had many fine characteristics which had heretofore passed unnoticed. And to distract Frederica from her usual bout with morning sickness, Zoë was all too willing to enumerate them. In addition to his brilliant mind, incisive wit, and charming personality, he possessed a kind heart, perfectly straight teeth, and a mane of dark, unruly curls. And then there was his shameless grin, with half a dimple on the left side. And his eyes! Oh, they were an oddly mesmerizing shade—or so Zoë claimed—of dark brown rimmed in bottle green.

But when Zoë began to sigh over the size of his thighs, Frederica shoved away the chamber pot and suggested perhaps Zoë ought to marry him and take a turn heaving up her hot chocolate. Zoë had just laughed and threatened to snatch back Jennie, whom she had magnanimously surrendered to Freddie for the trip to meet Bentley's family in Gloucestershire.

And soon enough, they were at the church and standing in the midst of a ceremony so simple and so elegant Frederica's breath caught. Though not wildly fashionable, St. Martin-in-the-Fields was one of London's most beautiful churches, and for her wedding day, it blazed with a thousand candles and brimmed with vases of white lilies, all of it trimmed in gold satin ribbon. She found herself deeply touched that Bentley had arranged such a lovely ceremony.

Then the Reverend Mr. Amherst came out, looking

very different in his flowing vestments. And the next thing Freddie knew, her knees were nearly buckling, and Bentley Rutledge was sliding a warm, heavy chunk of gold onto her hand and pledging his eternal love in that husky whisper she loved so well. After that, she had only the vaguest memories of having her cheek repeatedly kissed and her hand pumped up and down as she'd stood next to her husband on the church steps.

But Bentley, never one to remain solemn for long, had been unable to resist a moment of levity. When the pews had completely emptied and the well-wishers were wandering away, he grinned, snatched her up by the waist, and kissed her again, right in the churchyard, twirling her round and round in a heady circle, just as he'd done on Boxing Day. And suddenly, quite unexpectedly, Frederica felt happiness spring into her heart. There was a sense of unalloyed delight in his touch, and his face had not held the expression of a man who'd gone to the altar against his will.

And when he put her down, all she could do was catch her breath, snatch his hand, and stare at the monogram on his signet ring. "Why did you never tell me your real name was Randolph?" she asked on a happy laugh.

During the ceremony, it had struck her as a reassuring, more steady sort of name. She was the Honorable Mrs. Randolph Bentham Rutledge. It was a staid and sober mouthful, harking back, she supposed, to her hopes of safe, dull, and ordinary. But when he kissed her and twirled her around in the churchyard, he became again just Bentley. Her friend. Her lover. Now her husband. And she was suddenly, and quite inordinately, glad.

But she'd had little time to ponder her happiness. Suddenly, Mr. Kemble, Elliot's former valet, was making her a sweeping bow, kissing her most elegantly on the hand, and waxing even more poetically than Zoë had done as he told her what a sterling example of English manhood she had married. Later, she discovered in her carriage a beautiful wedding gift: a ten-piece rococo tea set made of antique silver, along with a thick ivory envelope on which was written, in perfect copperplate, "G. J. Kemble's Infallible Intemperance Remedy." A recipe for some sort of foul-sounding morning-after cure was tucked inside. That had been a sobering stroke of reality.

No, it had not been her fantasy wedding. But there had been a sense of promise in it, and perhaps that was more realistic than any of her girlish dreams? The question had tormented her as they returned for the wedding breakfast at Strath. There, however, the food had tasted like paste in Frederica's mouth, and she had begun to feel a little frightened at the thought of leaving her home and her family. Another round of well-wishes, however, and there was no avoiding it. Somewhere near mid-afternoon, she and Jennie had been bundled into a sleek black traveling coach bearing the crest of the Earl of Treyhern and driven away from Strath. And away from the only family Frederica had known since leaving her homeland.

Her husband had traveled beside them, mounted on a fine bay mare who strutted alongside the carriage as if it were she who was newly wed, flicking her ears attentively to Bentley's every murmur and motion. That prancing horse, Frederica suspected, would not be the last of her competition. Indeed, at every village and crossroads they passed, there seemed to be someone who wished to greet him like a long-lost relative. Even the farmers plowing in the fields and the cottage wives taking in their wash had stopped to wave and sometimes even pass a word or two over the hedge. Near Wallingford, there had even been a band of gypsies, their carts painted up in a wild array of colors and half a dozen black-eyed beauties hanging out of them, calling his name. Bentley just waved and rode on.

Frederica soon realized there was no hope of arriving in Gloucestershire that day. The afternoon clouded over, and a moonless night edged near. Shortly thereafter, they put up at an inn near Little Wittenham. At the reception counter, Bentley behaved like the most courteous of husbands. Too courteous, Frederica decided, when he tactfully arranged a small room for himself and a suite for her and Jennie. It was the polite and proper way for a husband to behave. But it was not, Frederica realized with some embarrassment, the way she had hoped he would behave. She sighed when she locked the door behind her and fell at once onto the bed, wondering if they would ever reach Gloucestershire.

Camden Rutledge, the Earl of Treyhern, was striding through the great hall of Chalcote Court when he heard the horse hooves come thundering into his courtyard shortly after noon on a cool spring day. Someone in a devilish hurry, he mused as a small shower of gravel spattered across a window. His butler went to the door while the earl collapsed into a nearby chair to await what was apparently a pressing matter. He stretched out his heavy work boots and slumped a little, watching dispassionately as Milford paid the messenger and sent him away again.

The earl had been up since long before dawn, having spent the morning with his steward and his employees, who were erecting a new granary on the home farm. The stonework alone had taken better than two months, and the earl had mashed three fingers in the process. Today, he was both bone-weary and irritable. Too irritable, he did not doubt, to deal well with the message Milford was now carrying across the hall, for the butler's expression was a telling one.

Milford sighed witheringly. "From your brother, my lord."

"The devil you say!" Awkwardly, Treyhern tore the seal with a finger which was missing its nail. His mood was not improved by what he read:

> *Dear Cam,*
> *Obliged to pinch your traveling coach from Mortimer Street. Arrive home tomorrow. Have got myself leg-shackled. Bride the former Miss d'Avillez of Essex. Very pretty chit. Can't think if you know her.*
>
> > *As ever,*
> > *yr. servant & brother, R.B.R.*
> *P.S. Do not kill fatted calf. A plucked and scalded rooster more in keeping with the occasion.*

"My God!" The earl jerked from his chair, his eyes still on the message. "Helene!" he roared, bolting off in search of his wife. "Helene! My God! I think Bentley has taken up opium smoking!"

* * *

Mr. and Mrs. Rutledge reached Chalcote Court in the early afternoon of the following day, and it took but a moment for chaos to break loose. Frederica was almost relieved when Bentley's family burst from the front door and into the graveled forecourt, waving and smiling as the carriage circled toward the door. She had not been brought up in a formal household, and really had no wish to live in one with strangers, even for a short while.

A lady and a gentleman, three children, half a dozen servants, and a damp, dirty spaniel darted about as their luggage was unloaded in a flurry of activity. Lord Treyhern tried to subdue the dog, despite the fact that he held a tiny infant in his arms. Lady Treyhern rushed forward to hug Bentley as he leapt down off his horse. Frederica was relieved to see that everyone seemed perfectly . . . normal. Better than normal, really. Warm and extremely relaxed. And suddenly, her marriage to Bentley Rutledge did not seem quite so dreadful a decision.

Soon she found herself being soundly hugged and kissed by Lord Treyhern and his wife, then passed along to their eldest daughter. Lady Ariane Rutledge was perhaps fifteen years old, blue-eyed and slender, with heavy, almost white-blond hair which put Frederica very much in mind of her cousin Evie. And then there was her smile, which was filled with warmth and mischief, and so much like Zoë's that Frederica felt her homesickness begin to wane.

Chalcote Court was by no means a large house, but it was old and extraordinarily beautiful. As its name implied, the house was set in a walled garden on a hill just above a quaint village. Beyond the walls, the squat Norman belfry of the village church could be seen. Soon they were shown into a long, sunny parlor, and a tray of tea and sandwiches was carried in behind them. Lady Ariane remained, while her siblings, Gervais, Madeline, and Baby Emmie, went happily away with their nurse.

Frederica was more than a little relieved to realize that Bentley had sent word ahead of their marriage. She was not at all sure that such a thing would occur to him. But perhaps she was not giving him enough credit? After all, he had thrown together a breathtakingly beautiful wedding at the last minute. Still, the warm welcome aside, it was soon quite clear to Frederica that the reality of the situation had not yet been fully absorbed by Bentley's family.

Lord Treyhern, who was just a leaner, less benevolent-looking version of his brother, smiled tightly but scarcely spoke six words. Lady Treyhern, however, was quite cordial—and quite French, too, though her accent was barely discernible. It was soon evident that there was a deep affection between her and Bentley. As Ariane served sandwiches and Helene poured, the five of them chatted about the warmth of the weather and their uneventful journey from London. But slowly, the conversation ground down to that pregnant silence which so often occurs after all the polite, mundane topics have been exhausted.

"Well!" said Helene brightly as she leaned forward to warm Frederica's tea. "Now that the niceties are out of the way, Frederica, you must satisfy our appallingly vulgar curiosity and tell us how long you and Bentley have known one another."

Frederica took back the outstretched cup and saucer. How long had she known Bentley? "Why, most all my life, it seems," she said quite honestly. "He has been my cousin Augustus's best friend for any number of years."

And indeed, it surprised her to realize she could scarce remember a time when Bentley hadn't been drifting in and out of their lives at Chatham Lodge, or a time when she had not enjoyed having him about. Helene settled back into her chair with a relieved expression, but the earl jerked at once from his. "Your pardon, ladies," he said stiffly. "Bentley, will you join me in my study? There is a most pressing estate matter on which I require your opinion."

Frederica watched as a dark look passed over her new husband's face. Stiffly, he rose. "Yes, of course," he said quietly. "I shouldn't think of depriving you of my bountiful wisdom." Together, they disappeared through a door at the opposite end of the room.

"His lordship disapproves," murmured Frederica as soon as the door closed.

Helene put down her teacup. "Oh, no, my dear!" she answered. "My husband is taken aback, that is all. Bentley's message quite shocked us, for we'd no notion he was contemplating marriage. But it is high time he did, and we are glad, Frederica—exceedingly glad—to welcome you into our family."

"I am honored."

Suddenly, Helene leaned intently forward. "Come," she said impulsively. "Let me show you to the suite of rooms I am having refurbished, and we shall see if they suit you. This is not a large house, but I think we can make you comfortable."

"Yes, of course." Frederica forced a smile. "How kind you all are."

Chalcote's study was much as Bentley remembered it. It was a large, darkly paneled chamber with a deep bay window, a massive mahogany desk, and enough books to fill a lending library. The only new addition was a litter of kittens, half of whom were asleep by the hearth with their mother, Matilda, a marmalade tabby who stared at him through drowsy, slitted eyes.

The other kittens, three fat balls of fur, were staggering about the coal scuttle on short, unsteady legs beneath the watchful eye of their grandmother, Boadicea, who had settled herself in a sphinxlike pose atop the *Times* on Cam's desk. Instinctively, Bentley headed for the fireside and one of the overstuffed wing chairs which flanked it. He was tired, his emotions already worn to a bloody nub, and he meant to take Cam's sermon sitting down—if he took it at all, which he often didn't.

"I collect you have ruined the poor girl?" said Cam, throwing down the gauntlet at once.

"Do you?" Bentley stretched his legs out and crossed them at the ankles, a desultory gesture which never failed to irritate his brother. "Is that your best guess, Cam? There's always rape, pillage, and kidnapping, you know. Or perhaps I just married her for her money."

His brother looked little chastened. "Well, whatever else can be said of you, Bentley, I don't imagine you'd marry a woman for her fortune," he said gruffly. "You don't like money well enough to bother."

"A compliment!" he answered bitterly. "How charitable."

His brother made an impatient gesture with his hand. "I merely wish to help, Bentley," he said. "If there is any scandal attached to your marriage, I should like to hear it now."

"I have no need of your help." Bentley kept his voice surprisingly calm. "As for scandal, I regret to say that there is a bit. Congratulate me, Cam. I am about to become a father again."

Bentley watched in mild satisfaction as a little of the color drained from his brother's face. "Again?" Cam retorted. "You have never been one, Bentley. Not in any meaningful sense of the word."

For some reason, Cam's response did not stir his ire as he might have expected. Part of it was Bentley's sheer fatigue. But there was also the calico kitten which had toddled over and crawled up Cam's trouser leg. It was hard for a man to seem like an overbearing jackass with a mewling ball of fur hanging off his knee.

"No, I haven't really been a father before," Bentley admitted as his brother unhooked the kitten from his trousers and tucked it under his chin. "But that is hardly my fault, Cam. Had I known my mistress had borne me a daughter, I would have cared for both of them as best I could. And I will care for this one to the best of my ability. Now, do you wish me happy, Cam? Or do you wish to continue lecturing me to no good end?"

"I have never wished you anything but happiness." Cam spoke very gravely. "And now, I wish it for your bride as well. You will, I trust, make her happiness your life's priority?"

Bentley sneered a little and stared into the morning's fire which was now dying in the grate. "I shan't deliberately make her miserable, if that's what you mean."

"It isn't," said Cam abruptly. "But I am glad to hear it. She seems a good, well-brought-up young lady. And quite remarkably beautiful, too. You are a most fortun—"

"Damn it, I don't need to you extol my wife's virtues!" Bentley interjected, jerking from his chair. "Or my good fortune. I have already noticed both. And you had best just stay away from her, do you hear me?"

Cam's head jerked up. "You brought your bride into this house of your own volition," he snapped, his eyes cold and hard. "Frederica is now my sister. Good God, Bentley! What kind of man would trifle with his brother's wife? Can you tell me that? Can you? And don't tell me I mistook your meaning."

But Bentley's heart had begun to race. The room was suddenly hot and airless. What the devil *had* he meant? *What?* He couldn't think straight. Couldn't breathe. As if to dispel the dreaded sensations, he dragged one hand through his hair. "Cam, I didn't mean—" he awkwardly began. "That is, what I meant was—oh, hell! I'm damned if I know what I meant. I think marriage makes a man lose his wits."

Slowly, the chill in Cam's gaze receded. "Mind the kittens, then," he murmured, "if you mean to hurl yourself restlessly about the room now."

Bentley was already halfway to the window. And he was restless, he realized. Worse than restless. And Cam had guessed it easily. But then Bentley was always ill at ease in this house. When he was away from Chalcote, he sometimes longed for it like a wistful schoolboy, yet when he returned, he soon became apprehensive.

Anxious. He kept waiting, waiting for something which did not happen, but which felt so near and so threatening it was like standing in a thunderstorm and feeling the anticipatory shiver of a lightning strike.

Aimlessly, he drifted through the room, picking up bits of bric-a-brac and staring through the window as if looking for trouble to come strolling down the carriage drive. On a distant hill, he could see old Angus and one of the younger farmhands plowing a south-facing slope, churning up the soil from a barren shade of dun into brown-black mounds, rich with promise. Was there any such promise, he wondered, in his life? If he churned at it long enough, would he ever reap a crop of real happiness—one which was fairly earned, instead of won on the turn of a card or stolen at someone else's expense?

He did not feel quite as content as he'd hoped, now that the worry of the wedding was behind him and reality stretched out ahead. And as much as he pretended otherwise, his brother's questions nagged at him. Could he give Freddie a happy future? Was that his duty? And what was hers? It seemed unfair that she should bear the same obligation toward him. He had thought that in bringing Freddie to Chalcote, he might banish some old ghosts, yet they seemed more alive now than ever. Had it been a mistake to come here?

It was as if his brother read his mind. "You had to bring her here, Bentley," said Cam in his solemn voice. "There will be talk, you know. It is best the two of you remain here for a long visit. The world must be shown that your marriage and your bride have the overwhelming approval of your family. It will go easier for her that way."

Bentley still stood, staring out the window. "You know who she is, then."

"The ward of Lord Rannoch, yes," said Cam. "And I know, of course, that she is . . . foreign-born."

"You mean you know she is illegitimate."

"Yes, that, too." Cam's voice was gentle.

Suddenly, Bentley turned from the window to face him. "I don't give a tinker's damn about all that, Cam," he said on a rush. "I like her. I always have. And I will take good care of her."

Contemplatively, Cam stroked the kitten with one finger. "You like her . . . but you do not love her?"

Bentley shook his head. "Not . . . love. No, not that. But I am not displeased with my lot. I shall make the best of it."

"Did Rannoch put a gun to your head?" Cam's tone was matter-of-fact.

Bentley laughed harshly. "By no means," he answered. "Indeed, I collect they went to quite some lengths to avoid me."

Cam made a pensive noise in the back of his throat. "When is the child due?" he asked. "Just how bad, Bentley, is this situation going to look for Frederica?"

The question struck Bentley like a tumbril of stone. "When?" he echoed. "Why, in the winter, I daresay . . ."

"Count off about forty weeks," Cam dryly suggested. "I am assuming here, you see, that your better judgment slipped but the once."

Bentley swallowed hard and did a little mental arithmetic. "Early November, then."

Cam groaned and seemed to sink a little lower in his

chair. Displeased, the kitten began mewling. Bentley reached down and peeled it from Cam's waistcoat, then put it gently back into Matilda's basket, where she began to twitch her whiskers at it, as if inspecting it for damage. Even the cat, it seemed, did not trust him. Hell, he did not trust himself.

"The blame for this delay cannot be laid at my door, Cam," he said, kneeling down to stroke the tabby. "I offered for Freddie at once. Long before she knew of the child."

Cam's brows went up again. "Did you?"

Bentley stood and spun around. "Good God, Cam! What manner of man do you take me for? She is a good girl from a decent family. I never meant to—"

"No, no," murmured Cam, lifting his hand wearily. "You never do."

Bentley stood over his brother now. "Damn you, don't start with me!" he warned, jabbing a finger in Cam's face. "We have come to blows in this room on more than one occasion, and, given my current mood, I am just itching to break something."

Cam jerked to his feet. "Just tell me this, Bentley," he said impatiently. "Have you given any thought to the future? Have you any notion how you mean to support that poor girl? You have no profession. You have been thrown out of every university in the kingdom. Indeed, you haven't even a roof over your head unless one counts Roselands, which is Helene's."

"I don't need your threats, Cam," he growled. "Just sod off."

His brother held up his hands, palms outward. "These are not threats, Bentley," he said, the strain telling in his voice. "I just need to be sure everyone is provided for."

"Oh, *you* need!" echoed Bentley caustically. "You have ever imagined yourself the patron saint of perpetual responsibility, haven't you? But this woman is my concern, Cam. Not yours. Stay away from her. And let me tell you this whilst I'm at it: card playing and risk taking are a damned sight more lucrative than one might imagine."

"Easy come, easy go," warned Cam, setting his work-roughened hands on his hipbones.

"This time, it shan't go anywhere," said Bentley grimly. "I'm hardly fool enough to think I can continue to live as I have. Remember, dear brother, I already lost one child to poverty. This time, my child won't be left in some charity orphanage to die a slow death from fever and starvation. This time, I *know*. So I won't be gallivanting off to India or to Italy or to any other damned place out of ignorance. And let me make it plain I do not need your help in supporting Frederica. I can afford, Cam, to keep my wife and child in a very grand style until hell freezes over."

Cam's shoulders sagged a little, but, oddly, he did not look surprised. "I am glad, then," he said, sounding quite sincere. "And so long as you are not looking for some sort of miracle or an improbable turn of fate to provide for her, then I shall refrain from giving advice."

"Ha!" snorted Bentley. "Now, *that* would be a miracle."

Chapter Ten

In the Garden Suite.

When Bentley stalked back into the parlor, Ariane was alone at the harp, plucking out "Scarborough Fair" with fingers which were light and sure. She lifted her gaze and surreptitiously winked at him, never missing a note. Cam came in behind him and bent to kiss Ariane. "What has become of the ladies, poppet?"

"Mama took Frederica up to look at the garden suite," she answered vaguely.

At that moment, however, both ladies appeared at the door. Helene's arm was circled lightly about Frederica's waist, as if they were old friends. "Ah, but we are back," said Helene, returning to the tea table. "Cam, you will be glad to hear that the work upstairs is progressing splendidly. The gentleman's bedchamber is finished, and the painters have moved their scaffold into the sitting room. Larkin is taking the baggage up now."

Bentley's head whipped around. "What's this, Helene?"

Frederica caught the sudden tension in her husband's voice. Everyone settled back into their chairs. "I am moving you and Frederica into the garden suite," Helene answered, picking over the remaining sandwiches. "I intend you to be frequent visitors here, so—"

"No." Bentley braced both hands on his chair arms, his knuckles white. "No, I do not want it."

Helene's gaze flicked up. "But it's no trouble, Bentley," she insisted, a cucumber sandwich pinched daintily between her fingers.

Bentley had half risen from his seat. "Helene, you don't understand," he said, his voice tight. "I don't want it. I want my old room."

"Your old room!" she echoed, clearly amazed. "But it's so small!"

"I like it," he insisted. "I am comfortable there. And that is the room I want."

Helene looked confused. "But, Bentley, think of the view from the garden suite! And your old room, why, it's far too cramped for two."

"I'm sure I shan't mind," Frederica interjected. She didn't care where they slept, but she was beginning to wonder at Bentley's strident refusal. He looked odd, almost as if he couldn't get his breath. And his expression, too, seemed stricken.

"Well, this is all rather silly, is it not?" asked Helene, still looking at her brother-in-law. "After all, what is one small gentleman's bedchamber to a good suite of rooms? Really, Bentley! Ladies require space. Where is Frederica's maid to sleep?"

"With the other servants," he said tightly. "Put her with Queenie. I don't want to be near any workmen. The racket will disturb our rest."

Frederica leapt to her husband's defense. "I fear Bentley is merely thinking of my comfort," she asserted. "You see, I've been a bit tired of late, and I often nap in the afternoon."

As she'd hoped, the tension in Bentley's expression eased. Helene exchanged a speaking glance with her husband. "Oh, I see," she murmured. "Well, I'm sure we can make do until the work is finished."

But Frederica could see from her husband's dark expression that he had no intention of falling in with Helene's scheme, now or ever. "Indeed," he murmured, jerking from his chair. "I'll just go and save Larkin a wasted effort, then, shall I?"

Bentley never returned to tea. Instead, Frederica and Lord Treyhern passed the time in a rather animated discussion about her travels. Frederica had been fortunate in that regard; Evie's work as an artist had frequently taken the family across the Continent, once as far as Warsaw. It was clear that his lordship had a fine grasp of history and politics, and he readily confessed his envy of her good fortune. But farming, he explained, kept him fixed at Chalcote for much of the year. The rest of his time was taken up by his Devonshire seat, Treyhern Castle.

Bentley had said that his elder brother was bookish, and clearly, Lord Treyhern had a brilliant mind. But the man she saw before her, with his work-roughened hands and unrefined clothing, looked more like a gentleman farmer than a scholar. He was also a surprisingly good conversationalist. Nonetheless, somewhere in the midst of her third cup of tea, Frederica found herself suppressing a yawn.

Helene noticed it at once. "I am sure, my love, that Frederica is quite worn from her journey," she interjected. "She should rest before dinner."

"That would be lovely," Frederica admitted.

This time, Helene took her up three flights of stairs and down a long, dimly lit corridor. At the end of it lay a large, single bedchamber fitted with masculine furnishings, a dark gold oriental carpet, and a triple window which overlooked the village church. Opposite the window was a massive Jacobean bed with a mattress higher than her waist and a footboard so tall it reached her chest. There was also a bathing closet and a small dressing room.

"This is beautiful," she said, turning a slow circle on the carpet. "Quite as nice as the garden view. Thank you, Helene."

Her new sister-in-law kissed her lightly on the cheek and left. Frederica drew in a deep, reassuring breath. Though her husband was nowhere to be seen, his wonderful masculine scent seemed to permeate the bedchamber. It had been his room since leaving the schoolroom, Helene had explained as they mounted the stairs. And, having seen it, Frederica was inordinately glad that this was to be the bedchamber they would share as a married couple.

Just then, Jennie stepped from the dressing room. "Good afternoon, miss," she said, shaking the wrinkles from one of Frederica's gowns. "Lovely house, ain't it? I've never been to Gloucestershire. It looks all quaint and country-like, don't it?"

"Yes, doesn't it?" agreed Frederica, poking through the open trunk. "London has encroached on Richmond, and even Essex. But here, this is like heaven."

Jennie smiled, but her eyes looked tired. "I've put your gowns up to hang just in there, miss. And now I'll take this dinner dress down for pressing."

"Thank you, Jennie," she said. "But first I'm going to take a nap, and I suggest you do the same. I'm told you're to share a room with someone called Queenie. I gather she's one of the housemaids?"

Jennie wrinkled her nose. "Aye, I've seen her," she answered darkly. "And a saucy piece she is, too."

Frederica was taken aback. "Will that be a problem, Jennie?"

Jennie looked slightly ashamed. "Oh, no, miss," she said reassuringly. "She's friendly enough, I'm sure. I'll just go along now."

But as soon as the door closed, Frederica realized that the dressing case containing her face flannel and toiletries had gone missing. Yet she was sure that she had seen one of the footmen carrying it up the stairs. It had been left, no doubt, in the suite. There was a bell pull in the room, but Frederica had already noticed that Chalcote kept few servants, and she was loath to call Jennie back.

Frederica retraced her steps to the staircase, a twisting, Jacobean monstrosity of carved oak almost black with age. It was no trouble at all to find the suite Helene had shown her. But when she arrived, she saw that the door to the lady's bedchamber was cracked. How odd. This floor was rarely used, Helene had said, and the suite had lain vacant for some years. Gingerly, she pushed open the door on its well-oiled hinges. As it had earlier, the faint, sweet scent of lilacs floated from the room. Almost at once, however, Frederica sensed someone's presence and drew back.

Bentley?

Her husband stood at one of the deep, narrow windows, his back to the door, his hands braced wide on the embrasure. His shoulders were hunched as he stared into the garden, yet Frederica could sense the tension in his posture. She started to enter. Suddenly, with a slight strangling sound, Bentley jerked from the window and turned. His expression could only be described as stricken. It was as if his whole body trembled. He strode through the room to a tall mahogany clothes press, ripping open the double doors as if he feared Satan himself might be hidden inside.

The cabinet was quite empty. For a long moment, Bentley simply stood, staring into its depths, his knuckles white against the wood. It was very odd, but even from across the room, Frederica could smell the musty, sickly sweet scent of lilacs grow thicker. With a vile curse, he slammed the doors shut and turned away. But a latch slipped free, and one door fell open again, swinging eerily outward in the fading light. Heedless of it, Bentley began pacing the floor, his tread echoing heavily in the empty room.

Frederica watched, uncertain what she ought to do. She had intruded on some private moment. But she was, after all, Bentley's wife. Was she not expected to comfort him, both in sickness and in health? And whatever the cause, her husband had the look of a man who was not well.

Suddenly, on another wretched sound, he rushed back to the window. This time, he shoved it wide, braced his hands on the sill, and leaned halfway out. Frederica could see the fabric of his coat stretch taut across his shoulders as he dragged in slow, almost ragged breaths. It was the unmistakable posture of a person fighting down nausea. Alarmed, she pushed the door open another inch. "Bentley?"

His reaction was explosive. "*What—?*" he snarled, spinning around to stare at her. But it was not Frederica whom he saw; on that, she would have staked her life.

"Bentley?" She stepped from the gloom into what was left of the daylight. "Are you . . . unwell?"

For a moment, he stood frozen to the floor. His face was devoid of any color, his lips thin and bloodless. And then he shook his head and closed the distance between them. "Freddie?" He settled one big hand on her shoulder. "What are you doing here?"

"My dressing case is missing," she explained, studying him carefully. "I wanted my face flannel."

At last, Bentley managed a weak smile. "I sent Larkin up with it," he answered, taking her by the hand and drawing her back into the corridor. "You just missed him. I shall take you back upstairs."

Stubbornly, she stopped. "Bentley, are you all right?"

The smile faded. "Wifely concern?" he murmured coolly. "What a novel experience, Freddie. The smell of paint makes me ill."

The fresh paint was two doors away, but she did not say so. "You looked as though you'd seen a ghost."

For a moment, he seemed to falter, and then he just laughed. "Darling, this is a moldering old pile of a house." Casually—almost too casually—he threw one arm about her shoulders and urged her down the corridor. "Has no one told you about the specter of old John Camden? He haunts this place, you know."

"What, in the clothes press?" she said dryly.

"Ah, Freddie love, one never knows," he murmured as they rounded a dark corner. Suddenly, something goosed her right in the ribs.

Frederica squealed, almost leaping out of her shoes. "Bentley!"

"Ah, see, there he is!" whispered Bentley, his lips pressed warmly to her ear. "Old John punishes the skeptical!"

He prodded her again, and this time, Frederica shrieked with laughter. "Stop!" she said between gasps. "Let be! People will think me mad."

But Bentley just kept dragging her along. "Oh, Freddie love, they already do," he answered as they reached the stairs. "After all, you married me."

Abruptly, she stopped. "Bentley, why can you never be serious?"

His humor faltered. "Why should I?" he asked. "Don't you find my brother serious enough for the both of us?" He caught her shoulders and tried to kiss her, but Frederica turned her face away.

"Don't." His voice was suddenly sharp.

Frederica turned back again.

His eyes dark and hard, Bentley lifted one hand and skimmed the back of it along her cheek, flesh barely touching flesh. It was a caress of quiet tenderness, even as his other hand gripped her shoulder quite ruthlessly. On a sudden flash of insight, Frederica saw the dichotomy, the potential for both cruelty and kindness which lay hidden in his eyes. There was nothing light about him now, and for an instant, it chilled her.

"Don't do that," he rasped. "Don't turn away from me, Frederica."

Frederica held his gaze unflinchingly. "Then don't hide things from me, Bentley."

He smiled faintly, but it was tinged with bitterness. "You have promised me six months, my dear. Six months of wifely obedience. Do you mean to honor that vow?"

"And you have given your own vows," she returned. "For example, you have promised to keep only unto me. Where is your honor?"

"Here," he softly answered, touching his left breast. "Have I given you cause to doubt it?"

Had he? No, not yet. Still, he was being less than honest about something. And eventually, she would discover what. But at this moment, she sensed they were balanced precariously on the fine blade of an argument. Their marriage was too new and too fragile to sustain such a wound. She would have to let it go—for now.

Suddenly, as if he could read her thoughts, Bentley flashed that too-charming smile of his, and all Frederica's doubts and fears were burnt away by the flame which leapt in her heart. Unable to resist, she closed her eyes and felt his lips brush over hers, as she'd somehow known they would. At once, a hot, sweet heat went swirling through her, just as it had that night in the garden. Bentley's mouth tasted of temptation and offered up promise. The promise of worldly pleasure, one which she did not want to refuse. He had taught her well in just one night, had he not?

Was he was both sinner and seraph, this beautiful man she had wed? Was she sorry she had done it? Not yet. Perhaps . . . soon? Or perhaps never, she decided as he took her mouth again.

At last, she tore her lips from his. "I am going upstairs for a nap, Bentley." Her words came out low and throaty. "Are you coming? Or am I to sleep alone again?"

She could feel his gaze on her, hot and hungry in the gloom. "Did you miss me last night, my sweet?"

Frederica swallowed hard. "Yes."

"Upstairs," he rasped. "Now."

Helene's husband and stepdaughter had vanished by the time she returned to the yellow parlor. It took no real gift of prescience to know where her husband had gone. Into the study to lick his wounds, if he had any, and to cool his temper, which he always had after a private meeting with his brother. She found Cam sprawled on his back across the hearth rug, staring at the ceiling as the kittens staggered over him like furry Lilliputians. His coat and waistcoat lay heaped upon the chair.

"Hello, Gulliver," she said, lightly prodding his ribs with her toe.

Cam frowned up at the ornate plasterwork. "I daresay you mean *gullible,* don't you?" he grumbled. "I should have dragged Bentley outside for a bloody good hiding."

Helene sank down onto the floor, tucking one leg up beneath her skirts in a most unladylike posture. "Don't argue with him," she chided, settling one hand on his thigh. "Really, my love, you both quite waste your breath. Now, roll over onto your stomach. Your back aches again, I see."

Cam set away the kittens and rolled over with a grunt. Helene pulled his shirt loose and slid her hands over muscles which were far too tight. "I thought so," she murmured. "How many beams or rafters or what-evers did you heft this morning?"

"Not enough," he muttered into the carpet. "The poor girl is with child, you know."

"Ah," said Helene, gently massaging his lower back. "I feared it must be something like that. He was prickly as a hedgehog at Emmie's christening. But Bentley will make a responsible father, Cam. You'll see."

"Damn it, he does not know the definition of the word *responsible,*" her husband fumed. "He is about as constant as a will-o'-the-wisp."

Helene propped her chin on one hand. "Yes, I dare-say that was once true."

But Cam did not hear her. "Good God, he is the worst sort of womanizer! And now look! She is but a child, Helene."

"Is she? How odd! She told me she was eighteen."

"An innocent!" he continued, oblivious to her gentle sarcasm. "A sweet girl from a fine family! We are bloody lucky Rannoch did not kill him where he stood."

"I believe you exaggerate, my dear," Helene soothed. "Young love run a little wild is hardly a killing offense."

Cam turned his head to look up at her, and his per-sistent cowlick flopped to one side, tempting one of the kittens to swat at it. "Young love?" he said archly. "Is that what you think it was, Helene? Bentley has been bedding women on a daily basis since he was sixteen— probably a damned sight younger—and, trust me, love never had anything to do with it. I have every notion he has worn calluses on his pri—"

Helene threw up a hand. "Don't say it, Cam!"

The tips of Cam's ears turned red. "Father encouraged this, you know," he said grimly. "Toward the end, not a week went by that Bentley wasn't caught diddling one of the dairy maids or shoving himself under the skirts of some tavern wench. Father thought it a great joke."

"Given Bentley's charm, I rather doubt he had to coerce anyone, my love," murmured Helene.

"Charm?" Cam looked at her incredulously. "Good God, Helene! He even tried to seduce you! I wonder you've forgotten it!"

Lightly, she laughed. "He did no such thing, Cam. He wanted to hurt himself and to strike out at you. He never meant me any harm. Nor does he mean Frederica any harm. She is a lovely girl. For my part, I think him very lucky.".

"Yes, well, and what of her? What is to become of her, Helene?"

Helene sat back on her heels and considered it. "Bentley will love her and take care of her," she finally answered. "I have every confidence."

Cam struggled to sit up on the hearth rug. "Then you have far more confidence than I, my dear. When will you admit that Bentley brings his troubles on himself?"

Helene lost her temper. "And when will you admit that Bentley has a—a problem?"

"Beyond his tendency toward irresponsibility, do you mean?"

"I mean something seriously wrong, Cam," she insisted. "Perhaps I have not explained this clearly enough to you these last few years."

"What?" he challenged. "What could possibly be wrong?"

"Damn it, I don't know!" she exploded.

Cam patted her gently on the cheek. "Now, don't curse, Helene!" he said, standing up and offering her his hand. "Just give in gracefully, and admit that you've been looking in those big black books of yours again so that you might put some multisyllabic Latin word to a young man who was simply spoilt by his father."

She glowered up at her husband's proffered hand. "Spoilt?" she retorted, spurning his assistance and rising unaided. "And in what way was he spoilt? Your father scarce had two shillings to rub together."

"Spoilt by bad habits," he said gently. "Exposed to things which were not appropriate. Told things, encouraged in things, you know what I mean."

"Oh, I begin to see," said Helene. "And all this was Bentley's fault, was it?"

Cam had begun to shove in his shirttails. "I—no, it wasn't," he admitted. "But they are very like, Helene. Yet no matter what he seems to think, I could never hate him."

"Oh, he hates himself enough for the both of you," she said quietly. "No one with any sense of self-worth would run such risks or throw away his life so cavalierly. But that is what Bentley thinks he deserves."

Her husband looked at her, his gaze softening with worry. "Helene, your heart is in the right place. But that is all I will accede to just now."

Helene managed a smile and picked up his waistcoat. "Then let us quarrel no more, Cam," she said, holding it open for him. "Instead, let's plan what we can do to help Frederica. A new marriage can be hard slogging under the best of circumstances."

"Yes, of course," he agreed, shrugging into his clothes. "What shall we do, Helene, to signal our approval?"

"I shall take her to call on all our neighbors," she mused. "Perhaps she can even help me in the village school. Joan, I am sure, will welcome her at Bellevue. And Catherine can have us all to dinner."

Cam was doing up his buttons. "Oh, dash it!" he interjected. "Forgot to tell you. Cat sent round some chicken-scratch note about Max's grandmother. Old Mrs. Castelli has been flogging her business manager again. The poor devil has threatened to quit unless Max gets her out of his hair. They set off for London this morning."

"Well!" said Helene on a laugh. "Cat will just die when she learns of all the excitement she's missed. Now, come along, my love. You need a long soak in a tub of hot water to loosen those muscles. And then, perhaps, some other sort of therapeutic treatment might be in order, hmm?"

Chapter Eleven

In which Lady Madeline explains Everything.

When Frederica pushed open the door to Bentley's bed-chamber, the sun was sinking fast, the low shaft of light casting a golden glow over the room. In the massive hearth, someone had built up the evening's fire, and her dressing case sat by the bed. She heard the door latch behind her, heard Bentley snap the key in the lock. And suddenly, she felt just a little nervous.

But why? He was . . . just Bentley, wasn't he? That flash of darkness by the staircase had meant nothing. She was tired, her imagination overwrought. And yet she sensed in him a need, something only hinted at in his eyes and in his touch. She wanted him, too. She'd taken the risk of wedding him. So, nervous or not, why shouldn't she enjoy the advantages? And her husband definitely offered some advantages. Winnie had been right about that.

Bentley strode around the foot of the bed toward the hearth, still attired in his heavy riding boots and snug breeches. He paused and turned to face her, lifting his arms. "Mrs. Rutledge?" he murmured, lightly arching one brow. "Would you do me a wife's service and help me from my coat?"

Frederica went to him at once, and, reaching up—far up—she slid her hands beneath the superfine fabric and over his shoulders. It had been a long day, much of it spent in the saddle, and he smelled of horse and sweat and of something uniquely his. The warmth of it enveloped her as he turned, his arms coming out of the coat. Frederica had seen many men in their shirtsleeves. But never one quite so fine. His shoulders were wide and solid, and his dark, overlong hair curled gently about his shirt collar, in stark contrast to the pristine white cambric.

She must have been gawking. "My dear?" he said quietly. "The waistcoat?"

Frederica returned her eyes to his. He really wished her to undress him! It seemed a deeply intimate thing to do. And rather exciting, too. Still, her unpracticed fingers made an awkward job of the buttons. When the last fell free, Bentley's long, dark lashes swept down. "Thank you," he murmured, and let the waistcoat slide to the floor.

She could smell a trace of soap in the heat which rose from his shirt. "I'm afraid I do not know how to take loose your cravat," she said.

Those melting brown eyes flared open, catching hers as he slid one finger beneath her chin. "I will teach you, Mrs. Rutledge," he said with his wicked smile. "I will teach you all that you need to know."

Oh, he was good at this, her husband. His touch was soft as silk, his voice dark as sin. A sudden, misplaced memory flashed through Frederica's mind—a vision of him lying atop her in the grass at Chatham, his head thrown back in ecstasy. In response, a melting heat began to unfurl in her belly. He smiled at her now, a slight, knowing tilt at one side of his mouth, as if he'd guessed her deepest thoughts.

His hands closed over her fingers, and she felt the raw sensuality coursing through him. He gazed into her eyes, then pressed her hands, palms open, to his body. Swiftly, his eyes never leaving hers, he loosened the knot in his neckcloth and unfurled it from his collar.

From the corner of one eye, she saw it fall to the floor. Frederica wet her lips. Whatever he was, whatever else she felt for him, she desired him physically, and with a white-hot need that went coursing through her blood and chasing up her spine. Suddenly, he stepped back, yanked his shirttail free, and drew it over his head.

At once, her eyes went wide. Heat sprang to her cheeks. His chest was perfectly smooth and layered with muscle which looked as if it had been sculpted from stone, then warmed with God's own breath. In the firelight, every muscle took on a shape defined by shadow and flame.

Bentley touched her face again. "You approve, sweet?" The finger traced down her throat, along the curve of her collarbone, leaving a melting trail of fire. "I'm glad, Frederica, for I should like to please you. That is one thing, at the very least, I can do for you. And it is one thing I do well."

She remembered Winnie's whispered gossip and blushed hotly. He smiled and bent his head to kiss her throat. The finger slid around the neck of her dress again, plunging deeper. Her breath was hard to catch. Her breasts seemed to swell, to grow heavy with heat. Her nipples went hard, and with a little sound in the back of his throat, Bentley's hand slid down to cup her breast.

"You like this?" he rasped, touching his tongue to the tender spot behind her earlobe. "Tell me."

Frederica tried, but only a strangled sound came out. He thumbed her taut nipple through the fabric, and she exhaled on a shiver. "We have this, Frederica," he said in some satisfaction. "Remember that. If we have nothing else, we have this."

She wanted to cry out that this was not all, that there had to be more. But was it true? At the moment, she was not sure she cared. She just wanted Bentley to take her to bed again. And she began to see quite clearly just how she'd got herself into this mess. It hadn't had anything to do with feeling spurned or hurt, had it? She had used Johnny as a bad excuse. She had felt an irrational desire for this man—a man who had always intrigued her. A man who was beautiful, tempting, and more than a little dangerous. She had wanted his hot brown eyes on her. Had wanted his incredible body with a lust which should have felt sinful but did not.

Then, as now, her whole body ached from the sweetness of his torture, yet he'd scarcely touched her. He set one hand on her waist and bent his head to brush his lips along the turn of her jaw. His sharp teeth scored her flesh as he moved down her throat, the pain a slow, sweet agony. Her mouth opened on a sigh, and she pressed her lips to his neck, willing herself not to beg him.

"Ah, Frederica," he groaned.

And then his hands skimmed up her back, making short, expert work of the pins in her hair. The buttons went next. The dress suddenly relaxed and sagged off her breasts. He knelt and, for an instant, bowed his head until it brushed her thigh. Reaching beneath her skirts, he rolled down her stockings, his rough fingers catching in the silk and teasing at her flesh. Then, with an unhurried touch, he stripped her, garment by garment, until nothing remained but her lawn shift.

"Take it off," he rasped.

Frederica's eyes shot to the heavy draperies which framed the window.

His hands went to her shoulders. "No," he whispered, as if reading her thoughts. "You are mine. I want to see you in the daylight."

He had paid the ultimate price for her. Was that what he meant? She almost turned away, but he caught her and pulled her into his embrace. "Don't be afraid."

"I'm not." But she was, a little. Her breath ratcheted sharply upward.

He pressed himself fully against her, and she could feel the thick, jutting bulge of his arousal. She shifted, but he mistook her movement and set one hand low on her spine, trapping them thigh to thigh. He bent his head to brush his lips over her temple. And then he whispered those three little words she was half afraid to believe in. "Just trust me," he said. "Trust me to take care of you, Freddie."

She felt her knees nearly buckle. He drew her deeper into his embrace and kissed her, crushing the breath from her lungs, and she was lost. His hands moved on her restlessly, down her spine and over her hips, rubbing her through the thin shift and driving her need sharply upward. Frederica pulled away, fisted her hands in the sheer fabric, and drew it up and over her head.

His eyes moved down her throat, her breasts, and

lower. "Beautiful," he choked. And then he drew her into his embrace on another groan, pulling her close as he wrapped one hand in her hair. His heat and scent were stronger now. She could almost feel the pulse of life pounding through his body. He pulled her between his hard, muscled thighs, crushing her against him with a force she had not expected.

"Tell me, Frederica." His fist in her hair, he dragged her head back until their eyes met and the flesh of her throat was exposed. "Tell me you burn for this as I do. Have I corrupted you already? Or are you yet too innocent?"

Her arms had gone instinctively around him. Frederica looked up to see that Bentley's eyes were hot and wild. Unable to bear it, she let her lashes drop shut. It was futile; she had no resistance to him. "I burn for you," she whispered. And it was true. She could keep no distance between them.

He smiled, but it was a smile tinged with that odd, world-weary sadness she'd already come to recognize. Pushing her down onto the bed, he stood over her, jerking off his boots and stripping away what was left of his clothing. She gasped when his breeches and drawers slid down his thighs, allowing his erection to spring free, fierce and thickly veined.

Good heavens. Surely not?

"Oh, it fits, Freddie love," he whispered. The unabashed grin was back. He was naked now, and glorious beyond words. One could not grow up in a household of men and not catch the occasional glimpse of masculine flesh. Yet she was unaccountably sure she'd known no man who would look like this with his clothes off. Wild, that was the word for Bentley Rutledge. Sleek, beautiful, and uncivilized. He made her think of temptation in the Garden of Eden. He caught her wrist and drew her almost to the edge of the bed. Frederica gulped air, and he set his hands on her shoulders and pushed her down beneath him, his weight following her onto the bed.

Under them, the mattress groaned. She lay on her back, he on his left side, facing the fire as he curled around her. Bentley watched not her face but his hand, as it weighed her breasts and stroked her nipples until they peaked harder still. And then he bent his head and drew one areola between his teeth, gently biting. On a sharp cry, her whole body arched upward, and, in response, he threw one thigh over her body, forcing her back down again.

Sweet. Exquisite. He drew heat and fire from her with his mouth, sucking and tugging, urging her toward madness. His broad palm slid lower, caressing her lightly along her ribs, lingering tenderly over the swell of her belly, then, finally, easing between her thighs. He parted her legs and drew his fingers up through her flesh, causing her to gasp and writhe. He controlled her every sound and shiver. He drew them, coaxed them, like a master.

"Oh, please . . ." she heard herself whisper.

And then he rose up over her, dark and powerful. His upper arms were sinewy with muscle layered over heavy bones. His thighs were thick and taut, lightly dusted with black hair which grew thick and dark at their joining. His erection throbbed and twitched, and he touched himself, sliding his hand down his shaft as if restraining his impatience. "Open your legs," he commanded.

She did, and eagerly, too, drawing up her knees to cradle him. But he did not mount her and thrust himself inside her as she had yearned for. Instead, he knelt between her thighs, smoothed both hands over her belly in a soft, slow circle, then bent his head to gently brush his lips there. Twilight was near, the golden glow heating the room with color. He looked up, his gaze softening as he stroked her abdomen. He was thinking, she sensed, of the child. Frederica felt a new sort of joy burst into her heart. Her husband closed his eyes.

Bentley felt the sun warm his shoulders as he struggled to steady his breathing. To slow down his thoughts. He wanted—no, needed—some sort of distance from this. It was too much. Too real. This wasn't just a need for sexual satisfaction. Bentley wanted *her*. Wanted her so much that something inside him throbbed—and it was not, God help him, the organ between his legs. The sensation alarmed him now, as it should have done all those weeks ago. This intensity of need, this desire for someone—not just carnally but almost metaphysically— was not meant for him.

Was it because of the seed he had planted in her womb? He kissed her there over and over and thought of the child they had made. Was that why she felt so different? Was that why he couldn't detach his mind and simply focus on the physical satisfaction his body craved? Without opening his eyes, he skimmed his hands over her firm, flat belly. No, he thought not. Feared not. He had never wanted Mary this way, couldn't imagine it, even knowing that she'd borne him a child.

God Almighty, how he wanted to just fuck his wife. How he wanted to pound himself inside her, to thrust and grunt and mate with her until his breath came hot and fast, until all his thoughts went black, and until the sweat ran off his face and down his throat. Until he'd had his fill, and she—a woman who should have been one of his usual, nearly nameless lovers—was left panting and screaming beneath him.

But it wasn't going to be quite like that, was it? No, not that easy. In the falling darkness, he shook his head and softly swore. Frederica called out his name, a faint, tremulous question. Plaintively, her fingers brushed his thigh. Still, he did not answer.

No, he could not do it. Not like that, with distance and dispassion. Instead, he was going to make love to her, with all his presence of mind, with every shred of his awareness. It would not be just the scratching of a physical itch, with all the impassivity that the phrase implied. But instead, a holy act. *The marriage act.* A joining of his body to hers, in a way which he already knew would feel worshipful.

But it did not seem like the sort of sex that a man like him had been meant to have. He opened his eyes and slid his palms down her inner thighs. Her skin was golden in the light, her eyes wide with surprise. He lowered himself, delicately touching his tongue to her most intimate place, and Frederica cried out softly. Her hand lifted, fluttered uncertainly, and he captured it, entwining their fingers and drawing her hand to her belly as he listened to the low, hungry sounds she made.

Soon she was panting, almost thrashing. With the strength of his arm, he forced her body to yield, forced her bare buttocks hard against the counterpane, stilling her to his mouth. He was surprised at the swiftness of her response. She was a truly sensual creature, his delicate, almost fragile wife. He could feel her quicken, could feel her hips fight to rise upward.

But he wanted to pleasure her, long and hard, and not because he wanted to prove himself but because there was a new and sudden joy in it. Still, it was all too apparent that Frederica was not going to last. He let go of her hand and slid his fingers around her thigh. She shivered again and begged him for something in a low, raspy whisper. In response, he slid two fingers inside her. Her head went back, her whole body arching, and she cried again, like a wounded animal, a quiet wail of desperation.

There was no holding her back. Frederica's hands came down, one clutching her own thigh, the other frantically fisting in his hair. With one last perfect stroke, he touched her with his tongue again, and she shattered. He let her body rise to his mouth, reveling in the tremors which rocked her. He felt wave after wave roll through her, and when the last shudder died and she was left sobbing, he rose up and dragged his body over hers.

Was she really crying?

Oh, Christ Jesus. Tears he could not bear, and Bentley could see one leaking from her eye onto her temple. Worse, she was gazing at him with an expression which went far beyond appreciation and looked perilously close to utter adoration. Good Lord, he did not deserve that. Not tears, and surely not adoration. A fragment of memory, a warning—something Amherst had said in the church—came back to him. *The dreadful day of judgment, when all secrets of the heart shall be disclosed.* Oh, she would not look at him then with eyes so warm and melting, nor would she offer her embrace so easily. But, for now, her arms were still open, and his name was on her lips.

And so he took his cock in one hand, and, with the other, he opened her, drawing back the warm flesh. He considered it but a moment, could not wait, then shoved himself deep on one true stroke. Frederica cried out, but he knew instinctively it was from pleasure, not shock. She rose beneath him, arching to him again, and he heard himself begging her for what he did not want.

"Love me," he whispered, throwing back his head. "Oh, Freddie, love me. Please."

Love me. His words were like magic to Frederica's ears. Bentley looked so unexpectedly vulnerable. She held him, melting her body to his, matching their motions, and offering up her pleasures, guided by little more than instinct and eagerness. He moved inside her slowly, tutoring her with every stroke, his eyes shut tight, his strong arms trembling. In response, she slid her hands down and over the taut muscles of his buttocks and heard his groan of pleasure.

Her eyes drank him in. She watched the tendons of his throat cord and tighten and the sweat of his brow bead on his face as he thrust himself inside her. When it trickled down his neck to pool in the hollow near his collarbone, she delicately touched her tongue to it, and, atop her, her husband's whole body shook. Again and again, he whispered her name, his voice hoarse and hungry. She rose to meet him, instinctively tightening herself about his manhood and thrilling to the emotions, both pleasure and pain, which contorted his face.

And then the long, heated strokes of his body began to inflame her. Frederica let the rhythm take hold, let it drive her hips upward to meet him. Greedily, she gave herself over to him, to the bliss she sensed dangling just beyond her reach. Bentley's eyes flew open, and he knew. A black curtain of hair shadowed his face now, and still he did not break his cadence. Again and again, he drove into her, his lean body drenched with sweat, tempting and taunting her with the promise of pleasure renewed. She ached, oh, how she ached. For this. For him. For her husband.

He stroked her again, high and deep, harder and harder, until Frederica cried out. Her body melted, turned to lava, and began to flow around him. He clutched her shoulders with his hands and pounded himself into her. And then he cried out, a low, soft sound of anguish. Frederica felt the hot rush of seed spurt into her, again and again, until their passion was spent and his chest heaved with the effort of it.

He fell against her, gasping for breath. "Freddie," he finally murmured, collapsing fully on top of her. "Oh, my God."

Then she felt a moment of alarm shoot through him. Abruptly, he rolled to one side, taking her with him. His gaze held hers, soft in the dying light. "The baby," he whispered. "We shouldn't . . . ? "

Out of sheer exhaustion, Frederica fell onto her back. "No." Her voice was certain. "No, Bentley, that definitely does not hurt the baby."

"No?" he asked tentatively. "Are you sure?"

Frederica managed a weak smile. "Absolutely."

He kissed her once more, and then, without another word, Bentley curled his body around hers, rested his hand on her belly, and promptly went to sleep.

It was some time later—days later, it felt—that Frederica was roused by a light knock at the door.

"Mr. B.?" came a cheerful Cockney voice. "Mr. B.? Move sharplike, ducks. I've got yer 'ot water 'ere, and Mrs. Naffles is taking yer apple tart out 'er the oven."

The following morning, Bentley awoke to a remarkable realization. He'd slept through the night, something he'd not done at Chalcote in better than fifteen years. Pushing up onto one elbow, he stared through a shock of hair to see a pale sliver of sunlight cutting through the draperies, draperies he vaguely remembered pulling shut after dinner last night.

A faint noise caught his ear. With a little grunt, he rolled over to see Freddie stifling a yawn and staring at him with a soft, contented gaze. For a moment, it was as if his heart stopped. A flood of tenderness rolled over him, a most extraordinary sensation. And not an unpleasant one. Yet in some ways, it was more disconcerting than the rush of emotion he'd felt last night making love to her. Good Lord. This just got worse and worse.

To cover his bewilderment, Bentley scrubbed a hand down his face. "Morning."

"Good morning." She reached out to thread her fingers through his hair. "Sleep well?"

"Like a dead man," he laughed, rolling toward her. "I think I can get used to this, Freddie love."

She laughed. "Used to what?"

He nuzzled his face against her neck. "Waking up to find you in my bed."

Freddie smiled and stretched her lithe body like a cat. "Can you indeed?"

"Hmm, let me be sure." Bentley took her by one shoulder, pushed her away a little, and let his eyes drift over her face. "Oh, yes, you make a ravishing sight first thing in the morning. Devilish convenient in a marriage, I'd say. Some women, you know, don't wear so well."

Freddie gave him a sly grin. "Had some rude awakenings, have you?"

Bentley winced. "Aye, a few," he admitted. "But none I'd married, thank God."

She laughed, and, in response, he threw one arm around her, rolling onto his back and dragging her into the crook of his arm. Heaven help him, she fit perfectly there, too. He saw that the coverlet had slipped down to reveal the curve of her breasts, round and delicate beneath her nightdress, and the feeling of tenderness surged anew. To push the feeling away, he ran one hand beneath the covers and stroked her belly. "Freddie love, are you eating enough?" he mused. "Oughtn't you be getting fat or something?"

Freddie's lips formed a little pout. "Evie says I'll be as big as a house by Martinmas," she said. "Perhaps I won't look so attractive then."

Impulsively, he captured her lips with his and kissed her hard. "You'll be even more so," he whispered, the fervency in his voice surprising even him. He settled his hand squarely over her womb. "Yes, *more* beautiful, Freddie. You'll be lush and womanly, round with my child. How could a man not find that attractive?" His lips moved over her face, sprinkling little kisses. "Ah, you'll be so pretty I won't be able to bear it. You'll have to beat me away with the hearth broom."

She erupted with laughter then, and, impulsively, he tossed the covers back, then set his lips where his hand had been. Through the thin fabric of her nightdress, he could smell the heat of her skin and a hint of some flowery soap. "Do you hear that, sweet pea?" he said into her navel. "Your mother will be so irresistible, and your father so greedy, you can expect months of jiggling and jostling."

Frederica was still laughing, her head thrown back in the pillow. She was trying to drag him back up again, and eventually he relented. "*Sweet pea?*" she echoed.

"Well, it is a girl, you know," he warned, settling his head on her shoulder. "I can tell."

Frederica shook her head. "No, it's a boy," she retorted. "Winnie has already said so."

"Oh, *Winnie* has said so? And fatherly instinct counts for nothing, eh?"

"That's because you don't have Winnie's special stone," she said with a wink. "It's foolproof."

Bentley cocked one brow. "Oh, I've got some special stones," he said with a suggestive tilt of his head. "Want to see 'em?"

He could see Freddie struggling to keep a straight face. "No, this is a magical stone on a string," she insisted, pinching something imaginary between her fingers and waving it over her stomach. "A black onyx she bought from a witch in Florence. You suspend it over the mother's womb on the new moon, and if the babe is a girl, the stone spins clockwise. If a boy, counterclockwise. It was never wrong with Evie."

"Well, it's wrong this time," he muttered, burying his face against his wife's neck and giving her a little nip.

"Ouch!" said Freddie. "Do you want a daughter so badly? Don't men always want sons?"

Beside her, Bentley shrugged. "Perhaps if they have a title to pass on," he mused. "But I don't, and I think little girls are pretty, and they smell better than boys. I remember quite fondly Ariane as a child. And then there are Madeline and Emmie—not to mention Anaïs, my sister's girl."

Freddie settled back into her pillows. "I just think you are charmed by anything remotely female, and they are equally charmed by you," she said. "But I say that boys have an easier time of it in this world. They have options. Opportunities in life to do and be what they wish."

Bentley lifted his head and looked at her quite seriously. "Our daughter will have options and opportunities," he vowed. "I'll make sure of it. Why are you so worried, Freddie?"

Frederica shrugged and began to pick absently at the hem of the coverlet. "Oh, I daresay I'm just being foolish," she softly admitted. "I suppose I'm speaking more of myself than my child." She lifted her eyes to meet Bentley's, her gaze suddenly steady and serious. "But whatever our child's sex, Bentley, and whatever comes of this marriage, I do know that my child will walk an easier path through life than I. I haven't thanked you for that, and I should have."

Bentley felt his chest grow tight with some unexpected emotion. "I'm no selfless saint, Freddie," he said quietly. "Don't make me out one. I had my own reasons for marrying you."

For a long moment, she was silent, and then, inexplicably, Freddie turned the subject. "I enjoyed meeting your family yesterday," she said. "I especially liked your brother. We had such a lovely chat last night at dinner."

"Oh, I noticed Cam's attentiveness," said Bentley coolly. Her talk of marriage had struck a painful chord in his heart, but he liked this topic little better.

Freddie shot him a probing look. "At first, I feared he disapproved of our marriage," she continued. "Did you not think him a little distant during tea yesterday? But Helene said he was merely concerned."

"Aye, Cam's a great one for concerning himself with other people's business," Bentley muttered. "And never you mind whether he approves or not. We'll never be dependent on his charity."

Freddie looked at him in mild surprise. "Why, I never dreamt we were," she said softly. "What are you talking about?"

Bentley frowned up at the ceiling. "Forget it."

Freddie shook her head. "I'm not sure I should," she persisted. "The tension at tea was like shoe leather, Bentley. And things improved little during dinner. You seem not to like your brother. And he seems not to trust you."

"Aye, well, you've the right of that last part."

Freddie was silent for a moment, then she sighed. "Helene said the two of you sometimes don't get along." She stroked a soothing hand through his hair. "How may I help, Bentley?"

By staying the hell out of it, he wanted to snap. But he knew better. In her delicate state, that might cause her to cry, and God only knew what that might make him do. Fling himself at his brother's feet, kiss his boots, and beg forgiveness, most likely. Besides, her tears notwithstanding, Freddie just wasn't the type to stay out of trouble or blindly take orders. At Chatham, the chit had been allowed—no, *taught*—to debate, question, and think. She'd likely crossed her fingers during the word *obey* in their marriage vows.

"I just want us always to be close to our families," she resumed, threading her fingers through his and giving his hand a little squeeze. "It is important to me. And to our child."

Bentley gave a bitter laugh. "Playing peacemaker, Freddie?" he asked, his voice deceptively light. "Don't. My troubles with Cam needn't concern you."

Freddie, however, was gently insistent. "But of course they concern me, Bentley," she said. "I am your wife now. We're going to build a family together, and I am just trying to understand your—"

Bentley cut her off with another bark of laughter. "Don't bother!" he said, shoving violently at his pillow. "I don't even understand myself half the time."

"Bentley, I won't be shut out of your life."

"Oh, for pity's sake, Freddie!" he interjected, sitting abruptly up in bed. "This is our wedding trip. Why fret over things that don't matter?"

"Nothing matters more than family, Bentley." Freddie's tone was suddenly adamant. "To me, family unity is the most important thing, to be preserved before all else—and that includes one's pride. Should I have made my feelings clearer on that point before we wed?"

"Aw, Freddie, it's awfully bloody early in the morning for a high dudgeon!"

But she continued, her voice gentle but persistent. "No, you must listen to me, Bentley," she answered. "You see, I had no family. Not until Evie took me in. You cannot imagine how frightening that is. You have all this—" Here, she paused to make a sweeping gesture. "Caring relatives, this wonderful home, and an ancient heritage. And you aren't treasuring it, Bentley. You should be, for it is a precious and rare thing. I don't want our child to grow up in a family fraught with anger and dissension. I won't have it."

"Then you married into the wrong family," he snapped, wishing instantly to snatch back the words.

But his bride didn't give him the backhanded slap he deserved. Instead, she turned and set her open hand over his heart. "I married you because you convinced me that we both want what is best for this child," she whispered. "Was I wrong?"

For a time, Bentley just stared into the depths of the room.

"Bentley, was I?"

"No," he finally whispered. "No, you weren't wrong. You know how I feel, Freddie, about this child."

She left her hand on his chest, her palm warming the skin beneath. Her touch felt good and comforting. And if a man had to upend his whole life to suit a woman, a little comfort wouldn't go amiss, he supposed. "I know, Freddie, that you are right about Cam," he finally admitted. "But just let me handle this in my own way and in my own time, all right? Just . . .

don't rush me. Cam and I, we rub along pretty well most of the time."

"But you will make peace with him, won't you?" she softly pressed. "You will try, and soon, for the sake of our family?"

Slowly, he nodded. "Yes, but this trouble between Cam and me is so old no one really remembers what started it," he said, knowing full well that his words were at least half a lie. "I realize that's hard for you to understand, for I know how happy your family life was at Chatham Lodge. But ours was not like that, Freddie. Cam didn't even have a childhood, and Catherine was—"

Just then, the doorknob rattled, as if someone were struggling awkwardly with it. Finally, the door squeaked open, and Bentley turned to see little Madeline's head pop in. When she saw him looking down from the bed, she grinned, and slammed the door behind her. The little girl did not wait to be invited up. Instead, as she often did when Bentley was at home, Madeline darted straight for the bed, which was taller than she was.

Good Lord. As much as he loved Madeline, he was a little sorry he'd unlocked the door and bloody glad he and Freddie had some clothes on. He hoped someone had explained the new sleeping arrangements to the children. But apparently not, for when Bentley caught Madeline's hand to haul her up the last few inches, she crawled on top of him, saw Frederica, and froze. "Oh!" she said softly.

Bentley chuckled. "Surprised, moppet?" he asked, lifting her up and settling her onto his knees so that they faced one another. "You remember Freddie, don't you?"

Madeline just stuck her thumb in her mouth and eyed her new aunt suspiciously. Gently, he leaned forward, kissed her atop the head, then eased the thumb back out again. "I brought Freddie home yesterday because she's my wife now," he continued, catching Madeline's tiny hands in his. "Husbands and wives sleep in the same bed, don't they?"

Almost reluctantly, the child nodded. "Mama sleeps in Papa's bed."

Bentley shot Frederica an apologetic look. "Do you mind?" he mouthed, tilting his head toward Madeline.

With a warm smile, Frederica shook her head. "Good morning, Madeline," she said, leaning forward to brush the child's dark hair from her forehead. "Did you sleep well?"

The little girl nodded hugely. "Yes," she answered. "But Gervais didn't. He had a nightmare. A weally bad one. He cried because he's a big old baby. I never cry." Then Madeline turned impatiently back to Bentley. "Uncle Bentley, will you take the dogs out? Can I go? I have a gun now. Aunt Cat bought it in London. I alweady can shoot it."

At Frederica's alarmed expression, Bentley winked at her, then shook his head. "Oh, not today, Madeline," he answered.

The little girl threw her arms over her chest. "When?"

Bentley yawned. "Oh, perhaps tomorrow, moppet," he answered. And then, as if to divert her, Bentley gave the child a wide-eyed look. "Madeline, want to know a secret?"

The little girl's eyes rounded. Solemnly, she nodded.

Bentley patted Frederica's belly again and cocked one brow at his niece. "There's a baby in here."

"Weally?" breathed Madeline.

Bentley nodded. "Another cousin, like Armand and Anaïs."

Madeline's eyes were fixed on Freddie's stomach. "Can I hear it?"

When Bentley nodded, Madeline scrambled over and set one ear to Frederica's belly. Over Madeline's mop of curls, Frederica scowled at him. Bentley just shrugged and shot her an apologetic glance. "There's no hiding it for long," he murmured. "So we'd best just brag and look besotted. That way, all the wags can whisper it's a grand romance."

He watched a little wretchedly as Freddie's scowl melted to a wistful smile. Absently, her right hand began easing up and down Madeline's spine, her touch instinctively soothing. Her sudden sadness he understood. Freddie wasn't going to have a grand romance, was she? And that was partly his fault. But as he watched her with Madeline, he took comfort in one thing. Freddie was going to make a wonderful mother. And suddenly, Bentley knew without a doubt that he was already besotted with his bride.

Just then, Madeline's head jerked up. "I do hear it!"

"Oh, my!" Frederica pressed her hands to her cheeks. "Do you? What does it sound like?"

Madeline made a strange growling sound, like a pair of quarrelsome house cats, then slapped her hands over her mouth and giggled.

Hunger pangs, Bentley guessed. But just the same, a

sense of joy leapt in his heart. "What a frightful racket!" he said. "I'd best have a listen."

With Madeline still giggling between them, Bentley twisted himself around until his ear was on Freddie's belly. He looked up and winked. "By gad, you're right, Madeline!" he said. "I hear it, too!"

"Do you?" asked Freddie dryly. "And what is he saying? 'Please stop squishing me'?"

"She," corrected Bentley airily. "She is saying . . . well, let me see." He wriggled his head around for dramatic effect and gave Freddie a surreptitious pinch. "Ah, yes! I hear it. I want . . . I want . . . Papa to . . . to—to—to . . . to what? Good heavens, I can't make it out!"

"Listen! Listen!" cried Madeline. "What does she want?"

Bentley pretended to press his ear a little more firmly. "To take me on . . . on a . . . why, on a picnic!" he finished. "Yes, yes, that's it, Madeline! A picnic!"

Frederica burst into laughter. "On a picnic?" she said, jerking abruptly up in bed. "Are you sure?"

"Quite," said Bentley, sitting up and dusting off his hands theatrically. "Well, that's decided, I think! Freddie, you'll have to come along, of course, attached as you are. I'll have Mrs. Naffles fix us up a hamper this afternoon."

But Frederica seemed to have taken sudden offense to his plan. All the color had drained from her face, and her eyes were wide. Abruptly, she shoved Bentley onto Madeline, then bolted for the bathing closet. Alarmed, Bentley followed, grabbing Madeline as he went. "Freddie?"

But the only answer was the dreadful sound of her

retching. He could see one dead-white hand clutching at the door. Without thinking, Bentley put Madeline down and hastened in. She was bent over the close-stool, her other hand braced unsteadily on the back. "Oh, God." He touched her lightly. "Freddie?"

Freddie made a threatening sound in the back of her throat. "Go. Away."

But a second spasm wracked her slender frame, and Freddie heaved again. Bentley grabbed her hair, dragging it back from harm's way, then set what he hoped was a soothing arm about her waist. Another spasm, this one worse. "Go away!" she choked.

Instead, Bentley leaned forward with her. It seemed the thing to do. Sure enough, Freddie relented and let her weight sag into his embrace. Instinctively, he bolstered her up and kept her hair in place. Another spasm, this one just a dreadful, protracted gagging sound.

Watching her suffer, Bentley felt like the worst sort of scoundrel. Why, oh, why, could he never keep his cock in his trousers? "Aw, Jesus, Freddie," he whispered on the next spasm. "This is my fault, isn't it?"

"No," Freddie whispered weakly.

"No, it's not," echoed a small, authoritative voice somewhere near his knees. "It's that baby's fault. The one in her belly."

Bentley looked down to see Madeline peering up at them, her dark curls contrasting against his white drawers.

"Oh, Lord!" groaned Freddie over the close-stool.

Madeline was still explaining. "See, babies kick and wiggle a lot."

"Do they?" murmured Bentley.

Madeline nodded. "And then they squish your innards, see?"

"Innards?"

"Guts and gizzards and livers," she clarified, causing Freddie to gag violently. "And that makes you weally sick."

"Oh," said Bentley weakly. "I see."

Hugely, she nodded. "I know 'cause my mama's innards was squished, and she had the pukes every day 'til Emmie popped out."

Paternal indignation struck. *"The pukes?"* he returned, tightening his grip on Freddie just as she retched again. "Who taught you that?"

Madeline shrugged. "Don't wemember," she said defensively. "But I heard Queenie tell Mama that the pukes was all Emmie's fault."

"Oh, God!" choked Freddie.

"They weren't Emmie's fault," hissed Bentley, clinging to Freddie as she shuddered. "And stop using that word! Besides, babies don't pop out! They . . . well, they're *brought.* By the stork."

"What's a stork?" asked Madeline suspiciously.

"Oh, you just had to start this!" said Freddie on a gag.

"A great big bird," snapped Bentley. "It brings babies into the world."

The little girl thrust out her lip. "S'not what Queenie said. She said Emmie popped out quicker'n a buttered pound cake. I don't think birds like pound cake."

The visual image was Freddie's undoing. She promptly turned round again and heaved up the rest of her dinner.

* * *

Just a few short hours later, however, Frederica found her situation much improved. The midday sun was warm on her back as she lay prone across an old wool blanket, propped up on her elbows so that she might better view her husband's face. Bentley lay on his back, with one knee drawn up and an arm thrown over his eyes, as if to shut out the sun. His coat, waistcoat, and neckcloth lay carelessly heaped in the grass. In sleep, his handsome visage had softened, and, despite the faint beard which already shadowed his face, he looked somehow younger. Almost innocent.

At that thought, Frederica suppressed a laugh. What a foolishly romantic notion! Had she allowed the strange events of this morning—and this pleasant afternoon—to go to her head? Perhaps. But why not? There was no denying that both had touched her deeply.

"We've got to get you out of this house for a few hours," Bentley had said, as he'd hefted the basket which the kitchen staff had set out. "You must be sick to death of people you scarcely know barging in. Next we'll have the village tabbies scratching at the front door, and they won't take no for an answer."

Frederica welcomed some time alone with her husband. How extraordinary life seemed in the light of a new day and in this new place, she mused, absently studying the blanket's fringe. She was a married woman—married to Bentley Rutledge, a charming rogue she'd thought she'd known for half her life. But she was now beginning to believe she barely knew him at all. With Bentley, it felt as though she were moving through life in some sort of dreamlike state, caught between her old, very ordinary existence and this astonishing and enigmatic new one. Still, Bentley was an enigma she meant to solve. The success of their marriage, she greatly feared, might well depend on it.

At least the walk here had cleared her head and chased away the last of her nausea. The children, as it turned out, had been engaged to have luncheon with their cousins at Bellevue. So Frederica and Bentley had set out alone walking briskly for a mile or better. Bentley had chosen a spot high on a hill above Chalcote, near a copse of trees along the footpath. There he had tossed out their blanket, proclaiming it his favorite hill in all of England. And Frederica could understand why. From its lofty apex, one could see for miles over woodland and wolds dotted with stone cottages, peeping church spires, and the occasional soaring roofline. The River Coln cut through it, snaking past green pastures speckled with sheep.

Stretched out on their blanket, they had feasted on a meal of cold chicken, fruit, cheese, and crusty bread. Frederica had nibbled slowly, with Bentley poking the occasional sliver of apple or bit of cheese into her mouth, as if she needed encouragement. Afterward, he had propped himself back on one elbow, crossed his boots casually at the ankles, and regaled her with tales of Madeline's antics, while she had watched, charmed, as the faint breeze played with his hair.

Frederica tilted her head to one side the better to study her husband's profile. Indeed, now that she thought on it, there was more than a little resemblance between Madeline and her uncle. Perhaps it was no wonder Lord Treyhern had that permanent furrow in his brow.

Frederica thought again of the discord which seemed

to exist between Bentley and Treyhern. A certain amount of competition between brothers was normal, she knew. Gus and Theo were forever bent on besting one another at every masculine pursuit. The gray cloud hanging over Chalcote, however, did not feel anything like sibling rivalry but more like some deep and impenetrable sorrow. Like a wound which had festered too long, one which Frederica believed had to be healed.

Suddenly, the deep toll of a church bell reverberated through the air. Frederica turned to look at St. Michael's bell tower, glowing golden in the sun. Soon the chime and clang of bells was sprinkling over the hills like a cool, sweet rain, and Frederica began to imagine she could stay like this forever, lying in the sun with Bentley, awash in the sound of church bells.

Alas, life was never that simple. Where, she wondered, was this new life with Bentley taking her? They had never discussed it, which was troubling. How long would they stay at Chalcote? Had he given any thought to where they would live as a family? In town? In his cottage? And could they ever be truly content, when this marriage had been thrust upon them by bad luck and imprudence?

"Lost in thought?" whispered a husky voice near her ear.

Frederica startled so badly her chin slipped off her fist. Bentley laughed and rolled onto his back again, dragging her with him. "Why so pensive, Freddie love?"

Sprawled across his chest, Freddie relaxed. "Oh, I don't know," she said wistfully. "I just feel . . . oh, a little lost, somehow."

"Lost?" He brushed the back of his hand over her cheek. "Tell me about it, sweet?"

Frederica laid her head on his chest and stared into the berry thicket. "In the dark," she clarified, steeling her nerve. "Bentley, shouldn't we be making plans? You know—for the future?"

She felt a laugh rumble through his chest. "Oh, I daresay!" he teased. "After all, we've been married three whole days."

Lifting her head, Frederica looked at him in mild frustration. "Oh, Bentley, can you never be serious?"

Something shifted and changed inside him then. She could feel it in his voice and in the gentling of his touch. "I'm sorry, Freddie," he answered, his breath stirring her hair. "I've never been much of one to make plans for the future, but—"

"Why?" she interjected curiously.

Gently, he ignored her. "But if you'll tell me what you want to know, I'll try to start. Now, what worries have I neglected?"

Frederica shifted her gaze from his face to stare into the green distance. Somehow, it made it easier to talk. "I just need to know what you are thinking, Bentley," she began, as if a dam had burst. "What's on your mind? What are you feeling? You can't be as blithe as you seem. And are you happy with me? Are you truly glad about the child? And I want to know how long are we to stay here at Chalcote, and where we will live when—"

"Do you dislike it here?" he interjected, stemming the flow. He slipped a finger beneath her chin and lifted her face to his. "If you do, Freddie, we'll leave tomorrow."

She shook her head and returned her gaze to his. "No, I love it here," she whispered. "I think it is the most beautiful place in all the world. But this is not our home, Bentley. Are we to visit here, then go to your cottage in Hampstead? Are we to buy a house in town and live in it together?"

Bentley could hear the disquiet in his wife's voice. It wasn't as if he'd given no thought to such things. He'd merely been taking his time about it. Freddie, however, needed a home and a degree of certainty in her life. Most women did, yes. Freddie, however, more so than others. He needed to remember that. "Do you wish to live in town, Freddie?"

Again, she shook her head. "Not really," she admitted. "But I thought you would be . . ."

"Would be what?" he pressed. "Bored to tears in the country?"

"Yes," she admitted with a shrug.

And suddenly, he knew that she was wrong. He loved the country, and there was no better place to raise a child—no, *children*. He wanted more than one, he was sure. And he wanted to raise them here, because, for all its memories, both good and bad, this village was still his home. It was just that here, there was never enough elbow room between Cam and himself. That was what drove him away, time and again. That, and the need to escape . . . something. Himself, perhaps.

Bentley kissed her brow. "Then we'll buy ourselves a house in the country," he said. "I daresay I always assumed we would."

"Can—well, can we afford it?"

He looked at her and laughed. "Lord, yes," he said.

"Two or three, I daresay. Of course, Roselands is pretty—someday I'll take you there and show you the magnificent rose gardens—but the house won't hold that cricket team you accused me of having." He lifted his arms a bit and hugged her to him. Perhaps this business of planning a future was not so hard as he'd thought. "What else, Freddie love?"

She lifted her head and looked him straight in the eye. "I want to know if you have a mistress," she said, her voice quiet but steady. "If you do, I'll tell you straight out, I'll not have it. I should have said so before we wed. And I think you should tell me about your child, the one you mentioned in the music room that day. Is the child being properly cared for? And is it a boy or a girl?"

Bentley's breath seized. Ah, now the questions got harder, didn't they? He could feel the tip of that metaphorical knife pressing against his vein. Bentley had no recollection of having mentioned Mary or Bridget. Had he? Probably, damn it. He drew a deep breath. "I had a mistress once, and she bore me a child," he began a little gruffly. "A daughter, Bridget. But she died when she was small."

"Oh," said Frederica softly.

He heard the catch of sorrow in her voice, but he simply could not bear to tell her the details. No, not just now. Not when the promise of their own child was so new and sweet. "Now, what else did you ask?" he said, collecting himself. "Ah, the mistress! No, I've never been one for keeping women. And there won't be another, Freddie. Not while we live beneath the same roof."

"But where is she?" Freddie rolled away, and sat up. "The little girl's mother?"

Ah, he hated this. *Hated it.* "She died, too," he said, rising to his feet. "A long time ago. And if I have answered those questions to your satisfaction, Freddie, I'd rather we not speak of it further."

"Yes, all right." She moved as if to rise, and he offered down his hand, drawing her smoothly to her feet. Restlessly, he began to stroll toward the copse of trees, her hand in his. "And you asked if I was happy, Freddie," he said, pausing to kick a stone from their path. "Yes, I'm happy with you, if that's what you mean. As to how I feel about the child, well, I'm sorry it all came about as it did. But I can't say I'm not glad."

"I am glad, too." She looked up at him then, and through her long, heavy lashes, he could see a teasing smile in her eyes. He had put it there, he realized. He had made her, fleetingly, happy. And he became suddenly conscious that he desired her. That he needed her beneath him, breathless and hungry—and not just to satisfy his lust or to please her but to seal the words they'd just spoken.

His wife's thoughts were apparently elsewhere. "What do you wish to name this child?" she asked, setting her other hand lightly on her stomach. "If it's a boy, would you like Randolph?"

"God, no!" His reaction was explosive. "That's been a damned millstone about my neck. I'd not be so cruel as to pass it on."

"A millstone?" She blinked at him. "I think it is a lovely, proper-sounding name."

Bentley laughed a little bitterly. "My dear, you never

met my sire," he said. "There wasn't a less lovely, less proper man in all of England. No, not Randolph. Choose something else. What about Frederick, after you and your father?"

Her gaze softened. "And if it is a girl?"

Bentley frowned. "Can't say," he mused. "Cam and Helene have snatched up all the good family names. What was your mother's?"

"Luciana," she said. "Luciana Maria Teresa dos Santos d'Avillez."

"Well, that's pretty," he said. "And impressive, too."

That time, the smile reached her eyes and her mouth. And there was, he thought, a soft sweetness in her expression. He stopped on the path and stared down at her. It wasn't love he saw. No, he was not fool enough to think it was that. But a bit of hope, perhaps? And he had managed to answer most of her questions and hold her tight.

So perhaps—just perhaps—this shipwreck of a marriage could be salvaged after all. And perhaps it was not so base, this almost ceaseless desire he felt for her. Perhaps he really could have a normal life. Was that what he wanted? He'd never dared consider it.

Her brown eyes were warm now, drifting slowly over his face as if she were memorizing his every feature. In response, he lifted both his hands and touched her, stroking his thumbs along her jaw, then sliding his fingers into the hair now loose at the nape of her neck. Frederica turned until her breasts were pressed almost fully against him and rose onto her tiptoes, dropping her lashes shut on a sigh.

It was as if she'd answered a question which had hovered unspoken. Still cradling her face in his hands, he kissed her, his lips slanting over hers, gentle at first. Then harder, more demanding. Ah, God, how he wanted her! She sensed it and opened beneath him. On a moan, he took her mouth, thrusting suddenly and desperately. Something of his savage need reached her then, for she tore away from him.

"Come," she whispered, dragging him into the forest away from the footpath. He followed her, watching as she pushed deeper into the trees, her skirts trailing through a swath of springy, pale green ferns. The cool shadows enveloped them, almost—but not quite—concealing them. And then she stopped beside a stout young oak, set her spine firmly against it, and drew him suddenly against her. "Make love to me," she whispered when his lips touched hers.

Bentley felt the earth lurch beneath his feet. "Here? *Now?*"

She brushed her lips along his jawbone. "Aren't you supposed to be a wicked rake?" she teased. "Yes, here. Now." Then, touching his earlobe with the tip of her tongue, Freddie let her mouth slide down the tendons of his neck. Bentley swallowed hard, his throat working up and down beneath her searing lips. He heard himself make a sound, an almost inhuman groan, and then he was touching her—her shoulders, her breasts, the curving weight of her buttocks. The lushness of her body filled his hands; the scent of her filled his nostrils.

Freddie was already tugging desperately at his shirt-tails. The starched cambric tore free, and her hands skated beneath, warm and eager. She slid her palms slowly up his ribs and then set them flat against his chest. Lightly, her thumbs teased at his nipples, and Bentley felt his entire body draw taut with raw lust. His need for his wife had been simmering now for the better part of the day, and Bentley did not wait for a second invitation. After a fleeting thought for their privacy, he reached down and grabbed a fistful of muslin, jerking her skirts roughly upward.

His mouth never leaving hers, he pressed her harder against the tree. He could hear the rough bark abrading her hair and her dress. He felt blindly beneath her skirts, searching for the slit in her drawers. He found it, eased one finger into her heat. Yes, she was eager. Soon he could feel her trembling.

No shy lass, his pretty wife. Her hands came around his waist, then lower, as if she wished to drag his hips against hers. He couldn't wait. It was time to lay her down in this soft bed of ferns and thrust inside her until she exploded beneath him. He opened his mouth to say so, but he lost what concentration he possessed when Frederica drew one hand to the front of his trousers. She began to jerk almost desperately at the buttons. But she was tight against him, and the buttons were awkward. With an impatient sound in the back of her throat, she gave up. Instead, she let her hand ease down the front of his trousers, massaging the straining bulge of his cock.

"Ah, Freddie!" he groaned, pushing a little away from her. "Both hands, love. The buttons—take—oh, Lord."

With a soft hiss, she tore into them again, freeing some, ripping one off. It was enough. She shoved away the linen of his drawers, and Bentley's erection sprang free. Roughly, he lifted her, his hands filled with her buttocks. "Your legs," he rasped. "Ah, God, Freddie!"

Instinctively, she threw one around his waist. He lifted her higher and, with one good thrust, drove his hips up, impaling her on his cock. Frederica let her head fall back against the tree, her breath already coming in hot little pants. "Oh, God, oh, God," she chanted as he shoved into her again. "Oh, Bentley. Do it like—ah, yes. Like that."

Bentley spared no thought for their surroundings. He kissed her again, his mouth rough and unapologetic. The coarse tree bark caught at her hair, freeing a hairpin, and her dark, heavy tresses began to slide free. Again and again, he drove into her, shoving her against the wood. The young oak shuddered, its branches and leaves quivering over their heads with his every thrust. Frederica clutched at him, her eyes tightly shut now, her face a mask of desire and urgency.

There was a feeling of shared desperation between them. He thought again of their sweet interlude on the blanket. She wanted him—wanted him, he thought, for more than just this, his pleasuring of her body. The possibility left him awestruck. No woman had ever made him feel he had anything else to offer. Wrapped around his thrusting body, it was as if Frederica instinctively offered him a precious gift. He closed his eyes and took it. Treasured it and savored it. He held himself in check as long as he dared, drowning himself in the soft sighs and feminine scent of her. *His wife.* And when he felt her body tauten and tremble, he called up his every skill, until she was shuddering against the tree, her head and shoulders thrown back, her body exultant. And then she cried out, reaching for him blindly.

Her fingers dug into his flesh. "Oh, Bentley. Oh!"

He let himself go then, pumping his seed into her body, over and over, thrusting high on powerful surges of relief and joy. They seemed to stretch into infinity until, at last, he fell against her in a state of perfect bliss. Clean and new. And somehow a better man than he'd been before.

After what seemed like an eternity had passed, his wife lifted her head from his shoulder and stared down at the leafy carpet beneath their feet. "Oh!" she said, as if awakening from a dream. "How perfectly amazing! I did not know one could do this standing up."

"Freddie love," he groaned, letting her slide slowly down his length and onto her feet. "You did say *now*."

Chapter Twelve

※

In which Our Hero is caught Playing parlor games.

At Chalcote, the next fortnight passed in something of a haze for Frederica. May came to the Cotswolds in an explosion of greenery and birdsong. Bentley's family continued to be kind and to ask few questions. At church, she met their cousin Joan, who was married to the rector, Mr. Rhoades. Afterward, as the congregation flooded from the church, Frederica remarked upon the crowd. Helene just laughed and said the village had turned out to glimpse the woman who'd brought Bentley to heel. But Frederica was not at all sure she'd done any such thing. He was little changed on the surface, behaving as cheerfully and carefree as ever.

To Frederica's relief, there was no recurrence of the strange incident in the empty bedchamber. And yet something between them did not feel precisely as it ought. Despite their moments of intimacy, it was as if a level of closeness which she had expected in marriage simply did not exist in theirs. Perhaps she was expecting too much of a union made under such hasty and unfortunate circumstances.

But Bentley was quite obviously attracted to her, and in that regard, Frederica suffered no disappointment at all. Not a night went by without their making love at least once. Moreover, he was not above catching her alone in the middle of the day. Then, he would simply lock the bedroom door, throw up her skirts, and pleasure her fast and furiously. It was desperate, passionate, and wonderful. And yet, when it was over, Bentley would sometimes apologize, as if he feared he'd taken liberties he ought not enjoy. That made no sense at all, when she herself had so obviously enjoyed it.

There were other things, too, which reinforced her notion that Bentley was keeping something from her. Most nights, after making love, Bentley would simply leave the bed as soon as he thought her asleep. Sometimes, she would wake to find him standing at the windows in his dressing gown, a snifter of brandy in one hand, the other pressed to the panes of glass, as if he felt himself imprisoned. Once, she went in search of him, only to find him alone in the yellow parlor, with the marquetry game table laid open. Backgammon pieces lay strewn across the baize surface, and at least three long-dead cheroots had been stubbed out in an empty glass. Bentley sat with his boots propped high on the table edge, but he had nodded off.

Some nights, he simply vanished. The next day, he might mention having gone to the Rose and Crown for a pint, but for the most part, he said nothing. Of course, he always returned to their bed in the wee hours of morning. They would make love again, then drowse in one another's arms. But eventually, Frederica would be forced to get up and dart into the bathing closet to wrestle with her morning sickness. Bentley was always greatly alarmed. She was, he still insisted, far too thin and eating far too little. Soon he began to speak of summoning a doctor.

During her first few days at Chalcote, Frederica confessed her condition to Helene, in the hope that she could assuage Bentley's fears. That had been a mistake. Helene had once miscarried and knew all the symptoms, so Frederica ended up with two nursemaids and twice as many questions. Each morning, Bentley would pace the floor of their bedchamber until she was well again and then provide Helene with a full report.

But once the morning's melodrama was over, Frederica would see little of her husband. As if set on escaping the house, Bentley seemed to be forever striding off with his gun in hand and a pack of bird dogs at his heels. But he almost never returned with any game.

Then there was the troubling fact that Bentley never mentioned their future together unless she pressed him. It was as if he did not think of it, and yet Frederica knew from their conversation at the picnic that this was not entirely true. Certainly, the child was in the forefront of his mind. She could tell by the way he touched her, always stroking her belly, looking by turn both worried and pleased. But they did not revisit their discussion of where they might live or what they might name the child.

Perhaps there was a reason for Bentley's silence? Six months, he had said, they must stay together. And he had promised his fidelity while they lived beneath the same roof. Was he waiting to see if she would leave him? Or was he wondering if he would prefer to live alone? Good God, she hoped it was not that. Despite his odd reticence, he continued to surprise her with his consideration and his gentle ways. And, in truth, Frederica was becoming just a little afraid she was half in love with her husband.

So, rather than remain alone with her questions,

Frederica began to spend the days with Cam and Helene. She and Cam shared many interests, and it was a pleasure to while away part of an afternoon just talking with him. At dinner, they would discuss politics and history until Helene began to yawn and Bentley began to scowl.

Helene, too, was warm. Chalcote had several tenant farms, and Mr. Rutledge's new wife, she explained, was expected to visit every one. There were also the children's lessons to attend to. Although a governess had recently been engaged for Gervais, Helene managed Lady Ariane's studies herself. Helene also called at the village school twice a week, where she taught Latin to some of the older pupils; soon Frederica was pressed into service, too. And a few days after her arrival, Frederica was invited to tea with Joan Rhoades, whose grand estate, Bellevue, adjoined Chalcote.

At first, it had been a pleasant afternoon. Bellevue was even more beautiful inside than out, and the Rhoades children were impeccably mannered. For better than an hour, she and the rector's wife made idle chitchat about gardening, needlework, and child rearing. But soon Frederica began to feel as though Joan had something unsaid on the tip of her tongue. Eventually, however, it was time for Frederica to go. She thanked her hostess profusely and set down her saucer.

"We are very close in age, you know," Joan finally blurted as Frederica began to gather her things.

Awkwardly, Frederica stood. "I beg your pardon?"

Joan blushed. "I'm sorry," she said, rising to show Frederica to the door. "That did not make sense, did it? Bentley and I, I meant to say. We were born but a few weeks apart."

"Oh, I see," Frederica managed.

But Joan had begun to look acutely uncomfortable. "As young children, we were, well, inseparable, really," she continued. "We were forever slipping away to see one another, for we had no other playmates our age."

Frederica had tried to smile. "I am glad he had you."

At the door, Joan lingered uncertainly, her hand on the knob. "And it is no wonder that when we grew older, people thought—or, rather, assumed—that we . . . well, that we would remain close."

Frederica had lifted her brows. "And are you not?" she asked, confused. "Close, I mean?" Surely they were; she had seen Bentley with her, and they seemed on quite good terms.

But Joan had shaken her head emphatically. "Oh, no—not—well, not in any way other than as dear friends. And cousins. That is all."

Frederica had smiled and tossed her shawl over her shoulders. "And what dearer friendship is there," she had asked, "than the one which binds a devoted family? It is my hope that the two of you will remain close all of your days, Joan."

Then, as if on impulse, Joan had kissed her. "Ah, I can see why Bentley loves you so very much, Frederica."

That had shocked her. "Why he loves me?" she had stammered.

At last, Joan's smile actually reached her eyes. "I always know what Bentley is feeling," she said. "Usually long before he does. Now, may I call you cousin, too? I'd like us to be friends. And if you have questions, about anything at all, will you feel free to ask me?"

She should have seized the opportunity to question

Joan about Bentley's past. But, more than a little confused, Frederica had returned Joan's kiss and taken her leave. Joan's words had stirred a sense of hope which Frederica did not wish to consider too carefully.

After her visit to Bellevue, Frederica worked even harder to to stay busy at Chalcote. Her afternoons were often spent in the nursery or the gardens with the children. Little Gervais and Madeline were so delightful it eased her homesickness considerably. Gervais possessed his father's solemn eyes but had clearly inherited Bentley's laugh. And despite her initial shock at finding Frederica in her uncle's bed, Madeline quickly developed an attachment to her new aunt. The baby, Emmie, was not yet three months old, but already she would smile almost flirtatiously at her uncle. In fact, all of the children adored Bentley and would lure him into the nursery at every opportunity. There, Madeline would ride him, pull on his ears, and poke through his pockets while Gervais showed off his toy soldiers or set up his chessboard.

Bentley seemed especially close to Lady Ariane, whom he treated as more of a friend and equal. Ariane was indeed a very mature young lady. Oddly, Frederica could not but notice that none of the younger children resembled her in the slightest. Many days had passed before she learned Ariane was not Helene's child at all but the child of Lord Treyhern's first wife, a young woman who had died tragically and whom no one, not even Ariane, ever mentioned. According to the gossip Jennie brought from belowstairs, Helene had been employed as some sort of governess for Ariane after her mother's death. It was said that Helene had been trained at a special school in Switzerland and had traveled to Vienna to study the controversial new field of mental diseases, all of which sounded fascinating. Had Ariane suffered such a disease? Neither Helene nor Ariane ever spoke of it. So Frederica did not ask.

And so her days passed with a soothing sameness, until one morning she awoke to find that Bentley had not returned to their bed at all. Strangely ill at ease, she sat up and drew on her wrapper. The mantel clock was indecipherable in the gloom. Padding across the rug, she drew the draperies back with one finger. Dawn was edging near. Where on earth was her husband? Could he have fallen asleep again in the yellow parlor?

Her anxiety inexplicably worsening, Frederica put on her slippers and crept downstairs. On the ground floor, she could hear the stirring of the scullery maids in the kitchen wing as they built up the fires and took down their pots. But the rest of the house still lay in silence. When she reached the parlor, she was surprised to see that the door was already open. Without another thought, she pushed it wide and wandered into the dimly lit room.

It was then that she felt instantly sick. One of the housemaids stood near the hearth, caught in her husband's embrace. She heard his low, rumbling laugh and saw his hand grab the woman in a most vulgar way. The servant drew back in mock indignation. In response, Bentley dipped his head and kissed her, full on the mouth.

Frederica must have cried out. The woman lifted her head and stared across Bentley's shoulder, catching Frederica's gaze. Her expression was one of pity.

Nausea roiled up in her belly then, forcing Frederica to clap one hand over her mouth. She remembered little after that. She must have rushed from the room, for the next she knew, she was turning the last landing of the staircase. Behind her, she could hear Bentley's heavy boots thundering up the stairs, swiftly closing the distance. Once, he called out her name, the word urgent and pleading. Frederica just gritted her teeth.

Damn him, she thought. *Damn him straight to hell.*

It was as if what little security she possessed had shattered. She felt hot, urgent tears well up behind her eyes. What a fool she was! This had been inevitable. Bentley Rutledge was pathologically incapable of fidelity. Had she not known it from the start?

She knew the servant, too. She was loud, and not the least bit attractive, unless one counted her mop of blond ringlets or her overripe figure. And she was forever cooing over Bentley, calling him 'ducks.' Queenie, her name was. *A saucy piece,* Jennie had said. That, apparently, had been an understatement.

His footsteps were closing in. "Freddie!" The word was sharp with warning.

Frederica did not heed it. She threw open the door just as Bentley reached the top of the stairs. Without looking back, she slammed the door and twisted the key. Violently, he wrenched at the doorknob. When it would not yield, his fist came crashing down. "Open the damned door, Frederica!" he barked, beating on it. "Open it this instant!"

Frederica had thrown herself across the bed. "Go to the devil, Bentley Rutledge!" she shouted, loud enough to be heard through the heavy oak.

This time, he kicked the door so hard she saw the bottom give. "Open it, Frederica!" he roared. "Open it, or I swear to God, I'll start a row that'll have Cam and Helene and half the house up here!"

That frightened her. Temper was one thing, but the English did not approve of vulgar displays of emotion. That much she knew. In a panic, she fisted her hands in the bedcovers.

"Freddie!" Bentley pummeled at the wood until the hinges rattled. "Damn you, Freddie, don't make me break down this door!"

Dashing the backs of her hands beneath her eyes, she dragged herself off the bed and went to the door. He came in as soon as she turned the key, shoving the door so hard it swung round and struck the wall behind it. He slammed it shut again, then stared at her through eyes which were aggrieved yet grim. "By God, woman, don't you ever do that again." His voice was low and fierce. "Don't you dare lock my own bedroom door on me. Do you hear?"

She watched him stalk across the room with his lean, predatory grace. But Frederica turned her back on him, refusing to be cowed. His hand touched her shoulder, gentle but resolute. She wheeled around at once and caught him hard across the face with her open palm.

"Don't you touch me!" she hissed.

She saw the sting in his eyes. A terrible, dark look passed over his face. His fingers dug into her shoulder. "Why, you black-eyed Portuguese witch," he rasped. "You don't give a man much of a chance, do you?"

For that, she tried to strike him again. But this time, Bentley snared her hand. Frederica barely restrained the urge to spit in his face. "If you mean to suggest I am no milk-and-water English miss, you're right!" she snapped as he dragged her body hard against his. "And if you expect me to stand by whilst my husband fondles the servants and makes a fool of me, you're wrong!"

Bentley's lips thinned in frustration. He looked mean and cold-hearted, his face made more grim by a blue-black shadow of beard. "By God, Freddie, it isn't like that."

"The hell it isn't," she retorted. "It is exactly like that. What kind of idiot do you take me for?"

Bentley shook his head, and for an instant, she thought she saw fear in his eyes. "I don't," he said quietly. "Freddie, if you would just let me explain——"

She jerked her face away. "There is no explanation," she whispered. "None which I care to hear. Now, if there is anything of the gentleman left in you, Bentley Rutledge, get out. Get out, and leave me in peace. I feel ill. I do not need you, and I do not want you here. I never have, and I said so from the very first."

She felt his hand go limp, then slide away. "Aye, so you did," he said softly.

The next sound she heard was the door clicking softly shut. And with it, an awful sense of hopelessness settled over her. She threw herself back across the bed and sobbed as though her heart was breaking. And it was, she finally realized. It was. She had stupidly given it to Bentley Rutledge, and he had trod all over it.

Chapter Thirteen

In which Lord Treyhern's matutinal Respite is Ruined.

The Earl of Treyhern was a man of deep-seated habits, and it had long been his custom to breakfast alone in the dining room every morning at six o'clock sharp. And every day, he partook of the same repast: black coffee and two slices of bread, lightly buttered. He did not encourage—and did not enjoy—any alteration to this routine. So he felt vaguely put upon when his younger brother stalked into the dining room at five minutes past the hour, wearing a grim expression and yesterday's clothes.

The rumpled attire was of little consequence. Bentley's days and nights had always tended to meld rather haphazardly. But today, Bentley did not appear to be plagued by the effects of a miserable morning after, as one might have expected. He looked more as if he were dreading what might lie ahead. Indeed, his brother looked so wretched the earl had not the heart to send him away. And that was saying something.

"Morning," he grunted by way of greeting. "Coffee?"

With a terse nod, Bentley went to the sideboard. He set a cup on a saucer with a violence and seized the coffeepot in what looked like a death grip. After filling the cup, he set it down on the table, yanked out a chair, and hurled himself into it. "Just tell me one bloody thing,

Cam," he demanded, staring sullenly at the black brew. "What the devil do women want?"

Treyhern made a little *tsk*ing sound from the side of his mouth. "It's a mystery," he confessed, buttering another bit of bread. "And an ever-changing one, at that."

Bentley lifted his eyes from his coffee and held his brother's gaze with a gravity Treyhern had never seen before. "I mean, do they want a fellow to slice open a vein and bleed for them?" he asked. "Is there no latitude? No explaining one's self? Not one inch of slack in their reins or one ounce of mercy in their hearts?"

"Oh, God." Treyhern had to bite his cheek to keep from laughing. "What have you done now?"

For an instant, Bentley hesitated. "Nothing."

"Nothing?" Treyhern arched one brow. "Do you wish my advice or not?"

Bentley bristled at once. "I don't want a damned thing from you."

The earl lifted his coffee cup and stared across the rim at his brother. "Well, pardon the hell out of me, Bentley," he answered. "I could have sworn I just heard you asking my opinion."

His brother's eyes seemed unable to focus clearly. "Sometimes, Cam, I am not sure I can trust you to have my best interests at heart when it comes to my wife," he whispered. "Sometimes I am afraid . . . that you should like to see me fail at this."

"Well, I'll be damned!" said Treyhern, his voice sharp with pain. "How can you say such a thing?"

"I don't know." Bentley shook his head as if to clear his vision.

"Bentley," said Treyhern more kindly. "Why don't you just tell me what happened?"

His brother had the grace to drop his gaze. "I just gave Queenie a good squeeze on the arse, that was all," he quietly confessed. "And—well, I tried to kiss her. Sort of."

The earl put his cup back down with a clatter. "Christ Almighty, Bentley!" He shoved away his plate in disgust. "Not the staff again! And especially not Queenie. It was your idea to bring her here so that she might escape just that sort of thing!"

"Blister it, Cam, it wasn't like that!" he said stridently. "It was a peck! Just a little peck! And a bit of a grope. It cheers the old gal up to have a fellow make over her a bit and try to steal a little pinch now and again."

Treyhern was a little mollified. "Cheered your new bride up, too, hmm?" he muttered. "Did she catch you red-handed?"

"More or less," Bentley admitted, propping his elbows on the table and his head in his hands. "Don't know how the devil I'm to explain myself, either, when she won't let me back in my own bloody bedchamber."

Treyhern pondered his brother's predicament with more than a little satisfaction. It looked as though Frederica might succeed where he had failed. At least one of Bentley's bad habits was about to be shed. "Well, old boy," he said very gravely. "There is nothing else for it. I am afraid you'll have to go to Cheltenham and buy some jewelry."

"Jewelry?" said Bentley querulously. "I generally save that until they are crying."

"Oh, she's crying," said Treyhern quite certainly.

"Depend upon it. She is facedown on the bed, sobbing her heart out even as we speak."

Gingerly, Bentley rubbed his jaw. "Well, she wasn't sobbing when she backhanded me," he said. "She was spitting like a hellcat, and cursing, too. That Iberian temper of hers is going to be the death of me. I'll tell you, Cam, it sometimes seems this marriage business is nothing but a damned misery."

"Oh, it can be," the earl agreed, laying aside his butter knife. "It most assuredly can be." And Treyhern could not think when he had enjoyed another man's misery so much.

"Ahem!" said a voice from the door.

Treyhern looked up to see his wife standing there, her arms crossed in recalcitrance and one shoulder propped against the doorframe. She looked stunning, too, in his favorite amethyst-colored gown, with her heavy black hair twisted up in a simple style. But her left eyebrow was arched halfway up her forehead, which meant she'd been there awhile. Oh, hell.

But he did not say that aloud. Instead, he smiled and came at once to his feet. "Good morning, my dear," he said. "Will you take coffee?"

Bentley was already circling around the table to pull out Helene's chair. "Thank you, I will," she murmured, tossing Bentley a chary glance over one shoulder as he scooted her forward.

Bentley returned to his seat and resumed his sulky posture. Cam put down her cup and pressed a light kiss to the top of Helene's hair. "You're up early, my love."

"How could one help but be, given all that racket upstairs?" she answered, her dark gaze sliding back to her brother-in-law. "Bentley, what was going on?"

His words terse, Bentley told her, and, to his credit, he did not whitewash one word. "It was stupid," he admitted when he'd finished his story. "But it was just an accident."

Helene looked at him very oddly. "Things like that are never accidents, Bentley," she said quietly. "You did it, and you did it quite deliberately. What you should ask yourself is *why*."

"What the devil do you mean, *why?*" Bentley's voice was arch. "I did not set out to antagonize my wife, if that is what you mean."

"Really?" asked Helene softly. "Are you quite sure? It sounds like deliberate sabotage to me. No man in his right mind goes about kissing and fondling the servants, convinced that his wife won't eventually take notice."

Bentley gave a snort of laughter. "Sabotage?" he said. "Really, Helene, I begin to think Cam is right. You have been reading too many of those . . . those psycho—psy-chie—aw, hell, those big black books of yours."

Helene's eyes flashed dangerously. "Perhaps, Bentley, your purpose might be better served by asking yourself why you feel unworthy of your wife's devotion." It was the harshest tone Treyhern had ever heard his wife take with his brother. "Frederica has been looking at you with utter adoration in her eyes for weeks now, and yet you spare her scarcely a moment of your time."

At that, Bentley really did laugh. "Oh, my wife is not neglected, Helene. Of that you may be sure."

Helene pushed herself a little away from the table. "Let me tell you something, Bentley," she said in a warning tone. "There is a little more to marriage than tossing up a woman's skirts and giving her a good poke two or three times a day."

"A poke!" sneered Bentley. "My dear Helene, I can hardly speak for my brother here, but I do assure you that I can do a vast deal better than po—"

The earl jerked from his seat. "By God, that's enough!" he said, hurling down his napkin in disgust. "Bentley, you've long been beyond shocking me, but Helene, I am appalled. We are not having this discussion in mixed company."

"Fine," snapped his wife, shoving back her chair. "Then I shall leave, and you may explain it to him, Cam. It is assuredly more your duty than mine, though why you've waited nearly three decades to get the job done, I'm sure I don't know. And let me suggest that perhaps your advice ought to contain something just a tad more substantive than 'Buy her some jewelry'!" And on that, Helene whirled about in a flash of purple silk and stalked back out of the dining room, leaving the two men to stare at her untouched coffee.

A grim silence hung over the room. Bentley broke it by smacking his palms together briskly. "Well!" he said. "Just what is it, brother, that you are supposed to explain to me? Something to do with how to keep harmony in one's marriage?"

The earl slumped back into his chair. "I'm damned if I know," he confessed. "All I'm sure of is that my wife is infuriated, my breakfast has been ruined, and the rest of this bloody day is certain to go right to hell."

Bentley nodded. "Shall we take the curricle to Cheltenham, then?" he suggested. "Because, frankly, Cam, I think Helene is going to look quite dashing in some new sapphire ear bobs—and you're going to need them. Especially if all you've been doing is *poking* her."

Propped up on a heap of pillows, Frederica was still trying to hold back her tears and her temper when she heard the door crack open again. Foolishly, her heart leapt in the hope that it was Bentley returning to fling himself at her feet and beg her forgiveness. But it was not. It was worse, even, than that. It was the woman called Queenie, and she carried a tray containing a little plate of dry biscuits and a steaming cup of tea. Frederica was so taken aback words failed her.

Queenie, too, looked acutely uncomfortable. "Now, just look 'ere, Mrs. Rutledge," she began, setting down the tray. "No need ter go gettin' yourself all sniveled up."

Frederica stiffened her spine. "Sn-sniveled up!"

Queenie nodded knowingly. "Aye, you're in a family way, that's plain enough to anyone with eyes," she said, pulling a little packet from her apron and dumping its contents into the tea. "Makes a gal peevish and sickly. So I'm going ter make you up this tonic—I learnt a trick 'er two during me game days—and it's prexactly wot I make up special for 'er ladyship. Suffers the collywobbles somethin' terrible when she's breeding, the poor lovey does."

Frederica crumpled her handkerchief in her fists, refusing to cry in front of this woman. "I beg your pardon?" she said stiffly.

The housemaid would not look her in the eye. Instead, she took up a teaspoon and began to stir the tea. "Now, I knows it ain't my place ter mention it, ma'am, but wot you thought you saw in the parlor this mornin'—why, t'weren't naught but Mr. B. trying to flatter an old woman's vanity." She shrugged and put down the spoon. "Thoughtless of 'im, o' course, but there you 'ave it. Mr. B.'s a leap-first-and-look-later kind o' fellow."

For reasons she couldn't begin to explain, Frederica found herself taking the proffered teacup. She wondered vaguely if the servant would try to poison her. The contents looked muddy now but oddly effervescent.

"Drink it!" said Queenie stubbornly. "All of it, quick-like."

Strangely enough, Frederica did. It tasted dreadful but not deadly.

Queenie took the empty cup. "No, Mr. B. don't want me, ma'am," she continued a little sadly. "It's just a little game we play. Done it for ages, we 'ave. But 'e's a married man now, and that sort o' foolishness 'as ter stop, aye? And 'e'll realize it, too, and do wot's proper. Arter 'e's had time to puzzle over it, anyways."

"Oh, he'd better puzzle over it," said Frederica darkly.

The woman's hard face broke out into a surprisingly lovely smile. "Just give 'im time to get used to bein' married, ma'am," said Queenie. " 'E's a fine man, your husband. Better'n 'e likes to let on. And better'n Lord Treyhern knows, too, I sometimes suspicion. A proper favorite with the staff, Mr. B. is."

"So I begin to see," murmured Frederica. "But I still don't understand that part about flattering your vanity."

"Oh, on account o' I used ter making me livin' on me back," she said lightly. "Afore Mr. B. and 'is lordship brought me to Chalcote. Right arter that wicked man made off with little Ariane and her ladyship, it was."

"On your back?" said Frederica, still a step behind. "And what wicked man are you talking about?"

"Ooh." A look of acute discomfort passed over Queenie's face. "Let's just say I once had me lots o' gentleman admirers, an' leave it at that, eh? And that wicked business—well, you'd best ask yer husband about that. I can't be speaking out o' turn. But I'll tell you straight out, that fellow wanted killin', and Mr. B. done the job proper. No one blamed 'im one whit."

"W-wanted killing?" Freddie began to wonder if the woman was right in the head.

Queenie pursed her lips and passed her the plate. "Now, eat one or two o' these sea-biscuits, ma'am, and lie back down. In five minutes, you'll be fit to cut a jig." The housemaid shot her a warning look. "Then I'm thinking you'll want to dress and go down to the dining room, 'cause Mr. B. and his lordship are like to 'ave a regular set-to over this."

"Will they?" Frederica murmured. "Yes, I daresay you're right. They seem always to be circling round one another."

Queenie had bustled over to the hearth and was shaking the ash out of the basket grate. "Oh, that's just the sort o' men they are, ma'am," she said, her ample rump swaying back and forth in the air. "Like barnyard roosters—but wot man worth 'is salt ain't, eh? Still, it did get worse, some do say, when 'is lordship snatched Miss Belmont out from under Mr. B.'s nose. I daresay Mr. B. was fair fond of the girl, her being a taking little thing, but Miss Belmont didn't 'ave aught ter do with it,

Naffles says, and who'd know better than she?"

Miss Belmont? Who was Miss Belmont? Frederica
nodded, just to keep the woman chattering.

Queenie clattered about with the coal scuttle for a
moment. "O' course, she had the last laugh, didn't she?"

"I'm sure I don't know," Frederica answered, but
Queenie was so caught up in her morning tasks she
seemed not to notice.

"Aye, run orf to Gretna Green, didn't she!" Queenie
chuckled. "Never wanted neither Rutledge, for all their
good looks and charm. No, wanted the poor curate,
Miss Belmont did! And him without so much as a pot
ter piss—" Abruptly, Queenie's rump went down and
her head snapped up, so fast her mobcap flew askew.
"Oh, gawd!" Her voice was a horrified whisper. "There
I go carrying tales, Naffles will say." She snatched up the
coal scuttle and bobbed a quick curtsey. "I'll send Larkin
ter make up the fire, miss."

Then Queenie disappeared in a streak of black
worsted, her wild blond curls bouncing along behind
her. Deeply, Frederica sighed. The woman was being
truthful; whatever he'd been about, Bentley could not
possibly have been trying to seduce her. But it seemed
somehow a small consolation. Her only hope was that
the rest of this miserable day would disappear as swiftly
as Queenie, but it wouldn't. She already guessed as
much. And she was to be proven right.

Sometime in the late afternoon, without being entirely sure how he'd got there, Bentley found himself
standing on the hill above the village again, staring into
the distance at Chalcote, St. Michael's, and the church-

yard, feeling trapped between his past and his present. It had been a glorious day. Even now, the afternoon sun was still warm on his shoulders, despite the clouds gathering on the horizon. Overhead, a hawk made a slow, lazy circle, his plumage dark against the sky. And yet Bentley could take little pleasure from it.

He had ridden halfway to Cheltenham this morning before realizing he was off on another fool's errand. Cam was wrong. Frederica would not be appeased by some outward gesture, no matter how grand. A piece of jewelry would simply further enrage her, and, worse, it was apt to put out an eye when she hurled it back in his face. What she wanted, whether she knew it or not, was something far less token. He had not been entirely jesting when he'd made his remark at breakfast about slicing open a vein. That was what he was beginning to feel might be expected of him.

What a fool he'd been to think he could make a marriage work when he had so damned little to put into it. Besides the sex, of course. It had always been his saving grace, that well-honed skill between the sheets. Hadn't many a woman told him so? Still, he was a bit ashamed of how frequently he lusted for Frederica. Sometimes he could not bear to lie with her, so acute was his need and so deep his disgust. He would not have used a well-paid whore the way he burned to use his own wife. He could not think when he'd last been faithful to a woman, but, by God, there was nothing left to wring out of him now, even if he wished to go elsewhere. And he didn't. Damn all, he didn't.

Ah, God, he was in trouble. And marriage, he feared, was not the half of it. He paced slowly along the ridgeline, leading his horse. What on earth would he do, he wondered, if Freddie left him in six months? Or in six years, come to that? His blood ran cold at the thought. He'd hated giving her an easy way out of this marriage, but he'd been desperate to have her. Besides, a man could not force his wife to live with him, could he? No, not unless he held the children hostage. The law permitted it, yes. But it was cruel.

Moreover, like some lovelorn fool, he'd already given his word that he would not force her. And now he was caught. She was like an addiction, his innocent little wife. Never mind that night in the damned garden. He had sensed the danger long ago. And he had confirmed it the moment his lips had touched hers last Boxing Day. It had been the strangest thing, that simple kiss. It had stirred in him some deep, dark yearning.

Shutting away the thought, Bentley lifted his gaze, squinting in the direction of Bellevue, its white stone walls glowing in the afternoon sun. He'd spent much of the day drinking ale and throwing dice in a wayside near Withington, so it must be nigh on three now. At Bellevue, Joan would be putting the children down for their naps, and Basil would be locked in his study. Gathering his reins, Bentley found his stirrup, hefted himself back into the saddle, and nudged his horse south. He was not interested in that long talk Joan kept mentioning, but perhaps—just perhaps—that long walk might do him some good. And it would delay his going home until he could think of what to say.

He arrived to find Joan in and glad to see him. While he sent his horse around to the stables, she went to fetch her cloak, and soon they were meandering through the gardens which surrounded the house, in the direction of the ornamental pond. They reached it in companionable silence, strolling along the edge until they arrived at the miniature Grecian temple which jutted out into the water. Much of Bellevue was, to his ordinary eye, frightfully elegant, but there was no denying its beauty. And the place had gardens—especially rose gardens—to die for. Usually, he could only fantasize about what he'd do with all those gardens if they were his. Today, however, the old daydream brought no pleasure.

"What's wrong, Bentley?" Joan's words cut into his consciousness. "Something is, I can tell."

Only then did he realize he had stopped on the path and was staring blindly across the pond. Well, perhaps he'd come to talk after all. "Good God, Joan," he murmured. "I seem to have bollixed up my whole bloody life. Where does one start?"

"At the beginning," she said, steering him toward the little bridge which arched over the water and into the temple.

"Ah, the beginning!" he said bitterly. "You already know the beginning, Joan. You know where I went wrong, and you're about the only person who does. Though I've always thought Cam suspects."

Joan touched his hand. "Don't be silly," she whispered. "He doesn't, and it wouldn't matter now if he did."

Bentley gave a bitter laugh. "If you think that, my dear, then you don't understand human nature."

But Joan persisted. "I disagree," she said. "But just tell me what is wrong now."

And so he told her everything, more or less, leaving

out any details which might serve to embarrass his wife. He surprised himself by telling her how he and Frederica had come to be married, and of the devil's bargain he'd had to make with her just to get her to the altar. He even told her of the inexplicably stupid thing he'd done this morning and of Frederica's reaction to it.

Joan scowled at him. "You will be lucky if she does not go home to her family at once, Bentley," she said darkly. "Were I in her situation, I would be considering it."

He braced his hands on the stone balustrade and leaned out over the water's surface, a mirror image of undulating blue and white sky. "No, you wouldn't." Bentley said it quite certainly.

Her deep green eyes lit with humor. "Is that why you once seized on the notion of marrying me, Bentley?" she murmured. "Because you thought me some milquetoast of a girl who would put up with your wicked ways?"

Bentley shrugged. "I wanted to marry you, Joan, because it never occurred to me that anyone else would have me," he said quite honestly. "You were my best friend from childhood."

"And yet I scarcely saw you once you went away to school," she said, her voice teasing. "You never wrote and rarely visited. You never bothered to court me, Bentley, or even to hide your philandering ways."

He laughed bitterly. "That never occurred to me, either," he answered. "You were always there for me, Joan. I somehow thought you always would be. And when I came home to find that things might change— that you might marry Cam—I felt as though the only sure thing in my life was being cut out from under me. As though it was his way—or God's way—of punishing me. For if you were his wife, then you could not be my . . . my anything."

"I never thought of it that way."

"Ah, but you had the last laugh on all of us, Joan," he said ruefully. "Cam and I both got put in our places, did we not? And by old Basil. Who'd have thought! And Cam got Helene, whom I'm convinced he'd loved all along."

Joan's eyes lit with a smile. "I think you're right."

"But what of you, Joan? Are you happy with Basil? You look it, you know."

"He suits me, Bentley, perfectly," she agreed. "And I should have been miserable married to you—"

"I hear that a lot," he interjected dryly.

Joan scowled at him. "—or to Cam," she finished. "Cam always seemed too omnipotent to me, and you seemed, well, just too potent, I suppose." At that, Bentley laughed quite honestly for the first time all day, but Joan was still speaking. "And now, dear cousin, may I tell you that secret?"

He threw one arm about her shoulder as they strolled around the circular temple. "I can guess it," he said, gazing absently about. The birds, he saw, were trying to wedge a nest atop one of the Ionic columns. "You are with child again, are you not? I know you too well, Joan, to miss that softening of your face."

She blushed. "Yes, there is that," she admitted. "The baby is due in October, not too many weeks before yours, Bentley."

"That will be nice, Joan," he said quietly. "Perhaps, if

Freddie doesn't leave me, our children can be both friends and cousins as we were."

At that, she looked a little sad. "Ah, it will be difficult," she said quietly. "We are leaving, Bentley. We are going out to Australia. Basil has been offered a post at the seminary there. That is his dream, you know. He means to give up the living of St. Michael's. We shan't make it public until Cam can find another rector, but I do not think, Bentley, that we will be coming back."

Bentley wheeled around to face her. "Oh, Joan, that is so far away," he answered, setting his hands on her shoulders. "Are you quite sure—yes, I can see in your eyes that you are. Oh, I am sorry. The Chalcote of my boyhood will never be the same."

Joan looked up at him with a knowing expression. "The Chalcote of your boyhood vanished long ago," she said quietly. "For good or ill, nothing is as it once was. I think you know what I mean?"

Bentley let his hands slide away. "Perhaps," he said quietly. "But I'd prefer to speak of something else."

"Then go home," Joan answered. "And start talking—really *talking*—to your wife."

He leaned forward and kissed her lightly on the brow. "I should," he said, his voice suddenly distant. "I can't put it off much longer, can I? I wonder if she will even be there."

"Most likely," said Joan gently. "But you have much to atone for. And I think, too, Bentley, that you need a friend. I am glad to be that friend, you know. At any time. For any reason. Just like in the old days."

"I know." But the doubt was plain in his voice.

She squeezed his hand. "I mean it, Bentley," she

insisted. "I am in the vestry almost every morning now. You have only to pop in, you know, if you need to talk."

He flashed her his crooked grin. "You do not worry, Joan, that St. Michael's will come crashing down about our ears every time I enter?"

Joan just rolled her eyes at him. And then, intuitively, they linked arms and began the walk back to Bellevue.

But once his horse had been brought round, Bentley could not quite bring himself to go home. Instead, he took the long way back, making his way slowly through the village. At the foot of the hill, he paused in the middle of the lane, listening to the Rose and Crown's sign as it screeched back and forth on its metal rings. The air had grown heavier, and now a stiff wind was blowing up from the Severn. There would be a storm, he thought, before morning. Surely no one would begin a long carriage trip under such conditions?

But perhaps that depended on how eager one was to get away. It would be just like Freddie to do something rash. He could already picture himself chasing her all the way back to Strath House, which was just what he'd do, too. But she might have been on the road for hours now. And so, still a little fearful of having to face an empty bed, Bentley dismounted and headed toward the taproom door. If a large traveling coach had been seen leaving Chalcote today, someone inside might make mention of it. Certainly someone might mention buying him a drink, which he could bloody well use.

Inside, the tavern was already filled with smoke, conversation, and the strains of a fiddle. A crowd had gathered about the hearth, three of them with musical instruments and all of them tapping their toes. Perched on a stool between them, a Welshman in a Royal Fusiliers uniform was singing a lusty ballad in a pure, rich baritone. Bentley flung himself down at one of the trestle tables near the kitchen, lit the first of many cheroots, and cast his eye about for someone to dice with. Play cards with. Fight with. Anything to save him from his thoughts.

But it did no good, for the thoughts came anyway. He no longer seemed able to shut them out. So he just sat there, miserable and sad.

Over time, the smoke and the crowd thickened beneath the low, timbered ceiling until the black beams were almost lost in the haze. Absently greeting those who passed his table, Bentley lost track of how long he sat there. He'd lost his taste for a drink, too. And no one seemed interested in cards or dice or any other sort of vice, for the Welshman held everyone in thrall.

Occasionally, he caught sight of Janie wandering through the crowd, setting down platters of food and tankards of ale. She kept cutting her glittery gaze in his direction, but there was no warmth in it. He was sorry she was angry, for he'd been fond of her. But he had more pressing problems than Janie's pride, so Bentley just looked away.

Janie, however, had never taken inattention well. Sometime after dark, she came swishing past his table, a tray of dirty dishes held high. She cut him one last spiteful glance, then, at the last possible instant, her elbow clipped the back of his settle. A half-empty brandy glass bounced off his head, then clattered across his table. Dregs flew, and glass shattered. A half-eaten bowl of boiled cabbage upended on his boot. The fiddle died. Somewhere near the hearth, applause broke out.

Forcing his usual good-natured grin, Bentley jerked to his feet, bowed, and began wiping at the brandy which had soaked his lapels, all the while battling to keep his temper in check. With a sweet smile, Janie plucked a small towel from her apron, tossed it down, and sashayed away. Bentley peered down at his coat again. Ruined, he decided, dabbing at the wool with Janie's towel. And now Kem was going to kill him, for it was the green one he'd fetched down from Savile Row. Worse, the stench of alcohol covered him.

Oh, hell and damnation. It really was time to go. The next thing to bounce off his skull would probably be a whole hare jugged in gravy. This was probably God's way of telling him to take his arse home, get on his knees, and start begging his wife's forgiveness for being such a thoughtless cad. If, of course, he could find her.

But it was Cam, in a manner of speaking, who found Freddie for him. After stabling his horse and giving her an extra measure of oats, Bentley let himself into the house through the kitchen. There, he swilled down a glass of milk, rummaged through the cupboards, oiled a squeaky hinge on the stillroom door, then, having run out of excuses, made his way down the passageway toward the stairs. He had passed but halfway along, however, when his brother's voice boomed out. Bentley jerked to a halt. The study door was thrown wide. The family paragon sat at his desk with his shirtsleeves turned up, a branch of candles ablaze, and a half-dozen ledgers stacked at his elbow, the very picture of hard-nosed efficiency.

"You called?" asked Bentley, propping one shoulder on the doorframe.

Cam had risen and was stalking around his desk. The verbal thrashing he'd taken from Helene this morning had obviously worn off, leaving him in what looked like one of his grim, pious moods. "Where the devil have you been all day?"

Bentley forced a casual smile and looked Cam up and down. "Oh, here and there," he finally responded. "Why? Did I need permission?"

"Your wife's, perhaps!" snapped the earl. "I thought you meant to make amends! Instead, it looks as though you've frittered the day away and given no thought to her."

Bentley let his gaze drop. One of Cam's cuffs, he absently noted, was badly stained with ink. "Not that it's any of your business," he said with a shrug, "but I've thought of little else."

"You should have done your thinking upstairs."

"Why is it, Cam," returned Bentley, "that you are always full of advice when it isn't needed and never around when someone could really use your help?"

He forced his gaze up, but Cam didn't seem to have heard him. Instead, his face had taken on a darker hue, and his nostrils were flared, as if he smelled something disgusting. "Sometimes, Bentley, I can scarce fathom your stupidity," he said on a second sniff. "Have you done nothing but drink all day?"

Bentley curled his lip. "Not precisely."

"Not precisely—?" Cam's tone was bitter. "Smells to me as if the bloody stuff's leaching out your pores now. Your bride upstairs will doubtless be charmed."

She was still there! Fleetingly, he closed his eyes, but when he opened them, Cam and his nostrils had stepped closer. "Damn it, Bentley," he hissed. "You're sotted as a pig, when you should be attending to your wife. What in God's name is wrong with you? Can you explain that to me? Can you?"

What was wrong with him? Nothing. Everything. His life was a mess, and he didn't know how to fix it. "Just bugger off, Cam!" he finally snarled, pushing away from the door. "I've had little enough to drink, damn you. Janie just got a bit miffed with me, and—"

Cam exploded. *"Janie!"* he roared. "Surely, Bentley, you jest? Surely you did not leave the mess you'd made here and leap straight back into bed with her again?"

That was the last straw. Bentley's nerves were shattered, his nice green coat was ruined, and now he was accused of being both a cheat and a drunk. Something inside him snapped. He planted four fingertips squarely in the middle of Cam's chest. "I said bugger off!" he growled, shoving him. "It's none of your goddamned business if I fucked every woman from here to Newcastle this afternoon. And it's none of your business if I'm drunk as Davie's sow and planning to divorce my wife tomorrow. In short, Cam, you are just a holier-than-thou, interfering pain in the arse, and I wish to hell you'd shut up."

Cam's fist caught Bentley solidly beneath the chin, snapping his head back. Suddenly, it was as if the bell had clanged at Gentleman Jackson's. Bentley felt a red-hot rage flash through him. By God, it felt good. And it felt even better when he hit Cam back.

It was a solid blow to the left jaw, and it sent Cam

reeling. He caught himself on his desk and came back with fists flashing. A few more punches were thrown, and fewer dodged, but soon it degenerated into wrestling. This time, Cam somehow got him down first, planting one boot firmly on his chest. Bentley caught him behind the knee and jerked hard. Cam fell, catching his chin on his desk as he went. With a curse, he sprawled across Bentley, then tried to scrabble onto his feet.

Bentley caught him around the waist, hauled him back down again, and grabbed a fistful of hair. It was his favorite thing to do, scrub Cam's face in the carpet. By God, he hadn't had a chance like this in years. But Cam somehow flopped back over, taking Bentley with him. Over and over they rolled. And then, just for an instant, they froze in a parody of violence, face-to-face, puffing and grunting like King George trying to truss in his trousers.

Suddenly, Cam's eyes narrowed to tiny slits. "It's on your bloody coat!" he roared. "You little shite! It isn't on your breath! It's on your coat!"

"Aye, and what of it?" grunted Bentley, seizing the moment to roll over swiftly, taking Cam with him.

Cam shoved him forcibly away. "By God, you're sober as a parson," he growled. "Why didn't you say so?"

"Why should I?" Bentley rammed his head back down again on a grunt. Somehow, they'd rolled off the carpet, and Cam's skull thudded onto the oak floor with a sickening crack.

"Ow!" Cam's eyes flashed. "Damn you, Bentley, I'm going to make you rue the day you were born." He grabbed a chokehold on Bentley's neckcloth and gave it a hearty twist.

"I already do," gagged Bentley. Somehow, he pried Cam's hands loose. Fists and elbows began to fly, and Bentley managed to split Cam's lip. Cam drew back an arm with bloodlust in his eye, but suddenly, a dreadful screech rent the air.

"Get off!" And then Frederica was on the floor beside them, dragging at Bentley's arm. "Get off this instant, I say!"

Bentley was disinclined to do any such thing. But Cam, the damned sissy, stopped. So what choice did he have? He let Freddie drag him off, giving Cam one last jab in the ribs with his knee as he went.

Freddie saw it and slapped him hard across the thigh. "I said stop it!" she demanded. "Good God, are you both run mad?"

She was in her nightclothes, Bentley realized, with her hair already loose about her shoulders and her high, lovely cheekbones flushed with pink. He swallowed hard. Lord, he kept forgetting how damned pretty the chit was. Well, except for that mean look in her eyes.

Cam staggered to his feet. "Your pardon, Frederica," he said, touching the back of his hand to his split lip. "We did not realize a lady was present."

"And you think that's an excuse?" she shot back. She had a ruthless grip around Bentley's wrist and the other hand set stubbornly at her hip. "I am shocked, my lord! Shocked at the both of you. Grown men rolling around on the floor like a pair of temperamental ten-year-olds!"

Bentley shook his head. "Freddie, you don't understand—"

She whirled on him then. "No, I certainly do not!" she agreed, her black eyes flashing. "And don't you dare try to explain it! I don't know why the two of you cannot get on. But if you have a legitimate quarrel with your brother, Bentley, then call him out and settle it like gentlemen!"

"Call him out?" Bentley was horrified.

Cam looked sheepishly at his brother. "Your pardon, Frederica," he said again. "There was a, er, a slight misunderstanding. Bentley and I—well, neither of us really wishes to shoot the other. No, I don't think it's come to that, has it, old chap?" He cocked one brow in his brother's direction.

Bentley had shaken off his wife's grip and was meticulously righting his clothing with far more attention than the task required. "No shooting necessary!" he snapped. "Just a misunderstanding, Freddie. Tempers get short, things get out of hand. Means nothing."

Both Freddie's brows flew up. "Nothing?"

Cam had gone to his desk and had begun shoving ledgers under one arm. "I'll just be off to bed now," he murmured, taking up the last one. "Put my candles out, Bentley, before you turn in."

Chapter Fourteen

⚜

In which Mrs. Rutledge puts her foot Down.

It was a long trip back up the stairs to his bedchamber. Bentley followed Freddie, watching the sweet sway of her hips, his heart growing heavier with every step. He had felt perfectly justified in swinging at Cam downstairs. So why now did he feel such a fool? And what could possibly persuade Freddie that he was worth hanging on to?

His worst fears were confirmed when he pushed open the door and followed his wife inside. Two of her bureau drawers were open, and a pile of clothing lay on one chair. He could wait no longer. He seized her by the shoulders and turned her about. "Are you leaving me?"

The raspy whisper had caused Frederica to jump. "What?"

"Are you leaving me, Freddie? If you are, just tell me. Just say so. Good Lord, I can't bear the waiting."

Frederica could hear the anguish in his voice. In the lamplight, she looked past his shoulder, and saw her open bureau drawers reflected in the pier glass. To soothe her nerves, she'd been sorting her clothing, but the task had brought her no consolation. So she'd been on her way to the kitchen for a cup of warm milk when she'd heard the thumping and cursing from the earl's study.

His eyes never leaving her, Bentley stripped off his coat and neckcloth and flung them onto the bed. She went to the bureau and closed the drawers, half afraid to speak. His gaze burned into her back. *Was she leaving him?* No. No, she wasn't. But a little part of her wanted to; wanted to turn tail like a frightened rabbit and run home to her family.

Well, by God, she wouldn't. She was *married*. She might be in over her head, but she could learn to swim. And Bentley Rutledge could bloody well learn to control his temper—and to communicate with something other than his fists and his penis. Neither of them was getting out of this marriage, not without a fight. She turned to see him closing the distance between them, his hands fisted at his sides, his eyes running down the length of her nightclothes.

"Are you leaving me, Freddie?" he rasped. "Just answer yes or no. For God's sake."

She blinked and shook her head. "I'm not leaving," she said, watching his shoulders sag with relief. "All I'm doing is sorting stockings for Jennie to darn. Now, what were you and Cam doing?"

He shook his head a little sadly. "Acting like lunatics," he said. "Cam accused me of being drunk— which I'm not—and I was in a low mood, feeling sorry for myself and scared sick over you. And one thing led to another, then Cam hit me. Or I hit him. Hell, I don't even remember. It happens like that sometimes with us."

"Where have you been all day?" she asked very quietly.

For an instant, his eyes closed. With his shirt open at

the throat, she could see the muscles of his throat work up and down.

She had gone down to the dining room this morning as Queenie had suggested, only to find that her husband had torn off on horseback some half an hour earlier, and no one knew where he'd gone. "Cheltenham, perhaps," Lord Treyhern had murmured. "He'll be back."

And so he was. But he was late, and he looked like hell in his two-day beard and yesterday's clothes. He reeked of smoke and brandy, and his expression was stark in the lamplight. Still, he was home. And he was safe. A sense of relief, swift and unbidden, rushed through her. "Where have you been, Bentley?" she asked more tenderly.

He shoved a hand through his hair. "Ah, God, I hardly know," he muttered. "To Withington and then to Bellevue. And down in the village at the Rose and Crown."

"You look tired."

"You look beautiful," he said quietly, still unable to hold her eyes. "I can't think why you're still here. I thought . . . you mightn't be, you know? I kept thinking I'd come home, and this room would be empty."

Perhaps it was as close to an apology or an explanation as she was apt to get. It would do—for the nonce. She reached up and stroked the backs of her fingers across his stubbled cheek. "We promised one another six months," she said, her voice soft but steady. "Six months to learn how to go on together, if we can. And that's what we are doing, I daresay. Learning . . . how to go on?"

It was more of a question than a statement, but

Bentley did not answer. Instead, he captured her hand in his, drew her fingers to his mouth, and set his lips against them. "This morning, you said you didn't need me," he whispered, his long lashes dropping nearly shut. "And that you'd never wanted me. But, Freddie, I've always known that. You didn't have to say it."

Frederica shook her head. "I *shouldn't* have said it—"

"Shh," he said, cutting her off. "I knew you didn't really want me, from the first moment you touched me that awful night. But I was weak. I couldn't say no. I'm not the man for you, Freddie. And now I have spent the whole bloody day wondering why I forced this marriage. I don't know why I didn't trust you to do what was best for the child. I don't know why I ever insisted on involving myself. And I damned sure don't know how to make you happy."

"Oh, Bentley." She shook her head and set one hand on her abdomen. "We have a child to care for. Stop feeling guilty for what we—yes, *we*—did. I am not precisely unhappy, or at least, I wasn't until this morn—"

"Christ, I know!" he interjected, dropping her hand. "Old habits die hard, I reckon."

Frederica pursed her lips stubbornly. "Well, a few of those old habits are going to have to go, Bentley," she said, her voice gentle but unyielding. "I won't have it. You can use these six months to decide if I am worth the inconvenience."

"It was just a flirtation," he protested weakly. "I wasn't unfaithful and didn't mean to be."

But Frederica was done with her tears. Moreover, she was done with making excuses for her husband, too. "But that sort of behavior is disrespectful of me," she said firmly. "It is as good as a public statement that you don't care about my feelings."

"But I do, Freddie," he whispered. "Don't you believe that?"

Frederica hesitated. "I'm not perfectly sure," she said quite honestly. "I don't know what you feel or think, Bentley. I know that we have a powerful passion between us, and that it has only grown stronger. But that day—in the music room at Strath, remember?—you said we could make something more of it. And yet I don't . . ." She shook her head and looked away.

Intently, he seized her shoulders. "Don't what?"

"I don't see you trying to do that," she whispered. "We . . . never talk. We never plan. We don't share our fears or our feelings, Bentley. We have passion but no intimacy. At times, I feel as if I hardly know you. Yes, we are good together in—in that one way. But I keep waiting for something more. Yet I don't know what *more* is. I feel very . . . oh! Just stupid and inexperienced and—" Suddenly, her voice broke, and those tears she thought were done with sprang forth anew.

Bentley heard the catch in her voice the instant the tears welled up in her eyes. Cursing himself, he gathered her into his arms and swept her off her feet. He went to the bed then and settled himself against the headboard, cradling her in his lap. And while she wept, he held her tight, making soft, soothing noises outwardly and kicking himself inwardly. She was right, too, God help him. And she meant to insist, didn't she? It was to be that bleeding vein after all, if Frederica had her way.

Well, that he could not do. It was the worst of all alternatives. Instead, they would probably just go on like this, muddling through tearful arguments and half-told truths, with Frederica fleshing out bits and pieces of what would never be a whole relationship and himself trying to hold it all together as he always did, with his charm and his grin and his cock. Jesus, it would be like trying to stack a bloody hayrick on a windy day. But he would have to try because—and this was the most agonizing part of all—he loved her. Not falling-in-love love. That, he feared, had happened long ago. And not head-over-heels-in-love, with all the tumult and uncertainty that implied.

No, while standing by the lake with Joan and hearing her put into words his greatest fear—that his wife might well leave him—he had known that he loved her. Known it with a certainty. He just loved Freddie, purely and simply, whether he deserved her or not. And if he lost her— if he could not find a way to keep it together—oh, God. It did not bear thinking about.

It was pathetically funny now when he considered it. He had tried so hard to have this marriage—have her— on his own terms. He had tried to force Freddie into it for all the wrong reasons, telling himself that he had ruined her. That she was with child. That he had no choice. But hot-tempered Freddie had refused him his usual easy path to self-deception. Instead, she had made him threaten, cajole, and eventually beg. There was no honest way he could now tell himself that he'd done it for her sake. She had stripped away his excuses with her obstinacy and made him see that he was doing it out of pure, premeditated selfishness. But now she threatened to strip away a vast deal more than his excuses. And it would feel as though she were stripping away his skin.

Her tears were subsiding now. Bentley dipped his head and pressed his lips to her temple, which felt feverish, just like little Madeline's after a crying jag. He had cradled her—and Gervais and Ariane, too—after untold scraped knees and scoldings, so often he knew the stages. Next would come the hiccuping sobs and then a measure of embarrassment. Frederica had curled herself against him, her left cheek pressed against his neckcloth, her right hand open against his chest.

But his wife surprised him by falling asleep, the deep, heavy sleep of one who has been eviscerated by turmoil and worry, and has finally found respite. Bentley tucked her gently under the covers, shucked off his clothes, and joined her, cradling her back against his chest. With her hips nestled against him and his face buried in her hair, he tried to find his own peace, but, as it often did, it eluded him.

Had he been wrong to marry her? That old sense of having sullied something precious tried to get a toehold in his brain. Ruthlessly, Bentley shoved it away. He had to. He could not fall into that old mental trap. What he and Freddie had—almost had—was right. *It was.* And his marriage had no chance of survival if he couldn't remember that much. But already, he was beginning to toss and thrash. And Freddie needed her sleep. Gently, he uncurled his body from hers, trying to slide from the bed as was his habit, but this time, she gave a soft cry of disappointment.

"No," she murmured, barely conscious. "Don't. Don't go away anymore."

Her tender plea broke his heart. He could not leave her, though he knew he should. So, with her shoulders warm against his chest and his arm wrapped round her waist, he closed his eyes, half of him praying for sleep, the other half fearing it would come.

Frederica was not sure how long she drowsed. She was tired. Tired and shattered and so lethargic that she almost could not rouse herself from her dreams. But something danced there, just on the edge of consciousness, urging her from the depths of slumber.

Suddenly, she came fully awake to a strangled cry. Hers? No. Disoriented, she sat up, grappling for awareness in the pitch black. She was at Chalcote. She was with Bentley. She shoved a hand through her hair, dragging it back off her face. What had awoken her? Had she dreamt it?

Beside her, Bentley thrashed again, his powerful legs jerking the bedcovers halfway off. Another awful sound, this one choking in the back of his throat and coming out little more than a whimper.

She rolled against his left side then, circling one arm about his waist and pressing her lips to his collarbone. Even drenched in sweat and gasping for breath, he felt safe and solid. She laid her head against his chest and was shocked to hear his heart hammering.

"Bentley?" she whispered. "Wake up, love. It's a dream. A bad dream."

"Wha—?" As if to stop someone, he tried to throw out his left arm.

In response, she nestled her body more fully against his and, to soothe him, stroked one hand down his length. But her arm brushed something hot and heavy. He was incredibly—fully—aroused.

He shuddered at the light touch. "No!" he rasped, as if the words were ripped from the bowels of hell. "No, stop!"

Frederica jerked her arm away at once. But oddly, his hand followed her, capturing her fingers and dragging them to the weight of his erection. "I thought . . . you wanted me," he rasped, pressing her hand crudely against his swollen flesh.

"I—I do." Tentatively, she circled her fingers around his shaft, and he groaned.

"Aah, God, yes," he whispered, rubbing her hand up and down. "Yes. Yes, do it, damn you."

Something felt very wrong. "Bentley?"

She felt him jolt fully into consciousness, his whole body going as rigid as his erection. "What?" he rasped. "What is it?"

"I'm here," she soothed. "You're dreaming. Just a bad dream."

"Freddie?"

"It's all right, Bentley." Awkwardly, she moved nearer, sliding one leg over his, intending to embrace him. But he cursed violently and shoved her off.

"Don't!" he said roughly. "Don't ever—Jesus, don't smother me like that! God damn, why is it so infernal hot in here?"

Frederica sat straight up. "What's wrong, Bentley?" she gently demanded. "You were dreaming something. What?"

He made a soft, hissing sound through his teeth. "Nothing. I don't remember."

"Bentley, I'm your wife," she pressed. "Won't you tell me what's wrong?"

"Nothing's wrong, Freddie," he insisted. "It's just that it's so bloody hot in here I can't get my breath."

But a cold rain had begun to hammer at the windows, and Frederica thought the room quite chilly. Bentley, however, was drenched in sweat. "Shall I open a window?" she offered.

He dragged his right arm from beneath his head and rolled up to face her. Even in the gloom, she could feel his eyes searching her face, as if wondering what he'd said or done. Urgently, he murmured something, then cursed under his breath. He breathed in and out slowly, twice. Then she felt his body shift and heard the old bed creak beneath his weight. He dragged himself over her, and, sensing his need, she reached out to him, glad for the heat and heaviness which pressed her down into the mattress.

A little roughly, he wedged his hard thigh between her legs, nudging them apart. In the darkness, his mouth desperately sought her cheek, her forehead, and then her lips. "Just kiss me," he whispered, his voice but a rasp in the darkness. "Come, kiss me, Freddie love."

She rose against him then, opening her lips fully beneath his, allowing him to explore her depths and drag her down into the warm, surging desire. Her questions melted away as he thrust his tongue into her mouth with a fierce, driving rhythm. Outside, the storm ratcheted sharply upward, spattering rain against the windows and enveloping them in a sudden sense of intimacy and isolation. She sighed and let her palms slide down his sides and over his taut buttocks. But he captured her hands and shoved them high above her head.

"Come to me, wife," he murmured, lifting his hips

above hers and driving suddenly, savagely, into her body. "Come, we are as one. Love me. Make me whole."

The storm broke shortly before dawn, but Bentley did not permit himself to drift off again. Instead, he watched his wife drowse beside him until the misty light began to cast shape and shadow to the bell tower beyond his window. Freddie lay almost on her stomach, her face turned to him, one small fist curled against the pillow. The counterpane had slipped down to expose the delicate bones of her shoulder blades and a lovely expanse of warm, olive skin. He felt desire stir again—sweeter and less savage, yes. But unwanted. Ruthlessly, he tamped it down and sat up.

Good God, he had not handled himself well last night. And he was afraid of what she might say or ask this morning. He was ashamed of the way he had used her, riding her like some sort of demon, rutting and thrusting in some blind attempt to . . . to what? To drive away the remnants of that bloody awful dream which seemed to come all too often. And had he pleasured her? Had she even come beneath him? Damn it, he did not know, so desperate had been his urge. The memory of it left him feeling . . . unclean. As if he had debased someone else to save himself.

He tore himself from the bed, realizing that he could bear to stay no longer. He was half afraid to leave her, though, for she was always so ill in the mornings. It was the child, he knew. Dear God, how many burdens would he lay on her before all was said and done? It was as if the walls were closing in on him again. He had to get out. Get some air. There was work to be done this day.

Swiftly, he washed and shaved, staring at the mirror as he did so. He looked like hell this morning, the candlelight emphasizing the hard lines around his mouth and the drawn look about his eyes.

As a boy, he had been physically beautiful, and almost impishly charming. But he had never, ever been innocent. And now, he could look at his reflection and foresee a time when his physical beauty would fail him. When charm would become eccentricity. When all he would have to fall back on would be what little he had managed to build. With his wife.

How could she then find him appealing? Even this morning, it might as well have been a week since he'd shaved, so black was the swath of beard his blade scraped away. He wondered Freddie had let him come near her last night. With a soft curse, he splashed off the last of the soap, threw on his most comfortable clothes, and left.

Chapter Fifteen

In which Our Heroine has a very Grave encounter.

Frederica awoke to a room filled with light. She stretched all the way down to her toes before suspicion struck, sending her straight upright in bed, her eyes fixed on the mantel clock. Good Lord, a quarter past nine! She threw back the covers and jerked on her wrapper just as Jennie bustled through the door. The maid carried a covered dish and a cup of chocolate.

"Oh, miss, are you awake, then?" she chirped, taking the tray to the small table between the windows. "I peeped in at eight, but you was dead to the world."

"Good morning, Jennie." Hastily, Frederica tied her wrapper. "Have you seen Mr. Rutledge today?"

"Gone off a good hour ago, miss," she answered. "I didn't hear where. Now, sit yourself down and try to eat a bite. Mrs. Naffles was having the sideboard cleared, so I snatched up what was left."

Jennie lifted the cover, and the heavenly scent of bacon wafted up. It was only then that Frederica realized she was not ill. In fact, she was ravenous. She sat down at the little table and sipped her chocolate. "I've never in my life missed breakfast," she said sheepishly. "Did anyone notice?"

"Just Mrs. Naffles," she answered. "She said she'd

have the girls cook something fresh when you got up, but—"

"Oh, no!" Frederica cut her off. "This is fine, Jennie. Doesn't the day look lovely? Will you lay out my gold walking dress? I think I shall take a walk."

Once dressed and downstairs, Frederica learned that Lord Treyhern was locked in his study with his ledgers, and Helene was with Ariane, studying French grammar. Frederica saw Mrs. Naffles near the conservatory and inquired about the nicest route for a walk.

The elderly housekeeper shifted her pile of linen onto one hip and peered over her small wire glasses. "Oh, well, there's the footpath behind," she said cheerfully, tilting her head toward the conservatory doors. "Go left, and you're but two miles from Coln St. Andrews. Straight past the stables takes you over the ridge and on to Bellevue. Or turn right, through the kitchen garden—"

"Ah, yes, to go past the orchards to the church," finished Frederica.

Mrs. Naffles nodded. "And on through the churchyard to the village, if you like a shortcut. That's the way Mr. Rutledge goes most times. A-whistling his way past his own grave, we tease him."

Lightly, Frederica lifted her brows. "Did he go that way this morning?"

"He did say something about calling at the saddler's," she said vaguely. "But that was some time past. You might, though, catch him coming back." The old woman smiled and went on her way. Frederica went out through the conservatory, but in the rear gardens, she ran into Madeline and Gervais coming through the back gate with Gervais's governess.

"Good morning, Mrs. Rutledge," said Miss Taft brightly.

"Good morning." Frederica looked at Gervais. His hands were grubby, his knuckles stained with grass. He looked earnestly back at her, his dark brown hair tossing in the breeze. Both children sported warm clothing, damp shoes, and pink noses.

"For you," Gervais announced, jerking a bouquet of daisies from behind his back.

"Oh, lovely!" Frederica knelt to take them.

On a loud snuffle, Madeline threw one arm around Frederica's neck and offered a second nosegay, this one a tad bedraggled. "Uncle Bentley helped pick 'em," she announced.

"Why, it is beautiful, too!" Frederic added. "Thank you."

"We're studying flowers," bragged Madeline. "And bugs. Weally ugly ones with hairy legs."

"Not bugs," corrected Gervais. *"Bees.* Bees make flowers."

"That's almost correct," Miss Taft interjected. "Bees fertilize flowers."

Frederica smiled at the earnest little faces. "And did Uncle Bentley participate in this lesson?" she asked. "I can scarce imagine it!"

Lightly, Miss Taft laughed. "I fear he was a most disruptive student," she said. "So he was assigned to help Madeline pick her flowers whilst Gervais and I discussed cross-pollination. There was, unfortunately, a vast deal of laughing and falling down involved in their process."

"I wonder who looks most untidy?" Frederica

mused, brushing some grass from Madeline's coat sleeve. "I daresay Uncle Bentley shall need a good dusting off, too."

"And I was supposed to pick only yellow ones and white ones," sighed Madeline, reluctantly unwrapping herself. "Uncle Bentley didn't follow instwuctions."

"No, he never does, does he?" murmured Frederica, studying the nosegay's gaudy colors. Swiftly, she kissed both children on their cheeks and thanked them again. Then, wishing everyone a pleasant morning, Frederica went through the gate and down the hill, wondering where her husband was.

It was a short walk past the kitchen gardens and down the hill to St. Michael's. A door set into the wall gave onto the churchyard, and it groaned open when Frederica lifted the latch and gave it a hearty shove. Once inside, she made her way along the back wall, keeping to the path which led to the village gate. This part of the churchyard was dotted with monuments and gravestones, a few worn nearly smooth with the passage of time. Others were covered with gray-green lichen or tilted into one another at drunken angles.

There were also a great many trees, especially yew trees and thick hollies. At the top of the gentle ridgeline, Frederica stepped from behind one of them, then drew back at once. A few feet away, a woman wearing a cloak of billowing olive merino was on her knees before one of the graves, arranging an unusual bouquet of wildflowers and cattails. Her soft coloring and simple clothing blended so perfectly with her surroundings Frederica had the impression of having espied some ancient woodland priestess laying an offering.

Frederica moved to retrace her steps, too late. The woman's ears were keen. She jerked up her head, then gracefully rose. She was tall, with high, strong cheekbones, a wide mouth, and a pair of perceptive brown eyes. Eyes which were vaguely familiar and thoroughly unsettling.

"I do beg your pardon," said Frederica. "Is this the path to the village?"

"Yes, down the hill and through that gate." Her cloak was worn and quite damp around the hems. It swept over the stubbled grass as she came closer.

Frederica thanked her and set off again.

"Wait, please." With an enigmatic smile, the woman pushed back her hood to reveal a plain arrangement of heavy chestnut hair, then thrust out a gloved hand. "I collect you must be my new sister," she said in her soft, husky voice. "I am Catherine. Good morning."

Bentley's sister? Good Lord, was this fey, unaffected creature the Viscountess de Vendenheim? "What an unexpected pleasure," said Frederica, curtseying awkwardly, still clutching her own flowers. "Forgive my interruption."

But Lady de Vendenheim had laughter in her eyes. "Lud, child, don't curtsey to me!" she said. "You make me feel quite ancient, when I am—oh, well, perhaps a month or two older than your husband."

Oddly, the viscountess wore driving gloves. Her hand was still stubbornly extended. Frederica took it and blushed. "You look very like him."

Lady de Vendenheim's wide mouth turned up at one corner. "Oh, we are very like in a great many ways," she admitted, motioning Frederica toward a bench on the other side of the yew tree. "Come, will you sit?" she asked, strolling across the grass. "I was just leaving some flowers on Mother's grave. Today is the anniversary of her death."

They paused near the end of a row of lichen-covered gravestones, a few of which were inscribed with the Rutledge name. Beyond them, however, were two uneven rows of older stones and several table tombs inscribed with Camden.

"The family plot, my dear," she murmured, gesturing about them as she sat. "And it's some family you've married into, I'll warrant you that."

Lady de Vendenheim, it seemed, was as plainspoken as her brothers. Laying aside her flowers, Frederica joined her on the bench. "I see many stones marked Camden," she commented. "It is also a family name, is it not?"

Her gaze oddly distant, Lady de Vendenheim nodded. "My mother's family built this church and village," she said. "She married into the Rutledges of Devonshire."

"And inherited Chalcote, did she not?"

The viscountess smiled tightly. "Much good did it do her," she said, motioning toward the flowers she'd just put down. "Her name, as you see, was Alice. She died young. So young that Bentley barely remembers her. She never really recovered from his birth, and he suffered greatly from the lack of feminine influence."

"Was there no one to mother him?" asked Frederica softly.

The viscountess shrugged. "There was Cassandra, I suppose," she said doubtfully. "Cam's first wife.

Unfortunately, she was not the nurturing type. Besides, Bentley was—oh, about Gervais's age when they married."

"Where is she buried?" asked Frederica.

The viscountess pointed at a wide spot between her mother's grave and the two smaller stones which ended the row. "There."

"I . . . but I don't see anything."

The viscountess flashed her enigmatic smile again. "The marker is missing," she said. "There was a latent fault in the stone. Can you believe that? It sheared apart a few months ago, smack between the words *Beloved Wife and Mother.* The stonecutter is making a new one, but frankly, it may have been a sign from God."

Frederica hardly knew how to reply. "She hasn't been dead long?"

The viscountess shrugged. "Some would say not long enough."

"Oh." There it was again. That startling Rutledge candor. "She was not . . . well liked?"

"Oh, she was liked well enough in some circles," murmured the viscountess. "Cassandra found country life tedious, so her friends and cicisbei flooded in from town by the carriage load. Between her and Papa, living at Chalcote was like living in Brighton Pavilion."

"I can scarce imagine that," said Frederica. "It seems so peaceful now."

The viscountess gave a sharp laugh. "Perhaps, but it used to be one endless stream of revelry—until Cam's patience snapped. He took the whip hand with Cassandra, sent her lovers packing, and confined her, more or less, to the house. Lud, I can still hear her raging at him over it! Swearing she'd get revenge, swearing she'd kill him—my God, it was a nightmare! Really, now I think on it, it's a miracle Bentley and I grew up to be normal at all." She looked at Frederica and winked. "Well, almost normal."

Frederica smiled. "It sounds as though Bentley was very much alone."

Lady de Vendenheim shrugged. "Well, he was Papa's little shadow," she admitted. "Not that that was especially wholesome. And there was Mrs. Naffles. And me. That's it, really."

"Your mother had no female relatives?"

The viscountess shook her head. "Only her sister, Agnes Belmont," she said. "But Aunt Belmont had little use for us poor relations."

Belmont. Why was that name familiar? Frederica smiled. "Bentley says John Camden's ghost haunts Chalcote," she said. "Do people really believe that?"

Lady de Vendenheim's smiled turned mischievous again. "Oh, some do," she admitted. "Grandpapa threatened it, you know, when he divided the land between Mother and Aunt Belmont. Their children were supposed to marry and reunite Chalcote with Bellevue, so that his spirit might rest in peace."

Suddenly, insight flashed. *Bellevue. Belmont.* Was Joan the girl Lord Treyhern and Bentley had both wished to marry? Good Lord! Queenie had said as much, but Frederica hadn't been listening. She must have grown very still, for Lady de Vendenheim laid her hand lightly over hers. "You have heard, I daresay, some silly talk about Bentley's having been in love with Joan. There is nothing in it, my dear. Nothing save two brothers who were snarling like mongrels over a bone which neither really wanted."

"Yes, I see." But the thought of her husband wanting to marry Joan bothered her. She searched desperately for another topic of conversation. "And where is your father, my lady? Is he buried here as well?"

"Lud, call me Catherine!" she said. "Yes, he is there, just beyond Mother's grave."

Frederica looked at the inscription. "Oh, dear," she murmured. "He did not reach a great age, either. Was he sickly?"

"Heavens, no. In the pink of health, unless one counts thirty years of drinking, dicing, and whoring. Eventually, that catches up with a man. Papa finally had a heart attack whilst *en flagrant* with Ariane's former governess." Beneath her olive cloak, Catherine lifted her shoulders in a gesture of resignation. "There was no hushing it up, of course. So Papa died as he lived, the talk of all Gloucestershire and half of England, too."

She spoke of her father almost emotionlessly, much as Bentley had done. "Whose are the newer gravestones?" Frederica asked, to turn the conversation. "Those at the end, marked O'Gavin? Or do they belong to the next row?"

"No." Catherine grew very still. "That is ... well, that is Mary. A woman with whom Bentley had a—a sort of relationship. When he was very young. A brief relationship. And—well, a child. Bridget. She is buried there with her mother."

It felt as if all the air left Frederica's lungs. "Oh, I ... I see," she managed. "I—I would not have noticed, but the names . . ."

"Yes, they were Irish," interjected Catherine into the awkward silence. "Mary was from St. Giles, a poor, wretched place. But I collect my brother was fond of her. Or perhaps he just felt sorry for her? With Bentley, one never knows."

Frederica could think of nothing to say. Bentley's sister looked at her in exasperation. "Sometimes," she pronounced darkly, "I should like to throttle my brother. He told you none of this, did he?"

Frederica's eyes flew open wide. "Oh, yes, a bit."

The viscountess looked a little mollified. "Well, at least he did not leave it to me to do all the telling," she muttered, jerking to her feet. "Really, the details are quite sad. She was, of course, his . . . well, his mistress. That's as good a word as one can put to it, I daresay. And, unbeknownst to him, she bore him a child while he was away in India, but she gave the child up. To a charity school in London's docklands."

"Oh!" said Frederica, hastening after her. "Not . . . like an orphanage?"

Catherine pursed her lips for a moment. "Just like an orphanage." Her voice was bitter. "And of course, the child died, as do most who are left in such appalling circumstances. I still cannot think why she did not come to us or to one of Bentley's friends. But we shall never know why, for Mary died not long after. Both were buried in London, in paupers' graves, more or less. And when Bentley learned of the child, he . . . well, he just—" Catherine made an eloquent gesture in the direction of the graves.

"My God, he had them *moved* here?" Almost unconsciously, Frederica laid her hand over her belly.

The viscountess was quiet for a time. "It's quite odd, is it not?" she finally blurted. "I mean that Bentley, of all people, would be so obsessed by such a thing? And he *was*. But Basil, oh! He was none too pleased with the notion of burying Catholics at St. Michael's. But Bentley wouldn't be gainsaid, and Cam, who holds the living here, finally agreed because Bentley was so . . . so distraught. My God, I've never seen a man so angry at the world. Not Cam. Not even my husband—and he has a temper like the devil himself."

"He just wanted them to be remembered," mused Frederica. "And safe, in a manner of speaking. I think that speaks well of him." In fact, she found Catherine's story somewhat reassuring, for it went a long way toward explaining Bentley's almost irrational fear of being cut out of his unborn child's life.

Bentley's sister looked at her curiously for a long moment. "You are a most unusual girl, my dear." Catherine resumed her sedate pace, her expression thoughtful. Frederica picked up her flowers and fell into step beside her, for it seemed to be what the viscountess expected.

She touched Catherine lightly on the elbow, and the viscountess stopped. "Did you know that I was orphaned as a child?" Frederica asked. "In Portugal, during the war. I was fortunate that my English cousins were willing to take me in. Perhaps that is why I appreciate Bentley's distress."

Catherine slipped her arm through Frederica's. "I think my brother most fortunate in his choice of a bride," she said quietly. "I confess, I had very much feared he'd got himself into trouble again, when, in fact, it appears that he might have done quite the opposite."

Frederica flushed with pleasure. "Thank you."

Catherine bent down to swipe the dead leaves from the base of one stone. "It would be dreadful to be buried where no one would mourn your loss, would it not?" she whispered.

"I shouldn't wish it," Frederica agreed.

Catherine stood up abruptly, the moment of intimacy gone. "Those are unusual bouquets," she said. "Did you bring them for anyone in particular?"

"I cannot claim such thoughtfulness," Frederica admitted. "Gervais and Madeline gave them to me. I think I shall leave them here on their grandmother's grave. Today, that somehow seems fitting."

Catherine smiled, and Frederica realized how much she liked Bentley's sister. "Well, Frederica," she said briskly. "May I take you up the hill? Cam is expecting me. My curricle is just outside the gate."

Frederica could not hide her surprise. "Did you drive yourself all this way?"

"I always do," she said on a laugh. "I'm frightfully outré, you know. And today I've a pair under the pole, matched grays bought just last week at Tattersall's. But I promise I shan't overturn us!"

But Frederica wished to linger. "Thank you, but I believe I'll go into St. Michael's for a bit," she said. "It was a pleasure meeting you."

Catherine kissed her lightly on the cheek, then pulled her hood over her hair and set a brisk pace toward the gate. Frederica laid her flowers next to Catherine's and went down the green slope toward the church.

St. Michael's was a fine old building, parts of it quite

obviously Saxon. The door, perhaps, was amongst them, for it looked a bit rotted and was stuck half open, its lower edge caught on the flagstones, swollen from last night's damp. The heels of her half-boots clicked faintly on the flagstones as she went up the aisle. The church was dark and peaceful at this hour, the sun not yet having touched the stained-glass windows. She did not go to the family pew at the front but instead hung back, sliding into a seat near one of the huge Norman arches. She had scarcely adjusted her skirts before she heard voices echoing from above.

Curious, Frederica craned her neck, looking all about the vaulted ceiling. Nothing. But the voices came again. The soft echo of a woman speaking, then the quiet rumble of a man's response. They were coming, it seemed, from the belfry. Frederica strained her ears and caught the soft scuffle of footsteps coming down the twisting stone steps.

Frederica relaxed into her seat. It was just Joan and Basil, most likely. Peeping around the stone column, she caught the flash of a woman's dark brown skirts. But as the man came fully into view, Frederica realized it was not the rector. It was her husband. His broad shoulders filled the doorway which gave onto the chancel. Around one shoulder he carried a coil of rope, tattered and filthy. At the bottom, he turned and lifted up his empty hand to assist the woman down the last of the steps.

Joan and Bentley? They lingered for a moment in the doorway, their gazes locked. Frederica knew she should announce her presence, but instead, she watched as Joan lifted one hand and laid it lightly over Bentley's heart. It was an intimate act, a gesture between close friends. Between cousins. That was all.

"Bentley, you are sure?" Joan's whisper carried through the chancel.

"I am sure," he said swiftly. "Do it as soon as possible, and do not let Frederica catch wind of it."

"I think you should tell her, Bentley," she said quietly. "Do what's best for your marriage, not what's best for me."

"Ah, Joan, must we speak of it any further?" His voice was suddenly edged with grief. "I cannot imagine our being separated like this. It did not quite hit me, I think, until today."

"Already I miss you," she replied. "More than I expected."

Bentley carried her hand to his lips. "We have shared so much," he said. "Some of it inappropriate for a gently reared girl's ears, I'm sure."

"Dear God, was it any more appropriate for you?" Joan whispered. "Why must you always act as though you need forgiveness?"

"I have much to be forgiven for." he said, striding toward the door. "I always knew what I was doing, Joan."

"Did you?" He stopped in his tracks at her strained voice. "There were occasions, I'll warrant, when you did not. As for Frederica, however it has come about, she is your wife now. You are bound to her in the eyes of God, and it cannot be undone. If you need forgiveness, ask her for it."

Bentley spun about. Joan still lingered in the doorway, the gray stone steps twisting up into the shadows behind her. "There are some things worse than honesty, Joan," he rasped. "And few things more malignant than the unvarnished truth. I think truth is a comfort I can ill afford." And then he turned, the rope still slung over his shoulder, and strode across the floor.

Joan started from the stairwell. "I am sorry, Bentley," she said. "You were good to climb up and replace that bell rope. Thank you."

He stopped then and bowed his head without looking back. "It was no great task to swap out a bloody rope, Joan," he answered gruffly. "I'll send some men down in a day or two to take this door off. I'll plane it down so that we can get the deuced thing shut when it rains."

Joan stood with her hands folded. "I'd appreciate that."

Without another word, Bentley slipped through the door. Then Joan turned and went through the heavy draperies and into the vestry.

Chapter Sixteen

In which Signora Castelli lays her Cards on the Table.

That evening, the family traveled to Catherine's home, Aldhampton Manor, for dinner. Catherine had insisted that everyone should come, including the children, who were to dine in the nursery with Armand and Anaïs. Frederica was to travel in the first carriage with her husband. In Chalcote's courtyard, however, little Madeline threw her arms around Bentley's knee and could not be pried loose until Bentley, laughing, leaned down and caught her up in his arms. At the same time, Gervais had begun to clamber inside to join Frederica. And so it was that the four of them set off together, with the rest bringing up the rear.

Gervais had brought a traveling game board, which he quickly unlatched to reveal a tiny set of dominoes. It soon became obvious he was intent upon playing a match with his uncle. Madeline, who had crawled onto Bentley's lap, thrust out her lower lip. "I want to play, too," she said, reaching across the aisle to grab a fistful of the ivory rectangles.

With all the arrogance of an elder brother, Gervais jerked back the board. "You don't even know numbers yet, you silly!" he insisted. "You must know numbers to play."

In the shadows of the carriage, Madeline turned her

face into Bentley's shirtfront, one small hand fisting angrily in the folds of his neckcloth. "I'm n-not silly!" she snuffled. "I'm not!"

"No, sweetie, not a bit of it." Bentley kissed her softly on the temple, oblivious that Madeline was ruining what had been, for once, a beautifully tied cravat. Against the broad width of his chest, Madeline's fist looked no larger than Bentley's thumb.

"Uncle Bentley, make him let me play!" she begged.

Gervais made a stubborn face. "She don't know how!" he protested. "She'll just ruin it."

"It is a difficult game," Frederica agreed, tucking an arm around the boy. "But we have a long drive ahead. Perhaps, Gervais, you could teach Madeline?"

Bentley nodded. "Devilish hard," he agreed with mock gravity. "But I daresay Madeline could outplay me. After all, I once mistook a two for a three in a perilous match down at the Fiddling Dog. I'd wagered my horse and my boots and had to walk home in my stockings!"

A gurgle of laughter erupted from his cravat. "Dogs don't fiddle," said Madeline, finally lifting her head to look up at him.

Bentley raised both brows. "That's just what I thought!" he admitted, smiling down at her. "But I lost a wager on that one as well—not a whole horse, mind, just two guineas—because the Fiddling Dog in London has one!"

His eyes round, Gervais scooted halfway off the bench. "A real one? A live one?"

"Ah, well, not anymore." Bentley pulled a long face. "The poor mite got clipped by a mail coach flying down High Holborn Road. But the tapster stuffed him and mounted him on his hind legs in the middle of a trestle table. And he's playing a little fiddle about this long—" Here, Bentley unwrapped his arm from Madeline's waist and marked off approximately twelve inches. "And he has it tucked up under his chin just so. Looked to me, Ger, as though that dog knew his business."

"I want to see him," demanded Gervais, his tiff with his sister forgotten. "Uncle Bentley, I want you take me to London and show me the fiddling dog."

At once, Madeline fell in with his wheedling. "Me! Me! I want to go!"

Bentley began to look a little uncomfortable. "Well, it mightn't be the sort of place your mama would let you visit."

"Why?" Gervais looked intently up at him. "Is it a low public house?"

Bentley drew back with mock indignation. "A what?"

Freddie leaned forward. "I believe he said a *low public house,*" she repeated, carefully enunciating each word. "But surely you'd know nothing of such places, my dear?"

"Oh, no, he knows all about 'em," corrected Gervais innocently. "Papa says that's where Uncle Bentley can always be found. With some barmaid wiggling round on his knee, I heard him tell Mama."

"What, just one?" Freddie grinned. "My dear, you can scarcely live up to your black reputation like that. Not when you have two knees!"

Bentley gave Gervais a dark look. "Do you want to

play dominoes, Ger, or do you want to flap your jaws all the way to Aunt Cat's?" he challenged. "Frankly, I think you're trying to avoid a thrashing."

"Play! Play!" Madeline began to bounce in Bentley's lap. Another tussle ensued over possession of the board, but Bentley interceded, peeling Madeline's plump little fingers from the handle.

"I know what we'll do," said Frederica, catching Madeline's hand and giving it a reassuring squeeze. "We shall have a team competition."

Gervais looked skeptical. "What's that?"

Bentley shrugged innocently. "Oh, team dominoes is a bruising sport," he said in a grave voice. "Played by only the most hardened of gamesters, in the darkest and lowest of public houses. We shall choose up teams and go in turns drawing and playing. Ger, I'd suggest you grab Aunt Freddie there for your team. She's a wicked good player. "

"Oh, indeed!" murmured Frederica dryly. "I frequented many a low public house in my salad days."

Gervais looked up at Frederica with new admiration. Madeline began to clap her hands. "And you be on my team!" she said, wiggling around to look at her uncle. "Be on mine!"

Bentley dipped his head and gave her a loud, smacking kiss on the cheek. "Absolutely!" he said. "As Ger pointed out, a hardened gamester never plays without a pretty girl on his knee for good luck."

Frederica shot him a strange look, and Bentley hastened on. "Now, Gervais, old man, if you will lay out the dominoes facedown, we shall let Aunt Freddie take the first draw."

And for the next half-hour, they played in companionable good spirits, with Bentley dandling Madeline on his knee and gently guiding her hand each time it was her turn to place a domino. He really was quite good with the children. His nieces and nephews adored him, and these weeks at Chalcote had shown Frederica that his patience with them was immeasurable. It was a little hard to believe she'd once assumed he would make a terrible father.

She wished she were as confident in his ability to be a good husband. Despite a quiet, pleasant afternoon, Frederica had not been able to get past the discussion she'd overheard in St. Michael's this morning. What had it meant?

Do what is best for your marriage, Joan had said.

I cannot imagine our being separated like this, he had answered.

It had sounded almost like a lovers' parting. Yet she was certain that was not the case. Bentley was, or certainly had been, a womanizer. But even his own sister did not believe him to have been in love with Joan. In the lamplight, she lifted her eyes and looked again at her husband.

Madeline sat in his lap, her mop of honey-brown curls tucked beneath his chin, one shoe bouncing against his shin in one of those timeless rhythms which only children can hear. If it hurt, one certainly could not discern it, for Bentley uttered not a word of complaint. Instead, he had one arm wrapped about the toddler's waist, and together they were counting aloud the dimples on a playing piece. Yes, he would indeed be a good father. And on that simple acknowledgment, it felt as if

God had reached down and lifted at least one of her burdens from her heart.

Frederica smiled and ruffled a hand through Gervais's soft hair. "I think," she said, tapping lightly on one of their dominoes, "that we can give them a proper thrashing if we play this one right about now."

Upon reaching Aldhampton, Bentley was immediately intercepted by another set of toddlers. Lord and Lady de Vendenheim had twins, perhaps a year younger than Madeline, and they, too, clearly adored their uncle. Anaïs and Armand were lively children with soft black hair, dark eyes, and skin as olive as Frederica's. Just looking at them made her feel more at home.

Frederica was surprised to learn that Lord de Vendenheim's grandmother and cousin were visiting. While wine was passed around the drawing room, introductions were made. Then, hastily excusing himself, Bentley went off to wrestle on the carpet with Madeline and the twins. No one in the family seemed to mind the shrieks and giggles or the loud thumping noises which ensued when Bentley galloped on hands and knees across the room. Catherine got up once or twice to move a vase or a fragile ornament from the path of the storm but otherwise seemed nonchalant.

Gervais, being above such juvenile antics, went at once to his father to regale him with tales of the domino match. Soon the adult conversation turned to food and wine. It was then that Frederica realized they were in for a treat. Max's grandmother and cousin had brought their chef from London. The two ladies were from the north of Italy and very particular about their meals.

It did not take long for Frederica to see that the elderly Signora Castelli was a tiny, silver-haired tyrant, while her cousin and companion, Mrs. Vittorio, was younger, plumper, and full of good humor. As the *signora* eyed Frederica up and down, her gold-knobbed walking stick clutched in her frail fingers, Mrs. Vittorio described the culinary masterpieces which she had planned for dinner. Catherine, her enigmatic smile firmly in place, seemed perfectly willing to have her position in the household usurped by the pair.

Soon Bentley's knees gave out, and all the children save Ariane dashed off to the nursery, amidst a great uproar over a matched pair of rocking horses which the *signora* had brought from London. The bell for dinner sounded, and, as he usually did at Chalcote, Lord Treyhern escorted Frederica in to dinner. She was secretly a little disappointed, for she had half wished to be seated next to Lord de Vendenheim, a man who looked utterly fascinating.

She watched him as the family began to make their way around the table. The viscount was quite the tallest gentleman in the room, with slightly stooped shoulders and hands which looked at once thin and powerful. His hair and his eyes were black as jet, and on the last finger of his right hand, he wore a cabochon emerald as large as a ha'pence—except that on his hand, it did not look large at all. De Vendenheim, too, was olive-skinned and far darker than his children. His nose was strong and hawkish, his face lean over hard bones, and his hair too long, and drawn severely back off his face. Whereas Lord Treyhern was dressed for country comfort, and Bentley was dressed with an almost studied casualness, Catherine's husband wore solid black.

Although his title was French, de Vendenheim spoke with an accent which definitely wasn't. There might have been a hint of German or Italian to it, but even Frederica, with her well-traveled ear, could not place it with any certainty. But wherever he'd come from, de Vendenheim did not look like a man to be trifled with. Helene was seated next to him, and they were clearly old friends. Soon they were chatting about a new leaf mold which was plaguing the vineyards in Helene's homeland.

Lord Treyhern leaned a little toward Frederica. "Perhaps you did not know Catherine's husband is in the wine business." he said. "Or I should say his grandmother is. Max tends to ignore it."

"Oh," said Frederica, confused. "I thought Bentley mentioned something about his having been with the police."

"Yes, that, too," agreed Treyhern. "And rather ruthless at it, if what one hears is true."

Frederica's eyes widened. "He does not still . . . ?"

Treyhern looked a little grim. But just then, two footmen came around, one laying salad plates and another serving from a crystal bowl.

Helene nodded, and her plate was summarily filled. "This looks delightful," she exclaimed, picking through it with her fork. "Tell me again, Mrs. Vittorio, what are these greens?"

"*Spinacio,*" interjected the *signora,* staring across the table at Frederica.

"*Si,*" agreed Mrs. Vittorio, with a wave of her hand. "Spinach. Very young. Very tender."

The last footman had reached Frederica. He filled her plate and started to withdraw. But the *signora* snapped her fingers at him. "More!" she commanded, gesturing toward Frederica. *"Subito!"*

The footman paused but an instant before heaping a second serving on top of Frederica's first. The old woman took up her fork and jabbed it at the overfilled plate. "Eat, *carissima,*" she commanded in a voice like gravel. "You need it."

Frederica ate. The frail old woman might have hobbled into the dining room on her fancy stick, but Frederica was not fooled. She did not doubt that should one displease the *signora,* she would happily pick it up again and give her victim an energetic flogging.

The remainder of the meal went on in the same fashion, with the *signora* deciding what and how much Frederica would eat, and no one at the table quibbling with it, as if there was some tacit agreement to humor the old woman. The eating, however, was no chore. Every course was scrumptious. But soon the meal was over, conversation fell away, and the ladies rose. The *signora* picked up her stick and struck the floor one good blow with it. All heads turned her way.

She was staring at de Vendenheim. "You will take your *porto,* my grandson, in the withdrawing room," she said. It was not a request.

A faint smile curved one corner of de Vendenheim's mouth. "Certainly, ma'am, if that is your wish."

The old woman did not deign to answer him but instead turned and marched toward the door. De Vendenheim had motioned to the footman that the decanter and the tray of glasses should be taken into the next room, so Bentley leapt up to open the door for the *signora*.

On the threshold, however, the old woman paused, set the tip of her stick against his toe, and leaned into him. *"Il Cavaliere di Dischi,"* she whispered. "We meet again. And we have unfinished business, *si?*"

Bentley flashed her his laziest smile. "Of what sort, ma'am?"

The old woman squinted one eye at him. "Come into the book room," she rasped. "I would speak with you in private. Bring your *porto,* if you wish it. In fact, I suggest most heartily that you do."

Ten minutes later, Bentley found himself carrying a glass of port into the darkened book room. *Bloody hell,* he thought as his eyes adjusted to the light. *How the deuce did I get rooked into this?*

She was already there, the crazed-demon-wine-merchant-from-hell, sitting in the shadows like some black widow spider awaiting her victim. Signora Castelli was not unknown to him. Bentley had had a run-in or two with the spooky old woman before, but he was damned if he knew what she wanted with him now.

The *signora* sat ramrod stiff at a small pedestal table, dressed as always in solid black silk, with a heavy gold crucifix suspended from a strand of jet about her neck and rubies the size of raspberries hanging off her ears. "Come closer, *Cavaliere.*" Her voice was soft and hoarse in the gloom. "I am old, and my eyes grow weak. But such a beautiful man as you—ah!—even I must wish to get a good look at that, eh?"

"I strive to please the ladies," he lightly responded.

The old woman cackled at that. *"Si,* so you do," she agreed. "That is half your problem."

Bentley laughed and crossed the room to the table near the hearth. A small fire burned there but shed little light over the room. The *signora* looked at him, half her face illuminated by the fire, the other cast in shadow. Bentley sat, and she drew her single candle nearer, causing the light to dance eerily over her features. Then she picked up a bundle of black cloth from the center of the table, deftly unrolling it to reveal a thick pack of cards, very old and worn.

"Oh, no," said Bentley, pushing back his chair. "No, *signora.* You have the wrong fellow at your table tonight. I have no wish to see the future."

The old woman smiled thinly. *"Si,* because you fear it, *Cavaliere,"* she muttered, getting up from the table and hobbling slowly toward the hearth. "We all do—if we are wise."

Bentley stood. "Really, Signora Castelli," he said. "I appreciate the gesture. But I'm rarely accused of being wise, and I far prefer to let life surprise me."

She turned on him then, her expression grim. "Your wife is three months gone with child, *Cavaliere,"* she snapped. "All is not well in your marriage. And I should think you'd had surprises enough for a lifetime."

Bentley felt his heart flip over and drop into his gut. As usual, the *signora* knew things which were none of her business. Though the state of his marriage might be easily guessed, his wife's condition was not generally known. What else, he wondered, might she suspect? He found it acutely uncomfortable to be in her presence.

But she's just an eccentric old woman, he reminded

himself. Cam had told Catherine of Freddie's condition, and Catherine must have told the *signora*. That was all there was to it. He watched her pause before the chimney piece, her shoulders narrow, her back bowed with age. "Why do you not go into the drawing room and read for some of the ladies, ma'am?" he suggested. "I am sure Helene would find it vastly diverting."

The old woman tossed one last disdainful glance over her shoulder, then extracted a screw of paper from her pocket and shook its contents over the basket grate. Planting one hand firmly on the mantel, she leaned into the hearth, bending so low Bentley feared she might tumble in. The glowing coals began to sizzle and pop. The smoke whitened, then began to spiral and snake toward the damper. Signora Castelli stooped lower still and thrust her deck of cards fully into the updraft.

Bentley was out his chair before he knew it. "Good God, Signora!" Wrapping one arm swiftly about her waist, he seized her hand and jerked it back. "Mind what you do!"

The old woman had the gall to laugh at him as she rocked back onto her heels. Bentley clamped a hand about her wrist and turned her arm this way and that. Amazingly, not even the black lace of her cuff had been singed.

"What, do you see any burns, *Cavaliere?*" she cackled. "No, I thought not."

Bentley released her hand and gently took her elbow. "You were fortunate, Signora," he said, steering her to her chair. "What on earth did you mean to do?"

With great effort, the *signora* sat back down. "The cards must be purified," she whispered, cutting a glance over her shoulder. "Only in this way is the vision cleared."

Bentley returned to his chair. "With all due respect, ma'am, it sounds like a pack of nonsense to me."

Signora Castelli pointed a bony finger at him. "You have enough evil surrounding you as it is," she warned. "You need none to linger behind from someone else's reading." So saying, she slapped the pack of cards down between them. "Touch the cards, *per favore*. Take them, stroke them, and turn your mind to the unseen."

Bentley managed to wink at her. "Signora, my luck always runs best when a fine-looking woman shuffles. Have at it, why don't you?"

The old woman made a chiding sound. "You are such a coward!" she challenged. "A pretty English coward who is scared of *i tarocchi*. Do it! *Subito!* Think of your wife and child."

Bentley leaned halfway across the table, propping himself on one elbow. "I'll tell you, Signora, I don't know how the deuce Max puts up with your managing," he said with a smile. "Your good looks and your charm notwithstanding, of course."

But her eyes—at least the one illuminated by the firelight—commanded him. "Do it!" she hissed. "Then cut three times to the left with your left hand."

Later, Bentley could not explain what it was that possessed him, but it was as if his fingers belonged, fleetingly, to someone else. Next he knew, he was handling her damned cards. Then cutting them. With his left hand. To the left.

"There!" he growled, finished.

The old woman swept them up again, shuffling with

fingers which were surprisingly nimble. Expertly, she snapped out two rows of ten and a cross of six cards. Bentley watched, mildly curious. He'd seen her play her little parlor game before, had even let her read for him once. Each time, the pattern she laid was different. This one was downright strange.

The *signora's* black eyes flicked up at him as she methodically turned the top row. "We look only at the present and future, *Cavaliere*," she explained. "The past, it is known to us. Too well, *si?*"

Bentley tried to relax in his chair. "You must suit yourself, ma'am."

With a grunt, the old woman began to study the row, pausing from time to time to tap upon one of the cards or to mutter to herself. Then she turned the bottom cards slowly, her face turning progressively paler and her hand trembling. Damnation. He hoped the old girl didn't give herself a heart seizure. De Rohan—or de Vendenheim, or whatever the hell he was calling himself nowadays—would have Bentley's head if his granny turned up her toes on his account.

"Odd, very odd!" said the *signora*. "Your past bleeds into the present, whether I will it or no." She had finished the bottom row now. Some of the cards, Bentley noted, were upside down. He knew that was usually bad news. Funny how he remembered these little things. The *signora* went then to the cross she had laid and turned the top card, making a soft sound of approval in the back of her throat. "Ah, *eccellente!*" she whispered.

Bentley looked at it. It was the card she called *Il Cavaliere di Dischi*. The Knight of Pentacles. The card was so faded he could barely make it out, but no matter.

He'd seen it before. The drawing showed a medieval warrior dressed in a red tunic, mounted upon a wild white horse which he struggled to control. His face was hidden from the viewer, his body hidden behind a massive shield.

She pecked at it with her fingertip. "The white horse is the symbol of purity and of prophecies," she said darkly. "And of a higher, better spirit which struggles to be seen. But the red tunic of the horseman—ah, yes, that and the first card here—" Lightly, she touched a card on the top row, the Three of Chalices. "These tell us you struggle also with sin, Mr. Rutledge. And that behind this shield you seek to hide your true nature."

Bentley managed to laugh. "Well, I don't know about any better spirit, ma'am," he answered. "But that part about sin isn't far wrong."

"Ah, *Cavaliere,* you are so brave and so foolish." She turned the next card, the Seven of Swords. "Ah, yes, impulsive action now is dangerous," she whispered, almost to herself. "You have been waiting. But this card is *sottosopra*—"

"Upside down."

"*Si,* you remember well," she agreed, touching the trump beside it. "Together, these represent a man, someone in a position of authority. Someone you fear, perhaps? Or do you fear the loss of his respect? *Maledizione,* it is not clear!" Swiftly, she turned two more cards. "Ah, you fear retribution. Tit for tat, as you English say."

Lazily, Bentley twirled his wine glass by the stem. "How intriguing," he murmured nonchalantly. "Will he be successful in his nefarious plan?"

The old woman nodded. "*Si, è probabile.* But I do not read his cards, do I?"

Bentley felt his blood run cold. He put down the glass. A thought—a fear so deeply repressed he hardly knew he had it—leapt unbidden to his mind. But surely he did not imagine . . . did not really believe . . .

"You have something in your mind, *Cavaliere,*" she whispered, so softly he had to strain his ears. "Be sure. Be sure you understand the nature of sin. I think, perhaps, that you do not."

Bentley picked up the wine glass again and tossed off half his port. "I don't know what you are speaking of, ma'am."

Signora Castelli smiled thinly. "*Va bene,*" she said with a shrug, touching the next card. "But you wish to escape something. I see it—an ugly thing which binds you like prison shackles to the past."

"There are a thousand things in my past I should wish to escape," he answered dryly.

The old woman pointed to a card in the top row, a hideous drawing of a man standing before a bowl of blood. "This card, it tells me you have made a useless sacrifice. More than one, perhaps. I see devotion which was false and remorse which is futile. You must put down your shield, *Cavaliere,* and make this sacrifice no longer."

Bentley found himself leaning over the table. "What sort of sacrifice?"

The old woman pointed at a card below and shook her head. "Ah, *caro mio,* that I cannot say."

"Good God!" he exclaimed. "Then what bloody good does any of this do?"

Lightly, she arched one brow. "Oh, now you do wish to consult the cards?" she challenged. "You see the truth which can be drawn from them, eh? The things we know but do not know, all the same, *si?*"

Bentley felt like ripping his hair out by the roots. "I swear you talk in circles, Signora," he growled.

The old woman lifted one shoulder. "Life is but a circle, *Cavaliere,*" she responded. Then her fingers brushed another card, the Six of Swords, which bore a drawing of a stooping man carrying many heavy weapons upon his back. "But in your circle of life, there has been much evil. Your innocence was stripped away, and with it went your life force. Your joy. And for a time, it left you angry and adrift. It burdened you. And made you reckless. *Si,* very reckless, as one who does not value what God has given him."

The old woman had bats in her belfry, and Bentley had no wish to listen further. "Have done with this foolishness, Signora Castelli," he snapped. "It grows late, and my wife needs her rest."

The old woman scowled at him. "Then take your wife home, Mr. Rutledge, and take very good care of her," she advised, making a sweeping gesture over the table. "That is what the cards tell us in the end. You must take your every step now for the good of your wife—your family now, as it were—if you cannot do it for the good of yourself."

Suppressing another curse, Bentley pushed back his chair. "I can't think why everyone has taken it in their heads that I'm beating my wife or some damned thing," he fumed. "I am taking good care of her. As good as I know how."

At that, the old woman smiled gently. "Ah, *si,* I think you are trying," she admitted. "Come, calm yourself now, *Cavaliere.* I will perform for you a divination."

"A what?"

The old woman shook her head. "Just ask a question aloud," she insisted. "Something which matters a great deal to your heart. And the cards, they will answer it. It need not be something dark or mysterious."

Oh, hell, why not? Bentley quickly shoved away the first question which popped into his mind and struggled to find another. "Very well, then, Signora," he responded. "I should like to know if my child is to be a boy or a girl. Would your amazing cards like to hazard a guess?"

"Oh, *si,* that is simple," the old woman answered, her hand going to the unturned cards at the bottom of the cross. She flipped them and then fell strangely quiet. The silence made him nervous.

"Well?" he finally interjected.

"Ah, *Cavaliere,* I cannot say," she whispered after what seemed like an eternity.

"Bloody hell!" Bentley exploded. "Cannot or will not?"

Slowly, she shook her head and lifted her puzzled gaze to his. "*Cannot,*" she said softly. "I cannot see. The card does not tell. It is . . . most unusual." The old woman pressed her fingertips to her silvery temple. "Ah, I grow old, Mr. Rutledge," she said, closing her eyes. "I think, perhaps, that I lose my touch, *si?* Perhaps we should finish this another time, when the visions come more clearly."

"By all means." A little shaken, Bentley drained the last of his port, put down his glass, and jerked to his feet.

Chapter Seventeen

❧

In which Mrs. Rutledge begins snooping Around.

The following morning, Frederica went down to the dining room to find Helene and Ariane finishing breakfast. The gentlemen had already gone off on the day's business—Cam to Bellevue to meet with Basil on a parish matter, Bentley down to St. Michael's with a couple of brawny men set on removing the damaged door. Frederica filled her plate but picked at her food with little enthusiasm.

Suddenly, something beyond the window caught her eye. She looked up to see that the painters were loading their scaffolding onto a cart in the carriage drive. "Look!" said Ariane, tossing down her napkin. "They must be finished with Mama's old rooms."

Helene had returned to the sideboard to refill her coffee. "They have indeed," she answered. "All that remains are the draperies. Frederica, I still think you and Bentley should move into them."

Frederica looked up uncertainly. "The garden suite?"

"Yes." Helene smiled. "Shall we go have a look?"

The refurbishment did indeed look splendid, Frederica agreed a few minutes later. They entered through the sitting room which connected the two bedchambers. In this room, much had changed. Walls which had been cracked and badly papered were newly plastered and painted in a warm shade of yellow. The oak parquet had been polished to a soft sheen, and the delicate rosettes of the Jacobean ceiling had been meticulously restored.

"Oh, Helene, it really is beautiful!" said Frederica.

Helene had drifted toward the window with a pile of fabric samples. "Yes, but it needs some contrast in the draperies, don't you think?" she mused, holding one of them up.

Just then, one of the scullery maids appeared, red-faced, in the open door. "Oh, beg pardon, your ladyship," she said breathlessly. "Mrs. Naffles says can you please come down to the kitchen and have a peek at the joint what's just going on the spit? 'Tis too lean, she thinks, and it mayn't do for dinner."

"Oh, I'm sure it's fine." Helene set the fabric samples on a table near the door and turned to look at Ariane. "Why don't the two of you choose a fabric for the lady's bedchamber?"

Ariane snatched the top two swatches. "I like these," she announced as her stepmother departed. "Let's see, Freddie."

Gingerly, Frederica pushed open the door and wandered in with a mix of reluctance and curiosity. She could not put out of her mind the last visit she'd made to this room and the horrific expression on Bentley's face. Inside, the smell of paint had finally overpowered the scent of lilacs. The old glazed chintz curtains had been torn down and tossed in a heap at the foot of the bed. The walls had been rehung with blue watered silk, and a new Axminster carpet in shades of blue and yellow had been partially unrolled in one corner.

Ariane looked at the walls, then at the fabrics she had carried into the room, one a jacquard rose, the other a red and ivory stripe. "Well, so much for these!" she said, tossing them into the air. She flopped down on the bed with an indecorous bounce. "Anyway, Freddie, you should choose the color. This is to be your new room, isn't it?"

"I'm not sure," answered Frederica, drifting through the room. "Would you mind?"

Ariane lifted her head and looked at her blankly. "Lud, no. Why?"

Frederica cut her eyes away. "I heard you say these were your mother's rooms."

"Oh, yes," said Ariane. "But take them, Freddie, if you like."

"I'm not sure Bentley is willing to leave his old bedchamber," Frederica murmured, smoothing a hand down the surface of the clothes press. The vision of her husband slamming the doors shut flashed through her mind. "No, I fancy we shall stay where we are. Perhaps, Ariane, you would like to have this room?"

"Oh, it's quite too large for me." Ariane had bounced herself off the bed and was beginning to poke about, picking up bric-a-brac and peeking into drawers. "I should feel lost here."

But Frederica barely heard the last, for her attention had been captivated by a beautiful blanket chest which sat at the foot of the bed. The old curtains had been piled on it, and Frederica impulsively pushed them onto the floor. The top of the chest was hand-carved into an arrangement of vines and leaves, and in the center, they twined about a monogram.

"C—L—H," she murmured, wiping away a trace of dust. "Look, Ariane, this must have been your mother's before she wed."

Ariane crossed the room. "Oh, I remember that," she mused. "It was her dower chest. I wanted to put my doll collection in it, but the key was lost."

Frederica knelt on the rug and examined it. "But this is a simple lock," she said. "And a beautiful chest. You should have it. Let me give the lock a try."

"Can you get it open?"

Frederica laughed. "Probably not," she said, squinting into the lock. "Oh, yes, this is nothing. Just decorative, really." Carefully, she drew out the pearl scarf pin she was using to hold her lace fichu together. "We had an old chest at Chatham Lodge with just such a lock," she said, probing deep with the pin. "We never did have a key."

"Did you open it like that?" Ariane was amazed.

"For years and years," said Frederica. "If it got accidentally locked, we'd use a hairpin, a scarf pin, or sometimes just a nail." Deftly, she twisted her wrist. Something inside gave way with a metallic *snick!* She laid the pin aside, and she and Ariane lifted the lid, its hinges screeching. But inside, the chest was deceptively small. A moth-eaten shawl lay in a drawer tray on top, while two wool blankets and some old silk bed hangings filled the bottom.

"Look!" said Ariane. "That's Mama's favorite!"

"This?" Frederica pulled the frothy pink garment from the drawer tray. The scent of mildew and lilacs was overpowering.

Ariane wrinkled her nose. "Ugh, it smells." They

peered into the chest just as a whole family of silverfish went scurrying from the tray. "Oh, that isn't large enough for my dolls," she added, her tone one of disappointment.

"Let's be sure." Still on her knees, Frederica lifted the tray, laid it aside, then scooped up the blankets. Three old books, a cloth-bound journal, and several mismatched stockings had been tossed into the bottom. But it really was quite small inside. With a sense of disappointment, perhaps more for herself than for Ariane, Frederica dropped them back in again. It would have pleased her to give the child something of her mother's, but Ariane did not seem to miss Cassandra Rutledge.

Frederica looked again at the chest as she set the tray back into its slot. What was it about its odd shape? It really did remind her of the chest Evie used to store pigments and oils. "Ah!" she said, her hand going to the notched drawer in the bottom. There was no drawer pull, but it was a simple matter to open it, once one realized that the carvings made little handles.

Ariane peered into it, curious. "Oh, just the rest of Mama's journals," she said, her voice oddly flat. "She was forever writing in them, or to her friends."

And too busy, if Ariane's tone could be believed, to spend much time with her only child. Frederica laid a hand on Ariane's shoulder. "Do you miss her dreadfully?"

Ariane wouldn't look at her. "A bit," she said. "We used to take long walks together."

Frederica was confused. Perhaps Ariane and her mother had been close after all? Ariane had easily identified the journals and the shawl. Ah, well. Time to leave well enough alone. Frederica was clearly confusing her own childhood longings with Ariane's. If the girl wanted the chest, the journals, or anything else to remember her mother by, she could claim it without Frederica's help.

With a smile, Frederica gently lowered the top and stood. But she must have risen too quickly. The floor seemed to dip, the room to spin. Her vision went gray around the edges.

"Freddie?" Ariane's voice came as if through a tunnel. "Freddie, are you all right?"

Frederica seized of one of the bedposts, and the room steadied. It was nothing. Her imagination. "I'm fine—I think," she said, still clinging to the bedpost.

But suddenly, the door which gave onto the main corridor swung inward. "There you are, minx!" Lord Treyhern stood in the doorway, smiling at his daughter. "The post has come. Milford has a letter from Henriette Middleton, and guess who it's addressed to?"

Ariane leapt off the floor with a shriek, kissed her papa soundly, and flew out of the room, leaving the door swinging wide behind her. "Good morning, Frederica," said the earl, stepping fully into the room.

"Good morning," she returned. "Have you settled your business with Basil so quickly?"

"Ah, very much so, it would seem." Treyhern looked suddenly sad, then brightened. "Well! How does the place look?"

"Lovely," she answered. "The sitting room is vastly altered. Have you not seen it?"

Treyhern smiled a little ruefully. "I haven't," he admitted. "Shall I see what my guineas have got me?"

He disappeared into the sitting room, and, with a sense of relief, Frederica sank down onto the edge of the bed. The weakness in her knees was disconcerting. For long moments, she breathed deeply and listened to the earl's movements as he roamed from the sitting room into the gentleman's bedchamber and back again.

For an instant, she let her eyes drop shut, but when she reopened them, Treyhern was staring at her from the doorway, his smile fading. "Frederica?"

Swiftly, he crossed the room to the bed. Hoping to allay his alarm, Frederica tried to stand. A mistake. The swimming sensation struck again. She felt her knees give. "Oh!" The edges of the room began to darken. A pair of powerful arms came around her, and the whole world spun away.

"Steady, Frederica," said a distant voice. "Steady. I've got you." But everything had taken on a dreamlike quality. In the background, a roar, like a waterfall in her head, almost obliterated the heavy footfalls now treading into the room from the corridor. Suddenly, she felt the earl's body stiffen.

"Why, you son of a bitch!" thundered an angry voice.

Bentley took one look at his wife in his brother's arms and knew that his worst nightmare had come true. Frederica had one arm around Cam's neck. Her lace fichu had slipped off one shoulder, and her face was turned from the door, her cheek pressed into his shirtfront. Rage exploded in his head, hot and blood red. Swiftly, he closed the distance, tearing his wife from Cam's embrace.

"She's ill, you fool," growled Cam as Frederica sagged against him.

But fury and fear blocked out all logic. Acting on instinct, Bentley caught Frederica against his body and slid one arm beneath her knees. "Get your goddamned hands off my wife," he snapped, scooping her up. "Touch her again, and I swear, Cam, I'll kill you where you stand."

His brother's expression was inscrutable. "She swooned." Cam said the words slowly, as if addressing a child. "I caught her."

"Damn you, just shut up," he answered. "I can take care of my wife."

Cam's eyes narrowed. "So you have repeatedly claimed," he replied coldly. "Please do so now by taking her to her bed. I'll fetch the doctor."

A doctor?

Reality began to intrude on his rage. Frederica was almost a dead weight in his arms. True terror struck him then. Her eyes were closed, her skin pale as parchment. Against his chest, he felt her stir and moan. Swiftly, he turned and started from the room, cradling Frederica's body against his own. His brother was already striding down the corridor, his hands balled into fists, his spine rigid. Bentley hit the steps, bounding up them two at a time.

"Bentley?" Freddie whispered. "I . . . I can walk."

"No." The word was succinct but not sharp.

"Wh-what happened?" She struggled to lift her head from his shoulder. "Why were you shouting?"

"Hold on, Freddie," he answered, taking the last flight. "We'll get you into bed."

"No, no, I'm not ill," she protested. "I just . . . I don't know—fainted or something."

"It is the babe," he said grimly. "And it is my fault for putting you in this position." Awkwardly, he shoved the door open with his knee. He settled her onto the bed, but Frederica began struggling to sit up. He pushed her gently down again, cursing under his breath.

"It's all right," she responded, reaching up to caress his face. "I've felt faint before. It is perfectly natural when one is carrying a child."

Yes, that was true. Rationally, he knew it, but the thought no longer consoled him. What if something else was wrong? He took Freddie's hand in his and drew it to his mouth, pressing his lips to the backs of her fingers. He remembered Signora Castelli's divination—her inability to answer his simple question. He had not missed the troubled expression on the old woman's face. His blood ran cold. *God, no,* he prayed, *please, not that.*

But just then, Helene rushed in. "I met Cam flying down the stairs," she said, bending over the bed. "Oh, poor Freddie! Are you queasy?"

"I was a bit," she admitted, trying to sit up again.

Helene's gaze shot anxiously toward Bentley. "My dear, have you bled at all?"

Frederica blushed. "No." She tried to sit up, as if to reassure them, but Helene set a hand on her forehead.

"No, you really must lie still, my dear. Cam is fetching Dr. Clayton. Let us pray that everything is fine."

And everything did indeed seem fine, Dr. Clayton reassured them not an hour later. They stood in the corridor beyond Frederica's door—Bentley, Helene, and the doctor, speaking in anxious whispers. But Bentley could not keep his hands from shaking. It had terrified him, the realization that she was ill. And now he wondered if the doctor was telling him the truth. He did not know what he would do should something happen to her or the child.

"You mustn't force her to be an invalid, Mr. Rutledge," the doctor sagely advised. "Really, I see no need for alarm."

"She is well?" asked Bentley sharply. "The babe is well? You are quite sure?"

Dr. Clayton smiled. "As sure as one can be, Mr. Rutledge," he said. "The first months are risky, yes, but Mrs. Rutledge just had a fainting spell. Another week or two, and she'll be beyond most of this."

"You are certain?" asked a low, worried voice over Bentley's shoulder. Bentley turned to see his brother standing in the shadows of the corridor. So absorbed had he been by Dr. Clayton's words, he'd not heard his brother approach.

Helene went at once to her husband. "She is resting comfortably now, Cam," she said, setting one hand on his arm. "This sometimes happens, you know."

The doctor gave his leather valise a little pat. "It does indeed, my lord!" he said cheerfully. "My heartiest congratulations to you, Mr. Rutledge. Do not hesitate to send for me if you have any concerns at all."

"Yes, I shall," said Bentley softly. "Thanks."

"Yes, thank you, Dr. Clayton," said Helene. "I shall see you out."

Together, they went down the passageway toward the stairs. Bentley was left standing in the silence with his brother, and damned uncomfortable it was, too. Well, there was no help for it. He looked at Cam and stiffly inclined his head. "I beg you will accept my apology, Cam, for my ugly words," he forced himself to say. "I have no excuse—or at least none which I will trouble you with."

His brother stood silently in the shadows for a long moment, his hands clasped behind his back, his shoulders still rigid. "We will put it down, then, to your concern for your wife," responded Cam tightly. "Now, be so good as to excuse me. I've work to do."

And with that, Bentley's brother turned on one heel, leaving the yawning chasm of anger and misunderstanding between them yet another mile wider.

Good God, what had he done now? Bentley wanted to reach around and kick himself in the arse. And yet he inexplicably wanted to kick Cam, too. He wanted to hurt him. Strangle him. He felt somehow—in some sick, twisted way—that his brother was still, in part, to blame. Not for this. No, not exactly. But for something.

No, that wasn't right. It was his fault. Wasn't it? He'd always asked for trouble. Invited it with his very existence. Hadn't he?

God damn it, was he losing his mind? He wanted to cry out after Cam—to say what, he hardly knew. But he did not. Instead, without being fully aware of his actions, Bentley turned his back on his brother and slammed his fist into the wall with all his strength. Paint cracked, and plaster splintered. A soft white powder rained onto the toes of his boots. Bentley just stared down at it. The dust was very pale. His boots were very black. A drop of blood fell from his fist, bright and glistening against the gold carpet. But Bentley felt no pain. Instead, he focused his every thought on the contrasting colors—white and black, gold and red—willing himself to breathe and then to breathe again. Willing every other thought from his mind. Willing himself not to scream.

He was good at it. He did not scream.

In the end, Frederica decided not to go down to dinner, in part because she felt embarrassed for having caused so much worry. The family had run up and down the stairs all day, inquiring about her condition. Queenie sent up another potion from the stillroom, while Mrs. Naffles baked a lemon sponge cake just to tempt Frederica's appetite.

Despite her protests that she felt fine, Bentley would go to the door each time someone knocked and send them away again. He scarcely left her side, insisting that she stay in bed while he either read to her or watched her nap. She was touched by his kindness, even if she did feel it was unnecessary. It was as if something between them was slowly changing and deepening.

She suspected, however, that there were fences to be mended between Bentley and his brother, and the sooner the better. And she imagined they might be easier to mend if she were not around. So, as dusk neared, Frederica asked that a dinner tray be brought up to her room and ordered him to join his family downstairs.

Stretched out on the bed beside her, Bentley laughed, tossed aside the novel he'd been reading her, and kissed her slowly and deeply. "Ungrateful girl," he murmured, his mouth lingering over hers. "You won't get rid of me, you know."

Frederica felt the familiar surge of desire rush through her body. "Haven't you gone stark mad, being shut up with me all day?"

Bentley just laughed again and began to nibble at the swell of her bottom lip, sucking it between his lips and gently biting. Soon he'd worked his way down her throat, nipping and tasting, moving lower and lower, until, at last, she tried to push him away. "Go!" she ordered. "Stop trying to distract me."

With one clever hand, he tugged loose the tie at the throat of her nightdress—the nightdress he had insisted his invalid put on. "How heartless you are, Freddie, to use me and then toss me aside," he murmured, his lips sliding across the swell of her breast.

"You have never been tossed aside by a woman in your life, Bentley Rutledge."

He lifted his mouth from her breast and looked at her through a shock of disordered black hair. "But how can I leave my wife when she is so clearly in need of further ministrations?" he whispered, flicking a quick glance down at her nipple, taut beneath her gown.

Frederica squeezed her eyes shut. "You are trying to distract me," she said in a warning tone. "Go to dinner!"

For a moment, he stared at her through dark, somnolent eyes. "All right," he said more seriously. "Just promise me you will be in this bed when I get back."

"I promise."

He began to slide from the bed, but, on impulse, she stopped him. "Bentley, I—"

His gaze softened. "What is it, Freddie?"

She smiled crookedly. "I'm sorry, Bentley, that I gave you such an awful fright."

He shifted his weight until he sat on the edge of the bed. "You surely didn't mean to, Freddie," he said, gently stroking his palm over her hair. "I'm sorry I got you into this mess."

Frederica shook her head and swallowed hard. "How can it be a mess when . . . when I love you so?" she whispered. "I do love you, Bentley. I know it now. Shocking, isn't it?"

He looked at her strangely. "Freddie—"

She cut him off. "No, don't look at me like that! Don't smile at me as if I'm some adorable but misguided child. I'm not, do you hear me?"

For a long, silent moment, he held her gaze, as if looking beyond her eyes, beyond her thoughts, and into something deeper still. Then, as if waking from a dream, he shook his head, bent forward, and slanted his mouth over hers in a kiss which was infinite in its gentleness. When at last he lifted his head and began to pull away, she caught his hand again.

"Bentley?"

He turned back at once. "Yes, Freddie?"

"Are you . . . are you keeping anything from me?"

His eyes darkened at once. "Is that what those words of love were all about?" he asked a little roughly. "Emotional bribery, Freddie? It won't work."

But Freddie held firm. "Just answer the question."

He shook his head disbelievingly and cursed beneath his breath. "What would I possibly hide from you?" he asked. "What is it you suspect me of? Have I not danced attendance on you like the most faithful of lovers?"

"You have." Frederica pursed her lips. "That is not what I meant."

His expression gentled. "Then you have the answer to all the important questions right there, Freddie." His mood seemed light again. As if to prove it, he bent and kissed the top of her nose.

"And Bentley?"

"What?"

She gave his hand a reassuring squeeze. "Make things right with your brother, won't you? Will you try?"

His smile was faintly mocking. "It is not that simple, love."

"Why not? Families should always get along."

He looked at her very gravely. "You are my family now, Freddie, aren't you?" And then, as if to distract her—or perhaps to distract himself—he set his hands on either side of her shoulders and took her lips again. But this time, it was no sweet, delicate kiss. It was a kiss of urgent hunger yet almost sinfully slow and languorous. And it did distract her, damn him. Every serious thought flew from her head as Frederica felt her body melt against his, wordlessly begging for his touch.

To torment her, Bentley slid his tongue back and forth along the seam of her lips until she could not resist, and then he eased into her mouth on a groan. With slow, sinuous motions, he plumbed her depths, until Frederica's hands became restless on his body, sliding down his back, pleading and seeking.

And then, slowly, he pulled away and gave her a rueful grin. "Damn, Freddie, look at the time," he said. "You're making me late for dinner."

"You wretch!" Her words were but a whisper, yet he chuckled softly. "Can you never be serious five minutes running?"

Bentley shrugged, and made her no answer. After

dressing for dinner, he breezed past, pausing just long enough to kiss Frederica once more before leaving. Feeling the need to move and stretch, she got up and began to tidy the room. Her dress, chemise, and fichu still lay across the chair where Bentley had tossed them. Frederica picked them up and carried them into the dressing room. It was only then that she realized her pearl scarf pin was missing.

Frederica's heart sank. The pin had been a birthday gift from Winnie. Suddenly, she remembered having taken it off to pry open the lock for Ariane. She considered it but a moment before throwing on her dressing gown and going out into the corridor. Besides, she had been trapped in bed with her thoughts all day, and, for reasons she could not explain, she'd grown increasingly curious about the contents of that chest.

With everyone at dinner, it was no trouble at all to slip out and down the stairs. The corridor was dark, with only a wall sconce to light the landing, but she made her way to the bedchamber with no trouble. Once inside the room, however, it was very dark indeed. Frederica stubbed her toe on the chest, cursed soundly, then knelt down to feel her way around it. She found the pin just where she'd dropped it and paused long enough to jab it through her dressing gown.

Frederica stood up—slowly this time—then, on second thought, bent down and lifted the lid. Impulsively, she thrust her hand beneath the old blankets and, one by one, extracted Cassandra Rutledge's journal and the books beneath it. She felt a little guilty for doing so, but she was growing deeply curious about Lord Treyhern's first wife. What had she liked to read? What had her daily life been like? Ariane did not seem to pine for her mother. But whatever she'd been or done, Cassandra Rutledge was dead now. So what harm was there in flipping through a few old books to alleviate one's boredom?

Moments later, Frederica was back with no one the wiser. Eagerly, she dumped the books in the middle of the bed, then settled down beside them. The first was a tattered copy of an old gothic novel. Frederica tossed it aside and snatched the second, a book of French fashion plates, at least a decade out of date. She flipped through it, chuckling at the high waists, protruding feathers, and jutting breasts, then tossed it aside, too.

Then she grabbed the third, which was large but not thick. Illustrations, Frederica guessed. She looked at it curiously. The book was bound in a garish shade of red morocco, and if ever there had been a title stamped on the spine, it had worn away long ago. There was an inscription on the flyleaf, dated almost twenty years ago. Frederica peered at the flamboyant, feminine handwriting:

To my delightful Randolph—
Paris has many pleasures, and I have brought one
home to you. May it serve to tempt and to inspire.
                    —Your ever-admiring Marie

What an odd inscription. So the book was not Cassandra's at all. Instead, someone named Marie had given it to Bentley's father. With a shrug, Frederica flipped it open somewhere near the middle, and her eyes almost fell out of her head.

Good Lord! It was a picture book, all right. A collection of colored sketches which must have cost a fortune to produce. And they were nothing but blatant obscenity, brazen depictions of ladies and gentlemen performing sexual acts which were wicked beyond anything Frederica could possibly have imagined. A few more pages, and her heart began to pound with horror and guilt and pure old human titillation. Dear heaven, she thought, turning one page sideways to better study it. Could the human body really do that?

Her face felt afire. She wanted to toss the thing out the window lest her fascination be discovered. And she *was* fascinated. Frederica had not been raised a prude, but only after her marriage had she begun to realize the many ways lovers pleasured one another. Indeed, she had imagined her husband knew every trick in the book and had already taught her most of them. But as she slid back another page to see a drawing of a plump Parisian lady pleasuring two men at once—and using some orifices which were hard to conceive of—Frederica began to doubt that even Bentley had seen all the tricks in this book.

The next sketch was even more fascinating, in a way. A woman sat astraddle her lover, who lay flat on the bed beneath her, his arms folded beneath his head. She was touching herself on her breasts and between her legs as he watched. The reclining gentleman looked deeply appreciative. On the adjacent page, a man sat drinking champagne while his lover knelt between his knees with his erect penis in her mouth.

With each drawing, Frederica's eyebrows flew another notch higher, and she was ashamed to admit that it left her almost eager for her husband's return. But would Bentley approve of his wife having seen such a book? Even as it shocked her, the book made her feel inadequate. Clearly, there was much about pleasing a man she needed to learn. Was one supposed to know how to do such things instinctively? Had she, perhaps, been a disappointment to her husband?

Slowly, Frederica closed the book. She had much to think about. Certainly, the dusty old journal no longer held her interest. Feeling both confused and enlightened, Frederica gathered up all the books and shoved them deep into the recesses of the dressing room. Then she changed into her finest nightdress and crawled back under the covers to await her husband's return.

Chapter Eighteen

In which Our Hero is quite Taken Aback.

It was a known fact, so far as Bentley Rutledge was concerned, that a colder, more rigid man than his brother had never drawn the breath of life. The Earl of Treyhern had apparently been born a saint, and age had only made him worse. He was also industrious, intelligent, chivalrous, and a whole host of other adjectives which were ordinarily thought good qualities but merely served to get on Bentley's nerves. He'd never been able to measure up, so "Why bother to try?" had become his motto at an early age, an attitude encouraged by their father.

Other than an occasional reading of the riot act, Cam hadn't seemed to care that Bentley didn't bother. Perhaps there was nothing Cam could have done anyway. And yet some part of Bentley felt that his brother should have tried. But tried to do what? He did not know. Better than a dozen years separated them. To him, Cam had always seemed like a man grown, and, to use Joan's apt term, *omnipotent*. Sometimes he wondered if Cam had ever really given him a moment's thought after their mother had died. Instead, it seemed Cam had worried more about marrying a rich wife and keeping the whip hand on their father.

The sad truth was, though, that both had been necessary to save the family from ruin. Still, it sometimes felt as if Cam had been so bloody busy restoring the family's façade he'd ignored the deep fissures in its structure. Bentley was not jealous of his brother. No, he was . . . angry. Just angry. And left with this niggling sense of having been cast off by someone who should have been, well, *paying attention.*

There, he'd said it—at least in his head, thought Bentley, as he trod slowly up the stairs. And it sounded so lame, so pathetically little-boy-lost, that he'd sooner choke on it than say it aloud. He had never asked for Cam's help or love or attention, and he damned sure wasn't about to start now. Still, impending fatherhood began to stir up strange things in a fellow's head.

Their dinner tonight had been a damned misery. Cam had been cold and distant, and, as if to compensate, Helene had been annoyingly exuberant. Then Ariane had prattled on for half an hour about her friend Henriette's letter, and, for once, his niece's banter had made Bentley want to throttle someone. Even Mrs. Naffles's menu had been abysmal: a joint which tasted tough as saddle leather, accompanied by an array of overstewed vegetables.

Bentley's only hope of salvaging the evening was to go upstairs and make love to his wife. He only prayed Freddie felt up to it. Good God, he'd really come to depend on the chit. With Freddie, he could blind out the bad and think only of the future.

Was it wrong, he wondered, to spend his emotions inside his wife's body? No matter. So long as she'd have him, he didn't mean to stop. Until now, he had rarely stopped doing anything which brought him relief, pleasure, or satisfaction, choosing instead to live with whatever guilt resulted. He was fortunate that Freddie was always willing. No, *eager*. She was a wonderfully sensual creature, with her flashing eyes and warm skin. From the very first, her passion had delighted him, and her innocence had charmed him.

She was awake when he came into the room. Bentley gave her a cheerful, smacking kiss, sloshed out a dram of cognac, then fell into a chair by the hearth to kick off his shoes. Looking delightfully drowsy and disheveled, she slid from between the sheets and padded across the carpet toward him. To his surprise, she settled on her knees by his chair and began to help. "How was dinner?" she asked, her voice low.

"Bloody awful," he admitted as the first shoe slid away.

"I'm sorry." She tugged off the second, then looked up at him with a coy smile. "Can I do something to make you forget about it?"

Intrigued by the throaty tone of her voice, Bentley arched one brow and studied her. He had more than a little experience with the subtleties of feminine behavior, and Freddie was definitely sending some signals. Her hair was not braided. Instead, it formed a tumbling black waterfall about her shoulders, just the way he liked it. Her mouth looked full and tempting, and there was something in the back of her rich brown eyes which made his breath catch. And she had changed into her thinnest nightdress, one made of fine white lawn, so sheer it exposed her breasts, which had grown plump and round these past few weeks. Her nipples were dark, rosy circles, beautifully hard beneath the fabric.

"Freddie love," he said softly. "With breasts like those, you could make a man forget his own name."

Frederica smiled and flashed him a look which could only have been described as naughty. And then she shocked him by running her palms up the insides of his thighs and making a little sound of pleasure in the back of her throat.

"Mmm," he said. "Mind those clever hands, Freddie."

But she didn't. Instead, she leaned into him, allowing the neckline of her nightdress to gape wide. Bentley's mouth went dry. He watched her full breasts sway as her hands slid higher, her thumbs massaging deep into his thigh muscles, deep enough to make his cock twitch with pleasure.

Oh, Lord. He was already so hard it felt as if someone had shoved a double-barreled dueling pistol down his trousers. But when she slid her hands higher still, kneading him up and down though the fabric of his trousers, Bentley fleetingly feared he might explode still dressed. "Freddie love," he said hoarsely, catching one of her hands. "Best wait for me in bed."

She cut a sly glance up at him. "What if I can't wait?" she purred.

Bentley closed his eyes. "Just let me undress," he whispered thickly. "Then, I swear, sweetheart, I'll ease what's plaguing you, all right?"

Apparently, it wasn't. Freddie rose onto her knees, twined one hand behind his neck, and kissed him deeply. She eased her tongue into his mouth with slow strokes, forcing his breath to come hard and fast. A long moment later, she sat back on her heels and smiled. "I don't want to wait for you to undress," she whispered, toying with the close of his trousers. "Perhaps tonight we should do something different?"

He let her fingers go then, curious as to just how far the minx meant to take this and wondering what the devil had got into her. In response, Freddie slid one hand down his crotch, cradling the heat of his balls in her palm, while the other hand cleverly freed the buttons. He tried to snare her hand again. "Whoa there, Freddie." He choked out the words. "Sure you know what you're about?"

She answered him with a flirtatious smile, then pushed away the fabric of his shirt and trousers, crumpling his drawers in the process. His dueling pistol sprang free, hard, hot, primed, and cocked. To his shock, she slicked one warm, delicate hand down his length, drawing back his flesh and fully exposing his head. His entire body shivered. "Good God Almighty," he heard himself groan.

It was exquisite. She caressed him gently at first, with long, languorous strokes, cleverly mimicking the way he liked to move inside her body. Oh, she was a fast learner, his pretty wife. Again and again, she touched him, growing increasingly skillful—and increasingly demanding. As her fingers moved over his heated flesh, one hand slid back down to massage the weight of his testicles. At every turn, he meant to stop her. Wanted to stop her. But somehow, in the heat of things, she got his trousers halfway down his thighs and then down around his ankles, until he'd slid onto the edge of his chair, fully exposed to her touch.

It felt so decadently wicked to sit thus by a warm

fire, with the rest of his dinner dress perfectly intact, a glass of good brandy in his hand, and his wife on her knees, almost suppliant between his legs. Faintly, he knew he should push her away. Knew it was wrong to let Freddie—a gently bred girl—touch him in so vulgar a way. And wrong to want more. To want her mouth on his cock. There were women a fellow could pay if he needed that sort of thing. But it felt so good. Oh, sweet heaven, it felt good. Her next stroke tightened into a fist, drawing his skin so taut his whole body shuddered. "Aaah," he moaned, letting his head tip back.

It was then, at the very instant he wasn't watching, that his wife bent her head and took him deep into her mouth, plunging him into a smooth, sensual warmth which words could not describe. "Christ Jesus, Freddie!" he croaked, his whole body going rigid in his chair. His head jerked up, brandy sloshed onto the carpet, and his free hand clenched the chair arm, as though he were clinging to the last of his sanity. For a moment, he allowed himself the luxury of watching her lush lips slide along his swollen flesh. And then, reluctantly, he set aside his glass and took her face between his palms, gently forcing her head up.

"Freddie love," he managed to say, "you really oughtn't."

Her eyes widened. "Am I doing it wrong?"

Wrong? Hell, no. The sight of his cock glistening and damp from her mouth almost undid him. Bentley closed his eyes and pushed gently at her hands. "No, but this isn't something—" He searched his mind for the right words. "We just shouldn't."

"No?" He couldn't miss the uncertainty in her voice. "This isn't something you enjoy?"

He opened his eyes and forced himself to look at her. Freddie's mouth was pink and swollen, her eyes round and ingenuous. Good God, what a picture of innocence she was with that cloud of black hair and her nightdress sliding off one shoulder. And how desperately he wanted her. Wanted her to suck him dry. Wanted to take her face between his hands and watch himself thrust deep into her throat. Until he . . . until he . . .

Oh, God, no. This wouldn't do. His cock twitched insistently. Bentley swallowed hard and prayed for strength. "Freddie love, I always enjoy it," he admitted, his voice a raw rasp. "But you shouldn't . . . it isn't—" He couldn't think how to explain it to her. "Look, Freddie, this isn't something a wife does."

Freddie looked at him suspiciously, her eyes suddenly knowing. "Your whoring days are over, Bentley Rutledge," she warned, her voice lethally soft. "Remember that, and get it here, or go without."

Alarmed, Bentley shook his head. "No, no, sweetheart!" he choked. "I won't—absolutely wouldn't—even think about it." But it was a miserable consideration.

"So you should let me." With a sly grin, she dipped her head and nipped him hard on his inner thigh.

"Ow!" he squalled. "Damn it, Freddie, don't bite!"

"Can I have my way with you?" Her voice was sultry enough to melt glass.

She really was determined. In answer, he closed his eyes, framed her face in his hands, and guided her mouth back to his body. She swallowed his heated length with exquisite slowness. He savored the feel of his flesh sliding through her wet lips, over her sharp, white teeth, and down the velvety length of her tongue. He was at her mercy, and it felt dangerous. Erotic. Wicked.

With one hand on the base of his shaft and the other caressing his inner thigh, his wife touched him with exquisite skill, her mouth hot and tight, the strokes of her tongue growing increasingly intense. Damn, but she was good. For long, sweet moments, it went on. Soon, he could barely control himself. His grip on her shoulders was too tight, his motions too urgent. He knew he should stop . . . had to stop . . . right *now*.

"Ah, God, Freddie!" He ripped his flesh from her mouth, pushed her down by the shoulders, and followed her onto the hearth rug. He tumbled across her, frantic and clumsy, his ankles entangled in his trousers. Freddie's nightdress slid halfway up her thighs. Crudely, he rucked it up to her waist and heard fabric rip. He tore it off and hurled it into the shadows. Then he pushed her legs apart with his knee and shoved himself inside her on a jubilant cry.

To his shock, she was like molten fire beneath him. Her legs came up to encircle his waist, and her hips rose to meet his. She clung to him, trembling and needy. Stroke for stroke, gasp for gasp, she matched him, her eyes open wide, her lips slightly parted.

"Please, oh, please," she begged, her shudder deepening.

And Bentley tried to oblige her, but his vision was fading, and his whole body was shaking. Freddie's release came upon her with startling speed. By the glow of the fire, he watched as she lost herself in the rhythm, panting and arching beneath him, until at last she cried out. Twice. Three times. Deep, keening sounds of pleasure as she rocked and shuddered beneath him. And then his brain went black, and he exploded inside her. Inside his wife.

Oh, sweet heaven, how he loved her.

It was his first lucid thought when he returned to consciousness. He almost uttered it aloud, but the moment didn't seem quite right. His head was on the hearth rug, his nose buried in her wild mane of hair. He breathed deep, drawing in her heightened scent of soap and feminine heat. Freddie still had one leg curled about his waist. Bentley wondered what had got into her; he couldn't think what he'd done to deserve such a life-altering experience. He had believed it disrespectful—even crude—to let her do that to him. Was that true? He no longer knew. She had enjoyed it. God knew he had. And she felt perfect beneath him now.

He was going to regret this, perhaps, in the morning. And he was going to wonder what had put such a notion in his young wife's head. He'd just tell himself it was feminine instinct and hope that he was right. But he had no wish to think of that at the moment. Instead, he stumbled up onto one knee, slipped his arms beneath Freddie, and carried her to bed.

So often in Frederica's life it had seemed that happiness and security were things which fate had conspired to dole out to her in small, fickle dollops, like some too-rich treat. Often, as had been the case with Johnny Ellows, it soon became apparent that fate had done her a favor. Other times, the disappointment was an almost felling blow, never to be forgotten, such as that dreadful morning when she'd been turned away from her grandmother's door.

On this particular morning, however, Frederica awoke before dawn, feeling happy, secure, and quite thoroughly sated. In the darkness, she rolled closer to Bentley, who still slept deeply. With one arm thrown across his eyes, he lay naked on his back, taking up two-thirds of the mattress and all of the bedcover. On her side of the bed, Frederica shivered. The room was chilly, and she was too lazy to crawl from the bed to look for her nightdress or poke up the fire.

No, in her drowsy state, it seemed better to wriggle beneath the blankets and curl against her husband's side. He nuzzled her without waking, his morning erection tenting the blanket as she hooked one leg over his thigh. On those days when he did not rise insanely early, she would notice this remarkable phenomenon. Sometimes, he would ease her gently onto her back and put his phenomenon to good use, too.

At that delightful notion, she burrowed her face against his neck. Bentley still smelled of ash and smoke from last night's antics on the hearth rug, and of sweat and sleepy, musky male. Perhaps she was not quite so sated after all? She hitched her leg a little higher on his thigh. His erection brushed her knee, and she shimmied closer, sliding one hand over the taut plane of his belly, then down to the thatch of dark hair at the base of his manhood.

She so rarely got the opportunity to touch him this way. But this morning, her entreaties seemed to meet with Bentley's approval. As she stroked him, he made a sound in the back of his throat and began to move restlessly. Emboldened, Frederica crawled half on top of him and kissed him. In his drowsy state, he turned his face to hers, his mouth eager, blindly seeking.

Again, she caressed the warm, velvety length of his erection. The memory of last night returned, intriguing her. How thrilling it had been to pleasure him so decadently. Innocence, she'd concluded, was of little use to a married woman. She considered again the sketch she'd seen—the woman atop her lover, touching herself while he watched. A little thrill chased up her spine. Why not? Perhaps she could show her husband that she was not quite as innocent as he feared.

Slowly, she mounted him, setting her knees on either side of his hipbones. Bentley's face shifted, seemed to change somehow. Frederica felt a moment of uncertainty. But there was nothing uncertain about his erection, which moved insistently. Gingerly, she rose up onto her knees and eased herself down, slowly impaling herself on his shaft. Slowly stirring, Bentley moaned again. Frederica sighed aloud with pleasure. Then, like a cat in the cream pot, she closed her eyes, tipped back her head, and sank down onto his hardness again.

In that split second, all hell exploded. On a bloodcurdling roar, Bentley bucked up off the bed, pitching her backward. He came up like a madman, fists and elbows flailing. Something caught Frederica hard across the temple, and with an awful crack, her head struck the wooden footboard. "God damn you, get off me!" he roared. "Get off!"

He towered over her in the gloom. She must have

whimpered. He moved as if he might lunge again. Her heart pounded in her throat. She was afraid to speak. Afraid to move.

The bed creaked ominously beneath his shifting weight. He pinned her with his body against the wood. His hard, powerful hands slid around her throat. "Damn you." His voice was raw and rasping, like something torn from the pits of hell. "Don't ever touch me again."

Frederica huddled against the footboard. "Y-yes, all right," she sobbed, wondering which of them had lost their minds. "Please, Bentley, j-just let me go—"

Something in him changed at the sound of her voice, quick as a lightning strike. She felt his whole body jolt, and then Bentley's hands fell away. A long, awful silence hung over them, and then he exhaled sharply. "Oh, Christ Jesus."

He was awake, thank God. *Awake.* She went limp with relief. Bentley fell back onto his heels, and even in the gloom, she sensed his eyes burning through her. He cursed again, violently, and shoved both hands into his hair.

"Bentley?" she said softly, but he wouldn't answer. Instead, he leaned forward at the waist, still clutching his head, his elbows rolling forward, as if he wished to shut her out. As if he fought to turn inward and simply disappear inside himself. "Bentley, say something," she whispered. "Oh, please, just say something."

"Freddie?" His voice was choked with shock and horror. "Oh, my God."

She sagged with relief. He really had been asleep. But what on earth had set him off? It came to her in a flash.

It was what she had done. Crawling on top of him. That was something he had never let her do. In fact, everything they did in bed—or at least what *she* did to *him*—seemed tame compared with Randolph's wicked drawings. Vaguely—and a little sickly—she recalled his having pushed her away once before. *Damn you, don't!* he had said. *Don't smother me like that!* And yet that instance had been nothing like this.

Suddenly, Frederica felt the warmth trickling down her face. She touched her temple with her fingertips, and they came away sticky. She remembered her husband's heavy signet ring. "Bentley," she warned in a shaky voice. "I am getting off the bed now, all right? I need to light a candle."

He said nothing. In the darkness, she fumbled until the candle by the bed flared to life. Only then did he take his hands from his head. He turned and lifted his eyes to hers, his expression bleak and hopeless.

She realized it the instant he saw the blood. And she watched as the full awareness of what he had done struck him. His whole face crumpled, and tears pooled in his eyes. One hand reached out to touch her, but it could not quite span the distance across the bed, as if it were some awful symbol for the whole of their marriage.

"Oh, God, what have I done?" He looked down at the smear of blood on his signet ring. "Oh, Freddie. What have I done this time?"

Chapter Nineteen

A voice from Beyond the grave.

For Frederica, life turned suddenly surreal. It was as if the fear drained away but took her grasp of reality with it. More candles were lit, but by whom she couldn't recall. She had only the vaguest memory of Bentley leading her to the chair by the hearth and tucking her into her wrapper. Numbly, she watched him jerk on his clothes, then fetch a washbasin. He began to sponge the blood from her hair and her temple, his touch tender.

Strangely, it did not hurt. She felt almost nothing. Bentley kept murmuring softly, his expression stricken. *He was so sorry. So sorry. It was not her fault.* But Frederica could sense that beneath it all, he was frightened. Terrified, really, though that brought her little comfort.

As Bentley wrung the water out of her face flannel, Frederica looked down into her lap to see that her hands were starting to shake. Reality was setting in. Good God, she really was in over her head. She was not yet nineteen years old. And she was with child. And married—married to a man whose heart seemed to hold terrible secrets.

Perhaps it was time to face the fact that something was wrong. She loved him. But was that going to be enough?

Bentley touched her temple again with his fingertips. The examination was meant to be clinical, but his hand, too, was trembling. "Ah, God, Freddie, it's going to bruise." His voice hitched; not quite a sob, but something almost worse. "I wonder if you will ever forgive me."

He sat down in the opposite chair and took her hands in his. Abjectly, he lifted his eyes to hers but said no more. Frederica searched her mind for the right thing to say. "Bentley," she said softly, "what was it, exactly, that you thought? What were you dreaming?"

His gaze was instantly shuttered. "I don't remember."

He was lying. She sensed it. "You don't remember?" she gently probed. "Or you won't tell me?"

He jerked from his chair and began to pace toward the windows, one hand set on his hip, the other at the back of his neck. "Damn it, Freddie, I've no excuse for what I just did," he admitted. "I won't even try to make one. So what do you want me to say? What do you want me to do?"

Frederica was still shaken. "Just tell me the truth," she demanded. "I love you, Bentley, but you have to stop hiding things from me. And from yourself."

"Hiding?" he said, staring out the window. "Just what is it you think I'm hiding?"

Frederica's emotions snapped. "I don't know *what*," she responded. "How could I? Why, I hardly know anything at all! I am just a stupid and naïve girl—and when I try to be a good wife, when I try to—to please you, well—just look! I think we can see what happens."

He turned from the window and closed the distance between them. He took her hands in his and went down on one knee so that he might look her directly in the eyes. "Freddie, *you* are a *good wife*." He said the words slowly and distinctly. "It is this marriage which was a bad idea."

Frederica slowly shook her head. "Oh, no," she whispered, horrified. "Do not say that! We both chose this marriage. We have staked everything on it."

His lips thinned, and he shook his head. "Freddie, *I* chose it," he said firmly. "I chose it like some spoilt child chooses a toy which is too fragile for his touch. I wanted you. Hell, I think I've always been half in love with you. And I thought it might be a chance—a chance to . . . oh, God, I don't know what I thought! But if I'd truly loved you, well, I would never have tricked myself into believing what I wanted was best, would I? Not when there were a thousand better alternatives for you than a marriage to me."

"What are you saying, Bentley?"

Still on his knees before her, he seemed to look beyond her, to a point somewhere far in the distance. "That I care enough now to do the right thing instead of the selfish thing," he whispered. "I am saying that if you wish it, Freddie—if you wish, that is, to leave me—I shan't try to hold you to that foolish bargain we made."

It was as if he'd struck her a mortal blow, one far worse than a bruised temple. "My God, is that it, then?" she cried. "We are simply to give up? Over . . . over this?"

"Jesus Christ, it's not just this, Freddie! Don't you see?"

She shook her head. "No. No, I don't."

He closed his eyes for a moment and bent his head

until it rested on the backs of her hands, which he still grasped. For many seconds, he was quiet, and when he lifted his head, his eyes were shimmering with tears. "I just want you to do what you think is best for you, Freddie. And for the child. Whatever that is, for God's sake, please do it."

Freddie felt her throat tighten. "But you are my husband," she whispered. "I don't think either of us should take the easy way out. Why, if you are at least a little bit in love with me, and if I am head over heels in love with you, isn't it morally wrong to give up?"

Bentley's shoulders sagged—with relief, she hoped. "Then we need to get away, Freddie," he said softly. "I can't stay here. And perhaps if it was just the two of us, things would be better."

But Frederica was almost in tears now. "Going away won't help!" she cried. "It's like running away from your troubles, Bentley. You have to stop doing that. I want to know what is wrong with us. I want to fix it."

"Good God, Freddie, nothing is wrong with us. Is that what you were trying to fix last night? And just now? Were you trying to be something different for me? Don't."

"I only wanted you to—to stop thinking of me as such an innocent," she sobbed. "I wanted only to please you. To pleasure you. I did not mean to make you so angry."

He touched the wound at her temple again. "I was dead asleep, Freddie," he quietly reminded her. "I was so deeply asleep I did not know what I was doing." Then he looked at her more intently. "What on earth put such thoughts in your head? What could make you feel inadequate? You are perfect, Freddie, as you are."

Frederica stared at the floor, and he continued speaking. "Freddie, that was quite a trick you pulled on me last night," he said, his voice gentle. "I suppose I knew, even then, that we would need to have a talk about it."

She regarded him suspiciously. "Wh-what do you mean, *have a talk?*"

He made no move to rise, but he tightened his grip on her hands. "You are an innocent, Freddie—"

Frederica cut him off. "For God's sake, I shall go stark staring mad if you keep saying that! I am not an innocent. If I ever was, I certainly am not now."

Bentley looked as if it pained him to go on. "Yet the fact remains, Freddie, that what you did last night—"

"Oh, yes!" she interjected sardonically. "That thing you did not like!"

For a long moment, he was silent, as if considering his words. "I am not scolding you, sweetheart," he said gently. Then he rose from his knees, took the chair opposite, and cleared his throat. "Still, that little trick last night was not something which a gently bred lady should know anything about. And what you did this morning—well, God knows I'm not blaming you. I'm just trying to understand how you took it into your head to . . . to be so . . ."

He could not finish. Frederica saved him the trouble. She went into the dressing room and returned with Randolph's book, then dropped it into his lap. He recognized it at once. She knew that he did, for what was left of his color drained away. "Where in God's name did you get this?" he demanded, the tenderness leaving his voice.

"From the old blanket chest," she admitted. "The one in Cassandra's bedchamber."

She watched as his knuckles went white on the red leather binding, as white as they'd been the day he ripped open Cassandra's clothes press and slammed it shut again. "Freddie," he rasped, staring down at the book. "Had I wished for a wife with the tastes and talents of a whore, I would have married one."

The brutality of his words shocked her, but she hid it. "Well, I think that you are just a big hypocrite, Bentley Rutledge."

His jaw began to twitch. "Would you care to explain that?"

Frederica jerked to her feet and stared him down. "You're said to be the biggest whoremonger in six counties," she retorted. "And yet you want a wife who will be content to—to what? Just lie there underneath you? Is that what you wanted? Did I misunderstand? Should I stop moving? Moaning? Is it a sign of ill breeding when a woman has a cli—"

Bentley jabbed a finger in her face. "Just stop right there, Frederica!" he growled. "We haven't exactly been living like monks and nuns in here for the last few weeks. And yes, we've both damned well been enjoying it. But you listen to this, for I shan't say it again: Cassandra Rutledge was a manipulative bitch and a cold-hearted slut. No one in this house wishes ever to be reminded of her. Not me. Not Ariane. And least of all my brother. Stay out of her things. Stay out of her rooms. And don't ever mention her name again." This last was said as he strode toward the door. His hand on the knob, he whirled about to face her.

"Where are you going?" she asked weakly.

Some of the frustration went out of him at that. "To fetch your maid," he said, his shoulders sagging. "You need a plaster on that bruise. I am deeply sorry I hit you, Freddie. Deeply sorry. God knows I didn't mean to."

Frederica started toward him. "Are you coming back?"

He did not look at her. "I'm going to the workshop to plane down the church door," he said. "I need to work off some of this emotion before I explode."

And on that note, he jerked open the door, causing Queenie to almost fall into the room. Perched on the threshold, she teetered, the weight of her bosom seeming to tip her forward. Bentley caught her shoulder, too late. She flailed backward, smacking Bentley in the face with her hearth broom.

Without another word, Bentley steadied her, wiped the soot from his face with his coat sleeve, and slowly walked away.

Frederica watched her husband vanish into the shadows of the corridor. Too late, she realized Queenie was staring at her, an expression of pity on her face. Good Lord, were the servants listening at doors now? There had likely been no need. Bentley's deep voice carried. Frederica lifted her chin. "Queenie, it isn't what you think."

Queenie snapped into action and began bustling about the hearth. "Ooh, it ain't my place to think, ma'am."

For several minutes, Frederica sat, simply watching the servant work and wondering what to do with her life. She was unable to make sense of anything, least of all her own emotions. Just as Queenie finished sweeping, Jennie hastened in. "Oh, miss!" she said in a rush. "Mr. Rutledge told me to—oh, my God!" The maid knelt by Frederica's chair and pulled back her mistress's hair.

"It isn't as bad as it looks," said Freddie dryly. "But I daresay I've learned not to wake a man when he's in the midst of a nightmare."

Both servants looked at her with thin, nervous smiles. Heavens, did no one believe her? Frederica felt her face flush with heat. Murmuring some platitude, Jennie went into the dressing room and began to rummage about. At once, Queenie set the fender back in place and darted out after wishing Frederica good day. Suddenly, Frederica felt an overwhelming wish to be alone. She needed to think. Something in the back of her mind was troubling her.

Impulsively, she called Jennie from the dressing room. The maid appeared with a strip of bandaging in one hand. "Yes, miss?"

Frederica smiled sweetly. "Will you go down to the kitchen and send up a pot of strong tea?" she asked. "And after that, Jennie, I should really like to lie down. A plaster will only make this look worse. I'll ring for you later."

Her expression uncertain, Jennie bobbed a quick curtsey and left. At once, Frederica went into the dressing room to find Cassandra's books. She was not perfectly sure why she did so. She knew only that her relationship with her husband was fast approaching some critical point. A point at which they would either forge something of a real relationship or watch what little they had crumble. And for reasons she could not explain, she felt that the ghost of Cassandra Rutledge had cast a pall not just over this house but over Frederica's marriage, too.

She carried the books to the chair by the windows. Queenie slipped in with her tea but hastened away at once. Frederica took one sip, hoping to fortify herself, and then flipped open the journal, the one book she'd not yet opened. There had been no date on the green cloth cover, nor was there one inside. In fact, only the first six pages contained any writing at all. Disappointed, Frederica thought of the other journals she'd seen shoved in the drawer of the blanket chest, then glanced again at the one she held. Could this be Cassandra's last journal? One so new she'd not bothered to date it?

Again, Frederica wondered how long Cassandra had been dead. She began to skim the journal pages. It was more of a daily log than a diary. On the first page under *"Wednesday,"* Cassandra had made several unremarkable notations. It seemed her blue wool riding habit had arrived an inch too short. Milford was to be reminded to check the champagne reserves. A faulty clasp on her sapphire bracelet needed immediate attention. Paragraphs with more such minutiae followed in a dark, angular handwriting.

At the bottom of the second page, Cassandra made mention of the day's post: a letter from her father and a second from a gentleman whose name Frederica did not recognize. *"He says is back in England and desperate to see me,"* Cassandra had written. *"He begs me to contrive a meeting. Mortimer Street, next month."*

Mortimer Street? That was the address of Lord Treyhern's London town house. Her plan sounded vaguely improper, but Cassandra had noted it emotionlessly. Continuing on, Frederica saw no mention of anyone else, save Cassandra herself, on the first five pages. There was no word of time spent with Ariane or any reference to her husband. Instead, she remarked upon the tedium of village life and the insipidness of her neighbors. On the whole, her words described the life of a very dull, self-absorbed woman. Then, under *"Sunday,"* Frederica's eye caught a strange remark.

"Saw Thomas after his sermon today," she had written. *"Ephesians 1:7, redemption and forgiveness! Could not keep from laughing in his face."*

This aside was followed by a bitter remark about the Cotswold weather and its disastrous effect on her hair. Frederica flipped to the last page. Three paragraphs were scrawled across it and, after that, nothing. What had apparently been the last day of Cassandra's life was noted as a Thursday. Frederica skimmed the first paragraph. At once, her stomach began to twist into knots. Again, she read it, forcing herself to slow down. To be sure.

"Thomas came whilst Cam was at shearing," Cassandra began, her penmanship suddenly unsteady. *"The fool thinks to threaten me. What gall. Town beckons. Tonight I again pressed Bentley for help, but my precious grows stubborn. Most unwise. Confession, I reminded him, is good for the soul."*

Frederica squeezed her eyes shut and tried to force her breathing to calm. Good Lord, it sounded as if . . . as if . . . what? With a sick feeling, Frederica read the last two paragraphs. For the first time in days, she felt nausea roil up in her throat. She felt cold. Numb. Cassandra's veiled notes left little doubt about her meaning. An awful suspicion choked the breath from her lungs.

As if it had just burst into flame, she flung away the book. It landed on the carpet, then skittered into the night table with a thud. Frederica simply stared at it, unable to think. Whatever the truth, it was appalling. She did not want to know. *Never wanted to know.* But she already did. It simply wasn't that hard to read between the lines. The reality was more horrifying than any bruise her husband could have given her. Frederica sagged with a sudden sense of grief. Bentley had much to explain. His past was his past, yes. But this was . . . unthinkable. Her hands shaking, Frederica stood, went into the dressing room, and dragged out the first gown she saw.

Backlit by the glow of the blacksmith's forge, Bentley bent over the worktable and drove another smooth pass with his plane. A long sliver of oak curled in its wake, then tumbled softly onto the dirt floor. With the back of one hand, he wiped the sweat from his eyes, then straightened up. At the forge, old Angus was hammering out the first of what was to be a new set of hinges. If he'd thought of it, Bentley wryly considered, he could have dragged the project out until kingdom come by just building a new door altogether. That would have meant new planks, new joinery—hell, he and Angus could have felled and sawed the trees, too. Yes, if he'd been willing to use green lumber, he might have stayed hidden in the workshop for days—and doing the Lord's work, no less. Old Angus turned from the fire, then rooted around beneath his leather apron for his handkerchief. "The bolt holes," he called over one shoulder. "What's the distance? Measure center-to-center wi' that rule, ye ken?"

Bentley snatched the device from its peg, measured, and called out the result. Angus grunted, then took up his tools and resumed his efforts. The heat, the smells, even the rhythmic clanking of the hammer, were strangely soothing to Bentley's senses. It was peaceful here, in its own way. A man's domain, simple and purposeful, just as a man's life ought to be, were the world a perfect place. Certainly, there were no women here. And no memories of them, either.

Bentley picked up his plane and thought again of what he had done to Freddie. Good God, he was still appalled. Why her? Why now? It wasn't as if he hadn't suffered that damned dream a hundred times and in a hundred different beds. There had been a hundred other women in those beds with him, too, but he'd never hauled off and backhanded any of them. Of course, none of them had crawled on top of him when he was dead asleep and hard as Angus's hammer.

The trouble, of course, was Freddie. None of it was her fault. But she stirred things up in his head. She stripped away the detachment he'd come to count on. Forced him to a level of intimacy he almost could not bear. *They were as one,* the Reverend Mr. Amherst had told them. And that was just how it felt when he gazed into her eyes as they made love. He was there with her, in body and in spirit. He could not keep his distance and simply satisfy his physical ache. She aroused in him an ache of the soul as well. A yearning to be linked, heart to heart and mind to mind.

Good Lord. He could open neither his heart nor his mind to anyone. But neither could he seem to stop it when it came to Freddie. So it was just a matter of time. A matter of time before she sensed or saw something. Or asked some probing question he could not answer. She was no fool, his young wife. And she was right about something else, too. She was not all that innocent. She would be hard to deceive. Had he imagined he could? Or had he subconsciously brought her to Chalcote to help banish his old ghosts? Had he foolishly convinced himself that love conquered all? Well, none of it had worked, had it? He had been a fool to take her to the altar, whether she carried his child or no.

"Ho, laddie!" Angus's voice cut into his thoughts. "Would ye be warkin' or daydreamin'?"

Bentley realized he'd stopped in mid-stroke, bent halfway over the worktable with the curl of wood just dangling off the back of the plane. He jerked the blade back, cursing at the rough spot which remained. Another two strokes smoothed it away. A pity his nightmares were not so easily dealt with. Ah, but he would not think of that now. He would think, instead, of the shaping of this wood, and he would try to lose himself in the simplicity of the task.

Lord Treyhern was locked in his study when Frederica came downstairs. Through the heavy door, she could hear his voice booming, as if he were angry. She let her hand drop without knocking and turned away, but a pitiful noise caught her attention. She looked down to see one of the kittens mewling at the door. She scooped it up and pressed its yellow fur to her cheek, reluctant to leave it alone. Fortunately, at that very moment, Mrs. Naffles bustled past.

"Ooh, poor wee dear!" she cooed, dropping the kitten into the front pocket of her apron. "I'll take it in through the butler's pantry." Then Frederica explained her dilemma, and Mrs. Naffles was happy to help her, too. The workshops at Chalcote, she explained, were under the hill below the new granary.

The workshops consisted of a long row of stone shelters, some partially open, such as the blacksmith's shop, which belched white smoke from its chimney. Others were fully enclosed and fitted with squat double doors. From above, Frederica could hear a great deal of clanking and cursing. As she came down the path, she could look through the open blacksmith's shop to see a second room fitted with carpentry tools.

Her husband was bent low over a worktable, naked from the waist up. Sweat trickled down the muscles of his back. Frederica could see why when she paused in the entryway. Heat roiled from the forge, radiating off the stone walls. The servant they called Old Angus gave her a curt nod of greeting, then laid down his tools and left. His back turned, Bentley seemed oblivious to her presence as he ran the plane smoothly along the bottom of the door. For a long moment, she lingered, watching the thick muscles of his shoulders bunch then relax as, again and again, he slid the tool smoothly across the wood, making the blade sing with a soft, hissing rhythm. How like him to choose to do such manual labor himself. Clearly, he knew what he was doing, too.

As with everything he did, there was a lazy, almost effortless grace to his motions. And yet the power in his body could not be denied. With every stroke of his sculpted arms, the muscles of his back drew taut and drove the plane home. His torso glistened from the heat of the forge and the effort of his strokes. With his braces slipped off his shoulders, his dark trousers rode low on his tautly muscled hips, accentuating his narrow waist.

Was this how they lured you in, these fine, sleek specimens of male beauty? With such charm and strength, could they blind a foolish woman to what lay beneath? No. Frederica might believe her husband a rogue and a sinner. But she did not believe he had set out to lure her or to blind her to his character. Gently, she cleared her throat. "Bentley?"

His entire body went rigid at the sound. He straightened and half turned his head to look at her. With his face in profile, she could see the tracks of sweat which had run like tears down his face. But he stood almost stoically, some strained emotion flickering deep in his eyes. "Bentley," she said softly, "we need to talk."

She heard him curse beneath his breath. Then, with the plane clutched hard in his left hand, he slowly turned to face her. He put the tool down, dragged an arm across his face, then, with a brusque nod, strode past her and into the shade of a chestnut tree. In the quiet vale, one could hear nothing but birdsong and soughing wind. There was an old bench beneath the chestnut, and he motioned for her to sit. When she did, he threw himself down in the tufted grass, stretching out his long legs in front of her.

In that instant, however, Frederica forgot her husband's physical beauty and thought only of the awful task before her. It felt as though her heart was in her throat. The fear and doubt returned, and Frederica felt suddenly as though she were alone with him again, locked in the music room at Strath House, waiting to hear what was to happen with her life.

In the shade, Bentley leaned his weight back on his arms, then lifted his chin to look up at her. The heel of his left hand, she saw, was bearing down on an old chestnut burr, and yet he seemed not to notice. Frederica found that disturbing. And it was not the first time, now that she considered it, that Bentley seemed . . . well, not to *feel* things. Or, at least, not to feel them in the same way that others did. She must have been staring at him oddly.

"Well, have at it, Freddie," he said. "Bad news gets no better with waiting."

She felt suddenly ill and became graceless. "I want to know if it is true, Bentley," she whispered. "Is it true you had an . . . an *affaire d'amour* with your brother's wife?"

He turned his face away from her and gave a bitter, almost resigned laugh. "Damned if you aren't quick, Freddie," he answered. "But no, it was no love affair. Hell, I didn't even like her. But I fucked her often enough, if that's what you're asking."

Frederica felt her whole body go rigid. "Please don't use that word," she said. "It is vulgar and disgusting."

He looked up at her again, squinting his eyes as the sun dappled his face through the leaves. "Well, it was a vulgar and disgusting thing we did, Freddie." His tone was dispassionate. "So that's the only word which fits. I hate to break it to you, love, but life isn't all sweetness and light."

Frederica could only gape at him. "Good God, have you no remorse?" Her voice was strident now. "How can you just sit there and—and say that? 'I fucked her!' It's as if you're speaking of the time or—or the weather!"

"That's about how significant bedding Cassandra was," he answered. "And she was almost as unpredictable."

Frederica shook her head. "No," she said, her voice growing hollow. "Oh, no, Bentley. It cannot have been insignificant. Please, tell me . . . tell me you did not commit adultery so casually. So cruelly. Not with your brother's wife. Please tell me you feel guilt. Or regret. Or a modicum of shame, for God's sake."

He looked away again and was silent for many moments. "Well, there's the rub, Freddie," he finally said. "I just don't feel much of anything. I . . . I can't let myself."

"I don't understand you," she whispered.

He laughed harshly. "No, you *don't* understand," he agreed. "My head is like a bloody floodgate, Freddie. And if I open it, if I let myself think about what she . . . oh, hell, what does it matter? What would it change? I did it. I did whatever she wanted. And Cam, well, maybe he wouldn't have given a damn, anyway. If he had, maybe he'd have noticed. My God, it was right was under his nose, and for longer than I care to remember."

Frederica could hear his bitterness. "Oh, Bentley, you sound almost as if you wanted him to discover it!"

His head whipped around to face her. "I did *not* say that," he said roughly. "And you won't tell him, Freddie. I forbid it, do you hear?"

Slowly, she shook her head. "I don't mean to," she said. "I mean for you to do it, Bentley."

A muscle twitched in his jaw. "You must be mad."

Frederica reached out her hand, but Bentley did not take it. "Bentley, you have to, for the sake of the family," she whispered. "This is a part of what's wrong, why you can't sleep. Why you have nightmares. And it's why you two are forever at one another's throats. It's the guilt. But you can lance it by asking Cam's forgiveness."

Bentley's beautiful mouth thinned. "Over my dead body, Frederica."

Frederica wanted to cry. "Over the dead body of our marriage, more likely," she answered. "I love you, Bentley, but I can't stand all this bottled-up hate and rage."

He jerked to his feet. "You don't love me, Frederica," he rasped. "You just love what I can give you. The way I make you feel between the sheets. That's all I'm good at—it's all I've ever been good at—and someday, you'll realize it, too."

"Stop it, Bentley!" she cried. "Just stop it! I know my own heart."

Bentley hung his head. "You are a child, Frederica," he whispered. "And a damned fool, too, if you think confessing this to Cam will make things better."

Frederica held firm. "Do it, and make this right," she warned. "Or, I swear, I won't live with you as your wife. Bentley, I won't!"

He was staring blindly into space now. "Aye, that easy way out you spoke of holds some appeal now, doesn't it?" he answered softly. "I knew it would eventually. And it might be for the best, Freddie, given what happened this morning."

"Bentley, no!" Her words were a horrified whisper.

He shook his head and laughed again, soft and bitter.

"I'm just not marriage material," he replied. "You said it yourself weeks ago. Besides, this didn't stop with Cassandra. Do you imagine that she's the only married woman I've ever bedded?"

"Stop it, Bentley! I don't want to hear it!"

"Oh, come on, Freddie, why not?" His smile was bitter, his eyes ice cold. "You know what's said of me! I've slept with them all—randy widows, rich socialites, tavern sluts, dockyard whores—and I damned sure won't be looking up their husbands to apologize. That's the whole point, you see. *I just don't care.* It makes no difference to me. It's like scratching an itch. And Freddie, I itch a lot."

Frederica felt her indignation surge. "Do you?" she snapped. "Then why not sleep with Joan? You share more of your feelings with her than with me, it seems. And since you have no morals, there's always Helene. Yes, even better. And when you tire of them, why, you can start on all the neighbors' wives! That should keep you busy until New Year's."

She saw his every muscle strain with sudden rage. "Shut up, Freddie," he hissed over his shoulder. "I told you I'd be faithful to you, and goddamn it, I have been. Let's just end this farce of a marriage now, before we learn to hate one another."

"Is that really what you want?" she whispered. "To end it?"

"Didn't I say so this morning?"

In fact, he had not said that at all. But Frederica was too wounded to argue. "And so you will not speak with your brother?" she asked, though she could already feel him slipping away. "You will not swallow your pride and ask his forgiveness so that you can stop hating yourself?"

Abruptly, he jerked into motion. "Not this side of hell, Freddie love," he said, stalking off toward the workshop.

She followed him in and watched him drag his shirt on over his head. Frederica could feel the tears beginning to stream down her face. "What are you doing?" she whispered as he thrust his arms through his waistcoat. "Where are you going?"

He lifted his gaze and pinned her with it. "To get drunk, Freddie," he answered succinctly. "To get piss-pot, snot-slinging, dog-howling drunk. And I mean to stay so for a very long time to come." With that, he hooked his coat on one fingertip and tossed it over his shoulder.

But his departure was forestalled when heavy footfalls sounded on the pathway. Frederica looked up to see Lord Treyhern striding toward the shop, stripping off his coat as he came. He stopped short in the doorway and glared at his brother, his eyes hot with rage. *Good God, surely he hadn't overheard?* No, it wasn't possible.

"Frederica," the earl snapped without really looking at her. "Go back to the house."

Frederica drew back an inch. "I beg your pardon?"

"Go—back—to—the—house," Treyhern growled. "Go *now*. I shall deal with this."

Bentley hurled his own coat back down. "Damn it, by whose authority do you order my wife around?"

Treyhern was already rolling up his shirtsleeves. This looked grim. "Leave now, Frederica," he warned again. "Don't make me carry you, for I will if I must."

Bentley took a step closer to his brother. "Sod off, Saint Cam!" he snarled. "She's my wife."

Frederica's patience snapped. "No," she corrected. "No, I don't think so."

Bentley narrowed his eyes at her. "Freddie!"

Frederica tried to look haughty instead of hurt. "Don't 'Freddie' me!" she challenged. "You practically divorced me not two minutes ago! So why don't you just—just *sod off* yourself!" And on that note, she spun around and swished off, trembling with hurt and fury.

Bentley watched his wife stalk back up the path, wondering if she had any clue what she'd just said. He didn't see his brother hurl his waistcoat to the floor. And he certainly didn't see his fist come flying out of nowhere. But he felt it connect quite solidly with his jawbone. Bentley went hurtling backward, the edge of the church door catching him squarely in the lower spine. As he flailed for balance, Cam snared him by the shirt collar and dragged him up again.

Bentley didn't bother asking what he'd done—hell, there was no telling—so he pitched himself into the fray with mindless fury. On a quick bob, he missed the next fist and came up swinging. By God, he wanted to smash someone's face, and right now, smashing Cam's suited him just fine. Apparently, he was to see some luck at it, too. He caught Cam square in the nose, snapping his neck back, causing blood to spurt.

"You worthless scoundrel!" Cam roared, spittling red. "I'll teach you to go round punching innocent young ladies in the face." He tossed a regular rounder, but Bentley dodged it.

"I never punched anyone!" he shouted back, throwing a low blow to Cam's gut. It connected, and Cam landed on his arse, splayed limply across the dirt floor.

But Bentley had scrapped with his brother too often to count him out. Sure enough, Cam came up like a regular Tom Crib, one fist to the belly, then a knee almost square in Bentley's ballocks.

"Aaggh!" Bentley clutched himself. But a little ducking and jabbing, and somehow he forced Cam across the room. His brother was fast, but Bentley was experienced. A low blow to the diaphragm had Cam clutching his ribs and gagging. It was then that he caught Cam solidly in the jaw, pitching him back against the forge.

Never one to miss a good mill, Angus had come back into the shop. With a speed that defied his age, the old man grabbed his hammer just as Cam's skull cracked sickly against the stone, right where the hammer had rested.

Bentley had him then. He bent over Cam, chest to chest, forcing him back until the acrid stench of scorching hair drifted up. The coals still roared red-hot. Cam looked backward, wild-eyed, at the heat. Another six inches, and his shirt would be afire.

Old Angus tossed his hammer down with disgust. "Oh, I wouldna be sae quick a-killing my own blood kin, laddie!"

But Cam wasn't out. With one last grunt, he rammed his knee straight up.

God damn, not the knackers again! Gagging, Bentley let loose and collapsed into the dirt. Cam staggered up from the forge and stood looking scornfully down. "Don't—you—ever—" he panted. "Hit—that—girl—again."

Bentley lurched up onto his knees. "Go to hell, Sir Lancelot!" he spat. "You self-righteous prick!"

Old Angus had begun to wheeze with laughter. Cam,

unfortunately, had caught his breath. "You!" he roared, jabbing a finger at Angus. "You I can fire, you moth-eaten, mean-tempered old Scot!"

Old Angus just slapped his knee and wheezed louder. "Oh, good Lord, Cam, leave him be!" grunted Bentley, wobbling to his feet. "At least you've most of your hair left."

Cam turned his lordly glower on Bentley, but the effect was spoilt by the blood which had spewed from his nostrils. "And you!" he gritted, dragging his shirt-sleeve under his nose. "If you ever raise your hand to that child—hell, if you so much as raise your voice to her—I mean to finish this, do you hear me? And, by God, you won't walk away next time."

But Bentley had had enough. He snatched his coat from the dirt floor. "It was an accident, Cam," he snarled, stalking out of the workshop. "If you don't believe me, ask Freddie! God knows she's mad enough to tell you the truth."

Cam crossed his arms over his chest. "And just where do you think you're going?"

"Ask Freddie that, too," snapped Bentley, heading up the path toward the stables.

Chapter Twenty

In which Mrs. Rutledge receives a Birthday gift.

On the day her husband disappeared, Frederica locked herself in his bedchamber and cried for six hours straight. The burden she carried was awful, the loss of her marriage worse. And the most miserable part of it was, she had no one to confide in. She really had come to rely on Bentley—not just as a lover but as a friend, too. It was a startling realization, especially when she ought to hate him. Well, perhaps not hate. Whatever he was, she loved him. She was afraid she always would. And she had never felt so alone or so confused in all her eighteen years.

As the sun began to sink in a violet haze, Frederica crawled off the bed with one of Bentley's handkerchiefs clutched in her fist. It smelled like him, which made her misery all the worse. Snuffling, she went to the window and watched the path from the stables, just in case. But there was nothing. Darkness fell and, with it, an awful silence. Frederica began to fear she'd made a dreadful mistake. But there was no one—least of all Helene or Lord Treyhern—whom she could ask for advice. Oh, how she missed her family! Especially Zoë. And, strangely, Aunt Winnie. She understood men, and nothing shocked her. Frederica returned to the bed and fell into a fitful sleep, wondering whether to write to her.

The following morning, she got up late, had another good cry, then washed her face in cold water. She did not know what to say or do. Certainly, she did not know what to tell Bentley's family. The truth, perhaps, so far as she was able. It certainly would not do to just lie in bed and feel sorry for herself. One could wallow in misery only so long before self-respect was lost, and hers was wearing thin.

After ringing for Jennie, she packed up Cassandra's books, determined to return them to the blanket chest. But when Jennie came, she brought a message. "A stable boy come over from Bellevue afore breakfast, miss," she explained, shaking the wrinkles from Frederica's night-dress. "He said as how his mistress was wishing to see you today. She's to be in the vestry 'til noon, he said. And at home after that."

Frederica dressed in silence, wondering what Joan could possibly want. Had she already heard of Bentley's departure? Good Lord, did the whole village know Frederica's husband had left her? With a heavy tread, she went down to breakfast. Only Helene remained at the table.

"Do not despair of Bentley, my dear," she said, dispensing advice as she poured Frederica's coffee. "He'll be back. He always comes back, once his temper settles."

Frederica pushed away her plate. "I mayn't want him back," she complained. "I think a marriage is rather too important to be shoved aside with so little explanation."

"You are right," Helene acknowledged, sitting back down. "But he loves you, and he will figure all that out. And he'll apologize profusely, too. Just give him time."

Frederica lifted her gaze to meet Helene. "Do you think he loves me?"

She smiled vaguely. "Oh, he would never have married you, Frederica, if he did not." Helene sounded quite confident. "Trust me, Bentley does nothing unless he chooses to. He has been that way all of his adult life. Though as a child, I remember him as very sweet and biddable."

Her words confused Frederica. "Did . . . did you know him as a child?"

Helene blushed. "Oh, I lived here for a time as a girl," she murmured. "When Bentley was just a toddling babe. Had you not heard that old gossip? My mother, Marie, was Randolph's mistress."

Frederica almost gasped. *Marie?* But that was the name in Randolph's naughty book! Was that Helene's mother? Her blush had deepened. "But I went away to school in Switzerland when I turned seventeen," Helene continued. "Then Cam married, and I did not see the family again for many years."

Federica put down her cup. "Excuse me," she murmured, shoving back her chair. "I fear I have no appetite. I believe I will go for a walk."

Helene reached across the table and laid her hand over Frederica's. "I will leave you, then, to your privacy, my dear," she said softly. "But do not fret, for the babe's sake, yes? And if you want someone to talk to, you need only let me know."

Frederica nodded, then made her way from the dining room. Helene was so kind, and every inch a lady. How odd that the mysterious Marie had been her mother. There was a shocking tale hidden there, Frederica didn't doubt. Good Lord, was she the only one at Chalcote without a deep, dark secret?

Outside, the morning was quite cool, but Frederica walked almost blindly to St. Michael's without her cloak. She found Joan in the vestry, darning a choir robe. Bentley's cousin laid down her needle and rose at once, seizing Frederica by the hands. "Oh, thank you for coming," she said. "I was not at all sure you would after . . . after whatever has happened. Not that I know what has happened, mind. But Bentley did say—"

Frederica cut her off. "You have seen him?" she asked eagerly.

A little sadly, Joan shook her head. "My dear, I have not," she said quietly. "But there was something I was, well, preparing for you. For your birthday, I think? Really, I'm not perfectly sure. But late last night, Bentley left word at Bellevue that I was to give it to you now. And I was to give you this note which he left for you."

"My birthday?" Frederica took the two papers Joan thrust at her. "But that's months away. I can't imagine Bentley even knows the date."

"He said it was in December," Joan assured her. "Though I told him it was a vast deal of money to spend without so much as asking your opinion first."

"*My* opinion?" Frederica stared blankly at the papers. One was a note, fastened in red wax with Bentley's seal. The second was a thickly rolled document, tied in blue ribbon.

Joan looked suddenly nervous. "Oh, I really do not

like this," she murmured. "I wonder if I am making a mistake. I think Bentley has put me in a very bad position, and I should like to box his ears."

Frederica collapsed into a chair. "Am I . . . am I to open these?"

Joan shrugged. "That's what he told my butler," she said. "The rolled paper first. He was quite clear about that."

Frederica untied the ribbon. It was a legal document, affixed with various seals and signatures. She peered at it more closely. It was a deed. A deed to . . . *what?*

"Bellevue," said Joan, as if reading her mind. "That is the deed to Bellevue. It includes half of Chalcote's original acreage, just as it was willed to Mama." Then she laughed a little nervously. "It must stay in the family, you know, else Grandpapa John will haunt me all the way to Australia."

Frederica felt deeply confused. "I'm sorry," she blurted. "To Australia?"

Joan looked perplexed. "Basil and I are moving to Australia," she said. "Good heavens, didn't Bentley tell you?"

Frederica shook her head. "Not a word."

Joan laughed. "Oh, that would be just like him! I told him in confidence, yes. But I did not mean him to keep it from his wife!"

The deed trembled in Frederica's hands. Suddenly, at least a part of Bentley's surreptitious conversation with Joan made sense. "I do not understand," she whispered. "Are we to have . . . has Bentley bought . . . Bellevue? For me?"

Joan's face fell. "You do not care for it?" she cried. "I

mean, I realize it is rather large and almost frightfully elegant. But Bentley seemed so sure. He said you had remarked how much you loved Gloucestershire and that you longed for a house of your own."

Frederica wanted to cry. "But Bellevue is so gorgeous," she whispered. "Perhaps the most beautiful home I have ever seen."

Joan relaxed into her chair. "Oh, good!" she sighed. "It is to be yours, then. I never fancied selling it outside the family, so Bentley's offer was a godsend. Now, my dear, I suspect you should read that note in private. I have no notion what it says, but if Bentley wrote it in a temper, it will just be a pack of nonsense."

Frederica tried to hand the deed back. "Thank you, Joan," she said. "But I really don't know—that is to say—I might be going back to Essex for a time."

Joan eyed her stubbornly. "Oh, no, you shan't!" she insisted. "Do not step one toe out of this county! Bentley will just have to straighten himself out."

Frederica looked at her, curious. "Do you think he needs straightening out?"

But Joan looked away and began to fold the choir robes. "We all do, don't we?" she answered vaguely. "Some, perhaps, more than others."

Frederica gathered her courage. "You know about Cassandra, don't you?" she whispered. "I overheard you once, in the nave, with Bentley."

Joan's hands had frozen in mid-motion. "Oh, do not ask me about that," she whispered. "Oh, please do not! Once, we shared everything, Bentley and I. But now . . . well, you must speak to your husband."

"I'm sorry," Frederica answered. "But I never know

whom to ask about anything. I don't even know how she died."

For a heartbeat, Joan was silent. "We aren't sure." She was staring down at the stack of robes. "But the whole sordid tale was common gossip. Cassandra had a long affair with Thomas, my husband's cousin. He was our former rector."

Frederica's brows went up. "The *rector?*"

Faintly, Joan smiled. "Appalling, isn't it? And when she ended it, Thomas took it badly. They quarreled. A lamp was knocked over; an accident, we think. Cassandra died in the fire."

"Oh, my God." Frederica slowly sat back down. "And Thomas? What became of him?"

Joan's gaze flicked up from the robes, oddly emotionless. "Do you not know?" she asked very softly. "Bentley killed him. Shot him straight through the heart. He had no choice. Thomas was quite mad, you see. He had taken Helene and Ariane hostage. Did Bentley tell you none of this?"

For an instant, Frederica could not breathe. Could not think. It was as if the walls suddenly pressed in on her. She managed to shake her head. Later, she barely remembered taking her leave of Joan, but somehow, she made her way back through the chancel. A sheet of heavy canvas covered the gaping hole where the door had been taken down. Frederica pushed through it, then sat down on the doorstep to gather her thoughts.

Good Lord, she almost wished she had not asked Joan about Cassandra. Bentley had killed this man, Thomas? How appalling. And yet, he had had no choice. He had been placed, it seemed, in an untenable position. What must he have felt? What must he still feel? She remembered his letter then and pulled it from her pocket. His heavy scrawl was unmistakable.

> *My dear wife,*
> *I am aware that I have broken our agreement. Such, I daresay, is my honor. I hope you will enjoy Bellevue in good health. If it does not suit, contact my broker in Lombard Street. Stoddard is authorized to cover your expenses, including the purchase of another property. In this regard, please yourself, as it seems I am incapable of doing so. I will wait to hear the news of the birth. Kindly write to me at Roselands Cottage, North End Way, Hampstead.*
>
> > *With all respect,*
> > *R.B.R.*

Frederica's hands began to shake. She read the note again. *Oh, God.* This was it, then. He really had left her. And she had brought it on herself. She had made unreasonable demands. She had asked him to do something he was unable to do. Something which really had little bearing on them. On their future together. Was that right? God, she was so mixed up! Perhaps marriage did not mean one got the chance to pick apart the past. Perhaps it meant only that one deserved fidelity and affection in the here and now.

Frederica thought again of the deed Joan had given her. *Bentley had bought Bellevue?* It boggled the mind. And so he had been planning for the future, albeit in his own rather ham-fisted fashion. He had been trying.

Trying on many fronts, both of them. But would they have succeeded? She would never know now. She had spoilt it. Yesterday, she'd been quite confident in the rightness of her actions. Now, having seen the horror in her husband's face—and having spent the first of what might be a lifetime of nights alone—she was not so sure.

Frederica felt the hot well of tears again. It was time to go and have a good cry. But it would have to be her last, she vowed. She had a child to consider. And because of that, she was going to return to her family. Perhaps she was weak, but she did not think she could bear to go through this without their support. Resolved, she stood and shoved Bentley's note into her pocket.

It was then that she noticed the workmen on the hill by the yew trees. One of them turned, tossed a shovel onto his cart, and led his horse down the hill toward the village gate. In the empty spot in the last row of graves, she could see that a new marker had been set. *Cassandra's gravestone.* For reasons she could not begin to explain, Frederica wanted to see it. Would doing so make it all seem less harrowing? Would it prove the past was dead?

When she reached the top of the hill, the workmen were latching the gate. Frederica stood alone in the shade of the yew tree, staring down at the smooth, honey-colored stone. Irrationally, she wanted to hate this woman who was dead and gone. She wanted to hate her for what she had been able to reach out and taint, even from the grave.

No, seeing it did not help. Saddened, Frederica turned and started away. But halfway down the slope, something began to nag at her. As if pulled by a magnet, she walked back and glanced at the stone again. *The dates.* The dates were wrong. She stared at them, her hand trembling. She fell to her knees, her skirts pooling in the grass and fresh earth, and leaned forward to touch the last line. The year of Cassandra's death. The newly cut stone was rough as she traced it with a trembling finger. A cold realization was creeping over her.

God. Oh, God. *That could not be right.* Could it? Cassandra Rutledge had been dead better than a dozen years? But Bentley would have been . . . just a boy.

He was Gervais's age when they married, Catherine had said that day in the churchyard. *But Cassandra was not the nurturing type.*

Frederica felt nausea roil up in her throat, choking her. Good God! How could she have misunderstood? She had thought . . . she had assumed . . . *what?* The worst. Yes, she had believed the worst of her own husband—but no worse than he'd come to believe of himself. He had spoken of this, an appalling horror, with such icy detachment, it was as if he spoke of someone else and not himself at all.

I did it. I did whatever she wanted.

You don't understand. My head is like a bloody floodgate, and if I open it . . .

If I open it . . .

Frederica was still touching the gravestone. Horrified, she jerked back her hand as if scalded. And then she stumbled to her feet and flew through the cemetery, through the door in the wall, and all the way up the hill to Chalcote. Once inside, Frederica hastened through the cool, shadowy corridors, pushing open doors and flying up the stairs unhesitatingly. The garden suite was unlocked. She burst into the bedchamber and fell to her knees before the blanket chest. Without pausing to think, she jerked open the drawer and began to rip out Cassandra's journals, one at a time, until her arms were so full she could carry no more. Leaving the last two or three in the open drawer, she raced down the stairs and into Bentley's bedchamber, where she dumped the journals in a heap beneath the bank of windows.

She sat down, opening the first one she seized. Frantically, she read. At first, there were only veiled allusions. No proof. Just dark suggestions and sarcastic asides, separated by days, even months, of narcissistic drivel. For hours, Frederica kept reading, her heart growing leaden in her chest. She refused to see anyone who knocked. In the early afternoon, she finally accepted a luncheon tray from Queenie, but only for the babe's sake. While she ate, she returned to her vigil. As the light faded away to nothing, Frederica closed the last of the books with a hand that trembled.

Cassandra had been no fool. She'd been clever in her seduction. Oh, so very clever. And wicked beyond human comprehension. But it was there, between the lines, for anyone to see. The truth. The horror. Why had no one noticed what was happening? He had been a boy. Who was supposed to watch over him? *Protect* him?

Cam wouldn't have given a damn, anyway, Bentley had said. *If he had, maybe he'd have noticed.*

Answers. More answers. Oh, dear God, were they all there? If one had the courage to look? Somewhere in the depths of the house, a clock struck six, the sound low and mournful. And finally, Frederica gave way to that one last cry she had promised herself on the doorstep of St. Michael's. She cried from the bottom of her heart and the depths of her soul; deep, wracking sobs of despair which left her shoulders shaking and her ribs almost bruised. But this time, it was not herself for whom she cried.

Along the post roads of England, there were a thousand waysides like the Cat and Currier, places neither especially mean nor particularly dirty but with few pretensions to elegance. The Cat sported a dark, narrow taproom, a spartan dining room with a private nook or two, and, above it all, a half-dozen rooms to let. Situated as it was between Cheston-on-the-Water and greater London, Bentley frequented it often, for the Cat was the sort of place one could get a clean, louse-free bed and, if a man were so inclined, a clean, louse-free bedmate to warm it. And afterward, a game of dice or cards, perhaps a tad less clean, was easily had.

But Bentley didn't know what the hell he'd had when he woke up on this particular morning. Or was it even morning? Damned if he knew. Someone, however, had the gall to be pounding on his door. Well, damn them, too. With a grunt, Bentley rolled over.

But the rapping on the door grew louder and faster, until it was a great, thunderous tattoo in his brain. "Mr. Rutledge!" cried a shrill voice. "Mr. Rutledge, sir, it is half past noon! I must know if you mean to keep the room. And there is that small matter of last night's, er, expenses."

"Ummph," Bentley managed to groan.

The innkeeper took that as a sign of reluctance.

"No, I really must insist, sir!" The shrill voice notched higher. "These debts must be settled. There was a vast deal of damage to my taproom."

Bentley buried his head in his pillow. "Aw, fuck all!" he groaned. But sudden guilt stabbed him. *Why?* Then he remembered. Freddie had asked him not to use that word. And as foolish as it seemed, he'd meant to oblige her. Even if she wasn't to be around to hear—or, in this case, not to hear. Jesus Christ, his brains had turned to mush. Or perhaps they'd been flushed out through his kidneys in dribs and drabs by the gallons of brandy he'd apparently drunk last night.

But it had all been for naught, hadn't it? There wasn't enough liquor in all of Christendom to make him forget his wife. To make him stop missing her. To make him stop longing for the taste of her in his mouth and the warmth of her hand in his. Nothing had changed, and yet everything was different. They were as one. *They were.*

He didn't even know how or when it had happened. He knew only that he might as well cleave out his own heart, for, apart from her, he could not survive. He'd had time to think. Time to consider what she'd demanded. And now he knew. It was time to go home. Time to beg for forgiveness. First, God help him, from his brother. Then from his wife. She had left him no choice. He only prayed it was not too late.

In the passageway, the innkeeper was beginning to enumerate the smashed windows, broken tables, and shattered crockery which he'd been obliged to cart away. And then there was, apparently, the small matter of a missing mantelpiece. Good Lord, he was getting too old for this. What had he done last night? And with whom? Bentley remembered nothing—which had been, he supposed, his intent.

Suddenly, a second voice joined the fray. " 'Ad bit o' highjinks last night, ducks?" asked a perky female voice. "Aw, don't fret. Rutledge is good for the blunt. Now, just 'and me that key, wot?"

Beyond the heavy door, the innkeeper made an indignant noise. Curious, Bentley tried to sit up. In the corridor, a tussle ensued. "Aw, now be a good chap, an' give me that key," said the female amidst a good deal of grunting and thumping.

"Madam!" huffed the innkeeper. "This is a respectable inn!"

"Aye, an' I'm respectable as the old queen 'erself, God rest 'er!"

Another thump, a few more grunts, and Bentley heard the key scrape into the lock. Queenie burst into the room, her bosom leading like the prow of a battleship. The diminutive innkeeper was on her heels, leaping about like some overzealous rat terrier, trying to snatch back his key.

Irritated, Queenie spun about and slapped it into his hand. "Orf w'you then, me fine fellow," she said. "I've private business 'ere."

"I daresay your sort would," he said nastily. "Still, there is the small matter of what's owing for the damage."

Bold as brass, Queenie hiked up her skirts to reveal a plump, milk-white thigh with a green morocco purse strapped to it. The innkeeper gasped and averted his eyes. "This 'ere is wot you call an old-age pension, ducks," she chortled, extracting a banknote. She shoved it under his nose. The innkeeper took the hand from his eyes and gasped again. "Now, back downstairs, ducks, before I break one o' your arms," suggested Queenie sweetly. "Then send up a pot of strong coffee, two raw eggs, and a tankard of stout."

The innkeeper hastened away. Bentley wobbled up onto one elbow, the bedcovers slipping down to his waist. "My coat," he rasped, pointing an unsteady finger at a heap of clothing in the floor. "I'm paying you back, Queenie. Then get the hell out." But the room was spinning, and Bentley was forced to flop back down.

"I'll not be leaving without you, Mr. B., 'cause yer did me a good turn once, an' old Queenie ain't forgot it." She slid an arm beneath his shoulders and hefted him back up again. "So let's walk it off, eh?"

"Get out, blister it!" he growled. "I'm not decent."

"Ooh, lawks!" said Queenie in mock horror. "Me delicate sensibilities!"

Soon Bentley found himself sitting on the edge of the bed in his drawers. The room had almost stopped spinning. Queenie was peering into his eyes. "Yer do look a tad rough, Mr. B.," she said briskly. "But a tub o' hot water, some fresh togs, an' you'll be your fine old self again."

Bentley let his face fall forward into his hands. He'd left Chalcote too quickly to put up a change of gear. What a charming sight he'd make when he arrived home in filthy clothes and a stubbled beard. Freddie wouldn't want to forgive him.

But Queenie was gesturing at a valise by the door. "Packed 'em meself with none the wiser," she said proudly. "Forgot the razor an' strop, though. Then Milford sent the coachman ter drive me here, just like a fine lady. O' course it took us all day to run you to ground."

Bentley was on his feet. Queenie went to the door and bellowed for a tub of hot water. A harried serving maid rushed in with a tray, and, quick as a wink, Queenie mixed up a tankard of something frightful and forced it down his throat. A tub was carried in. Brass cans of steaming water followed. And through it all, she scolded and cajoled.

" 'Ow long yer been foxed?" she asked at one point. " 'Tis two days you've been gone from Chalcote, and poor Mrs. Rutledge is beside 'erself."

Two days? Where the devil had he been for two days? Bentley had vague memories of having won a small fortune at a boxing match somewhere. And even vaguer recollections of having lost it again in an all-night hazard game. But beyond that, memory failed. "Good Lord, Queenie," he muttered. "I have to get home."

Queenie dragged a screen before the tub and shoved him behind it. "Aye, that you do, Mr. B.," she said. "She's leaving, see? And 'er ladyship's in an awful taking over it."

His drawers half off, Bentley froze. "Who's leaving?"

"Mrs. Rutledge," said Queenie's disembodied voice. "That scraggly little maid o' hers fetched down the trunks from the attic, and the two of 'em were packing faster than the cat could lick 'er ear. Heading out at first light, they are."

Disappointment crushed him. But what had he expected? "I might just have to live with that, Queenie," said Bentley softly. "Frederica and I . . . well, we have an understanding."

Queenie snorted. "Maybe *you* do," she snipped. "But mark me, that wife o' yours don't understand nothing but she's got a babe in her belly and no husband ter 'elp raise it."

Bentley groaned and stepped into the water. "Don't do this to me, Queenie. I'm begging you."

"Aye, shut up in that room, she is, and crying the live-long day, I don't doubt," Queenie continued from a distant corner. He could hear her snapping the wrinkles from his clothes and then opening the valise she'd brought. "Won't eat, neither," she added on a heavy sigh. "Poor little mite won't be no bigger'n a squirrel when it comes."

The child. God, she was talking about the child.

Then Queenie's voice became sterner still. "So I'm packing up yer things, Mr. B. And yer going to make it up to 'er. Whatever it takes."

"I mean to try," he said, hastily soaping up. And he did. Because even he couldn't stay drunk much longer without doing himself some serious harm. Perhaps it was age, or just disinclination, but he could no longer run far enough, or wild enough, to escape it. Besides, this time, what had his running gained him? Hell, he hadn't even made it past Oxfordshire.

Still, two days of drunkenness hadn't washed away the memory of Freddie's last demand. But if he did as she asked, then Bentley would have no brother. As it was, however, he had no wife. Slowly, that little conundrum was coming clear to him.

Yes, it was a deal with the devil, this thing Freddie

was pushing him toward. But maybe it was the lesser evil. He loved Cam, yes. More than he wished to admit. Yet he was just so tired of this miserable, peripatetic life he'd been living. Tired of having no hearth, no home, no family of his own. And God help him if he didn't miss her. If he drank enough to get past that, they'd be shoveling dirt on his coffin.

He was sitting motionless in the tub when Queenie's voice cut into his consciousness. "Mr. B.?" she said, her tone gentler. "Look sharp now, ducks. It's a goodly ways home."

"Ah, Queenie," he whispered. "Those might be the truest words you've ever spoken."

Chapter Twenty-one

A Sad ending & a New beginning.

Some hours later, Bentley found himself standing before his brother's study, his hand lifted as if he'd every intention of knocking. God, it was a bloody hard thing to do. He wished he had a guinea for every time he'd stood in this same place, and feeling just this way, his stomach churning, his heart weighed down with that awful mix of guilt and anger, and always, always expecting trouble.

But this time, fate took charge, and the door jerked open, leaving him nose to nose with his brother. And what a beauty of a nose it was. Black and blue, the thing was swollen twice its size, with a streak of yellow dashed beneath the left eye for good measure. Broken. Badly. That was Bentley's expert assessment. And when the swelling went down, there would likely be a lump in the middle to forever mar his brother's beauty. If he hadn't been so heartsick, Bentley would have taunted the old boy unmercifully.

The earl's expression was inscrutable. "You look a nasty piece of work, old chap," he said, stepping back to let Bentley in. "A two-day drunk? Or has shaving gone out of fashion?"

Bentley rolled at once onto the balls of his feet. "If I am not welcome, Cam," he said quietly, "just bloody well say so."

With a crooked smile, Cam headed toward the hearth, settled into his favorite chair, and motioned to the one opposite. A kitten darted from beneath the desk, and, absently, Cam scooped it up. The thing was all legs and tail now, a pretty gray tabby. They would need a cat at Bellevue, Bentley mused. If they were going to Bellevue at all. He shut the door and joined his brother.

Cam cleared his throat almost formally. "Bentley, you must know that you've always been welcome here," he said, stroking one hand down the kitten. "I've never understood why you are forever suggesting otherwise. I'm glad you're home, and I know Frederica is deeply relieved."

Bentley let his gaze drop. "She does not know."

Cam's lips thinned in irritation. "Good Lord, Bentley, she has been beside herself with worry! You must go to her at once."

"I cannot," Bentley said quietly. "She won't have me. There's something I must do first. And when I'm done, Cam, I'll grant you one good punch before you throw me out for good. I suggest you aim for the nose."

Cam snorted. "Yes, mine's a damned ugly sight," he admitted. "But I won't be needing your free shot, Bentley. Frederica explained how she came by her bruise." He shook his head and swallowed hard. "Christ, I knew in my heart you'd never do such a thing. I beg you will forgive me. My nerves seem frayed of late."

"I can sympathize," muttered Bentley. "But it's no matter."

"It matters greatly to me," Cam answered. "I accused you of something deeply dishonorable, and I was wrong."

"Well, this conversation isn't finished yet."

Cam just looked at him strangely. "Go on, then. What do you wish to say?"

But Bentley couldn't find the words, could barely catch his breath. Good God, how did a man confess what had been hidden most of his life? "It's—well, it's about Cassandra."

Both Cam's brows shot up at that. "What can she possibly have to do with anything?"

"Signora Castelli says the past always bleeds into the present," Bentley whispered. When Cam just looked at him, he closed his eyes, and thought of all that was at stake. It was time to start talking, if he meant to do the job at all. "I want to tell you straight out, Cam," he began. "For there's no way to pretty this one up. Cassandra and I—well, we had this . . . there was a . . . thing between us."

Cam cocked his head to one side. "A thing?"

"Yes." Bentley drew in a deep breath and felt the walls begin to press in on him. "A physical—no, goddamn it!—a *sexual* thing."

Cam jerked upright in his chair, and the kitten bounded softly to the floor. "Cassandra who?" His voice was hollow, incredulous. "Not . . . oh, no. No, Bentley. You cannot possibly mean—"

Bentley cut him off. "For a long time, Cam," he interjected, hoping to stave off panic. "And the hell of it is, I knew it was wrong. It felt wrong. Bad. So I can't think how I justified it—in my own mind, I mean. But I guess I did. She said it was my fault, and I daresay it was. She said I was wicked—and I was. Everyone knows that. And what's worse, Cam, I was glad when she died. *Glad.* And I'm ashamed of that, too."

"You slept with my wife." Cam's voice was devoid of emotion. "Or, better put, my wife slept with you."

Nodding, Bentley stared into the blackened depths of the hearth. With minute concentration, he forced himself to exhale and then to drag in another breath, willing away the awful terror.

"Did Father know?" The earl's voice was a low growl. "Damn it, did he?"

Bentley couldn't look at his brother. "Yes," he whispered. "He would laugh and wink at me. He thought it a great joke. But I never—good God, Cam—I never thought it was a joke. I don't know what I thought. I just knew it was wicked. But I didn't stop. I don't know why."

He kept waiting for Cam to leap from his chair and pummel the living daylights out of him. But Cam seemed more distraught than angry. "Bentley," he continued, his words slow and distinct. "Perhaps my memory fails me. You are not quite seven-and-twenty, is that right?"

"Not quite," he agreed.

Much of Cam's color had drained away. "And when my wife died—" He paused and shook his head as if to clear his vision. "When Cassandra died, you were what? Sixteen?"

"Thereabouts."

Something inside Cam snapped. "Thereabouts?" he exploded, coming half out of his chair. "The devil can take thereabouts and fly to hell with it! Tell me—how frigging old were you?"

Oh, it was a bad sign when Cam started cursing. "F-fifteen," Bentley whispered. "But I had put a stop to it long before then, Cam. I swear to God, I had."

Cam fell back into his chair. His hands were clenched on the chair arms, his eyes closed and his face twisted with some awful emotion. "Fifteen!" he whispered, as if mentally calculating. "And scarcely that, by God."

Bentley barely heard the last. He did not like the color of Cam's complexion. "I'm sorry, Cam," he whispered, wishing his brother would open his eyes. "I'm glad it's out. And Freddie's right—it's been eating me alive. I feel so—oh, I don't know—just dead inside sometimes." He stumbled on, unable to stop himself now, the words falling faster and faster. "I know you hate me. Hell, sometimes I hate you. Father pitted us against each other that way, and quite deliberately, too."

"Oh, dear God!" The words were choked. "He probably put her up to this!"

Bentley shrugged. "I just want you to know, Cam, that what I don't feel is jealousy. I swear, it was never that. I have never envied you your title or position. And no one envied you your marriage to Cassandra. I can't tell you how this has tortured me. But now I have Frederica, whether I deserve her or not. And I want so desperately to make a life for her. A life for us, together. Yet I have given her a disgust of me. My own wife. And she doesn't even know—" His voice choked. "God, she doesn't even know the worst of it. And already, I think she wonders if she oughtn't leave me. Indeed, she has promised to, if I don't confess everything."

"*Confess?*" Cam made a strange noise in the back of his throat, then jerked from his chair and strode across the room to the deep bay window. He set one hand at the back of his neck and the other on the window casing, half leaning into it. Was he considering the wisdom of pitching Bentley out of it? For a long moment, Cam was still as death, save for his shoulders, which seemed to tremble, as if he were restraining some torturous emotion. Bentley began to wonder what his fate would be. He felt suddenly cold. Sick to his stomach. Would it be as she'd always threatened?

Yes, go on, tell him! He could still see Cassandra's lush pink lips mouthing the words. Could feel her hot breath on his cheek. *Yes, tell him exactly what you did to me, Bentley. What I did to you. But tell him how it felt, too, my precious. For you'll need that memory to warm you after he's turned you out into the street.*

Oh, Christ! Bentley closed his eyes. What had he set in motion? Was he to be turned away from his child-hood home, never to be allowed to return? And whom would Cam tell? Helene? Everyone? He wore his shame like a mantle of lead. It had been years since he'd cried, but now he felt that hot, dreadful surge behind his eyes.

Yes, confess it all, hissed the silky voice in his head. *Go on—tell him how it is with us. After all, you are so very good at it.*

"Oh, Bentley, I am appalled that I did not notice this!" Cam rasped from the window. "Oh, there were hints—deliberate ones, I daresay—when I look back." He made the strange choking sound in the back of his throat again, and it was only then that Bentley realized his brother was crying.

Bentley half rose from his chair. "Good Lord, Cam, you mustn't think—"

But Cam spun around to face him. "*Think?*" he choked. "I wasn't thinking! And I wasn't watching, either. That was the very trouble, wasn't it? My God! My God! Why has this never occurred to me? Am I a total idiot? I mean, she seduced my bloody rector, so it's not hard to believe she'd seduce a child, is it? But I noticed neither. I am ashamed, Bentley. Deeply ashamed."

In his fear and confusion, Bentley missed the point. "Now, Cam, I did not know she'd once been Thomas Lowe's lover," he said hastily. "I swear, not until I overheard him quarreling with her. Not that that makes anything I did any less ugly. I would like to pretend I was innocent of it all, but Cam, we both know that just isn't true."

Cam searched Bentley's face, his eyes aflame with some nameless emotion. "You were exposed to a world of sin and debauchery," he whispered, his hands drawing into fists. "But was that your fault? *No.* That was Father's doing, and I hope the devil's keeping him warm in hell for it."

"But I knew what I was doing," said Bentley quietly. "I knew."

Cam came at him then, crossing the room in three strides. "Oh, you knew, did you?" he hissed into Bentley's face, his cheeks still wet. "Tell me, then, how old were you when it started? Eleven? Twelve? Were you a virgin? Aye, of course you were. I see it in your eyes. And big for your age. Oh, Christ, that I remember! So, tell me, Bentley, how did it start? What did she do first? Fondle you? Kiss you? Deliberately expose herself?"

It was Bentley's turn to close his eyes. "Yes," he whispered. "All that."

Oh, God. All that and more. And it had been disgusting. Disgusting and fascinating and erotic, all at the same time. He had hated it, and wanted it. For months, it had felt as if his body belonged to someone else. As if he were just watching, some innocent bystander to a damning sin.

Cam's hand came down on his shoulder like a vise. "And then what, Bentley?" he demanded. "What next? Did she tempt you into her bed? Or just invite herself into yours?"

"Yes." He choked out the word. "That."

"When? How? Tell me!"

Bentley shook his head. "Oh, Lord. I just don't know," he whispered. "I don't remember. Does it matter?"

"Good God, of course it matters!" His brother's voice was fraught with emotion. "Tell me! Don't punish me for failing you. You think this is your fault? It's not, Bentley. It is not."

Bentley was deeply confused now. "One morning, then," he whispered. "In winter, I think. There was a dust of snow. And I woke up dreaming . . . something. God, I can't remember! You know how it is. You wake up hard as a bri—well, you know. And there she was, naked as the day God made her, already on . . . on t-t-top . . ." He couldn't get the rest of it out.

Cam's fingers dug into his shoulder. "God damn her!" His voice was an angry whisper. "God damn that bitch to hell!" Bentley could feel his brother's body shaking with rage.

"Cam?" Bentley whispered.

"How old?" he begged.

Bentley swallowed hard. "I don't know," he admitted truthfully. "I just don't know! Twelve, maybe? Or almost. That's all I'm sure of. Things like that are hard to remember."

"Bentley, things like that are not hard to remember." Cam had sat back down and let his face fall forward into his hands. "They are impossible to forget. And yet they are so appalling we can't think of them, so we . . . we put them away."

"Put them away? Away where?"

Cam gave a bitter laugh. "It is like this little black closet in our minds, Helene says," he whispered into the floor. "And she says that sometimes we shove bad things into it and try to lock the door. Yet they are always there. Always pushing and pounding and rattling the doorknob. And eventually, they get out. In a thousand little ways, they get out." Cam lifted his gaze and stared straight into his brother's eyes. "But listen to me, Bentley. This was not your fault. You were alone, with no responsible adult to turn to. I was always busy. Cat was just a girl. Father was useless. I wonder you survived it at all."

Bentley couldn't take it anymore. "Why are you whitewashing this, Cam?" he asked stridently. "For God's sake, don't make me out a saint! And don't make me out one of Helene's lunatics, either. I'm spilling my blood here. Hit me! Kick me! Call me out! I knew what I was doing. In a way, I enjoyed it. I must have. I kept doing it."

"Did you feel you had a choice?" he asked softly.

Oh, God. *He hadn't.* That was the appalling truth. He thought of all her demands, of the many trips he'd made down that long, dark passageway to her bedchamber with his heart in his throat and his palms sweating, and suddenly, his chest went tight. It was as if all the air had been sucked from the room. He couldn't breathe in. Blood pounded in his ears. His stomach turned. He felt—not like a man but like a child again, forced to admit his own weaknesses. Forced to admit he was—or had once been—at the mercy of others. It was a horrible thing. Humiliating. And in that instant, he wished the conversation were over. Wished it had never begun. And wondered if it wasn't easier, less painful, just to let Freddie go.

"Did you feel you had a choice?" Cam whispered.

Freddie. Oh, Freddie! He couldn't bear to lose her. Couldn't bear to lose his child. So he had to keep answering Cam's goddamned questions. "N-not at first," he admitted on a faint gasp. "She said . . . oh, hell! What does it matter?"

"It matters to you. You need to say it, Bentley. You need to get the words out."

Bentley drew a deeper breath and felt a hot, dreadful pressure behind his eyes. "I couldn't stop her," he rasped. "Once I'd given in to her that first time, she had me, and she knew it. I couldn't control myself, either. She loved that. She would laugh and say that a man couldn't, you know, *do* it unless he really wanted it."

"That is a lie!" Cam rasped.

"Is it?" asked Bentley. "I don't know. It seemed easier to just do it—to feel it and yet not feel it—kind of like pretending I was somewhere else. To just go through the motions until she was pleased, and I was . . . oh, hell, Cam! It was like some awful rash that you just can't keep from scratching, even though you know when you're done, your flesh will feel raw and bloody. And it did. Oh, Christ, it always did. And I thought if you found out, you would hate me. She said you would. She swore you'd turn me out."

"My God, what you must have been through," Cam whispered.

Bentley shook his head. "In the beginning, it wasn't so bad. She just . . . teased. She paid attention, Cam, and told me I was a handsome and charming young man. But then sh-she started touching. And saying things. And then she began t-t-to trick me into . . . into being alone with her. She would put her hands on me. And if I didn't return the gesture, she'd say she heard your footsteps. That she was going to call out your name. Or scream and tell you I'd forced her t-to touch me. Then she would laugh and say she was just teasing. So I tried to believe that. But you don't believe me, Cam, do you?"

"I believe you," he said sadly. "But I wish to God you'd told someone."

Sweat was beading on his forehead now. "I d-did tell," he whispered. "First, I told Joan. I told her when it started. The——the touching. The teasing. And then I told her about that first morning when I woke up to find Cassandra . . . on me. Joan insisted I tell Papa. And I did, Cam! But he just laughed, slapped me on the back, and told me I was the only real man he'd raised. He said you didn't want Cassandra and that someone had to do the job. He said it was good practice for me. So, after that, I kept my mouth shut."

Cam's fist crashed down on his chair arm. "He let you be hurt to spite me."

"I don't know." Bentley shrugged again. "But if I tried to refuse, she'd make it sound so . . . not innocent, no—I shan't insult your intelligence by claiming that—but just *physical*. She would cry and say that she was so lonely. She would corner me in the library or an empty corridor and t-touch me. And touch herself all over and say that she ached for it and that you w-wouldn't . . ."

"You're damned right, I wouldn't," rasped Cam. "I wasn't about to risk having an heir of uncertain parentage. You know what she and her friends were like. I daresay this was a part of her revenge on me for sending them away. First Lowe, until she tired of him. And then you. She used you, Bentley, just to get at me."

Bentley couldn't make sense of it all. "I—I don't know."

The hand clamped onto his shoulder again. "How long did it go on, Bentley?"

"I don't remember."

Cam's expression was pleading. "Tell me, Bentley," he begged. "Can't you see, I have to know? It was my duty to protect you. It is little wonder you have spent the last fifteen years being angry with me."

Bentley shook his head. He felt numb now. He didn't understand why his brother was going on so. "Cam, I was almost grown," he whispered. "I did not look to you for protection. And I certainly did not blame you. Lord, I hope I didn't. Did I?"

"Of course you did!" Cam whispered. "I failed you, and in your heart, you had to know it! You were a child, no matter what Father told you. I think I convinced myself that you were too much like Father. That you were beyond managing."

Bentley closed his eyes and swallowed. "You do not hate me?"

"How could I hate you?" Cam answered, his voice gentler. "I never have. I love you. All that I've ever done, Bentley, I've done for us, for you, Catherine, and me. But, Bentley, I'll never forgive myself for this. I was always so busy with crops and land and tenants. Always worrying over our finances and our reputation, when there were more important things."

Bentley felt as if he were slipping into some sort of dreamlike state. "Oh, I'm over it now, Cam," he lied. But this time, oddly, he *knew* he lied. "And to be honest, I've since done stranger things. This bloody world is full of women with bizarre appetites, and I've tried to please most of them. In some ways, the things Cassandra wanted me to do with her seem almost tame now."

"Well, I wonder why, Bentley," said Cam, his voice choking again.

Bentley smiled a little crookedly. "I didn't do everything she wanted, you know," he said. "Not always. And if I could refuse her some things—why, then I could have refused her everything, couldn't I? But I didn't. Not until I found out she'd been Lowe's lover first. And somehow, that just . . . well, it struck me as wrong. Just *wrong*. I mean, I knew I was nothing but Randy Rutledge's wicked little scapegrace. I knew I would never amount to anything, for I'd heard it whispered behind my back a thousand times. But Thomas Lowe was the rector! A man of God. Oh, I might have been a bit buggered-up in the head, Cam, but I knew that was not right."

"You hold yourself too cheap," said Cam softly.

Slowly, it was dawning on Bentley that his brother truly did not blame him, that Cam was not interested in vengeance or punishment. Instead, he seemed grief-stricken. Was Cam right? Was the sin Cassandra's and not his? Had Cam failed him? And had a part of him blamed Cam for it all these years?

"You remember I said I once heard her quarreling with Lowe?" Bentley interjected into the silence. "He was threatening to tell you everything, Cam—not just about their affair but everything—if she did not resume the relationship. Afterward, she panicked. She was desperate to get away and begged me to take her to London."

"You?" Cam lifted his gaze. "Take her to London?"

"She'd planned it all out." Bentley smiled bitterly. "I was to say I wished to read Latin at one of the schools in London. I was to wheedle and say it was my new ambition to prepare for a law career. And then she was to say she felt it her duty to accompany me and to open up the house in Mortimer Street. She said you would be so pleased I'd found a goal in life, and so happy I'd formed a maternal attachment to her, that you would agree."

"Well, she was a bloody lunatic," muttered Cam.

"I think she was by then," said Bentley softly. "I refused her, and she threatened me. She said she'd see you turned me out and that Papa couldn't stop you because you had become too rich and too powerful."

"Oh, Bentley!" whispered Cam.

Bentley shrugged. "I believed her. But fate took care of Cassandra, didn't it? She was dead within the week, and I told myself justice had been served—and that sooner or later, fate would do the same to me. I felt the ax hanging over my head for years."

Cam's hands were shaking. "Good God, Bentley, I am more sorry than I can say," he whispered, jerking unsteadily to his feet. "In the days to come, we will have much to discuss. I think we *should* discuss it. But for now, I know Frederica needs you. And you need her. I can't imagine how she knew of this, but she was right that you should tell me."

Bentley jerked to his feet. "Frankly, I'd prefer never to speak of it again, Cam, if it's all the same to you."

The earl shook his head. "There are things I need to say," he answered, walking toward the door with his shoulders slumped. "Things which are at least fifteen years too late. You need say no more unless you wish to. I shan't flail you with any more questions. Now, go, Bentley. Go and find your wife, and do whatever you must to set things right. Trust me, it is worth it."

And as his brother slipped from the room, Bentley realized that it was he who needed Frederica. He was shaken by what had just happened. But the panic was gone at last, leaving him to feel weighed down by a sense of loss and grief which only his wife's touch could dispel.

Frederica, it seemed, was nowhere to be found. Instead, Bentley found Jennie rummaging about in his dressing room. Freddie's trunks sat on the floor, filled to bursting, their lids still thrown back. He watched her for a moment and wanted to cry. "Jennie?"

At the sound, Jennie gave a little scream. "Oh, Mr. Rutledge," she whispered, fingertips pressed to her chest. "I th-thought—"

"That I'd drunk myself to death?" he supplied, more cheerfully than he felt. "Sorry, Jennie, no such luck. Where is Mrs. Rutledge?"

"Gone." Jennie's eyes were mistrustful.

"Gone to . . . ?"

Jennie's lip came out, but she finally relented. "Gone for a long walk, she said."

Bentley let his gaze drift over the trunks. The sight of them was like a knife in his heart. "Unpack these, Jennie," he said quietly. "Unpack every stitch, and put it all away."

Jennie looked at him querulously. "I was told we were to go home."

Bentley tried to smile, but there was a hard knot in his throat. "Well, perhaps you shall," he admitted, his vision suddenly clouding. "But perhaps, Jennie—just perhaps—this *is* home? In any case, no one will go anywhere in a great rush once all the trunks are unpacked, will they? I just want to buy myself a little time, Jennie, not imprison anyone."

At last, Jennie managed a weak smile. Then she turned away and began to lift out the stacks of clothing. Bentley started from the room, but when his fingers touched the doorknob, Jennie's voice stayed his hand. "Mr. Rutledge?"

Bentley turned. "Yes?"

Jennie made an awkward little curtsey. "Perhaps she walked over to Bellevue?" she suggested. "She had a paper in her hand. Scrolled, it was, and all caught up in blue ribbon."

Chapter Twenty-two

✠

The Golden Ring.

In the falling dusk, Bentley sat at the top of the hill, one booted leg drawn up, his arm slung over his knee. It was his favorite spot on earth, this serene little apex from which the whole of his world could be viewed, the place he'd picnicked with Freddie while they gazed at Chalcote and dreamed of names for their child. But this time, his back was turned to Chalcote, and he faced south. Toward Bellevue. And, he hoped, toward his future. But that would depend on Freddie, wouldn't it?

Somehow, he'd made his peace with Cam, and the result had been so contrary to his fears and expectations Bentley still had not come to grips with it. And in making that peace, he had done what Freddie had asked of him. So why couldn't he escape this sense of hopelessness? Perhaps because hopelessness had been his boon companion for so long now he did not know how to shake it off. Or perhaps because the horror of his past had been brought home to him yet again—this time in stark detail, forced on him by his brother's questions.

Dear God, he had spent some fifteen years shutting it all out, by any means possible. Casual sex, copious alcohol, carelessness, wanderlust, fury—name it, and he'd used it. Used it for all it was worth. And now, he wished never to think of it again.

The evening breeze ruffled lightly over his hair. The long, thin shadows which had edged the copse of trees below had vanished, softened to a violet haze. Already, the moon was a silver sliver in the sky, and the evening's first star had appeared. Where on earth was Freddie? He prayed his vigil was not in vain. Good Lord, he prayed everything was all right. After all he'd been through, Bentley still could not forget that awful evening in Catherine's book room. Could not forget Signora Castelli's hand lingering uncertainly over her cards. She had been unable to answer his one simple question. She had been unable to see the future. And, irrational as it was, that terrified him—because what if it meant there *was* no future?

Just then, he saw a shadow emerge from the copse. A slight, feminine figure paced up the hill, her shoulders rigidly set, her pace brisk. He stood, and for a long moment he watched his wife move toward him. Watched the breeze play with her hair and the shadows shift over her face as she came. Bentley stood, suddenly hesitant. He felt awkward, like a gangling, uncertain boy again. As she approached, Frederica's gaze was distant. She did not see him, and Bentley was unable to speak.

Instead, he simply stood, drinking her in. She looked so beautiful. So . . . right. Good Lord, how could you love someone so much? How could he ever have contemplated leaving her? And how on earth was he going to persuade her to take him back? What if his awkward confession to Cam was not enough to keep her? What if she had changed her mind? He had said some harsh and ugly things.

Then, suddenly, she saw him. Her head jerked up,

and her eyes flew wide. Her hair was in disarray, as if she'd rushed to put it up. Her skirts were hitched high in one hand, and the other clutched her shawl tightly between her breasts. For an instant, she froze. "Oh!" she said breathlessly. "Oh, thank God. It is true. Bentley, I've been so worried!"

Her words, and the relief which tinged them, told Bentley all that he needed to know. He threw his arms wide, and, with a tremulous smile, she closed the distance between them, hurling herself into his embrace and pressing her cheek to the wool of his coat. "Oh, Bentley!" she whispered. "You're home."

His shoulders sagged with an overwhelming relief. He brushed his lips over her hair, then her forehead, before setting her a little away from him. "Yes, I'm home, Freddie love," he said softly, trying not to cry. "For wherever you are, that is my home."

Her eyes darted over his face. "Have you just come from Chalcote, then?" she asked almost anxiously. "Have you been to the house?"

It was then that he realized how ill at ease Freddie was. Her face seemed thinner, her gestures anxious. "Only briefly," he answered.

A look of relief passed over her face. "Bentley—" she started. "That thing I asked of you? Before you left? I've reconsidered, and—"

"It's all right, Freddie," he softly interjected.

"But I just want you to know," she said, rushing through the words. "I was wrong. Deeply so. I have changed my mind. Completely. Do you understand?"

In the dying light, he could barely see the tears which pooled in her eyes. It made his own all the harder to contain. "Don't cry, Freddie love," he teased, bending his head to kiss her. "Oh, Lord, please don't. Every time you cry, I do something incredibly foolish."

But Freddie would not be distracted. "I'm too late, aren't I?"

Frederica watched her husband blink back his own tears, and an awful sense of guilt assailed her. She had learned of Bentley's return quite by accident, from one of the servants at Bellevue, and had hastened home with every intention of begging his forgiveness. But Bentley looked wan and shaken. She had never seen him so before. No, not in all the years she'd known him.

"Oh, Bentley!" she whispered.

There was no more anger in him, just that age-old weariness which was ever present in his gaze. "I have done it, Freddie," he said, his voice hoarse. "I have done as you asked, and it feels as if a weight has been lifted from my heart. He said it wasn't my fault. Everything I've thought true for all these years has been turned upside down, and I see now that you were right. I had to tell him. I had to free myself of it."

She looked at him then and felt the tears began to spill from her eyes. "But I was wrong to ask that of you," she whispered. "Oh, I did not know how wrong I was! Please, Bentley, why did you not say something? Why did you not tell me?"

He looked at her blankly. "Tell you what, Freddie?"

"How very young you were." Her voice choked. "My God, what was I thinking?"

He took her by the shoulders then. "Who have you been talking to, Freddie?" he rasped. "Joan? Who?"

She held his gaze steadily. "To Cassandra," she

answered. "I found her journals. They tell everything, if one knows what to look for. But when I saw the date on her tombstone—oh, my love, I knew. It is too horrible to contemplate. You were but a boy. A child."

He laughed, low and bitter. "Was I?" he asked. "I did not think so. My father didn't think so. He thought it was a great joke. You cannot imagine, Freddie, what I was like then. I went from eight to eighteen faster than most people can blink."

Slowly, Frederica shook her head. "I simply don't believe that," she whispered. "A child can be exposed to any manner of unwholesome things, but does that give them the ability to understand it? What he did was morally reprehensible, Bentley. And in the eyes of the church, what she did was incest, pure and simple."

He was startled by her use of so ugly a word. "I know what the church says, Freddie."

"Did you know it then?"

He hesitated. "I—no, I daresay I did not."

She pulled him down onto the grass and drew up her knees beneath her skirt. "You need to forgive yourself, Bentley," she said quietly. "You must accept that you were not at fault."

"In time, Freddie. I know that I can do that now," he whispered, his voice soft with amazement. For a moment, they sat silently as the horizon darkened and the stars came out, one by one. Bentley stared out across the fertile fields which his family had tended for some eight hundred years. The air had cooled, and night was not far away. On a sigh, he circled one arm about his wife and drew her snugly against his side.

"I loved this place as a child, Freddie," he said quietly.

"It was like my own little Garden of Eden. I ran wild, with little supervision or discipline. I missed my mother, but I was not unhappy. I never felt alone or wicked or unloved. Not then. The most terrifying thing anyone could have threatened me with was expulsion from my little garden."

"Is that what you feared?" she asked softly.

Without looking at her, Bentley nodded. "Oh, yes," he whispered. "Somehow, I let her convince me that was exactly what Cam would do. That he would tear me away from all I knew, all I loved. I do not think I have ever stopped fearing that. Indeed, at times I think I've tried to push him to it, just to have done with the waiting. I have always thought he hated me. My God, I wanted him to hate me."

Frederica set her hand in the middle of his spine and slid it soothingly up and down. "Your brother cannot possibly hate you."

"He doesn't," Bentley admitted. "So why can't I believe everything is all right now?"

"Because you have never liked yourself before," she whispered. "But I like you. And I love you, too. The past is over now."

Suddenly, her husband made a soft, choking sound. "Well, thank God, Freddie," he answered. "For I've known not a moment's peace in this place since she took it from me. Not here or anywhere else. Not for very long. That, and not my innocence, is what she stripped from me, Freddie. My sense of peace. Of belonging. And so I've always kept moving. I daresay that's why I came to Chatham Lodge so often. Because it was peaceful and because I envied what all of you had. It was like . . . like what I'd lost. A house full of family, filled with joy and love."

Surprised, she tilted her head to look up at him. "Is that what you felt?" she asked, amazed. "What a tender heart you have."

When he laughed dismissively, she cut him off. "Perhaps that sounds silly, but it is true. Why did you think we welcomed such a scoundrel into our midst? Because none of us had the heart to toss you out, not even Elliot. We liked you, Bentley, genuinely so."

He shifted himself around and drew her between his legs, urging her to lean back against him. "I valued that friendship, Freddie," he said, wrapping his arms about her. "More than you or Gus or any of them will ever know. And after . . . after what we did that night, I hung about here for days, just waiting for your answer. And when nothing came, I thought . . . Christ, Freddie, I thought I'd lost it all! Not just my friends. Not just my chance with you. But that sense of belonging. That sense of home and peace."

Frederica tilted her head to look back at him. "What are you saying, Bentley?"

He shrugged shyly. "That everybody needs a place to go, I guess. A place where they're always welcome, and for me, that place was Chatham Lodge. I had tainted everything here at Chalcote, because I couldn't keep my cock in my trousers. To think I'd done it all over again and lost you in the bargain—God, it was almost more than I could bear."

Lightly, she pressed her fingers to her temple. "Yes, but that part about waiting," she said. "What was it you thought you were waiting for?"

As if on impulse, he tightened his arms about her. "For your answer, love," he said, brushing his lips over her head.

She turned in his arms to face him. "To—?"

"Marriage," he answered as if it were obvious. "It hurt to realize you'd no wish to marry me, no matter what we'd done. I know you hushed it up. And I know, too, that the only reason you relented was because of the child. And because I bullied you. But Freddie, if you will just stay with me—if you will just give it a try with me at Bellevue—I swear I think we can make a go of it. I want to make you happy. I have fences here to mend, yes. But I'm not sure I can do it without you. I need us to be a family. A real family. What do you say?"

But Frederica was a half-dozen thoughts behind him. "Bentley, you never said one word to me of marriage," she whispered. "You—why, you left me in the middle of the night, never to be heard from again! Did you expect me to—to what? Go down to breakfast and announce that I'd surrendered my virtue to you? My God, Gus and Elliot would have killed you! And that I could not have borne. So, yes, I hushed it up. What else was I to do?"

Against her spine, she felt her husband's body stiffen. "Freddie, good God!" he whispered, his tone one of horror. "I never left you in the middle of the night! It was dawn—or so near it your bloody chambermaid practically burst in on us. I had to jump half naked out your window! Do you know how high up that is? Do you? I damn near broke my leg! I limped for a fortnight!"

Amazed laughter bubbled up in her throat. "Oh, Bentley! Surely you did not?"

"Dash it, Freddie, don't laugh at me!" he warned. "Not after the agony and doubt you put me through."

She tried to control her mirth, but the vision of her husband jumping naked out a second-story window was a bit much to bear with any semblance of grace. "Bentley, I am so glad to know now that you wanted me," she said. "But I am not omniscient. A word or a note would have been most helpful."

Her husband's anger had melted. "Freddie, my God, I did!" he whispered, looking vaguely mystified. "I wrote you a very pretty proposal. Spent an hour and every sheet of paper you had doing it, too. I set it on your bloody windowsill. Surely you do not mean to say . . . you do not suggest—"

"Oh, my God!" Freddie widened her eyes. "I wondered who'd used all my paper! You left a note? Where? When?"

"That very morning!" he said insistently. "Didn't you get it? I had to make sure you understood . . . how I felt. Bad, Freddie. I felt bad. But I felt other things, too. And I wanted to marry you, Freddie. I don't think I let myself know how much until you didn't answer me. But it took me so long to write that bloody note—I kept scratching through and ripping up—and by the time I had it right, the chambermaid turned up. Damn, Freddie it was a near-run thing."

Frederica felt an awful ache in her chest and an enormous knot in her throat. He had written her a proposal? A very pretty one, he said. And she believed him, too. After all they had been through, she did not know why it should matter so much to her, but it did. Oh, it did.

"And you wanted me?" she choked, one tear sliding

down her nose. "Not just the child but me, too? You are not sorry? You do not regret this?"

Bentley set one hand over her belly, barely rounded now, and made a soft circle with his palm. "Good Lord, Freddie, I regret almost everything in my life—but this? You? No, those things I'll never, ever regret." Suddenly, he cleared his throat, and his face took on an awkward expression. "Here, now, give me your hand," he said gruffly.

Curious, she did so. Then she watched as Bentley slid the heavy signet ring from his little finger. The same ring that had winked at her in the moonlight that fateful night at Chatham Lodge. The ring she had studied so intently on their wedding day. And the ring which had so cruelly grazed her temple. In the dying light, he held it up between them.

"Frederica d'Avillez," he whispered. "Will you marry me?"

Frederica smiled quizzically. "I already did."

Holding her gaze, Bentley shook his head. "No, that was a marriage with mights and maybes attached to it," he answered. "I love you, and this time, I want us to marry for better or for worse. Forever and ever. With no getting out of it and no looking back."

"Do you know, Bentley," she whispered. "I think I already did that, too. But yes, and yes, a thousand times over, yes."

And on the last yes, Bentley slid his ring down her finger until it rested loosely above the one he'd given her on their wedding day. Then he pulled her into his arms and kissed her, long and deep, the way he'd learned she liked it.

When he'd finished—and it was a good long while, since he was the sort of man who liked to take things slow and easy—Frederica let her head fall back against his arm. "Bentley Rutledge!" she whispered, her voice soft with amazement. "Do you know you are the sweetest, kindest, most perfect man I have ever known?"

And in that instant, she knew that it was true. For all his wicked smiles and slipshod ways, he had a heart of purest gold. He had always been a good friend. He had become a wonderful lover. And he was going to be a splendid father. In short, he was the very embodiment of that long list of qualities which she had always wanted in her perfect husband—well, all of them save one. But perhaps that one she could do without?

She stared into her husband's eyes and thought of that awful day the dressmaker had come to Strath. Of how she had cried in Evie's arms, because her life was to be forever half empty. She had pinned her hopes, she'd told herself, on romantic love. She had been waiting for her dream lover, that one perfect man who could make her feel safe and secure and deeply loved. She had wanted a man who was wise, well grounded, and worthy of her deepest respect—and one who was very, very ordinary.

"Oh, well!" said Frederica.

Then, laughing through her tears, she shrugged and threw her arms around his neck. No, Bentley Rutledge could never, ever be ordinary. Not in a million years. But then, a girl couldn't have everything, could she?

Epilogue

A Twice-Told Tale.

"Dearly beloved, ye have brought these children here to be baptized, and ye have prayed that our Lord Jesus Christ would vouchsafe to receive them, to release them from sin." A shaft of twinkling emerald light sliced across the Reverend Mr. Prudhome's prayer book as he solemnly worked his way through the ministration of holy baptism.

He motioned the godparents forward. Lord Treyhern and Lord Rannoch stepped up to the font, followed by their wives. Mr. Prudhome cleared his throat sharply. "Dost thou believe all the articles of the Christian faith as contained in the Apostles' Creed?" he intoned. "And wilt thou endeavor to have these children instructed accordingly?"

Beside him, Catherine gave Cam a subtle nudge, but, of course, it was unnecessary.

"I do believe them," Cam answered without so much as glancing at his open prayer book. "And by God's help, I will endeavor so to do."

The Reverend Mr. Prudhome—who knew precisely where his bread was buttered—smiled indulgently at his lordship. "And wilt thou endeavor to have them brought up in the fear of God?" he asked, the smile deepening. "And to obey his holy Will and Commandments?"

"I will, by God's assistance."

And so it went, line upon line, until Mr. Prudhome took the child into his arms. "Name this child," he instructed the godparents.

"Luciana Maria Teresa dos Santos Rutledge," said Cam, rattling off the foreign names as flawlessly as he would his own. Mr. Prudhome echoed the words as he dipped his hand into the font. Luciana merely gurgled and crammed one corner of her lace collar in her mouth. The rector swapped off infants and repeated his command to name the child.

"Frederick Charles Stone dos Santos Rutledge," said Cam smoothly.

Blister it! thought Bentley. *Perfect as always.*

In fact, none of the godparents missed a syllable. Frederick Charles Stone dos Santos Rutledge went quietly over the font. But when the cold water trickled down his bald head, he started, gave the Reverend Mr. Prudhome a bleary, cross-eyed look, then ripped off a belch which echoed off the rafters.

"God help us all," whispered Freddie beside him as the new rector wiped something from his crisp white surplice. "That one's a Rutledge for sure."

Moments later, the crowd was flooding into the churchyard, jerking their cloaks and coats snug as they stepped into the sharp, wintry air. On the top step, Bentley paused to rifle through his pockets until he found a ten-pound note. "Here," he said, shoving it into Gus Weyden's fist. "Don't spend it all on your red-haired opera dancer."

"What's this?" rumbled a vaguely malevolent voice behind them.

Bentley looked back to see Rannoch towering in the doorway. Undeterred, Gus grinned up at him. "Rutledge laid me a tenner the godparents couldn't say all those names without bollixing one of 'em up," he chortled, shoving the note into his coat pocket.

"Bentley!" Frederica jabbed him hard with her elbow. "You never!"

He winced and cut her a sorrowful, sidelong glance. "Have you any notion, Freddie, what it costs to feed and clothe two children at once?" he asked. "And then there's the schooling. The come-out. The grand tour. The marriage settlements. I tell you, one of us will be treading the boards and the other picking pockets in Covent Garden before this is over."

"God spare me!" groaned Rannoch. Behind them, he clutched at his chest, then pushed his way past and down the steps. Gus just winked, then hastened off to snatch little Luciana from the crook of Evie's arm.

Ignoring propriety, Bentley looped his arm around Frederica's waist, and together they stepped onto the grass. "Don't give Elliot a coronary, or Evie will never forgive me," she warned good-naturedly. "Besides, when you persuaded me to marry you, you said you were rich as Croesus."

"Shot it all, Freddie love," he said, stroking a hand down his lapel. "On all these christening clothes. Kem has expensive taste, you know."

"Bentley Rutledge, you are the most egregious liar!"

Just then, a shadow appeared at Bentley's elbow. "*Il Cavaliere di Dischi,*" rasped a low, soft voice. "*Buongiorno!*"

Slowly, and with a touch of dread, Bentley turned

around. Though the *signora* had been visiting at Catherine's for a week, she'd not been in attendance at the baptism. But here she was now, springing on him out of nowhere. He smiled, and offered his arm. "Good morning, Signora Castelli."

To his shock, the wizened old woman was grinning. He'd not thought it possible. "Twins!" she said, gleefully smacking her hands together. "Twins! Again! It is in the blood!"

Bentley smiled warmly. "I'm glad it pleases you, ma'am," he said sincerely. "All my teasing aside, it certainly pleases me."

The old woman elbowed him lightly. "*Si,* fertile fields, you Rutledges!" she cackled. "I have considered this well, *Cavaliere,* and I see now my error."

"Your error, ma'am? I marvel you even know the word."

The *signora* squinted at him. "The question we asked, it was impossible for the cards to answer, no?" she answered, opening her arms expansively. "And so I thought—*Dio mio!*—I really thought I had lost the gift! This glorious event I could not foresee! Now, your sister, the Lady Catherine—that I saw! Twins, plain as the nose on my face."

And a dashed impressive nose it was, too. "Did you predict that, ma'am?" he asked, curious.

Sagely, the old woman nodded. "*Si,* when I read her cards," she whispered, narrowing one eye. "But that is the difference, you see, *Cavaliere?* It was *her* cards which I read."

Throughout this conversation, Frederica had remained strangely silent. Bentley gave her hand an affectionate squeeze where it lay upon his arm. "Then all I ask, *signora,* is that you keep those blasted cards far away from Freddie here. If she's to go through another birthing, I'd as soon not know it 'til I must. These two shaved a score off my life."

"Ah, too late!" the old woman cackled. "Too late! Too late!"

"Too late?" *Too late for what?* Surely she did not mean . . .

Beside him, he felt Freddie inching away from his grasp. He gripped her hard by the elbow and turned to face her. Freddie had lost most of her color. She would not hold his gaze.

"Tell me," he rasped. "Tell me, Freddie, that this woman is insane. Deranged. Attics-to-let. Tell me you aren't—aren't—already—"

Her smile crooked, Freddie shook her head. "Oh, no, I only let her read my cards!" she protested. "Last night after dinner, when you went into the gun room with Max."

"And—?" he demanded.

"Well," said Freddie witheringly. "Remember, my love, when we joked about that cricket team?"

The old woman plucked at his coat sleeve. "*Sette, Cavaliere!*" she cried joyously. "*Sette!* A most providential number! In this marriage, you will be many times blessed! Thank God for that big house, eh?"

"*Sette?*" whispered Bentley, grappling with the bits of Latin and Italian which rolled around loose in his head. "*Uno, due, tre, quattro, cinque, sei, sette*—why, that's— that's—"

The old woman lifted her gold-knobbed stick and

shook it in the air. "*Si,* seven!" she shouted, like some deranged spectator at a hazard table. In the dispersing crowd, feet froze and heads turned. Helene coughed. Zoë giggled. And the Reverend Mr. Prudhome, who apparently did not approve of jocularity in the church- yard, smiled tightly and stalked back toward them.

The old woman just wrinkled her impressive nose, crossed herself, and hobbled away.

Freddie patted her husband solicitously on the arm. "Poor dear!" she murmured as Mr. Prudhome bore down on them. "Seven children! Let's tell Gus. Maybe he'll feel sorry for you and give back the tenner."

But Bentley was rapidly throwing off the shock. "Oh, I've a better notion, Freddie," he said, sliding one hand around to pinch her lightly on the derrière. "Why don't *you* feel sorry for me and let me start working on Number Three right after luncheon?"

And then Bentley Rutledge shocked them all—well, really only the Reverend Mr. Prudhome, who was new in the village—when he snatched his wife by the waist, kissed her soundly, then lifted her up and twirled her round and round the churchyard.